Enchanting the Heiress

Books by Kristi Ann Hunter

Hawthorne House

A Lady of Esteem: A Hawthorne House *Novella*

A Noble Masquerade

An Elegant Façade

An Uncommon Courtship

An Inconvenient Beauty

Haven Manor

A Search for Refuge: A Haven Manor *Novella*

A Defense of Honor

Legacy of Love: A Haven Manor *Novella*
from *The Christmas Heirloom Novella Collection*

A Return of Devotion

A Pursuit of Home

Hearts on the Heath

Vying for the Viscount

Winning the Gentleman

Enchanting the Heiress

To the Ultimate Planner
Ephesians 1:7–10

And to Jacob
Thank you for teaching me the power
of reading the Bible in context.

Prologue

DECEMBER 1817
NEWMARKET, ENGLAND

How could Jonas Fitzroy possibly follow his twin sister's directive to stop watching over and protecting her, when she actually believed in the crazy plan she'd just laid out to him?

"Stop talking for a moment and let me think," he said as he set aside the cloth he'd been using to buff the saddles filling the Hawksworth tack room. He'd been working at the estate for only a handful of months, but it had been a refreshing change of pace from the traveling circus he and his sister, Sophia, had worked with the past few years.

The only downside had been how difficult it was to keep his sister out of the curfuffle she'd created when she'd brought them here in the first place. One dangerous pitfall had led to another, but at least she'd fallen into all of them with good intentions.

This time, however . . .

He crossed his arms. "Am I to understand that Miss Hancock is telling everyone that the two of you are embarking upon a grand tour, but you're really only going to London? Once there, she's going to write Lady Stildon about the change in plan. Then, because Lord and Lady Stildon are so deeply in love, she assumes

Lady Stildon will share the information with her husband. Am I correct so far?"

Sophia bit her lip and nodded.

Though that part of the plan seemed far more complicated than necessary, Jonas couldn't fault the logic. Working at Lord Stildon's stable had allowed Jonas to see firsthand how besotted the couple was with each other. There was likely truth to the idea that Lady Stildon told her husband practically everything.

It was the next step in the plan that gave Jonas pause.

"Then, because Lord Stildon wants everyone to be happy, and because Lady Stildon will prompt him to, the news will be shared with Aaron. Upon hearing that you are close at hand and not on a boat bound for Europe, he will speed to London, declare his love for you, ask you to marry him, and bring you back here so you can start your lives together."

Sophia huffed and crossed her arms. "Well, when you put it like that, it sounds ridiculous."

"That's because it is." Jonas snagged the cloth and resumed working on the saddles. "How did you come up with such a scheme?"

"It was Harriet's idea."

Jonas almost groaned. "Of course it was."

"What do you mean by that?"

He shook his head. Couldn't she see it? "I'm very thankful Miss Hancock provided you a way to move back to Newmarket, but ever since you returned, she's been manipulating and maneuvering your life."

"I am her companion. I go where she goes. That's called having a job, not manipulation." Sophia rolled her eyes as she grabbed another cloth, then dipped it in the water and began cleaning the next saddle in line.

How much should Jonas push the subject? Miss Hancock was friends with Lady Stildon and a frequent visitor to Hawksworth, so he heard things, saw things, knew things about the independent heiress.

Like how she'd never had a companion before hiring Sophia. And how even though she claimed to have interest in pursuing the type of complex riding at which Sophia was proficient, she'd made no moves forward in purchasing a trained horse for herself. Money wasn't the issue, because she'd bought a brand-new dining set on a whim the last time Jonas had escorted her and Lady Stildon into town.

She'd once stooped in the stable's doorway unhooking and refastening the top button on her boot eight times in a row to ensure an encounter with Aaron Whitworth, the stable's manager.

More than once, she made last-minute plans that forced an unsuspecting Sophia into the company of Aaron or women who had months prior shunned Sophia's existence. Oftentimes these plans didn't leave his sister time to return home to change. Fortunately, Miss Hancock always happened to have some suitable accessory at hand or was able to convince Lady Stildon to loan Sophia a proper dress.

A proper dress that always seemed to perfectly fit Sophia's tiny frame and never had to be returned.

Jonas could only imagine who else Miss Hancock considered her personal puppet.

It made him clench his teeth to hear Sophia speak about dinners she'd decided to attend or ideas she'd had or some *chance* encounter with Aaron or a potential riding client. The only balm—and the reason Jonas had kept his observations about Miss Hancock to himself—had been Sophia's smile as she and Aaron did, indeed, grow their relationship onto a firmer footing that would eventually get his sister away from that woman's influence.

Miss Hancock could not possibly have *known* that would happen, though. She'd risked Sophia's heart on a hunch, a game, a whim.

Now it seemed the slow success wasn't enough for her.

"Why can't you simply let Aaron propose when he's ready?" Jonas slid the cloth along a stirrup strap and looked up to pin his sister with his gaze. "Why force him into it?"

"Because we don't know if he intends to ever propose."

Oh, how he wanted to pounce upon that *we*. Why did it matter what Miss Hancock knew or didn't know? What had happened to his optimistic, dreamy sister who always believed the best for her future?

"Why wouldn't he?" Everyone in the stable knew Aaron was enamored with Sophia, and his requesting her hand was only a matter of time.

Sophia sighed. "Because he hasn't yet."

"I'm fairly certain if you told him you didn't want to travel the world with Miss Harriet Hancock, he'd be down on one knee within the week." Jonas dipped his rag in the bucket and wet another section of saddle. Why couldn't people just say what they meant? This entire business could be solved by Aaron asking Sophia what she wanted in life and Sophia telling the man it was him.

Instead, they were both playing games, scared of what might happen if the other didn't want the same thing they did.

"But what if he doesn't?" Sophia whispered. "What if he says he doesn't love me, isn't ready to marry me, and considers me only a dear friend?"

Then Jonas's observation skills were more than a little lacking. Still, her concern was enough to weave the tiniest thread of doubt into his conviction. He'd spent all his life protecting his sister. She might be ten minutes older than he was, but that didn't matter. She was his responsibility, and since he didn't have the means to provide for her if she quit her job as Miss Hancock's companion, he was required to work within the parameters the position provided.

That didn't mean he had to like it.

"How is Miss Hancock's scheme different?" He'd try one more time to get her to see reason.

"Because Aaron gets to declare his views in a way we can all pretend doesn't hurt anyone." She dropped the cloth atop the saddle before hugging her arms around her middle. The light Irish brogue that had traced her words moments before thickened as she fought back tears. "I like Newmarket, Jonas. It feels more like home than anywhere we've been since we lost the family house."

Jonas understood her sentiment. In some ways, he felt it himself. The horses, the Heath . . . it was all like a little piece of Ireland. Except here people actually liked them and wanted them to stay around. At least, they liked Sophia. He was here because she was, and that didn't bother him at all.

Sophia saw things differently, though, and he wanted her to have what she desired. "Are you sure this is what you want? A home with Aaron, working and living in one place?"

"It is. I had other dreams only because I didn't know about this one." Her expression softened, and she sighed. "If Aaron loves me, that would be everything. But if he doesn't, I don't want to have to move on and lose my home."

Jonas groaned. For six years it had been just him and Sophia, and that isolation had nearly wrecked his people-loving sister. He couldn't ruin her friendships she'd made since coming to Newmarket, not even the one with Miss Hancock.

That meant he had to allow this ridiculous scheme to continue. Maybe he could make it a little less convoluted, though. "I'll give you and Miss Hancock time to get to London, and then I'll tell Aaron where you are."

Sophia blinked. "You'll just come right out and tell him?"

"Regardless of what Miss Hancock has told you, men don't think the same as women. Yes, I'm going to come right out and tell him. He'll either make plans to follow you to London or he won't. Either way, at least you'll *know* he's been informed instead of waiting to see if the gossip has traveled as far as you hoped."

Sophia frowned. "Aaron won't feel trapped?"

"I can promise you that whatever Aaron feels will be better than his trying to decipher what it means that you didn't tell him you were going to London yourself. This little gossip chain could make it appear you didn't want him coming after you at all."

All the color drained from Sophia's already-pale skin, making Jonas drop his cloth and circle the saddle rack to catch her should she suddenly faint. "Your plan," she scraped out before swallowing hard and licking her lips. "We'll go with your plan."

He felt no surge of triumph in her acquiescence. It meant he was now a part of this ridiculous manipulation. How could Miss Hancock think she could move people around like chess pieces? If she were wrong, this game held few consequences for her, but Sophia's happiness and dreams could be crushed. Did the woman see his sister as anything but an amusing toy?

For the next several days, Jonas's displeasure stewed until it resembled anger. What would have happened if Sophia hadn't come to him? How could he have protected her? It would have been his own fault, too, since he could have warned Sophia about her friend and employer earlier. He'd stayed silent only because there'd been no immediate danger and no one had asked him what he thought. Eventually, Aaron would have removed Sophia from the situation, so why should he push?

Apparently, because *someone* wouldn't allow the people involved to find their own way.

By the time the allotted number of days had passed, Aaron's despondency over Sophia's supposed trip had increased until his foul mood affected all his employees, including Jonas. Frustration with his sister, himself, the situation, and the aggravating Miss Hancock pushed Jonas into an uncommonly emotional state. He threw a saddle onto a bench, the jangle of metal and *thunk* of leather on wood gaining the melancholy Aaron's attention. "London."

"What?" Aaron looked up at Jonas with a frown marred by confusion.

"London," Jonas repeated. "She's in London."

"What's going on in here?" Lord Stildon asked, poking his head around the corner from the stalls.

Jonas's irritation grew with his audience. There weren't a lot of secrets in this stable, but he'd thought no one was here but the other grooms. Preoccupation with Miss Hancock's schemes and Sophia's distress had impaired his observation skills, it would seem.

Aaron stood and looked down at Jonas. "Why is she in London?"

"Because that meddlesome woman thinks true love will make you run after her. She doesn't understand love doesn't demand what it wants. Instead, it will sacrifice itself to give the other person what they need."

"Tell me what you know." Aaron lost the forlorn look he'd worn since Sophia's departure and once more looked like the strong, capable, honest man to whom Jonas was willing to entrust his sister's future.

"They're staying at Clarendon Hotel."

A lively debate and growing excitement ensued as Lord Stildon was joined by the rest of Aaron's friends, men of a higher class than Aaron and a far higher class than Jonas. Plans were made, ideas tossed about. What was never even asked was whether or not Aaron was going after her, proving Jonas's interpretation of the situation far more accurate than Sophia's or Miss Hancock's.

Finally, Aaron turned back to Jonas. "I won't have anything but a one-room cottage for at least a year."

That was far more than the twins had been able to claim since their father died, leaving behind a debt-ridden riding school and a family without means of support. "She spent two years sleeping under a wagon. I don't think she'll mind."

"Am I to assume, then, that I have your blessing?"

Jonas looked up at the man who'd given him a job in a stable when he was too injured to ride, the man who'd honored an agreement with Sophia even though he'd been tricked into signing it, the man who'd been honest enough to know he couldn't give Sophia what she claimed to want and so made a way that didn't involve him.

It wasn't his fault Sophia had changed her mind. Aaron had been honest and steady despite his faults and emotional issues. Jonas would never give up the job of protecting his sister to a less worthy man.

Especially since that man respected Jonas enough to ask for his blessing despite his lower station.

Jonas gave him a slight grin. "I wouldn't have told you where she was if you didn't. But if you think to marry her without me there, I'll retract it."

Within hours, Jonas found himself joining Aaron in a carriage bound for London, ready to save his sister from Miss Hancock's scheming hands once and for all.

As a final act of brotherly protection, it wasn't half bad.

One

"Please!"

—Sophia, in seventeen notes shoved under Jonas's door after her father said she could go for a ride only if her brother accompanied her.

He never received them, as he'd already been down at the stable, waiting for her.

Three Months Later

Jonas hadn't participated in anything resembling school for many years, but he was certain that his sister's definition of the word *simple* hadn't come from the same dictionary the rest of the English-speaking world consulted.

He flicked a glance in her direction to acknowledge that he'd heard her speak, then turned his attention back to the horse he was grooming.

Sophia sighed and set her fists on her hips. "You're being ridiculous."

"I'm being ridiculous?" Jonas tilted his head, his expression conveying his disbelief plain enough that sisterly intuition would not be required to discern it.

Although perhaps he couldn't trust Sophia's ability to determine the unspoken. After six years of traveling the country, scraping out a living from amongst those who would just as soon take advantage of them as leave them to rot in a ditch, she shouldn't have trouble seeing potential manipulation and deceit.

Yet here she was, happily suggesting that he deliberately deepen his connection to a woman who nearly wrecked—or at least seriously delayed—Sophia's chance to marry the love of her life. Jonas tried to be a forgiving man, but Sophia had been married for three months now, and Miss Hancock was still sticking her nose into his sister's life. The clothing recommendations, societal guidance, and client referrals wouldn't be a problem on their own, but when they all hailed from the same source and were wrapped in subtlety, they became a picture of controlled manipulation.

And there was nothing Jonas could do about it.

His sister was married and building a life of her own, had a husband to watch over her and a group of friends she loved dearly. Since she needed and craved all those connections, he was glad she now had them. If only the good didn't bring a little bad along with it.

Jonas shook his head and ran a hand down the horse's leg so he could lift the hoof and clean it. "This is not a *simple* favor you're asking. You know that. Nothing involving that woman is simple."

"Don't say *that woman* in such a tone. Harriet is my friend." Sophia crossed her arms over her chest and stuck her nose in the air, a sure sign that she knew her request had been far too large and much too understated.

Whether Harriet Hancock truly was a friend was debatable, but Sophia was right that he shouldn't disparage the woman. At least not out loud. He was aware of plenty of people who lived as they shouldn't, and he had no trouble keeping their names out of his mouth. He likely wouldn't have an issue with Miss Hancock either if she nosed into any life other than Sophia's.

This happy world his sister had found was so new and fragile, though. Jonas didn't want to see her crushed beneath the rubble if it fell down.

Since he couldn't say something nice, he said nothing at all.

His sister changed tactics. "Are you truly attempting to convince me you're happy here?"

He placed the hoof back on the ground and straightened to squint at her. "I *am* happy."

At least he wasn't *un*happy. His life was no longer filled with the stress of day-to-day survival, and the injury he'd sustained many months ago had healed enough that he barely noticed it unless he spent a long day in the saddle. Now he had a home with filling food and a real bed and enough money to purchase a sketchbook to draw in during his recently attained free time. All of that while staying in close proximity to his newly married sister.

What was there to be unhappy about?

She wrapped her arms around her middle and shifted her weight before pleading, "But couldn't you be happier?"

Could he? Probably. Life always held room for improvement, didn't it? He enjoyed working with the horses even if he didn't have Sophia's passion for it. Nothing else created a burning dream within him, so why walk away from a good thing?

He examined Sophia. *She* was happy, wasn't she? When she'd given up the dream she'd claimed for years in order to grab for a different future, she hadn't seemed to see it as a sacrifice. It had been a few months now, though. They'd lived in Newmarket longer than they'd lived anywhere since their parents died. Had his current contentment made him miss a change of heart in her?

"Could *you* be happier?"

"With my life? No." She sagged against the wall of the horse's stall, a dreamy smile flitting across her lips. "I'm married to the most wonderful man in the world." She coughed and glanced his way. "Aside from you, of course."

Jonas rolled his eyes and moved to the next hoof. It didn't bother him that his place in Sophia's life had shifted. A woman should love her husband more than her brother.

What *did* bother him was Sophia's growing obtrusiveness. This morning's suggestion might have been the craziest, but it wasn't the first. "Is it that I work for you now? Is that what's bothering you?"

"You don't work for *me*," she said, sticking her nose another notch in the air.

Where was the closest chair? She would have to sit down if she intended to tilt her head back any farther.

"But," she said, drawing the word out long and slow, "I can't help but wonder if you intend to work for Aaron forever."

"Forever is a long time. Who knows what God has planned for me?" Jonas shrugged and set the cleaned hoof back on the floor. "I can probably return to working for Lord Stildon, if that would make you feel better."

When Aaron had stopped being Lord Stildon's stable manager and instead become his racehorses' trainer, Jonas had made the change with him. Working with racchorses had sounded more interesting than maintaining a viscount's pleasure stable.

He could adjust if Sophia needed him to, though.

His sister sighed as her shoulders slumped. "You would still be a stable hand."

"The world needs stable hands." Who else would take care of the animals? Besides, horses were all he knew. They'd been raised on horses, spending as much of their childhood in the stable and riding rings as they had in the house.

"But you could be doing what you love." Sophia surged into the stall. "This could be your chance to spend your days drawing and learning new methods and perfecting your skills. You would have time and space and supplies to make art your life."

He had time and supplies to draw already, so what did Sophia think his life lacked? True, his current living situation, while better than it had been in years, was nothing close to the comfortable home, servants, and promising future they'd had growing up. Aside from sharing a tiny room above the stable instead of sleeping in the manor house, though, his life was much as it was before their father died. Was that what this was really about?

Soon, Sophia would have all that back. Once Aaron finished the renovations on the old stable he'd purchased, he planned to build his new family a house. Until then, he and Sophia were living in his modest private cottage.

Jonas shared a small living space with a dozen other grooms, but Sophia had never seemed to grasp that he didn't care. He didn't care where he lived, though he did rather like having a bed under a roof instead of a pallet under a wagon. He didn't care what he did as long as he was good at it and it filled his day enough to let him feel he'd earned his keep. He didn't even care with whom he socialized or if he socialized at all, so it was easy enough to spend time with Sophia's new friends.

Now that she was happily married, he didn't even need to do that anymore. If he distanced himself from the aristocrats and gentry Sophia dined with weekly, though, would she feel even worse about their different life situations?

At some point she would have to accept the disparity.

"My life is fine, Soph. It's good."

She crossed her arms again. "And what do you intend to do today when you finish with Sweet Fleet? Volunteer to cover the duties of another groom?"

He probably would do that, but it wouldn't fill all his time. "I've been drawing and reading. Lord Stildon has offered me use of his library."

They were enjoyable pastimes he'd been unable to indulge in for years, but neither activity inspired any great aspirations. Reading certainly wasn't going to create a sense of accomplishment, and he rather doubted drawing all day could replace the satisfaction of seeing the results of physical labor.

Why was Sophia suddenly so concerned? He leveled his gaze at her. "What aren't you telling me?"

She was small, but he wasn't so much taller that his size could intimidate her. His steady regard might, though. He narrowed his eyes and continued to stare.

Sophia deflated with a long, deep sigh and ran her hand over the horse's side, something she did whenever she was nervous and needed the calming strength of the powerful animals.

Concern replaced irritation as Jonas set the hoof-pick atop the stall divider and leaned against the stall door, blocking her exit while doing his best to appear as though he hadn't a care in the world. Something was going on here, and he wasn't moving until Sophia told him what it was. It was never a long wait for her to start, but the completion of her tale could be several minutes away.

"Harriet found the cottage," Sophia mumbled.

Jonas frowned. "Pardon?"

"The cottage." She ran one hand up under the horse's mane and tangled her fingers in the hair. "The one you hid in while you were healing and I was racing horses. The one where you did all those engravings."

Jonas rolled his shoulders. The week he'd stayed hidden among those crumbling walls had felt like the longest year of his life. He'd understood the desperation that had driven Sophia to take the job as a racehorse jockey, but he'd hated that her greatest chance at safely succeeding had been to go without him.

"I thought it was funny at first," Sophia continued without taking a noticeable pause for breath. "Seeing that place through her eyes, imagining why someone would carve images into every wooden surface that hadn't rotted away. It would be a fascinating mystery if I hadn't known it was you filling your hours and trying to distract yourself from worry."

As much as he wanted to deny her assessment, he couldn't. Hiding in that broken-down cottage while she went out and provided for them both had been nearly as painful as the injury that prevented him from taking her place.

The last thing he wanted to do was relive it for Miss Hancock's benefit.

"You're safe now," Jonas said, "and you've my permission to tell her the story. She knows your part anyway."

"Harriet was fascinated," Sophia said, without acknowledging what he'd said in the least. "The cottage is on her property, you know, and she's made us visit it on multiple riding sessions. She even attempted to do a print from some of the more complete engravings."

Now, that Jonas would like to see. That week had been his first attempt at the reverse carvings. Had some turned out well?

"I'm worried that simply explaining the origins of the carvings won't be enough."

Jonas frowned. "What do you mean? Does she intend to seek restitution?"

Sophia's eyes widened. "What? No. The opposite, in fact. She's been going on and on about how awful it is that some artist was desperate enough to live in that dilapidated building, and she's determined to find him and become his patron. It's an old idea, I know, but there's no other way for her to support someone while they find their style and perfect it. I'm afraid someone else will take advantage of this new fascination of hers. She has such a huge heart, and I don't want her hurt."

Jonas coughed to cover his snort of disbelief. Miss Hancock's elaborate machinations could certainly be the product of a wily mind, but a huge heart? No. That woman was the perfect example of what happened when people floated through life doing whatever they liked without applying themselves to any sort of endeavor.

"I'm sure Miss Hancock will soon find someone and something

else to obsess over." Jonas pushed the stall door open and stepped out. As he headed toward the saddle room, he listened for the click that ensured Sophia had remembered to close the stall door behind her.

"This could be a brilliant opportunity for you," Sophia said as she scurried after him.

"If those carvings inspired some sort of appreciation in her, she doesn't have the correct taste for an art patron. They were horrible."

"They were carved into rotting wood. Of course they're horrible." Sophia scampered around until she was blocking his path. "But there's potential in them. Look."

She pulled out a paper and unfolded it before shoving it at his chest.

Jonas took the paper and winced at the print. He'd attempted to depict a horse in the middle of a *piaffe*, but he dared anyone to identify it as such. The neck wasn't properly aligned with the body, and the head was far too large. The eye looked like it belonged in a caricature. "This is awful."

Sophia snatched it back. "Well, you did carve it with a hoof-pick."

"She doesn't know that."

A blush rose to cover Sophia's cheeks with enough speed that Jonas's stomach clenched. What had she done?

"I might have mentioned that some of the grooves looked to be the width of a hoof-pick."

"Soph." Jonas drew out the name on a groan.

"I wanted her to realize the genius of your ability."

"It's hardly genius."

She crossed her arms. "Says you. What do you know about it, anyway?"

"Not a thing, which is likely a sight more than Miss Hancock knows." Though Jonas wasn't tall, a lifetime of working with horses had made him strong, and it was a simple matter to lift his sister out of the way and continue down the line of tack.

"Jonas, this is your chance to study what you love." Sophia chased after him.

"I don't love it, Soph."

"Fine. Something you enjoy, then."

He couldn't refute that statement, so he ignored it instead, focusing on ensuring buckles were securely attached to saddles and none of the leather showed signs of cracking. Sophia sighed and moved to the other end of the rack, doing the same as she worked toward him so they would meet in the middle.

"This isn't only about you," Sophia said quietly. "I'm concerned about Harriet. She's determined to do this, and you're right, it might be a fleeting idea, but that's even more reason for you to accept it."

Jonas waited, but of all the times for his sister not to prattle on incessantly it was when he wanted more information. He sighed. "Explain."

"If she sponsors someone unscrupulous, it wouldn't take long for him to damage her irreparably. And if she found someone suitable but then lost interest, the poor artist would be devastated. She would feel awful and might do something foolish because of that."

"So your *simple* request that I uproot my life and become her latest project is for her benefit and not mine?"

She bit her lip, once again blushing until her cheeks matched the flaming red of her hair. "Yes," she said in a small voice.

To anyone else it would be offensive and preposterous. For Jonas it was the only thing that made the idea even partially palatable.

He shoved a hand through his own red locks. As irritating as he found Miss Hancock, she was Sophia's friend. She would likely claim him as one as well, since he'd allowed himself to be pulled into that group's gatherings more than once.

All those people, with their aristocratic blood and high-born connections, had accepted Sophia. They'd supported her, helped her, made this new life possible. Gratitude inspired him to offer something in exchange.

Even if *he* didn't believe Miss Hancock was in danger of landing herself in an untenable position, Sophia did. That concern, at least, Jonas could alleviate, though not in the way his sister seemed to want.

"I'll go see your friend tomorrow."

Sophia jumped up and down and clapped. "Oh, this is going to be fun. Promise me I can go shopping with you. I'm discovering I vastly enjoy the activity but only when I'm helping other people purchase things." She paused. "I still can't bring myself to spend money on anything for me."

Since he had no intention of shopping for art supplies or anything else, it was safe to promise, "You may shop with me."

She squealed and gave him a quick hug. "This is so exciting. Are you coming to dinner tonight?" She frowned. "Maybe you should go tell her today. I don't know if I can keep my mouth shut all evening."

"The practice of restraint will do you good."

She rolled her eyes. "Aaron finds my lack of restraint endearing."

"You could smile at Aaron and convince him mucking out stalls was a delightful chore, so I don't find that a ringing endorsement."

She waved his comment away. "What tasks do you have remaining? I'll finish them so you can get cleaned up and call on Harriet."

Jonas narrowed his eyes. "I'm not calling on Miss Hancock. It is, at most, a business meeting."

Finding the buckle on the saddle fascinating, she avoided his gaze. "Yes, yes, but either way you don't want to go covered in sweat and mud."

Checking the tack was his final chore for the day, so putting Sophia off would only be out of spite. He might as well get this over with. He moved toward the door. "Don't forget to check the bridles too."

"Be sure to wash beneath your fingernails," Sophia called. "And put on a clean shirt."

Did she think he didn't know how to wash simply because he lived above a stable? Jonas rolled his eyes as he pumped a bucket half full of water and hauled it up the stairs at the end of the building.

As he washed in his small room, he said a prayer of appreciation for the ready access to water and privacy. Then taking a clean shirt from its peg, he relished the fact that his clothing was neatly hung and folded into drawers instead of shoved into a satchel. As he saddled the horse he'd been loaned, he thanked God the tragedies he'd endured hadn't robbed him of his enjoyment of the graceful animals.

In truth, though his life had taken some hard and unexpected turns, things hadn't washed out that badly.

Hopefully, he'd soon be saying the same for this ridiculous errand his sister had sent him on.

Two

"We received a letter from the head of school today, telling us how well you are fitting in with the other girls. Your grandmother would be so proud of you."

—Gregory Hancock, in a letter to his ten-year-old daughter, Harriet, six weeks after she entered Mrs. Brider's School for Girls

Harriet plopped her chin onto her palm and stared out the window at ornamental trees swaying in a strange sort of dance to the accompaniment of a stiff breeze. There wouldn't be many dances in town for a few months. Most of Newmarket's populace had gone to London at the beginning of the Season, and those who remained were contenting themselves with a more casual social existence.

It wasn't particularly the dancing Harriet would miss, as she was rather indifferent about the endeavor, but casual gatherings brought difficulties. Formality kept a certain distance in the interactions, a lack of intimacy that prevented true friendships from occurring. The close friendships she'd stumbled into made her life richer but also complicated.

She turned from the window and glanced at her open diary

to peruse today's schedule. The page was empty aside from her weekly dinner with the aforementioned problematic friends. Her life didn't need more relationships, but her calendar was definitely lacking.

The stack of invitations was thin, and after adding the ones that wouldn't require too much conversation to her calendar, far too many blank spaces remained.

While the modiste in Newmarket wasn't her preferred clothing maker, an appointment or two could fill some time. A visit to the vicar's wife would take up an afternoon, perhaps more if the church had extra needs among the poorer parishioners.

Harriet would love to fill more of her days with walks, rides, and teas with her friends, but it was far too difficult to constantly keep up her guard around them, and she needed time away to strengthen her resolve.

It was both glorious and horrible to get a piece of something one wanted so desperately but couldn't completely enjoy. She really did need to see about setting her life in order so she could move on with it.

Until then, she'd simply have to walk that fine line between keeping friendships and keeping secrets.

With the invitations sorted, she turned to the even smaller stack of personal correspondence. A new letter from her father sat on top.

A smile drifted easily across her face as she read the words and absorbed the comfort of her father's familiar handwriting. The local children had recently discovered that covering one hole of the town fountain made the water shoot farther from the other openings, his factory had turned out more cast-iron pots and pans than ever the previous month, and the flowers that lined his path from the house to the factory had bloomed, bringing extra life and color to his day.

Those tales, as had become increasingly the case, were followed by the hope that she was experiencing the world and not simply seeing it, that she was filling her heart as well as her mind, that she was seeing the beauty around her and making the most of her treasured adventures.

She dropped the letter on the desk. What more did he want from her? If she could provide what he was looking for and convince him she'd accomplished what he'd dreamed for her, she could end this farce and move on with her life.

Blowing out a frustrated breath, she picked up her teacup and took a sip. Cold. She frowned at the cup. Very cold. How long had she been staring out the window?

A commotion at the door to the private parlor had her setting the teacup aside and quickly rising to her feet. The scuffle wasn't one of the servants, though. It was Sophia, and breath was bellowing from her chest as if she'd run all the way from town.

"Sophia?" Harriet rushed around the desk and crossed the room, arms outstretched and ready to catch the other woman if she collapsed.

Not that Sophia looked in any imminent danger of crumpling to the carpet. It took her only moments to bring her breathing to a moderate enough level that she could speak.

"Harriet, I've hatched a plan, and I need your help."

As Sophia began to pace the small area of clear floor, Harriet gaped. She wasn't averse to getting involved in a scheme or two. In fact, she saw helping people anonymously as her great calling in life, which frequently required her to hatch a plan herself.

This was the first time she could recall being asked to help with someone else's project.

"What do you need?" Harriet moved to one of the chairs situated in a small grouping across the room from the desk and sat.

"It's about Jonas," Sophia said as she came to a halt and gripped her hands together. "I told him you've decided to become a patron."

Harriet frowned. "Of what?"

"Art. Or rather, an artist."

Involving herself that directly in someone's life was not something she did. Ever. "Why am I doing that?"

Sophia huffed out a breath and dropped into a chair. "Jonas refuses to help himself or allow me to support him, but he can't resist aiding someone else. I can't stay long because he's no more than twenty minutes behind me. He can't know I came to you. I have Lawrence holding Rhiannon at the front door so Jonas won't see her."

Harriet nodded in approval at the forethought. Sophia's white horse was quite distinct, and there'd be no hiding the animal amongst the mostly empty stalls in Harriet's small stable. She kept three horses only to employ the two stable hands and because it seemed a requirement for good standing in Newmarket society.

"What do you need me to do?" Sophia needed help, and Harriet was glad to give it. Everything else could be sorted later.

"Do you remember the cottage?"

"The crumbling one with all the carvings?"

Sophia nodded. "Yes. I told him you're quite enamored with it."

"I am." It was both a fascination and a point of strife. Obviously, someone had taken refuge in the dilapidated structure, but they'd spent their time there creating instead of moping. That someone was living in such a way on her property was distressing, though. More than once she'd ridden by to see if the artist still lived there so she could provide better accommodations.

Sophia cleared her throat. "Yes, well, I need you to be determined to find the artist and become his patron."

As that wasn't entirely against the truth, she could manage such a claim. "And Jonas knows the artist?"

Sophia took a deep breath. "Jonas is the artist. That is where he hid before Aaron put him to work at Hawksworth."

"Oh." Having a stranger live in such squalor on her property was bad enough, but someone she personally knew? And Jonas Fitzroy? She'd given more assistance to an acquaintance at a tea shop than she'd been able to give him.

"For now just get him to accept your help." Sophia spread her arms and pressed her hands out as if assuring Harriet this would be easy. "We can decide how to encourage him to explore his talents later."

Harriet was up to the task, but this seemed very out of character for Sophia, who tended to bluster into situations with her heart on her sleeve and her mind five steps behind. "Why are you doing this?"

"Because I'm worried. Now that I'm married, Jonas has no one to see to, no one to push for. He's so comfortable wherever he is that he won't see how much more he could be for himself. I just know if he had the chance to discover how much he truly loves art, he'd see why he needs to pursue it."

"Isn't he happy?"

Sophia shook her head. "Jonas has always been happy—at least as happy as Jonas ever gets. He lives for those he loves. And I'm worried because right now he's alone."

Harriet narrowed her gaze. "You aren't attempting to play matchmaker, are you?"

Sophia laughed and pushed up from the chair. "I wouldn't dream of it. You and Jonas? I can't imagine a more mismatched pairing." She sobered and bit her lip. "I want Jonas to learn how to love himself enough to work as hard for himself as he does for others."

Before Harriet could answer, Sophia was turning for the door. "I have to go before he arrives." She waved at Harriet as she stepped into the corridor. "We'll talk more later."

Harriet rose from the chair and pulled her wrap tighter around her shoulders. Hadn't she just been looking for something to fill the empty time in her upcoming weeks? Life was always easier when she had a project. With her friends happily married, their children far too young to need her assistance, and most of her acquaintances hied off to London, she'd been at a loss to know who had problems she could potentially solve.

Now one had dropped into her lap.

Soon it would be in her drawing room.

She rushed through the door connecting the parlor to her bedchamber, exchanged the wool wrap for a silk one, and shoved her feet into proper slippers. A brief glance in the mirror assured her that her dark hair was still in place.

A knock preceded the entrance of Frances, one of the parlormaids. "There's a Mr. Fitzroy to see you, miss."

Sophia hadn't been joking about how close behind her brother would be. "Put him in the drawing room. I'll be down directly."

How should she play this? Surprise, obviously. Mr. Fitzroy wouldn't know that Harriet was expecting him, and he barely acknowledged her when they were at the same dinner party. Concern over Sophia? What else would make her friend's brother come by?

The staircase from the first floor split at a landing and marched down both outer walls of the ground-floor hall. Harriet took the staircase farthest from the drawing room, hoping to get a glimpse of Mr. Fitzroy so she could gauge his demeanor.

Was he happy to be here? Excited? Irritated? Indifferent?

He wasn't near enough to the drawing room door for Harriet to see him during her descent. Her brain churned through ideas as she crossed the marble floor and joined him. "Mr. Fitzroy." She pushed an element of stunned breathiness into the words. "What brings you here?"

He rose from the chair he'd settled in near the window and gave her a quick dismissive glance that dropped from her head to her toes. Then he looked up at the ceiling as if seeking guidance. Or possibly strength.

Harriet frowned. Shouldn't he be bursting with the news, either from excitement or a wish to have it done with? "Mr. Fitzroy?"

He sighed and gave her a nodding bow. "Miss Hancock."

She waited.

He remained silent.

She stepped farther into the room and sank into a chair.

He sat as well, still without speaking.

He did recall that he was the one who'd come visiting, didn't he? What would she do if Sophia hadn't informed her of his pending arrival?

Probably sit here in expectant silence much as she was now doing.

He rubbed his hands down his thighs, took a deep breath, and said, "Sophia tells me you've decided to become an art patron."

Direct and to the point. That was easy to work with. "Yes. Sophia and I did discuss such an intention."

Such direct and obvious involvement in another's life made her mouth go dry and a burning sensation rise in her throat, but this was Sophia's brother. For her friend, Harriet could somehow swallow the idea that she was fully responsible for someone's livelihood, distressing though it may be.

Maybe she could offer him a job instead? Being an employer was far simpler than being a patron.

When Mr. Fitzroy said nothing, Harriet pressed on. "Are you aware of an artist in need of a patron?"

His gaze narrowed. "She said you wanted a particular artist. That you were obsessed with the carvings in an old cottage."

Direct was all well and good, but the man seemed nearly accusatory now. Harriet crossed her arms over her chest and attempted to look intimidating. "And what if I am? It isn't every day that one finds such art amongst such destruction. It's a fascinating combination."

"To be sure, but are you partaking in a determined search for the, er, artist?"

What answer was he expecting to hear? Sophia wasn't known for considering all the angles of a situation before making her move. It might be prudent for Harriet to leave her options for helping Sophia's brother open. Best not to commit to only one path yet. "I am devastated that someone was that destitute so close to my home and I couldn't help them."

He considered her for a moment before asking, "Would you have helped them?"

Was Mr. Fitzroy generally such an unsociable fellow, or did he just not think much of her in particular? The flatness in his words could be interpreted as disdain. What had she done to make this man think her cold and uncaring? Or something even worse?

She folded her hands in her lap and arranged herself as a perfectly proper lady, all but daring him to find fault with her. He'd barely interacted with her and certainly didn't know her. "I support many charitable subscriptions and have been known to involve myself personally when warranted." She'd been bolder about it once upon a time, but she'd found organized groups could be far more efficient in some situations.

Mr. Fitzroy dragged a hand across his eyes. "I am well aware that you get involved." He sighed. "Sophia thinks you've gotten the idea of supporting this artist into your head and that if you can't find whoever carved up your cottage, you'll be taken advantage of by some other fanciful-minded bloke."

There was no faking Harriet's indignant huff. "Well, that isn't very complimentary." Sophia would be hearing Harriet's thoughts about that.

"Complimentary or not, Sophia thinks it's true, and that's why I'm here."

Mr. Fitzroy hadn't yet announced himself as the artist in the cottage, so she had to continue acting as she would if she didn't hold that knowledge. She cleared her throat. "I don't answer to you, Mr. Fitzroy."

He shook his head. "I'm not here to stop you. I'm just here to solve the mystery. The Bible says, 'The truth shall make you free,' and that's very much true in this case."

"I beg your pardon?" How had the Bible become part of this discussion?

"I am the one who did those carvings."

Harriet forced her eyes wide. "You're an artist?"

"If you want to call me that. It was only a week. I spent my time carving the walls to keep busy. Aaron discovered me and Sophia's horse hiding there and found us all new lodgings."

"And you're here to claim the patronage?" Could she manage daily conversations like this, even for Sophia's sake?

He shook his head. "I'm simply here to ease your mind that the artist isn't wandering around somewhere, in need of assistance."

Had Harriet truly been set on finding the artist, that information would have been all she needed. But Sophia wanted her brother to find something new to love about life. Harriet couldn't deny her friend's request. Besides, the man shouldn't throw his glorious talent into the rubbish heap.

"You work in the stable most of the day, don't you? That can't leave much time to hone your skills. Nor can it provide enough funds to procure the best tools."

"One doesn't need a great deal of time to pursue a hobby. That's the beauty of such a pastime."

"But it could be more."

"I think you mean *I* could be more." His lips twisted briefly into a bitter curl before he pushed to his feet. "I've done what I came here to do. Good day, Miss Hancock."

Why hadn't Sophia come to her first? They could have concocted something far less problematic than offering a patronage to a man who didn't want one. Now Harriet had to buy them a little time to construct a new plan.

She scrambled out of her seat, grasping at the only thing he'd seemed willing to share in order to prolong the connection. "I'd like to at least know about the cottage."

He paused and turned to look at her. "You have already been to see it. Several times, if Sophia is correct."

"Well, yes." Those carvings must have been something of a comfort to him, or he would have done something else to keep busy. Perhaps he just needed to be reminded of that. "That's only the end result. I want to know how it came to be."

"I carved up the walls."

"And the furniture, yes." All his work was obvious and easily accessed, so what else could she say? "I want to experience it." That should do it. She could make him relive his days in the cottage, ask to see him do a few carvings, offer different tools than whatever crude ones he'd used the first time, and slowly, slowly she'd convince him to pursue his hidden passion.

"Experience it." He shook his head. "You want to stay a week in that dilapidated building? I wouldn't recommend it."

Neither would she. "We can reenact it." Even she nearly winced at that ridiculous idea. But it was out there now, so she had to run with it. "You can show me through drawings. Or describe certain moments."

He looked flatly unconvinced.

"We can perform an experiment to see what your work would be like under less daunting conditions. The comparison would be fascinating." Harriet was rather proud of herself for that idea.

His lips pressed into a thin line, and her smile widened in response. Obviously, he was trying not to frown at her. Likely, he was also trying to come up with a good reason to tell her no.

"Shall we discuss it over tea? We can meet next week. I should be able to procure the needed tools by then."

His frown broke through.

Her smile grew larger. If he didn't want to see her again, he could simply turn her down and leave. But he was invited to the same weekly dinner she was. He tried to skip them, but Sophia only let him miss so many.

There was no getting away from her. Harriet would have a new project after all.

Three

"So many other girls are here, Papa. How do I know who I should be friends with? What would Mama have looked for?"

—Harriet, in a letter to her father one week after arriving at Mrs. Brider's School for Girls

Harriet's carriage rolled slowly down the familiar tree-lined drive leading to Hawksworth, each tree out the window marking how far she'd come over the past year. Really, over the past three years.

After coming to Newmarket, she'd spent her first year in near hiding. Then she'd begun to move around town, slowly expanding her connections and attending events as it became apparent that no one intended to call her out into the street and label her a liar. She could obtain any invitation she wanted.

For now.

As an unmarried woman of independent means, she was always welcome. Partly because no one knew who she would be if and when she married and partly because she drew men of great prestige who wanted to answer that question and secure her money.

It was enough to make a girl wary of gentlemen's attentions.

To walk the balance between aloof harridan and coquettish flirt, she'd become eccentric and blunt, moving people about as if it were her right to do so. It never ceased to amaze her how many people let her get away with it.

The persona didn't completely disappear when she attended these Tuesday night dinners. Whether she'd become this outspoken woman after practice or it had been lurking inside her all along, she didn't know, but it remained even though she felt completely comfortable with this group of friends.

Only one secret entered these dinners with her, and it was so deeply embedded that she didn't fear revealing it here. All she had to do was ensure they never grew suspicious that she was holding such important information from them.

Her smile widened as a footman handed her down from her carriage and she glided up the steps and through Hawksworth's large front door. Inside, she took a few moments to marvel at the curved front hall. She would have loved a house as unique as Hawksworth, with its round central section and maddening maze of curved passages, doors, and rooms, but it was far too large for a woman on her own and likely hadn't been available for purchase when her grandfather bought her property.

There was no need for the butler to direct her where to go. This group had been gathering weekly for months now, and they all knew how to move about in one another's homes. At least, they knew how to get to the drawing room and the dining room. It was that odd blend of familiarity and privacy that made her so at ease. And with the variety of backgrounds, classes, and wealth, past lives were rarely the topic of conversation.

Several people were already in the drawing room when she strode in. Bianca, who'd become Lady Stildon a few months ago, was seated in a circle of chairs, conversing with Sophia and Lady Adelaide. Their respective husbands, Aaron Whitworth and Lord Trent, younger brother of the Duke of Riverton, stood near the window with Hudson, the Viscount Stildon. The men were indulging in a heated debate, though it was sure to also be good-natured.

Rebecca and Oliver, known to polite society as Lord and Lady Farnsworth, were visiting his father, so Harriet hadn't expected to see them tonight. Yet none of the other occasional attendees appeared to have arrived either. Lord Rigsby, who had joined them only three other times, wasn't a surprising omission, but where was Mr. Fitzroy?

Her gaze flitted about the room as she made her way to the circle of ladies. Sophia's brother frequently found a wall to support when he was in attendance, but tonight the room appeared to be holding its structure all on its own.

Was the sinking twist in her stomach disappointment? Surely not. She'd never felt it before, and he'd turned down as many Tuesday invitations as he'd accepted in the last couple of months.

She lowered into a chair and focused on the conversation.

"We'll see how you like it when Aaron starts ordering his grooms to curtail your riding," Bianca said with a scowl. "I'm not foolish enough to risk falling off, and I'm not even asking to ride the racehorses anymore, but I see no need to resign myself to sitting upon a horse being led about by a stable hand."

Sophia sputtered a laugh. "I'm sorry. It isn't funny, but—" Another giggle burst free.

Bianca rested her hand on her middle. "It isn't as if I'll be able to ride forever anyway. Eventually, I won't fit properly in the saddle. I've no intention of galloping across the Heath, but I want to enjoy riding until I can't anymore."

Harriet was excited and somewhat trepidatious about the coming baby. When she'd befriended Adelaide, the woman's daughter, Caroline, had already been born. This would be Harriet's first experience supporting a friend through carrying and birthing a child. She assisted the vicar's wife with care baskets, but other than cooing appropriately over a bundle of blankets, she had nothing to do with the babies themselves.

Sophia scrunched up her nose. "Suddenly I'm not quite as excited about the prospect."

All the ladies looked to Sophia.

"Are you joining me?" Bianca asked.

"Not that I know of." Sophia shrugged. "But it could happen at any time."

"Well," Adelaide said, blinking her large blue eyes at Bianca through her dark-rimmed spectacles, "when you do come down from the saddle, you can join me sipping lemonade on the terrace. I learned the first time around that it's easier if I just let Trent coddle me." Her lips curved into a small smile.

Bianca and Sophia gasped, and each reached over to clasp one of Adelaide's hands while spilling out a rush of congratulations.

Harriet joined the excitement, portraying appropriate levels of enthusiasm. Inside, however, a queasy feeling was forming. She knew it, recognized it, and hated it.

Jealousy.

Avoiding the emotion had been an unexpected benefit of avoiding friendships, though Harriet hadn't realized it at the time. She'd been protecting herself as much as she protected her secret. Inevitably, female friends got married, had children, and grew families while Harriet went home alone, craving the one thing she couldn't have.

At least not yet.

Growing up, there'd been no siblings to tease or play with, no raucous family celebrations like the children in the village enjoyed. After her mother died trying to bring Harriet's sister into the world, a tragedy made all the more heartbreaking by the baby's death a few hours later, it had just been Harriet, her father, and his parents. And a house filled with so much silence one nearly choked on it.

How nice it would be to have a family of her own.

How nice it would be to have her father say she'd made him proud.

How nice it would be to have known how much trouble one little lie would cause.

How horrible it would be to disappoint her father now, after all these years.

She could make it right, though. Tie off the lie and start fresh. It had to be done soon. Her money could maintain her appeal to unmarried men for only so long, and her thirtieth birthday was looming. Soon she'd have to climb up on the shelf and become just as dusty and ignored as the dreams she'd banished there years ago.

Bianca and Sophia's effusive joy had obviously been Trent's cue to share the news with the men, as the debate gave way to back slaps and congratulations. The group then joined the women, each husband moving to stand behind his wife's chair, a hand on her shoulder.

No one stood behind Harriet. No one laid the weight of his hand on her shoulder in solidarity. There wasn't even anyone with whom she could share a secret smile as they both sat on the outside of the loving couples.

As her fingers twisted together in her lap, Harriet tried to remember the way she'd felt in the carriage, how thankful she'd been to have these couples in her life. This moment was uncomfortable, but the years of feeling utterly alone had been worse.

She could help these babies in many ways once they came into the world, couldn't she? She could be the adopted aunt who helped them explore all the curiosities their parents wouldn't.

After all, it seemed making other people's dreams come true was what she did best.

JONAS STOOD AT THE SMALL WINDOW overlooking the drive that passed the stable and curved up to the manor house. His sister and her friends had traveled up that drive an hour earlier, and soon they'd be dining in Hawksworth's round dining room.

An invitation to join them had been used to start a fire in the common room two days ago. Jonas always debated declining the weekly invitation unless Lord and Lady Stildon were hosting. There was no debate then. Walking from the man's stable to his drawing room made even Jonas comfortable, and he never felt out of place.

He had nothing against Sophia's friends—in truth, he dealt with them better than he did most people—but whenever he joined them he found himself in a corner keeping company with his own thoughts.

Since he'd declined last week as well he'd have to attend next week no matter where it was held. Sophia didn't like him to miss three weeks in a row. Fortunately, if they held to their pattern, next week's would be at Lord Trent's home. It had plenty of corners where he could contemplate new ideas in his own time.

His attendance would have to become more strategic as he now felt a need to stay away from Miss Hancock's home as well. At least until she and Sophia forgot about the art patronage.

It shouldn't take long. The more he thought about it, the less sense it all made. What could Miss Hancock possibly gain from his creating more engravings? It had to be for Sophia. Not directly, of course. Sophia had never been subtly manipulative in her life. Miss Hancock probably thought elevating Jonas from stable hand to artist would somehow help Sophia's reputation.

That might be true if anyone who would care even knew he existed. He'd met only a few people in Newmarket, and now that Sophia was married with a new last name, no one would connect them immediately. They wouldn't connect them at all if it weren't for their matching red hair.

Jonas joined the other grooms in the large stone common room where they dined on bowls of hearty beef stew and yesterday's bread. A large sofa and three chairs faced a fireplace at one end of the room, while a long table lined with benches took up the other half. Conversations bounced around, but Jonas didn't participate.

Ernest, with whom he shared a room, was equally as quiet, so they often sat to the side by themselves and observed the rest of the men. Jokes and stories made for good, easy entertainment before Jonas went to bed in a solid, comfortable place.

It was a better life than he'd had in a very long time. So why did Sophia and Miss Hancock feel the need to muck about in it? Whatever their reason, he could outsmart it. He could think of a way out of Miss Hancock's machinations that wouldn't upset Sophia.

He rose from the table and strode down the corridor behind the sofa. His was the last room and therefore the coldest, as it shared a wall with the open hayloft and was far away from the common room fireplace. Still, it was better than sleeping outside.

His few personal effects sat atop the small dresser at the foot of his metal bed—his father's Bible, the book he was currently borrowing from Lord Stildon, a miniature of his mother, and a chunk of the cottage table Sophia had broken off for him when he'd moved out. He hadn't known she'd done it, had intended to leave all the carvings behind, but he had appreciated her thoughtfulness when he found it in his knapsack.

With one finger, he traced the deep grooves of his work. They were rough and uneven, creating a poor depiction of a horse's head but a good memory. Miss Hancock claimed she wanted to know those memories, asked about experiencing life in the cottage. He could provide that answer and force her to stop pushing—or at least to admit more than good intentions were behind her offer.

Lately a niggling voice in his head had been telling him he should ask God if there was supposed to be more than survival in his days, but tea with Miss Hancock would never bring him that clarity.

Among the items Jonas now owned were a pen, ink, and a notebook. He could stop this farce before it even began and he could do it without having to meet with Miss Hancock again.

Four

"Don't say anything about our coming home early. Marilee is heartbroken that she's now too frail to travel the world."

—Harriet's grandfather, in a letter sent to Harriet's father when she was five, after her grandparents' planned trip to France was canceled when her grandmother became ill traveling to the boat

After a restless night's sleep, Harriet came down late for breakfast. Not that it mattered. Her small staff were the only other residents of the house.

She yawned as she settled into her seat. The lateness of her arrival meant the morning sun was now warming a square of floor instead of her chair, but she was too groggy to care overmuch.

What she needed was food and coffee, and with no one else for the staff to serve, both should be arriving soon. A stack of publications sat on the table, pressed and ready for her perusal. She pulled it toward her with disinterest that faded as she saw the sheaf of folded papers lying on top.

The outside was marked with a fine scrawl reading *For Miss Hancock*. There was no seal or postal markings, so the papers had been personally delivered.

Frowning, she unfolded the handwritten pages, easily ignoring the shuffle of feet and clink of china that marked the arrival of her breakfast.

Within two lines it was obvious Sophia had not given her brother's stubbornness enough credit. Nor had Harriet. She'd thought herself so clever by claiming to want knowledge of his time in the cottage, but he'd found a way to satisfy her request without disrupting his life in the least.

Blindly nibbling at her food, she read the pages. Then she read them again. Ten minutes later, she was as concerned for Jonas's wasted talent as Sophia.

The bottom portion of each page bore a sketch, bearing the obvious marks of haste and nonchalance but still displaying skill and detail. Neat rows of words filled the top half.

And what words they were.

Her empty coffee mug and plate were taken away, replaced by her morning tea. The brew sat growing cold as Harriet absorbed every nuance of the story. She read the entire account four times before finally setting the pages aside and reaching for her teacup.

Her mouth revolted at the chilled tea, and she pushed the cup aside. A steaming teapot, wrapped in a towel to keep its contents warm, and two unused cups sat at the ready, since this was far from the first time she'd gotten caught up in her reading. She poured herself a new cup to sip while she thought.

Obviously, she couldn't allow Mr. Fitzroy to have the final word in such a manner. His drawings were skilled, but many a good artist did nothing but dally due to lack of ambition. Should he apply himself, Harriet had no doubt he could make a successful career.

His words, on the other hand . . . She picked up the writing again to skim it. The ability to bring such life to a story should not be locked away from the world.

What he'd given her was a gripping tale of one man's struggle through one of the most difficult weeks of his life. She could hear the wind whistling through the broken remains of the walls, smell the dust that stirred whenever the horse pawed the ground, feel the anxious hours as he waited for news of his sister's day.

It was as good, if not better, than any book she'd read in more than a year.

Mr. Fitzroy would never want the sort of fame Byron and his colleagues found in the literary salons, but life as a novelist would be better for him, wouldn't it? No more ending the day covered head to toe in filth, no more working at the mercy of the weather, no more sharing a small room above a stable. He would be invited to parties and recitations, welcomed into drawing rooms.

Did he not understand what a gift he had?

Probably not. To him, this had simply been the most expedient way to give her what she'd claimed she wanted.

Now she wanted Mr. Fitzroy to embrace the gifts within him and find a purpose in life that only he could fill. Didn't everyone want that? Didn't everyone want to know they were special and in possession of skills that not everyone could claim?

She flipped to the third page to reread her favorite portion.

I've been in the vicinity of horses my entire life, but no amount of stable work or horse care prepares a man for living in a confined area with only an animal for company.

I found myself talking to Rhiannon, particularly in the echoing darkness of night when the crickets emerged to serenade quiet cottages and the weighty silken air made anything feel possible—even the chance that a horse might answer back.

She would watch with those soft eyes as I carved beside her, shavings dropping to the earth like fluttering moths, and approve—or not—with the twitch of her lashes. In a return show of appreciation, I would braid elaborate designs into her mane and tail, occasionally crowning her with an embellishment of leaves and twigs. Something of a mockery when one considered the jewels with which a wealthier owner would decorate her.

Using Rhiannon as a muse was a natural extension of the time we were spending together. I've never minded being alone, but by the end of that week, I was craving human companionship instead of the equine variety. It would have been easy to feel like my life was crumbling right along with the walls, weeds crawling between the cracks, but I liked how those spaces let the sunshine in. The glow in the midst of that musty cottage was a reminder that this confinement was only temporary and that one day—one day soon—I would be free to roam again.

She read on, almost calling for her wrap as she felt the damp night air he wrote of, then glad she hadn't as he described the stifling midday heat. Even though she knew everything that had happened since his days in the cottage, knew that Sophia was happy and well, she felt concern for her friend's safety and the weight of the many hours her brother spent wondering.

Harriet knew him to be a practical man, but he was so much more than she'd realized. He had the soul of a dreamer. Even if he didn't know it, this retelling was more than an efficient way to tell her of his time in the cottage.

It was a cry from his heart, asking her to help him find his destiny.

Just as Sophia's horse now got to ride freely over the Heath with her owner, Mr. Fitzroy needed to be freed of the constraints of practicality so he could see what he might truly become in this world.

He'd turned down her offer of a patronage even though he readily admitted to enjoying the creation of art. How could she convince him to devote time to writing? How could she make him realize he could transport people to another world with a skill such as his?

Right now, she wanted to ride out to that cottage and sit, waiting for the sun to pierce through the rubble and light on the crossbeams so she could watch the dust dance in the rays. She wanted to sit still in a corner until a bird swooped in and scratched at the earthen floor.

These papers described a harrowing and humbling experience, but amongst those heartrending moments was a true appreciation of the mundane. He'd seen the beauty in the entire experience, and he'd made her see it, too, in ways she'd never thought to look at anything before.

An idea sparked in her mind, at once both brilliant and terrifying. Mr. Fitzroy needed to discover his talent, and Harriet needed to free herself from the trap she'd accidentally created.

It was possible she could help Mr. Fitzroy and herself at the same time.

And it would require only one more little lie.

NO ONE COULD CLAIM that stable work was elegant, but Jonas found it fulfilling. Working with the circus, every accomplishment was soon lost under the bustle of the next move or even the next show. In those last months, when he'd been in agonizing pain, he'd considered success merely making it through the day. The next morning would find him right back where he'd started.

Each day in the stables brought the same tasks, but there was something peaceful about the maintenance, about knowing it would be worth it to mend that tack or give that horse a good rubdown after a hard workout. The extra efforts added up, and he could see the horses making progress in their training, feel the accomplishment of a clean stall he wouldn't be dismantling tomorrow.

He hadn't realized how much he craved that solid sense of peace, but now that he had it, he didn't want to be without it again.

After stashing the wheelbarrow, he returned to the stable to check on the horses and complete his duties for the day.

His path was blocked by his sister standing in the middle of the aisle, arms crossed over her chest, mouth pressed into a determined line. Several steps behind her, casually leaning against the wall near the door, was her husband and his employer, studiously examining the toes of his boots.

In none of their many encounters that day had Aaron indicated Sophia might be vexed. While it was gratifying to know the man considered his wife his first priority, a little man-to-man support in the form of a warning might have been nice.

Not that a warning would have increased the chances of Jonas salvaging his plans for a quiet evening with a book and his notebook.

"Good afternoon, Sophia. You look nice." Jonas gave her a polite nod as he looked over the ensemble. Her dress was simple but modern, falling gracefully from the raised waistline to the floor without a patch or a stain in sight. The cerulean blue was a nice complement to her red hair, green eyes, and pale, freckled skin that bore no sign of a day spent getting dusty and dirty with the horses. She invoked memories of their mother before the worries of life had worn on her in ways no amount of scrubbing could erase.

"Thank you." Sophia looked him up and down. "You look filthy."

Was she expecting him to look otherwise? "Comes with the job."

"You promised to call on Miss Hancock."

Jonas's eyes narrowed at her phrasing that implied his mission had been more social than practical. Arguing semantics would give the issue too much importance, so he cut off the inquiry entirely. "I did. Seven days ago, as promised."

She bit her lip and glanced around the stable before whispering, "Then why are you still here?"

"Because," Jonas said, leaning in to whisper back, "I was able to provide what she wanted in one day."

Sophia's disgruntled expression made him want to ruffle her hair the way he had when they were children, but he resisted the urge. Her coiffure might not be as elaborate as some ladies', but it had been intentionally arranged. Instead, he stepped around her, moving toward Sweet Fleet's stall. There really wasn't anything left to do other than check the horse's feed and water, but Jonas would clean the horse from ears to tail again if it thwarted his sister's new urge to meddle.

Aaron gave him a crooked smile and shook his head before lifting his gaze to examine the rafters.

"What are you doing?" Sophia asked, trailing after Jonas.

"Checking on the horses your husband assigned me?"

"You need to be washing up. You can do so quickly, then ride with us."

Jonas rolled his eyes and opened the stall door just wide enough to slip his wiry body through. He knew what she was referring to, but feigned ignorance was often a helpful tool. "Ride where?"

"To dinner. You missed the last two."

"I beg your pardon." He made a show of checking the horse's provisions. "I haven't missed dinner in months." He tossed her a wry grin over his shoulder. "It's been a nice change."

"Not dinner the meal, dinner the gathering."

He shrugged. "I don't care much about the gathering."

"Well, I do."

"Then why are you letting me keep you?"

He pulled a currycomb from his back pocket, clinging to the slim hope that he could stretch his acceptable absence string to three. Dinner once a month would be doable. Possibly even enjoyable.

Sophia growled under her breath and looked to her husband. Aaron gave a one-shouldered shrug and remained silent.

How far could Jonas push his sister before he angered her enough to upset his employer? Not that he was concerned about being fired, but he could certainly be assigned less pleasant tasks each day.

To be honest, he'd rather do them than go to the dinner party.

"Why won't you come with us?" Sophia stepped into the stall opening, effectively trapping him inside unless he wanted to bodily move her.

Jonas sighed and put away the grooming equipment he didn't really need. "Why do you care?"

"Because you need society."

"No. *You* need society. I find my own company fascinating."

"I find your company fascinating as well, and I would like it if you were at dinner so I could spend some time with you without choosing between my brother and my friends."

That was hardly fair. "A week has six other days. Choose one and I shall commit to joining you weekly for a dinner at which we actually speak to each other instead of merely exist within the same room."

"I choose Sundays."

Jonas nodded, hoping his face didn't reveal that she'd acquiesced far easier than he'd expected. "Sundays it is."

"But you should still come tonight."

Of course she wanted both days. Never let it be said that his sister didn't think she could have the moon and the stars. As much as he adored her dreaming optimism, it was darned inconvenient at times.

He wiped his hands on a cloth as he nudged her out of the way. After securing the stall door, he took her elbow and guided her out to the gravel drive, where they could have more privacy. The acoustics of Hawksworth's stone stable allowed for the easy overhearing of conversations, and the other grooms enjoyed spreading gossip like fresh hay in a clean stall.

Aaron fell into step behind them, looming, silent, and ready to do whatever was necessary to make Sophia happy—within reason.

Forcing Jonas to go to dinner was probably deemed within reason.

His best chance was to convince his sister that she wanted what he wanted instead.

Once they were a sufficient distance from the stable, Jonas turned to face her and rubbed his hands up and down her arms, a gesture he'd used to comfort her when they were children and she'd fallen from a horse. "I'm glad you have friends, Soph. Too often the only one you had was me. I'll always be here, but tonight you're going to visit with the other ladies over a fine meal, perhaps enjoy a game of cards. My presence is not required. In fact, I'll likely throw off the numbers."

"Last week we had one more lady than gentleman. Harriet was alone."

That statement brought to mind an image of Miss Hancock sitting in a shadowed drawing room, face pressed to a window as rain rolled down and tears threatened. Fortunately, that disturbing thought wasn't reality. In this case, *alone* simply meant she had to sit beside someone of her own gender. "She wouldn't have been better off paired with me. I don't talk much."

Sophia looked ready to stomp her foot on the ground like an angry horse. She couldn't refute his statement. He knew it and she knew it. The frustration creeping across her face proved it.

Then the frustration ebbed, and he could almost see a frightening new idea taking its place. Her shoulders relaxed. Her lips curved into a smile. Her eyes sparkled in triumph.

Now it was Jonas's turn to tense.

"The Bible says not to forsake the 'assembling of ourselves together.'"

Aaron started to laugh and quickly turned away to cough into his hand.

Jonas crossed his arms over his chest and narrowed his gaze. "When did you start quoting the Bible in an argument?"

"Aaron and I have been studying at night." She met his stare with her own. "And this is not an argument. It is a discussion between me and the brother who is hiding himself away because I've found a new life and don't need him the way I did before. It's making me feel guilty."

How did she know just what to say to make him feel obligated to acquiesce to her wishes? Very well, he knew how. More than twenty-three years of walking through life together every day. Of course she knew him that well. Didn't that also mean she knew what she was asking of him when she pressured him to be amongst people?

"I never expected to take care of you forever." He rolled his shoulders to try to rid himself of the itching thought that a part of him might have assumed that *would* always be his purpose in life. After all, he'd never taken the time to find another one.

"Please come." She clasped both his hands in hers. "I worry about you."

Jonas sighed. Sophia had waited for so long to find what she now had. She deserved to enjoy it. If worry over his perceived loneliness prevented that, he could survive an evening of inconvenience. "Very well. Give me twenty minutes."

Sophia beamed. "Thank you."

Jonas shook his head as he stepped around her and moved toward the pump to collect a bucket of water. As he passed Aaron, he muttered, "You couldn't have stopped her?"

Aaron shrugged. "Why would I? Your coming to dinner makes her happy." He tilted his head. "I prefer her happy."

Jonas considered, for perhaps half a minute, taking a perversely long time to wash and change clothing, but delaying would only alter his sister's good mood.

Before long he was tucked into his brother-in-law's new carriage, headed toward dinner.

He had deliberately not looked at this week's invitation note, so he didn't know for sure where they were going. His breath paused as the carriage reached the end of the drive. As long as they turned south, all would be well. The only house to the north was Miss Hancock's. Hopefully, Lord Trent's home, with its numerous nooks and alcoves and large collection of oddities to feign interest in, was tonight's destination.

"I do hope Harriet remembers it's dinner night," Sophia said.

"Why wouldn't she?" Aaron asked, saving Jonas the need to bite his tongue to avoid voicing his own curiosity.

"She's been quite preoccupied lately. I think she may be formulating another project."

If neither he nor Sophia were privy to any information about that project, they likely weren't the intended victims. A prayer of gratitude threatened to escape, but Jonas managed to muffle it into a strange sort of grunt which earned him a questioning look from the other occupants in the coach.

Aaron's mouth slid momentarily into a smile before his expression became as unreadable as it normally was.

Sophia frowned. "What was that for?"

"Doesn't she always have a project of some sort going?"

"She likes to help people."

Sophia appeared to expect a response, so Jonas grunted again. Let her interpret its meaning however she wished. She was bound to come to a better conclusion than his true reaction. Miss Hancock had a forceful personality, and he'd seen her use it to push Sophia into feeling like her idea was the only option. Even if people were better off after her attentions—and Jonas had his doubts about that after her interference in Sophia and Aaron's relationship—her methods were questionable.

Still, it wasn't his place to say anything about it so long as her good will was never again aimed at Sophia. Or himself.

Five

"One of the scholarship girls wore a hole clean through her walking boot today when she stepped on a rock. It looked dreadfully painful.

I think I've grown again, as my own boots are pinching my toes. Can you send me another pair? I've included a tracing of my foot."

—Harriet, in a letter to her father one month into her second year at Mrs. Brider's School for Girls

Harriet had claimed she wouldn't join Adelaide and Bianca in the nursery to inspect the new rocking cradle because she had no need of knowledge on the available baby paraphernalia.

She lied.

Her main incentive for staying in the drawing room, sipping a pre-dinner sherry and avoiding any emotional confrontation with what she wanted but didn't have, was a desire to watch for Mr. Fitzroy.

She'd given it a great deal of thought over the past few days, and she was convinced this idea was one of the best she'd ever had. Mr.

Fitzroy needed assistance. Harriet needed to move on with her life. Her father needed to believe his daughter had received the world.

Three rather large needs, all of which could be addressed at one time.

Now she just needed to put her brilliant idea into motion.

Tension eased from her shoulders as Mr. Fitzroy entered behind his sister and brother-in-law. Sophia, fortunately, was somewhat predictable when it came to her brother. His attendance was the one piece of her plan Harriet couldn't control.

Sophia came straight to Harriet's side and struck up a conversation, forcing a delay in the plan's progress. Talking to Sophia was never a hardship, but as Mr. Fitzroy greeted the men and then drifted off on his own, Harriet's feet itched to follow him, to force a moment of easy conversation.

The night was young, however, and soon Adelaide and Bianca would return. As long as Harriet found a way to have the conversation before they were called in to eat, all would be well. She had no guarantee Mr. Fitzroy would stay long once the after-dinner port had been poured.

Finally, she was able to excuse herself to the retiring room without incurring any suspicion. Then she took a meandering path back to the drawing room, pretending interest in Trent's extensive and unique collectibles. Mr. Fitzroy was likely using the same excuse. Hopefully, he'd be somewhere that allowed a short, private conversation.

Luck was with her, as he had removed himself to a small alcove to examine a suit of armor. He was still in the drawing room, but shielded from prying eyes, and if she circled through the music room and entered from the side, she'd have to walk directly past him to return to the ladies. Striking up a conversation about the armor would be the most natural thing in the world.

An accelerated pounding in her chest had her pressing a hand to her breastbone as she strolled toward him. How to approach him? Unlike Sophia's, Mr. Fitzroy's reactions were unpredictable. Yet his sister claimed he couldn't resist a direct request for help.

Harriet could easily believe it. He often worked extra hours. He'd even helped in her small stable when one of her grooms had a terrible cold. A straightforward inquiry was definitely her best choice.

Coming to a stop next to him, she gave the armor a long look before saying, "I need your help."

His head turned slowly to face her, his green eyes moving directly to hers, staring at her as he considered the statement.

It was unnerving, the way she could look straight into his eyes because of their similar heights. She had no way to angle her face and hide her expression or manufacture certain appearances. Yet something about not having to lift her chin to meet his gaze was comforting and intimate.

"You need my help." His voice was polite, but the words were slow and cold despite the light Irish brogue rounding them out. "With what?"

She could do this, and she could do it without lying. Much. "I've read your account."

"That was my purpose in delivering it to you."

The urge to kick him in the shin was strong, but she resisted. "I enjoyed it immensely."

His head gave a slight jerk sideways before tilting as his gaze joined hers with strong consideration. "I apologize that it was not what you expected."

She returned his examining stare. "What did you think I expected?"

"You felt sorry for me." He gave one shoulder a careless shrug, as if he'd fully explained himself.

"Did you think I wanted to writhe in tortured agony over your experience?"

"I think such would make you feel a more worthy rescuer."

He had a point, but she'd stopped wanting to rescue him by the end of the second page. Now it was about rescuing his talent from stagnating beneath his tired contentment. "'Tis far more worthy to be the discoverer of untapped treasure."

He frowned at her. "I beg your pardon?"

She gave a short nod. "As well you should. You have been hiding this light for far too long. Fortunately, I know how we can remedy that problem."

"What problem?"

"The problem of your learning how to share your words with the masses."

He rubbed a hand across the back of his neck and glanced toward the group of ladies talking in the main part of the room. "I'd rather you didn't share my story of the cottage with anyone. Sophia's part in such a tale certainly won't help garner her riding clients, and I've no need of pitiable looks or well-meaning handouts."

"I wasn't referring to those words exactly." His concern for Sophia and her reputation was understandable and admirable, but did he truly not see anything lacking in his own life?

From Sophia's stories, Harriet knew their early life had been decent enough, but the past six years had been marked by a focus on survival. It would be easy for a man to forget there was more to life than not dying.

She would help him remember.

And in the process of helping him find a new life, she would free herself to claim one of her own.

Stating approval of his work had caught his attention but not intrigued him enough to pursue it. If she wanted to help him in spite of himself, he would need to think he was the one helping her.

"I want to write a book," she said.

"I'm sure you've plenty of time," he returned.

That might have been meant as something of an insult, but she would not let it distract her. "I'm not a very good writer."

"Could be something of a problem."

"But I have such a wonderful idea."

"Write it anyway. Maybe it won't be as bad as you think." He shrugged. "If it is, you can write it again. It's bound to get better each time."

Why wasn't he jumping at this chance? Did he dislike her that much? Maybe he didn't see her need as important. She curled one hand into a hidden fist and forged on. "I was hoping you would help me."

His eyebrows shot up. "I've never written a book."

"But you do know how to write."

"I am capable of holding a pen, yes."

"I meant you know how to write well."

"My mother did put an emphasis on penmanship."

The man was being deliberately obtuse, and it was inspiring equal desires to growl in frustration and laugh in amusement. Neither would help her, so she gritted her teeth against both. His verbal sidesteps would not keep her from her goal.

"I would like to learn to write—to phrase sentences and put together the imagery the way you did."

Mr. Fitzroy frowned. "I don't know what I did. I just wrote it."

Of course he had. "That's how we'll do it, then. We'll write the book together."

"I beg your pardon?" The words came out thin and rough, as if choked by his own surprise.

One day he'd thank her. All she had to do was convince him to assist her long enough for him to realize he enjoyed working with words. Then he would forge ahead with his own project and she could use his practice work to enhance her letters to her father. After that, she could build the life she truly wanted.

Everyone would be happy.

But how to convince Mr. Fitzroy he wanted to participate? He'd never agree to her true intentions. "You could write a few portions of my story, and I'll watch your process and ask questions. When you answer them, we'll both discover what makes your prose special."

"But it isn't."

"I beg to differ. My tea was completely cold by the time I set your pages aside."

His face was blank as he looked at her. No frown, no smile, no grimace of irritation. "You want me to write a book you can then claim as your own."

When he put it like that, it sounded so awful. That was, in effect, what she was asking for, though, and she couldn't go backward now. She gave a bright smile and brazened her way through. "Yes. Travel journals are very popular. Just think how much people would enjoy a fictional story of a woman traveling the world, sending letters home to her father about her experiences."

"Why wouldn't they just read a travel journal?"

Why indeed? "Because travel journals look at the big picture. They miss the life in the little things, the beauty in the small moments." At least that was the complaint Father had when Harriet reworded passages of travel journals for her letters. "I want my story to focus on those details."

Mr. Fitzroy looked back at the suit of armor.

Harriet held her breath and her tongue. If she said anything else before he did, she'd appear desperate. He hadn't immediately said no, which had to mean something about her offer intrigued him, didn't it?

"Instead of the wonders of the Parisian architecture," he said softly, "you want to emphasize the flavor of the spiced pancakes at the street fair."

How did he know about spiced pancakes? That hadn't been what she was thinking, but that was exactly what she needed. "Yes. That's precisely what I mean."

He turned his head, considering her with eyes that seemed to hold dozens of thoughts and observations. "Why would I do this?"

"Because." Harriet swallowed. "It would give you the opportunity to do what you enjoy while maintaining your privacy."

"Who says I enjoy it?"

No one had, actually. Sophia was always talking about his art, which was decent enough, but not compared to his writing. "We could include pictures."

"Hmmm."

Did the man not see it? "When you had time to yourself, you turned to art. It's all over the cottage—even in the way you braided Rhiannon's mane."

He took a deep breath and gave a short nod. "I'll do engravings for your book."

It should be a victory, but engravings wouldn't help her. They wouldn't help her father. And in all honesty, she didn't think they would help Jonas. With a little practice he could probably be as good at them as anyone else, but with the writing? He could be extraordinary. Instinctively, she knew the writing could do far more for him than the engravings. "You didn't have the means in the cottage to write stories."

"You think if I had, there would be pages of prose instead of walls of engravings?"

She braced her shoulders. "Yes."

"I've the means now."

"And have you been writing?"

He looked away, making her think there was indeed a notebook of scribblings tucked away in addition to his sketchbook. What did he write? Stories? A journal? An account of his life? If she knew that, it would be easier to find the line between urging him to agree and pushing him into stubbornly saying no.

She had to move with delicate care. "It's a safe way to pursue a dream, really. Writing with me carries no risk or scrutiny."

"Writing in my room has the same benefit."

Why did the infuriating man have to be so logical? "But," she said slowly, buying a slight bit of time to formulate her next argument, "this would be a way to make others happy while remaining safely anonymous."

At least for now. Acknowledgment and acclaim could be added to this mix later.

"Why are you doing this?"

Harriet's mouth dried, and her tongue thickened. No one ever asked her that. On the rare occasion that she extended a direct offer instead of helping people on the sly, they simply accepted her enthusiastic generosity. "I . . . well . . . that is, I like to see my ideas fulfilled to their greatest ability."

Dark-red eyebrows curved in skepticism.

Perhaps a bit more honesty was in order. "I like to enrich people's lives, and I believe writing would enrich yours."

He snorted and shook his head. "You are unbelievable."

Which was why she needed him. Her father needed to believe she'd accomplished his goals. "Are you truly satisfied with storing your talents beneath the bed?"

His expression was the picture of calmness when he looked back at her and said in a firm voice, "Yes."

Well, there was no arguing with that. She wasn't wrong about this, though. She couldn't be. His own sister had contrived to get Harriet to help him. "Are you satisfied with my nagging you daily until you agree?"

He dragged a hand over his face. "You would, wouldn't you?"

She shrugged. "It's for the best."

"You know, I think you genuinely believe that."

"Of course I do."

"My patience will outlast your persistence."

Stubborn man. "You underestimate my determination."

"You underestimate how little I'm concerned with your opinion."

"I'm sure Sophia would agree with me." At this point, Harriet was ready to play dirty. She would help Mr. Fitzroy whether he wanted it or not.

He regarded her for several silent moments, then shook his head with a sigh. "I'll help you write the book."

Harriet almost clapped in glee. "Excellent. When would you like to start?"

"Next year."

"Tomorrow it is. I can ask Sophia to have Aaron rearrange your sched—"

"No. If I'm helping you, I'll do it on my own time."

She had just won a great victory, so what would it hurt to give him this? "When is your time available?"

"Late afternoons. Evenings. I also get two half days a week."

Harriet frowned. Those were the most easily filled times on her social schedule. She had no one but herself to answer to when it came to her whereabouts, though. She could adjust. "Very well." She narrowed her gaze. "You will show up, won't you?"

"'Let your communication be, Yea, yea.'" Jonas pressed his mouth into a thin line. "I said I'll be there."

Harriet blinked before murmuring, "How can one be so sure of themselves that they're certain they won't change their mind?"

It wasn't a question she truly expected him to answer, but she couldn't keep from voicing the wonder aloud.

He considered her before asking, "You really want to learn to write like me?"

She crossed her fingers behind her back like a child and lied for the betterment of two precious lives. And her own. "I truly do."

"I'll let you know when I can start." He gave her a short nod and turned away, crossing the room to join the other gentlemen and leaving Harriet staring at the armor.

She would be able to keep this all under her control.

Wouldn't she?

Six

"I have never considered my life to be one worth remembering in any particular detail, but the books lining Lord Stildon's shelves inspire me to ponder more upon that idea. Perhaps I should take more time to remember my steps, though I see no reason to revisit the hardship."

—Jonas, in musings written on the first page of the notebook he purchased the week after Sophia's wedding

Since Miss Hancock would bring his sister into the picture if Jonas delayed their meeting past another Tuesday dinner, he made arrangements to start working with her on Monday.

Part of him hoped the delay would allow her interest to be snagged by another project. Should that occur, he would graciously allow her to back out of the agreement. If it didn't, he'd use the time with the heiress to get an understanding of what drew her attention so he could keep Sophia—and apparently himself—out of her future plans.

By Sunday there'd been no message of cancellation and Jonas resigned himself to participating in whatever scheme Miss Hancock was concocting. He didn't for one moment believe she wanted to write a book, but he couldn't fathom what else she would do with the results of their collaboration.

Keeping his promise would provide the added benefit of satisfying that particular curiosity.

Aaron didn't train the horses on Sundays, but they still required care, so Jonas mucked out the stalls and refilled water and food troughs before cleaning up and walking into town to attend church. He'd do all the work again that afternoon, which kept him from being idle—a fact he was thankful for—but still left time to himself, time he wasn't yet accustomed to having.

After he'd seen to the animals in his care again, he wandered over to the Hawksworth horses. The other grooms thought him a lunatic for putting his hand to work he wasn't paid for, but he couldn't relax while someone else worked around him.

"I'll take that pitchfork, if you please." Mr. Knight, Hawksworth's head groom, extended his hand and wiggled his fingers.

Jonas looked from the man to the tool. "I assure you, I don't mind."

"It isn't your opinion I'm concerned about," the gruff man answered, the wrinkles of his weathered face deepening as he frowned. "If you wear yourself out, Mr. Whitworth will blame me, and I'm not going to risk it. You're done for the afternoon."

With a shake of his head, Jonas handed over the pitchfork. He wouldn't argue with the other man, especially since he oversaw that section of the stable. The time he'd been giving to extra tasks would soon be taken up by Miss Hancock's project anyway.

He climbed the stairs and found three other grooms playing cards at the table in the common room. He gave them a nod before continuing to his room. Once there, he stood in the middle of the space and rubbed his chest in an effort to ease the sense of restlessness. As thankful as he was for the home, he didn't want to spend his waking hours within the dark space. Playing cards in the common room wasn't much more appealing.

So what did he want to do?

The book he'd borrowed from Lord Stildon's library the week before sat atop his dresser, and he scooped it up before returning outside and setting off to find a tree he'd be comfortable sitting beneath. Once he'd fulfilled his agreement with Miss Hancock—which shouldn't take long, as what he knew about writing couldn't take more than three days to learn—he'd have to consider what to do with his life. He couldn't keep picking up extra jobs just to avoid thinking about it.

Sophia's claim that he'd focused his life on her had been mostly true. Jonas had never wanted much, so why not help those he loved attain their dreams? That was a noble purpose in life as far as it went, but it did leave him at loose ends now that his sister was settled and happy.

Jonas needed a new purpose, even if it did nothing more than keep him busy during his non-working hours. Without some sort of task, he'd go mad.

Once situated under the tree, he tried to lose himself in the pages of the book. The idea that he could create something similar was both laughable and compelling. If he were honest, it was also more than a little intimidating. He'd written a few pages in the notebook he kept in his dresser, but they'd mostly been accounts of events he'd seen, passing memories he wanted to capture, or lessons he'd learned during the day's work. It was more of a journal than any sort of story.

He'd never even thought to attempt such a thing. What had given Miss Hancock the idea he could teach her? One couldn't teach something they'd never even tried.

Didn't that prove his suspicion? If she truly wished to learn to write, she would have hired a master from nearby Cambridge.

This was something else, and once he learned her true motive, he would know how to proceed. As long as her ultimate scheme didn't involve Sophia, he'd be able to simply walk away from the entire business.

He shut a finger in the book to hold his place and looked up at the sky in thought. His sister was fragile right now. Impressionable. She'd spent years claiming an aspiration that had really been nothing more than her desperate need to have a hope to hold on to. Once the opportunity arose for something real and true, she'd craved it down to her toes. Still, she wasn't entirely comfortable with this fresh dream. Its picture was still forming, and Jonas didn't want anyone telling Sophia how it needed to be carved.

Particularly not someone like Miss Hancock.

Last Tuesday the ladies had talked about going shopping, and Miss Hancock mentioned needing a new ball gown. Did she intend to convince Sophia to buy a ball gown as well? Was she trying to put visions of grand amusements in his sister's head?

As if Sophia and Aaron would be welcome at an aristocratic ball.

Starting tomorrow, he'd be in a position to discover if Miss Hancock had intentions toward his sister. That made enduring the rest of her plan more bearable.

It also allowed him to put off the question that had been plaguing him lately.

What, exactly, *did* he want in life? Even as a kid, he'd been happy to go along with what everyone else wanted to do.

The problem was there wasn't anyone to follow now.

Jonas opened the book and once again tried to lose himself in the pages for the rest of the afternoon.

JONAS JERKED AWAKE, his eyes open and staring into the darkness, unable to find anything to focus on to remove the last image his dream-self had experienced. He scrubbed a hand across his face, and it hit the slickness of sweat on his forehead and skidded off onto the pillow. His mouth was open, breath running in and out of his lungs in a thankfully soundless charge.

A snore rose from the bed across the room, proving Jonas's sleeping journey to the past had disturbed only him.

He used the blanket to wipe the sweat from his face, then tossed it to the foot of the bed, allowing the cool air of the room to wash over him and finish bringing him into the present. The dream had been so real and yet so obviously not real at the same time.

One moment he'd been a young man of fifteen, walking down to the stable with his father to see the foal he'd been told would be his. A horse of his own to raise and train and ride. Sophia's had been born two days prior, and she'd spent every moment since watching the white spindly-legged foal scrabble around the paddock.

His Andalusian was brown, and he was already on his feet, rotating through experimentally lifting each hoof off the ground as if he had invented some new country dance. They'd named him Prancer, and it was the first time Jonas experienced an emotional connection to the family business.

In the next moment of the dream, he'd been riding Prancer, training him with a great deal of assistance from Sophia, putting in more care and hours than he'd ever done with a horse before.

Until it had all ended, and he was riding away from his father's stable, everything he owned strapped to his back or Prancer's, Sophia in the same situation by his side. The load had dwindled and shrunk over the years, especially when they'd been forced to flee across the Channel to escape the false accusations of their unscrupulous employer.

Then he'd been riding in the circus, making a show with Prancer and Sophia and Rhiannon, watching the money pile up in the owner's hat but never get passed down to them.

How long his dream-self had played through these memories, Jonas didn't know. Had he recalled them all in a moment, or had he been reliving them in the hours since his head hit the pillow?

It didn't matter. All that mattered was that last scene, the one that stayed in his mind. He'd been riding beside Sophia. The rain had been heavy for days, and the road was not well tended. He'd nearly quit the circus that morning when Mr. Notley insisted they press on despite the conditions. Sophia didn't know about that fight, didn't know he'd counted their meager savings to see if it would be enough to get them somewhere—anywhere they might find work.

It wasn't. So he'd mounted up and moved on.

In this, he knew he'd walked through every moment in his dream, relived every second in excruciating detail. The distant thunder that had jerked Prancer's attention. The mud that had sucked at his back hoof. Jonas shifting his weight so he could dismount and walk alongside the horse for a while but never getting the chance, because with the next step the ground gave way and they were both sliding.

The horse bucked, and Jonas went flying, landing on his backside with enough force to break his coccyx and send pain shooting through his entire body.

That was nothing compared to the pain he'd felt when he gathered himself enough to look around, when he'd seen the wide track of fresh mud down the side of the small ravine, when he'd hobbled to the broken body of his beloved horse.

The dream was a familiar one. Jonas always woke when he cocked the gun, and he was thankful for that small favor. The dream came often during those first weeks after the accident. Slowly, it had faded away, and he'd not had it once since coming to Newmarket.

Why had it returned now? What had he done to bring that memory to the surface? Was it the time he'd spent in contemplation yesterday afternoon, considering what he should do with himself now that he was alone? That was all he'd done differently the day before.

With his heart beating normally again and his skin prickling from the chill in the air, Jonas pulled the blanket back up and closed his eyes.

As he sought sleep once more, he couldn't help but wonder if the return of the dream was some form of warning.

Seven

"Let this book be the story of my own life."

—Jonas's father, in a prayer he wrote in the front of his Bible

Jonas managed to forget about the dream as he worked through the morning. Not until it was time to leave for his meeting with Miss Hancock did he recall it in vivid detail.

He'd cared for a lot of horses. In truth, he'd exercised, fed, or brushed every horse in the Hawksworth stable at one point or another, and he'd viewed all of them as a job.

All but one.

Whenever he'd requested personal use of a horse in the past three months, he'd been given a black Friesian named Pandora. It had gotten to the point that he didn't even ask anymore. It was understood that if he needed a horse, he was to take Pandora. They even asked him if he had plans to take her out before one of the other grooms exercised her.

The first time he'd been given the horse, Jonas assumed it was something of a joke. It was difficult for someone of his stature to swing the large saddle onto the horse's wide back and then clamber atop.

Riding the stocky horse was a pleasant change from the thoroughbreds he rode for Aaron, and no matter how Jonas tried to keep a practical view of things, the horse had become more than simply a mount. He'd even taken to sneaking a treat to her on occasion. Now he—and everyone else—considered the horse essentially his.

Pandora wasn't Prancer. Jonas hadn't been there for Pandora's birth, hadn't broken her to saddle—had in fact never trained the animal to do anything. Yet she was the one thing he would miss when it came time to move to Aaron's new stable. Pandora was a Hawksworth horse and would be staying right where she was.

After last night's dream, Jonas considered taking another horse to Miss Hancock's, but Pandora needed her daily exercise. So with gritted teeth and a litany of prayers, he threw the large saddle onto the mare's broad back and mounted up.

Since he was dealing with plaguing memories anyway, he took the long route, cutting across the woman's property to the cottage that had started this entire business.

He stopped Pandora a few feet from the door, or rather where the door would be if Sophia hadn't ripped it down in a rush to see him one day. Aside from carving up all the wooden surfaces and caring for the horse, Jonas had spent that one memorable week sleeping more than he ever had in his life. Idleness had troubled him almost as much as the injury, and sleep passed the time in a way that maintained his sanity.

The horse shifted beneath him, and Jonas nudged her forward. "Would you like me to put braids into your hair?" He eased his hand beneath the silky black mane that reached well past the horse's shoulder and gave her a strong pat. "I could do your tail and the feathering over your feet. It would take me hours, and I wouldn't have time left to see Miss Hancock."

He was talking to the horse like a friend, and that was dangerous. He steered her away from the cottage and continued toward the house, berating himself for coming this way in the first place. No amount of reminiscing would change what had been. Simply writing up the experience for Miss Hancock had been more than enough looking back.

Perhaps this trip by the cottage was beneficial after all, as a reminder of the lessons he'd learned within it. Normally he had little difficulty trusting God's hand in his life, but when he'd had nothing to do but think, that dependence had been harder to come by. *All things work together for good to them that love God*, so there had to be some benefit to this project he was embarking on with Miss Hancock.

Until he knew her true intentions, he'd act as if he believed her claims. He'd insist that since she was the actual author, she must rewrite everything in her own words. That should sufficiently annoy her into revealing her true plan.

The small stable behind Miss Hancock's house had eight stalls and two stable hands. Jonas considered caring for the horse himself, but a delayed arrival wouldn't get him out of this promise.

He'd been here before, delivering messages, helping Sophia, even attending Tuesday dinners. This time the house seemed larger. Why did an unmarried woman have such a large home? Even an independent spinster could make a statement with a far smaller abode.

One of the footmen met Jonas at the door. How was Jonas to act here? Men of his class normally knocked on the kitchen door, yet here he was striding in the front hall as an expected guest.

Lawrence didn't seem to know how to treat Jonas either, tossing him quickly fading smiles and starting and stopping a half-dozen sentences as they climbed the stairs.

Jonas just looked ahead, eyes fixed on the doorway in the center of the wall that led to the first floor. The public rooms were all on the ground floor, so he'd never been through that door.

At the top of the stairs, he was led to the left and shown into a large library. Windows marched down the entire south wall of the house, creating pools of light between tall decorative bookshelves. One end of the room held a grouping of sofas and chairs, while the other boasted an enormous desk.

Miss Hancock rose from her seat behind the desk, a wide smile on her face enhanced by the genuine welcome in her dark eyes. "You're here." She rushed forward, hands clasped together in front of her. "Lawrence, please have tea sent up directly." She frowned. "Along with sandwiches and biscuits."

Jonas avoided emitting a smirk of laughter. Was Miss Hancock among those who thought him far too scrawny for the work he did? The concern was harmless enough, as he enjoyed food and could eat piles of it without expanding in any direction.

The footman left.

Jonas waited.

Miss Hancock unclasped and reclasped her hands.

Jonas waited.

This was her project. He wasn't about to take the lead.

The grin of greeting she'd worn earlier was now stretched into a wide flat line that she might have thought looked like a smile. The lack of dimples and not even a flashing glimpse of teeth made it more like a grimace, and a comical one at that.

Fortunately, Jonas had a great deal of experience keeping his thoughts to himself and not laughing.

"Have you had a pleasant day?" she finally asked.

First refreshments and now pleasantries? Did she think this a social call? He struggled with inconsequential chatter in a normal setting. He certainly didn't expect it in what he'd hoped would be a professionally distant atmosphere.

"I wasn't sure if you'd come," she said when he didn't answer.

Jonas tilted his head. "I promised I'd be here."

"Yes, but some people view the homes of single women the same as the homes of bachelors."

"Ah," Jonas said, shifting his weight at the discomfort of such a subject. "I believe in such a case yours would still be the concerned reputation." He shrugged. "It's only me, though."

She stopped even pretending to smile. "What does that mean?"

Why was she confused? "That it's not all that different from having Lawrence bring you food or allowing the carpenter in to repair a door."

"Hmmm." Why didn't she appear happy with his explanation? He did manual labor for a living. They weren't equals. They weren't even friends.

Letting anyone into his life was difficult and exhausting. The idea of letting Miss Hancock in made his head spin faster than Sweet Fleet on a practice run.

Professional and focused was what they needed to be. "What do you want to write a book about?"

She glanced at the open door, then cleared her throat and gave him another tight smile. "I told you. A woman's travels."

"That's rather vague." Which made him all the more suspicious. "Where is she traveling to?"

"Oh." She spun back to the desk, where several books were piled. "Europe seems a promising idea. People are returning to Spain now and even France."

Jonas picked up a book titled *Travels Through the South of France*. He flipped to the first page, which bore the date 1809. "Do you think it still looks the same? Surely war has changed it."

"I think the culture would have survived. Big things might be different, but I want to celebrate the little things."

"The beauty in the moment."

She beamed at him. "Exactly."

The idea was a good one. A book about a traveler noticing and appreciating culture enough to interact with it and take her life in a new direction.

Still, a sense of unease remained. He shrugged it to the back of his mind and looked about the room. "I can bring you pages to use as examples. You can rewrite them in your own words."

A frown thinned her lips, and Jonas berated himself for noticing. He could only know it had thinned her lips if he'd paid attention to their normal fullness. And he hadn't. Of course he hadn't.

He pinched himself again. They didn't need two liars in this room.

"If we don't work together," she said, "I won't learn from you."

He picked at a callus on his thumb with his forefinger. "I don't think how I hold a pen will tell you much. You'll learn more from the sentences I write."

"But if you work without me, I can't ask why you chose those particular sentences."

Jonas sighed. "I doubt I'll be able to answer that question anyway."

"Of course you won't if you aren't here for me to ask." She smiled as he tried to trace her logic that was somehow right and wrong at the same time. It was a smile of pride, like a cat who had successfully cornered a mouse.

This mouse knew how to fight back. "We'll need another desk, then. We can hardly share the same work surface."

"Why not?"

Aside from the fact that her servants were probably belowstairs at this very moment speculating as to why Jonas was here? The last thing he needed was any of them walking in to find him shoulder to shoulder with Miss Hancock, heads bent over the same paper.

Currently, he didn't have a reputation in Newmarket. He barely even had a name. He wanted to keep it that way.

If he said that, though, his new adversary would only produce a counterargument. Instead, he went on the offense. "You are the named author of this book, are you not? You'll have to rework everything I write into your own words. Like a child copying his letters."

"I don't think I care for that comparison."

He did. It kept things far less complicated. The servants weren't the only ones who might have a problem with Jonas spending hours in such close proximity to Miss Hancock. "Aye, two desks. Definitely."

She gave a quick nod. "I'll have the writing desk from my private parlor brought in tomorrow."

Once more he waited for her to lead their direction. She didn't. The strained quiet stretched on until the tea tray was delivered.

Miss Hancock lurched toward the seating area and set about pouring tea and filling plates. Because he had no reason to turn down sandwiches, Jonas joined her.

She nibbled on one sandwich while he consumed two. When he set his teacup on the low table between them, she set her half-eaten sandwich aside, looked about, then jumped to her feet. "I'll just . . ." She crossed to the desk, scooped up a stack of travel books, and hauled them back to the seating area.

"I want the book to be a series of letters from the woman to her father. Perhaps we could read a few entries pertaining to the area we choose and decide what her first letter should hold." She dropped the books onto the table. "Then you could, I don't know, write up the experience?"

While she read over his shoulder? Was that how she intended this to work?

She settled onto the sofa and picked up a book. "If you move over here, we can both see the passage."

Jonas clamped his lips together to keep tea from sputtering out as he nearly choked on his last sip. What was this woman doing? He narrowed his gaze at her as she flipped through the book. Everything about her demeanor purposed a genuine determination to find a particular passage.

Sitting beside her on the sofa was an even more disturbing image than sitting shoulder to shoulder behind the desk, though. Still, there was no other way to view the same book, so he slowly rose and rounded the low table to sit beside her.

For the next half hour, her gaze never lifted from the books as she pointed out passages about France. Some of it reminded him of a place he and Sophia often visited in Ireland. They would take a picnic and ride the horses down to the stream before wading about in the cool water, occasionally splashing each other and the horses. "She could go for a walk through the woods."

Miss Hancock turned to look at him, blinking. "Why would she do that?"

The bafflement was too pure, too quick not to be genuine. If she were truly writing a book, she definitely needed help. "Because one book mentioned a large forest surrounding Chambord. Perhaps your character—what is her name, by the way?"

Her glance jerked to his and then slid quickly back to the book. "Oh, er, uh, Elsabeth. Elsabeth . . . Ridley."

Jonas nodded. "Perhaps Elsabeth stops her carriage on the way. She lets it continue down the road while she cuts through the trees."

Miss Hancock frowned. "But there's a perfectly good drive to take her straight there."

"Isn't that the point of this, Miss Hancock?" Jonas scraped a hand through his hair. "If you want to regurgitate the details of the site, you may as well publish a reading list of travel memoirs."

"You're right." She smoothed her hands over the open book. "And call me Harriet. If we're to be partners, formality seems unnecessary."

Formality was absolutely necessary. Objectively, he'd always known Miss Hancock was a beautiful, if irritating, woman. The focus and enthusiasm she'd displayed over the past thirty minutes had been something of a surprise.

An attractive surprise.

He'd had to be serious for so much of his life. First in learning his father's lessons and then ensuring his and Sophia's survival. There'd been moments of frivolity and fun, of course, but he'd never experienced the sheer joy of life Miss Hancock seemed to present, reckless though it may be.

It drew him. Sometimes he felt far older than the twenty-three years he'd been alive. Now that he had some security, shouldn't he change that? If only he knew how.

"May I call you Jonas?" Miss Hancock said, interrupting his introspection. "Or I can use Fitzroy, if you find that more comfortable."

"Either is fine," Jonas said without giving customary thought to his answer. He'd given up being insulted by informality the week he'd started his first service job.

"Jonas, then." She grinned. "I like being special."

Jonas would rather she be as inconsequential as everyone else. He scooped up the books and moved toward the desk. "I'll get started."

"Then I'll see to having the parlor desk moved."

He kept his gaze averted as he sat and opened one of the books, more ready than ever to lose himself in someone else's world.

Eight

"I see no need to tell your papa of your changed plans. You can still take a trip during your school break. I will simply bring you to Cambridgeshire with me."

—Harriet's grandfather, in a letter to Harriet during her second year at Mrs. Brider's School for Girls

"What would you think of our redoing the library?" Harriet mused as her lady's maid, Elsabeth, whose name Harriet had frantically thrown out a week ago as the main character of her book, delivered the post to the writing desk.

Harriet hadn't spent a great deal of time in the library until this past week, and the heavy furniture and crowds of books were making her miss the airy and feminine environment she'd created in her parlor.

"Redo it, miss?" Elsabeth looked about the room in confusion. "But you said a house needs a masculine library."

"Yes, yes, I did." But that was only because she'd envisioned bringing a husband here one day, even though he would have a home of his own and they would likely sell this one.

All the more reason to leave the library as it was.

But this fictional husband felt very far away today, and she was stuck working in the library until Jonas could be brought to see reason.

Maybe she would just buy another desk so she could return this one to her parlor.

"Maybe you could face the desk in a different direction," Elsabeth said. "If you turn it a little, you can see out the window."

"It's worth trying." Another desk would be a wasteful purchase if she managed to inspire Jonas soon. Although, hopefully, not too soon. She needed him to write several letters before he came to the realization that he enjoyed writing.

She accepted the post and sent the maid on her way.

A log collapsed in the fire grate, sending a crackle and a wave of heat throughout the room, though it dissipated quickly in the large space. Harriet glanced at the fireplace beyond the large desk Jonas had claimed. Three times this week he'd sat there, writing the pages that were now strewn across the desk before her, mingling with the scribbles she'd made that were supposed to be ideas and notes from travel books but were really shopping lists and menus.

How could Jonas find this activity so enthralling? His pleasure had to be genuine as she found pretending exhausting. Yet how could she make him realize he enjoyed it enough to pursue on his own?

A guilty prickle nudged the back of her mind, but she quashed it with the reminder that Sophia claimed Jonas *liked* being helpful. Harriet could almost convince herself that meant he'd be happy to know this project would eventually bring joy to three people.

And now Harriet needed to bring a little of that joy to her father.

She picked up Jonas's first attempt. A few lines had words crossed out, others had notes written near the side, and in a few places he'd written the same idea with three or four different phrasings. Even amongst the rough messiness, she could see the beauty of his words.

So far Jonas had written two letters from the fictional Elsabeth. One discussed the wondrous adventure of never knowing what she'd see out her window each morning. It was baffling how Jonas's imagination could create such thoughts from snippets in travel accounts, but there they were.

They'd decided to wait on the walk in the woods since Jonas didn't think the book should begin in the middle of a journey. He'd even suggested starting the tale aboard a ship, but Harriet had managed to convince him ship travel was utterly boring.

She could hardly tell him her father thought she'd taken a boat across the Atlantic Ocean two months ago. That had been part of her plan to slowly work her way home, pretending to move from the Caribbean to Europe. The next ship she reported to her father would be the one bringing her home to England to finally start her own life.

Father might think it strange that she opened her letter with a description of her morning instead of her next destination, but his appreciation of the expressed sentiments should cover any awkwardness.

After situating a blank piece of paper in the middle of the desk in front of her, Harriet reached into the drawer and worked her fingers to the bottom of the stack of letters so she could retrieve Papa's note from six months prior. She set his letter to the right of her blank paper and arranged Jonas's writing on the left.

It was a delicate business, writing these letters to her father. She received one from him every week, but given that he thought she was out traveling the world, she could hardly answer them in a timely manner. So she'd built in a six-month delay.

He thought he was sending his letters to a solicitor in London, who bundled them up and sent them via ship to her next destination. As far as he knew, the same solicitor was receiving a return packet of letters from Harriet and doling them out at the rate of one per week.

In reality, the solicitor was a store clerk who merely redirected the letters as soon as he got them, never the wiser that what he considered an heiress's eccentricity was really a lie that she'd buried herself into so deep it was hard to fathom a way out.

Harriet had spent a small fortune in postage allowances, since she had to wrap her letter to her father in another sheet of paper before posting it to London, but it was less expensive than actual travel would be.

Now she had a plan, though. If she strung her imaginary travels along for two more months, she could declare her intentions to board a boat for home and be ready to start her new life by early autumn.

As always, she reread her father's old letter before beginning her own. It was a familiar pattern. Tales of the village and factory, answers to the questions she'd put in her last letter, and admonishments that she see more of the world than just the sights.

Her tales of houses and natural wonders weren't enough to convince him she was living the richest, fullest life any young woman had ever had the privilege to experience, but what else could she pull from the travel books to make him happy? Should she discuss the quality of the soil? Criticize the people? Those were the sort of commentaries included with the travel texts, and she simply couldn't bring herself to mimic them.

In her opinion, snubbing her nose at conventional wisdom and traveling the world over with nothing but a paid companion and a manservant should be more than enough to convince anyone that she was claiming the dreams her mother and grandmother hadn't been able to achieve. Her father wanted more from her, though.

He wanted her to make a name for herself in foreign and exotic societies. How would he feel to know she *was* a respected—or at least fascinating—member of society? It was just smaller than he'd always imagined.

If all those years ago she'd admitted that she didn't want to travel, that she didn't share the dreams of past generations, would he be happy with what she'd achieved instead? She had friends and a good home. The community was vibrant and changeable enough that her small sense of adventure was well satisfied. She was happy to stay in one place and let the world come to her. A port town might have been better for that, but she didn't particularly enjoy what the salty spray from the sea did to her hair or the sticky feeling it left on her skin.

To her, Newmarket, with the draw of horse racing and breeding, brought plenty of variety into her life. During the peak racing season, the assemblies were packed and the society was enjoyable. Then everyone went home and she got to enjoy the comparative peace of the quiet town. It truly was the best of all worlds.

But she couldn't go back and undo her lie. The only way forward was to finish it. Then she could pretend to move into the house her grandfather had purchased as part of her inheritance and see about creating a family of her own without a single lie in her letters home.

She read through the old letter, smiling at the silly stories and terrible jokes. With a slight frown she looked at the drawer and recalled the last few letters she'd received. Such fun items had been missing.

All the more reason for her to send a series of bright cheerful letters and make her way home.

Harriet picked up her new metal-nibbed pen and dipped it in the inkwell.

My dearest papa,

Your appeal that I take the time to truly see the world and experience the beauty of the moment has not fallen on deaf ears.

Harriet took a deep breath, dipped the pen again, and then copied Jonas's words.

Each morning I kick away the covers, eager to rise and discover what new beauty God has painted.

I am like a patron in a gallery, stunned into silence as my eyes rove and search the great ever-changing work framed by my window. The living canvas before me is more inspiring, more affecting, than anything contained in a museum, for the masterpieces it contains are not made of oil and pigment but of stories and life.

They are present for only moments—a baby and his mother, a trio of boys playing a game for which only they know the rules, a harried housemaid with her flapping black skirt—but they leave a lasting impression.

The customs and sights of this place are strange to me—as foreign a thing as elephants and palm trees—but they are familiar just the same. People are never truly strangers.

A couple once spent a full quarter hour huddled in a doorway, using the rain as an excuse to remove the socially appropriate distance from between them. Love such as that can be found wherever people live.

Harriet read over the letter once more. Should she change some of it? Jonas wrote so beautifully that she couldn't imagine marring it with her own lack of eloquence. She could add some of her own thoughts, though.

I hope to have that one day too. I want a love like you and Mother had, like Grandfather and Grandmama.

Would Jonas's poetic words make her own look better or stick out like a pretty girl in a plain dress?

The thought inspired a memory, and Harriet quickly copied over the rest of Jonas's letter before adding her own final line at the bottom.

I believe it may be time to consider coming home, despite these wonders. The world can move on without me. I should move on for myself.

The wording might be awkward and stilted, but it was sincere. She folded and addressed the letter, then slid it into her pocket before going in search of Elsabeth—the real one.

Her lady's maid was in Harriet's dressing room, preparing a gown for that evening's card party.

"Are the dresses for Miss Sailors ready yet?"

Elsabeth set aside the ribbons she'd been matching to the dress and grinned. "Yes, ma'am. Just as you requested." She darted into the closet and returned with two gowns. Harriet had ordered the edges and hems of the longer dresses to be stained and ripped so that alterations to fit the young lady would remove any imperfections.

The result was perfect. "Excellent," Harriet said as she ran a finger over one particularly intriguing grass stain. "On Sunday I'll mention to Mrs. Sailors that I'll be sending you by on Monday with a pie or some other such trifle."

The maid nodded. "And I'll take these as well, claiming I'm on my way to the ragman to trade them." Elsabeth giggled. "Should be a simple matter to set them down while I'm visiting and conveniently forget them. It's a brilliant plan, miss."

Harriet thought so. As the youngest of three daughters, Miss Sailors lacked proper outfits for her entry into society. Not that the girl intended to partake of any high-society functions, but there was no reason she couldn't catch the eye of a local businessman or a tradesman's son.

A smile crossed Harriet's face. Some would think her assistance in fashion frivolous—and indeed there were times with far more dire concerns—but the way a woman presented herself to the world could change everything.

Satisfied that all was in order, Harriet gave Elsabeth a smile and left to see to her letter. Nothing was better than seeing others' lives improved by her quiet work.

She tapped the letter on her leg as she stepped out of the house. Soon Jonas, Sophia, and Papa would all be happier with the changes she'd inspired, and Harriet would be able to enjoy the fruits of the life she'd spent the past three years planting in Newmarket.

Truly, this was going to be wonderful for everyone.

Nine

"How bored would a man have to be to document the soil instead of the people or even the plants?"

—Jonas, in the middle of the notes he took while reading one of Harriet's travel journals

Despite the regularity of care horses required, Jonas's days had a remarkable amount of changeability. Some days he was convinced Aaron was trying to turn him into a jockey by assigning him to exercise the racehorses. Other days he spent all his time cleaning stalls and refilling food troughs.

Today was one of the latter days. He considered feeding the horse as important as riding it, but he was scheduled to go to Miss Hancock's that afternoon to work on the book. The distraction of a lively horse that required the rider to focus with a firm hand would have been welcome.

Instead, his efforts to distract himself with work had him completing his tasks more rapidly than usual.

"How long until Mr. Whitworth's new stable is finished? We need to get you out of here before you start making the rest of us look bad."

Jonas looked up from the feed bin to see Miles, one of the Hawksworth grooms, standing in the stall door. Despite the irritated words, the man wore a large, teasing grin. It was impossible to look at those teeth shining through the shadows and think the groom meant any offense.

With a one-shouldered shrug, Jonas turned back to the feed. "You could try to keep up."

Jonas didn't spill any oats on the floor, but it was a near miss. Why hadn't that reply stayed in his head? Normally he kept a polite distance from the other men, content enough to listen to their conversations but rarely contributing and never offering the pithy comments that sprang to mind.

Miles's loud laughter assured Jonas no offense had been taken.

It also drew the attention of everyone in the stable. Another man leaned around the edge of the stall door, his glances flitting about the stall prepared and waiting for its resident to return from that morning's training. "Is he finished in here already?" Patrick asked.

"It appears so." Miles nudged the other man's shoulder. "I'm hoping to see if he'll just keep rolling down the line with the mucking."

Patrick sighed. "We can't. Mr. Knight said reliance on Fitzroy is making us lazy."

"Nothing wrong with being lazy as long as you can shuck the habit when you need to," Miles said with a shrug.

Jonas said nothing. Mr. Knight could keep the other grooms from requesting Jonas's help, but he'd still find something to do. He'd managed to steer clear of idleness since he was a child. That wasn't likely to stop now.

"Cards tonight?" Patrick asked.

"Of course." Miles kicked at the fresh straw. "Are we dealing you in, Fitzroy?"

Jonas rubbed a hand across the back of his neck and moved toward the stall door. The two grooms stepped back but didn't divert their attention. They always told him he was welcome at the card games, but this was the first time he could recall being directly asked if he intended to join in.

He couldn't think of a good reason to turn them down. "Aye. I'll be in the common room this evening."

Once he was there, he could judge the room. If there was an odd number of men, it would be easy enough to step out. If not, well, a game of cards wouldn't hurt him.

"Excellent." Miles slapped him on the back before nodding toward the stable's open door. "By the by, I saddled Pandora for you."

Already? Jonas wasn't leaving to go write at Miss Hancock's home for a few hours yet. There stood Pandora, though, with the sun glinting off her dark mane. The black Friesian stood out in stark relief next to the pure white Andalusian on her other side.

"Why is Rhiannon here?"

Miles squinted and scratched his head. "I believe Mrs. Whitworth went up to the house to inquire after Lady Stildon, but she said you were escorting her on her ride this morning."

Jonas put away his tools and stepped outside, his mind heavy with suspicion. He enjoyed riding with his sister, but lately nothing was as simple as it appeared. He looked at Rhiannon, and the horse stared back. He refused to give in to the urge to ask the animal what her mistress was planning.

Instead, he stood beside the horses and watched the door.

It wasn't long before Sophia emerged, calling a good-bye over her shoulder and hurrying toward him. The skirt of her proper riding habit was hooked up on the side, and a hat with a ring of bright feathers sat atop her head. If it weren't for the no-nonsense hustle in her step, he would wonder if this was actually Sophia or another redheaded lass who had stopped by Hawksworth.

He moved to Rhiannon's side to help Sophia mount, waiting while she loosened the riding skirt and let its long panel fall to the ground. After boosting her into the saddle, he stepped back and folded his arms. "I hear I am to escort you this morning."

Sophia straightened her skirts and grinned at him. "Yes. We're going to meet Harriet, then ride along the Heath."

Absolutely nothing simple. "You ride together at least twice a month. Why do you need me?"

"Because," she said, folding her gloved hands primly on the pommel, "normally we ride her lands or the countryside. It will be more proper if we have an escort when we venture onto the Heath."

"You've done that unescorted before." He didn't even try to keep the suspicion from his voice. Had Miss Hancock placed this idea in Sophia's head? If so, to what purpose?

Her gaze dropped to the reins Sophia was weaving through her fingers. Jonas gritted his teeth. His sister was never insecure. Not when it came to horses and riding. What had that other woman done?

"Well," Sophia said slowly, "if I behave as Harriet's equal instead of her companion, it may improve my reputation. Having an appropriate escort may elevate my status enough that more ladies will be willing to take riding lessons from me."

Jonas wanted to argue, but Sophia's voice trembled such that he knew she needed a moment to collect herself. He turned and mounted Pandora, remaining silent until they were in motion, then asking, "Who suggested this idea?"

She gave him a beleaguered sigh. "Does it matter? For what it's worth, Aaron agrees."

In truth, Jonas partially agreed as well. Perception drove a great many opinions. It wasn't easy to ignore the nagging uneasiness, but he would. He gestured his hand wide, doing his best impression of a courtly bow from atop his dark horse. "Very well, milady. Lead on, and I will follow the appropriate two paces behind."

"*That* is hardly necessary," Sophia said with a roll of her eyes.

Jonas grinned. "Oh yes it is. Anything less will ruin the effect, and your reputation will never recover."

He couldn't refute the motivation she'd claimed, but he could ensure that any secondary plan—whether Sophia's or Miss Hancock's—was thwarted. He wasn't above twisting Sophia's every request in the opposite direction it was meant.

Sophia had never been one to manipulate, but happily married people liked to see other people happily married, and they weren't above scheming to make it happen. Even she couldn't dream up a match between him and Miss Hancock, though.

They rode in silence—or rather he rode in silence, refusing to respond to Sophia's prattling commentary on everything they passed, like any good servant would—and soon they were on Miss Hancock's land. She was already mounted and rode toward them as soon as they became visible.

Her eyes widened as her gaze connected with Jonas's. Was that surprise? Hadn't she been the one feeding Sophia ideas about her reputation? Perhaps she just hadn't expected him to be the escort.

The women quickly fell into conversation, and after four glances back at Jonas, Miss Hancock seemed happy to ignore him. He took the opportunity to pay careful attention to the conversation that flowed between the two, since normally he heard of their talks only from Sophia's perspective.

He had to admit Miss Hancock seemed to genuinely like and respect Sophia, but how deep did the friendship really go? While his sister seemed to hold the other woman in great confidence, the most revealing thing Miss Hancock shared during the entire ride was that her cook was determined to perfect her recipe for Welsh rarebit and cooked it at least twice a month. Miss Hancock hadn't had the heart to tell the woman she hated mustard.

Jonas shook his head. If she truly despised it that much, she'd have done something about it. After all, the cook worked *for* her.

"Shall we run?" Sophia finally suggested.

Jonas almost groaned in gratitude. Plodding along was far from enjoyable, and running horses made it difficult to carry on a conversation. As they rounded the Heath on the edge close to town, they slowed back to a walk, briefly greeting a group of young women strolling along the edge of the Heath.

The women didn't even glance at Jonas before returning their attention to the unmarried men on their daily rides. One of the ladies had a dog on a rope but wasn't paying it much attention as it sniffed along the ground, tail wagging faster as it approached a cluster of bushes.

Sophia choked out a laugh and said in a low voice, "How can they possibly hope to attract a horseman that way? Men come to ride, not look for brides."

"Not everyone is as focused on the saddle as you, my friend," Miss Hancock said with a shake of her head as she turned to look back at the women. "Some of the men are here to be seen just as much as those young—Oh my!"

Miss Hancock's sudden alarm had Jonas jerking his attention to her, then following her gaze to the group of ladies and the dog that was now surging toward the bushes, obviously having learned that whatever animal he'd been sniffing at earlier was still in residence.

His owner hadn't been holding the rope tightly, and it slipped through her hands. She was now trying to scramble after it without appearing too unladylike.

The dog had other ideas.

A rabbit darted from the bush toward the ladies, and the dog spun around to give chase, barreling directly into his owner's chest and sending her crashing to the ground.

By design or instinct, the girl's arms wrapped around the dog, confining it to the place where they'd both fallen, but the animal attempted to continue its pursuit. Paws scrabbled across his mistress, turning her coiffure into a nest of tangles and her dress into a muddy canvas.

Once the girl got the rope wrapped firmly around her hand, she released the dog. He charged forward but soon came to the end of his lead. His pulling made it difficult for the girl to rise, and her friends weren't inclined to get close enough to help her lest they suffer a similar fate.

That poor girl. Newmarket was quiet this time of year, and news of the social variety was slow. It could take days or even weeks for something more exciting to happen.

"Sophia, my friend, I challenge you to a race." Miss Hancock's sudden declaration rang boldly through the immediate vicinity. "What shall the end marker be?"

"Er, the weigh house?" Sophia's voice was hesitant.

Miss Hancock's was not. "Very well. Shall we put a wager on it?"

Jonas kept an eye on the dog's pitiful owner to see if she truly needed assistance. He was the only one, though, as all other attention became solidly fixed to the two ladies on horseback.

He brought his gaze back to the women he was escorting. To anyone else, Sophia appeared cool and composed, but Jonas knew better. She didn't mind being in front of people, but she liked to know her lines when she was. Miss Hancock was taking her into unknown territory. Had Sophia ever made a wager in her life?

Jonas nudged Pandora a step closer.

Sophia cleared her throat. "What did you have in mind?"

Miss Hancock looked to the sky and tapped her lips with one finger. "I think," she said slowly, "that whoever loses must attend Mrs. Wainbright's card party tonight in their least flattering gown." She turned a haughty look to Sophia. "You should know I intend to win. I've a gown that endured a very unfortunate mishap when being laundered. It now boasts large purple splotches amongst the pink."

Sophia's already pale skin whitened even more until she nearly matched her horse. After looking around at the crowd and swallowing hard, she said, "All right. It's a wager."

The tremor within the agreement brought a frown to Jonas's face. It was nearly impossible for Sophia to lose this race since she was easily five times the rider Miss Hancock was and sat atop the better of the two horses. But why would Miss Hancock, who claimed to care so much for Sophia's future, take such a risk? A loss could mar Sophia's reputation, while a win could bring to mind her short but very scandalous career as a jockey.

Did Miss Hancock crave attention that badly, or did she truly not understand Sophia's position?

"Mr. Fitzroy," Miss Hancock called over her shoulder. "Do be a dear and call the start, won't you?"

He had no choice but to comply. Sophia had already agreed to the race, and he was stationed as a groom and a servant. He couldn't call either of them to task in front of so many people.

Moving Pandora to the side, he got into position and then counted off the start. The two ladies kicked their horses into a run to the accompaniment of numerous cheers and whistles.

From his position, Jonas could see that no more than ten strides into the race, Miss Hancock started pulling up. Not enough to bring the horse to a stop or draw the notice of the people behind her, but definitely enough to ensure she would not come close to winning this race.

Jonas glanced from her to the transfixed crowd and back again. This scheme had no rhyme or reason to it. What was motivating her?

As his gaze swung back to the crowd, a motion in the distance caught his eye. The disheveled young lady was hurrying back to town, her dog trotting beside her with his tongue happily lolling out the side of his mouth. She'd been all but forgotten in the excitement of an impromptu challenge and the prospect of Miss Hancock making a social appearance in a horribly ruined dress.

Jonas hated to admit it, but that meddlesome woman just might be a bit of a genius.

Ten

"There is no error in the books."

—Jonas's father's solicitor, in a note responding to Jonas's inquiry about the accuracy of the debt recorded in the family ledger following his father's death

Four hours later, Jonas's mind still hadn't decided where to land on Miss Hancock.

He was no longer certain that her habit of sticking her nose into other people's business was an entirely horrible trait, even if he still couldn't consider it a favorable one.

Mounting Pandora for the second time in a single day conflicted his emotions even more as feelings of ownership and camaraderie he didn't know what to do with swirled through him.

On the ride to Miss Hancock's, he futilely searched for a reason to be late. Instead, he felt a spark in his chest that might almost be labeled excitement as he walked into the house.

Why would he be eager to work on this book? Was the work he was doing for Aaron not enough? Was he feeling lost without his sister to watch over? Thoughts like these had never crowded his mind before, and were as unwelcome as the myriad of emotions.

A lot of things in his life weren't making sense anymore.

Perhaps *that* was why he was tempted to take the stairs to the library two at a time. On the written page he could make people and behaviors logical again. On the surface of that enormous desk, everything made sense.

Or at least it had.

Jonas came to an abrupt halt in the doorway of the library and stared at the large box sitting in the middle of what he'd come to consider his desk.

Approaching it slowly, he took the box's measure and inspected it for markings or any indication of what the contents might be.

And what he was meant to do with it.

He could set it on the floor. Maybe move it to Miss Hancock's writing desk. The delicate piece of furniture, made of pale golden wood and boasting plenty of decorative scrolls, had been moved from its original place along the wall to the middle of the floor, nudged against the large desk so the surfaces were perpendicular to each other.

"Oh good, you found it."

Miss Hancock's voice drifted into the room moments before the woman herself flitted through the door in a walking ensemble of pink and white. Lacy ruffles fluttered as she swung her arm in an elaborate gesture of presentation toward the box, a wide smile on her face.

Jonas cocked his head in consideration and confusion—at both the box and the woman. "Did you think I could miss it?"

"You are quite adept at ignoring what you do not believe is your business."

"The world would be a better place if more people did so."

"No, it wouldn't." She crossed her arms over her chest. "It would just be lonely."

And one poor Newmarket lass would be suffering the jeers of everyone in town.

Jonas shifted his weight and his focus. One good deed did not erase the potential harm she could have done—could still do—with her meddling. There'd still been risk to Sophia that morning.

As much sympathy as he felt for the girl with the dog, her situation had been one of her own making. Had Miss Hancock truly done her a favor by rescuing her from the consequences of it? That sort of mishap wouldn't ruin a person, after all. What if the impromptu race had distracted one of the nearby gentlemen who otherwise would have thought to offer the young lady aid?

Miss Hancock didn't seem horrible and vindictive, might even envision herself riding to the rescue, but she couldn't know that her schemes and machinations would make the situation better.

After all, *eye hath not seen, nor ear heard, neither have entered into the heart of man, the things which God hath prepared for them that love him.*

Miss Hancock didn't know more about what was better for a person than God Himself.

The woman shifted, giving him an expectant look as if awaiting his answer to a question she'd never asked. All she'd done was disagree with his opinion. Was he now to disagree with her disagreement? Jonas held in a sigh. Sometimes the rules of conversation were exhausting.

"I am not lonely," he said. "Seeing no need to meddle in the affairs of others does not make me uncaring. It is simply that I have not chosen to immerse myself in the details of lives on which I have no bearing."

She sniffed. "We all have bearing on one another. It is our duty to make that bearing as beneficial as possible."

He had to grant a certain amount of truth to her statement. *As every man hath received the gift, even so minister the same one to another.* There was a line, though, between using your God-given gifts to help people and invading their lives with your own opinion.

Obviously, she didn't see that. "You believe, Miss Hancock, that you know what is beneficial for others?"

She gave a brief shrug. "Most of the time. I am on the outside looking in, and that gives me a clearer picture."

Jonas withheld his snort of disbelief, but the emotion must have shown in his face, because she lifted her chin with a haughty expression and continued. "Did you know I passed a young woman in the street today? Of course, we could have smiled and nodded and moved along as you seem inclined to think is proper, but then she wouldn't know that salt of lemon can remove ink stains."

"And her life would be the worse for it?"

"Her dress certainly would be."

Jonas stared at the utterly confounding woman. Was she implying that she had insulted another woman's gown and was proud of having done so? How could she go from saving one young lady from embarrassment to causing it for another? "Did she thank you for pointing out the flaw in her garment?"

"Why would I do a thing like that?"

Now he regretted agreeing to join the grooms in the common room this evening. There wasn't a chance he was leaving this room without an aching head.

Her exasperated sigh seemed to move through her entire body. "I would never insult another woman in such a way, particularly not a near stranger. She complimented my pelisse, and I claimed it was one of my favorites before casually mentioning how genius my maid was because when I got a smudge of ink on it, she managed to clean it with salt of lemon and a pewter plate."

There had to be more to this story for her to believe she'd come to the rescue of the other woman or her dress. "And was it your favorite?"

"Goodness, what does that matter?"

Because truth should be far from frivolous? "Well, did your maid truly get ink out of it?"

Her brows pulled together in a look of genuine confusion. "Why would I get ink on a pelisse?" She flipped a hand through the air. "No, she got ink out of my blue morning dress, a detail that was hardly pertinent in this case and would have made the conversation very awkward."

"Lies do have a way of smoothing the immediate awkwardness." While creating far worse problems later.

She narrowed her gaze at him, and for a moment it looked as if she planned to stomp out of the room. Instead, she said, "By changing the garment in the tale, I was able to impart useful information without making anyone uncomfortable. I merely adjusted nonessential facts to maintain the flow of the conversation. There *is* a difference between lying and adjusting the frame."

"You don't think she'll recall your little tale when she notices the ink on her gown later? She'll know you lied and will second-guess all future interactions with women she meets on the street."

"Why such a dire outlook?" She tsked as she shook her finger at him. "She'll likely never know. I spoke loud enough for her maid to hear, and she seemed very attentive."

"Are all of your days so full of good deeds?" Jonas asked dryly. How exhausting to go through life altering reality and looking for opportunities to nose into someone else's business.

"Only when I'm fortunate." Miss Hancock pointed at the box. "I've done that as well."

"Who is it for?"

"You."

For him? Jonas blinked at the box. It seemed a lifetime since he'd received such a present. There'd been Christmas gifts from his sister over the years, sometimes something as simple as a decoration of sticks tied together by shed strands of a horse's tail. But a large, new box? Not since his parents were alive.

"Why?" Jonas asked.

"Because I'll not be made a liar."

"Did you get me lemons and a pewter plate?" The glare she

gave him almost made him smile, but he fought to keep his face impassive. "Do those work on grass stains as well as ink?"

"I'm afraid I know nothing of such clothing needs." She stuck her nose in the air as her gaze took in his wardrobe. "Though I've not much to go on, as that is the same outfit you wear every time you come here, and you've another ensemble you wear to each dinner gathering."

Jonas cut his eyes toward the box, the gentle curiosity that had been simmering within him shifting to a boiling sense of dread. "It isn't clothing, is it?"

"Why would I buy you clothing?"

"Why would you buy me anything?"

She sighed and rubbed at her temple with two fingers.

What reason had she to be frustrated with him? Their relationship was one of forced proximity, of shared attachments. She shouldn't be gifting him something unless it would be helpful for one of those mutual acquaintances.

In truth, she shouldn't be gifting him anything at all.

He could, however, think of a half-dozen reasons she would see his having new clothing as beneficial to Sophia's reputation and her associated friends. Did that mean he was starting to understand her motivations?

Did he want to?

"What is it?"

"Sophia informed you that I claimed a desire to sponsor an artist."

Jonas narrowed his eyes at the sentence. Was it naturally formal or carefully worded?

Miss Hancock pointed at the box. "Consider yourself sponsored."

That was worse than clothes. "I didn't agree to be sponsored."

"Consider it payment for helping with the book, then. If it is to bear my name, you should be compensated." She smirked. "Unless you intend to accept my money."

"I didn't request payment." He shifted his weight once more. Why was it so difficult for people to understand that helping others was its own reward? It was a purpose in and of itself.

Miss Hancock stomped around the desk and jerked the chair back. "It's a blasted gift, Jonas Fitzroy. Now, sit down, open it, and say thank you."

Her stern scolding inspired a grin even as he admitted—if only to himself—that she had a point. He was being belligerent and ungrateful. Receiving the gift might make him uncomfortable, but that was no reason to make her feel poorly for giving it.

Plenty of other things should be plaguing her conscience.

He lifted the lid off the box, and all the air whooshed from his lungs as if he'd been thrown from the back of a charging eighteen-hand stallion.

Some of the contents were recognizable, but for others he could only guess at their purpose. Picks, scrapers, awls, and on top of the pile, a book. *The Artist's Assistant*. He reached for it and flipped through the contents before he could stop himself. It held instructions for etching, engraving, mezzotint scraping, and a myriad of other artistic pursuits.

No more hoof-pick carvings in half-rotten wood, it would seem.

He reached past the various sized scrapes and needles and picked up a wide flat blade with a wooden handle. How was this used?

Beneath the tools sat a leather pillow filled with sand, and at the bottom of the box lay stacks of fine, thin blocks of wood.

After gently setting the tool and the book back in the box, Jonas stepped away, his fingers trailing over the edge before falling to his sides. "I can't accept this."

"Well, I certainly have no use for it."

Several months ago, before Aaron had shown an interest in Sophia, before they'd built a life here, before there'd been any evidence that every moment of their time in Newmarket would be anything other than a painful memory, Miss Hancock had gifted Sophia a dress. She'd used that same line. *"I have no use for it."* As if she'd possessed it, tried it, and no longer wanted it.

He wouldn't doubt that she was a good enough actress to pass off such a line when it came to clothing. She'd probably given dozens of dresses away in just such a manner. Art supplies were another matter. "You will never convince me you simply had these items lying about and chose to clean out a cabinet."

"Why would I claim such?" Miss Hancock slid the lid into place. "I contacted a man in London and told him what I needed. The box arrived yesterday."

Jonas knew how long it took for supplies to arrive when ordered from London. "That would have required placing the order after our first conversation."

Before they'd discussed his work on the book.

"Of course. Did we or did we not discuss my sponsoring you as an artist?"

"I never agreed."

"You sent me a letter with drawings."

"You said you wanted to know what happened in the cottage."

"And *you*"—her arm jerked as if she'd started to poke him in the chest but then thought better of it—"are being selfish."

Jonas twisted his head to look about the library. "Have you a dictionary in here? Because I believe you just said my refusal of your gift is selfish."

She turned her dark eyes on him, for once her face serious and determined. "Your sister wants you to have these, or she wouldn't have told you of my curiosity over the cottage. If you won't accept them for yourself, accept them for her."

It was an odd definition of selfish, but he could see how she'd twisted everything to make it work.

That didn't mean he agreed.

"It doesn't work that way," he said.

"It does in my world."

"Your world is strange."

"And yet here you are in it." Miss Hancock folded her hands in front of her middle and smiled in triumph. "I'll drop the box by Hawksworth on my way to dinner tomorrow. It's not that far out of the way when I go to Trenton Hall. I can give you a ride if you'd like."

Arrive at the weekly dinner *with* Miss Hancock? That group of lovesick fools would see nothing but hearts and flowers. "I can ride with Lord and Lady Stildon."

"But you won't," she said with a sigh.

"How do you know?"

"Because you never do."

"The option is still available."

"There are many options available that you never choose to take." She gave a nonchalant shrug. "I've never heard of you punching a man in the middle of church, but it is within the realm of choices."

Jonas blinked. She was equating his riding in a carriage with a viscount to him punching someone in a church? "Those are hardly the same sort of consideration."

"And yet one must wonder which you would be more likely to do."

"You can't be serious."

"I'm always serious," she said. "Just not always solemn."

Jonas could accept the box and end this conversation. The fact that part of him didn't want it to end was frightening enough to overrule the part of him that didn't want the gift. "You may bring it by the stable."

The box should fit beneath his bed. Just because he accepted it didn't mean he had to actually do anything with it. His sister would be happy. Miss Hancock would be happy. Jonas would be able to get on with his life.

As every man hath received the gift, even so minister the same to one another.

Jonas shook his head to free his thoughts from the Bible verse as he set the box on the floor. It referred only to spiritual gifts, not random talents, and certainly not unsolicited presents.

He turned back to Miss Hancock. "Shall we get started?"

She waved at the papers stacked on the corner of the desk. "You'll have to work without me today. I had originally intended not to go out tonight, but I've changed my mind. I'll need the time to ready myself for the card party."

Had she forgotten that he'd been there for the bet and the race, or did she think he hadn't been paying attention? "Wearing your ugliest evening dress, if I remember correctly."

A strain of pink a shade darker than her dress stole across her cheekbones. "Yes, well . . ." She waved toward the desk once more. "I'll read over your pages tomorrow. Perhaps it's time for Elsabeth to tell her father about her walk in the woods."

Then she spun around and departed before Jonas could say more.

Not that he had anything to say. He'd been hoping to work alone since he agreed to this farcical endeavor, so why did the room suddenly feel colder?

Eleven

"I shall never begrudge the Lord granting me a child so early in my marriage, not when others strive so hard to hold their firstborn in their arms. I do wish, however, that I'd managed to see a bit more of the world before bringing Harriet into it."

—Harriet's mother, Susan, in her journal three months after Harriet was born

Read by seven-year-old Harriet three years after Susan's death

Harriet left Jonas's most recent pages in the library, but his words still haunted her as she sat in her parlor, contemplating whether her life was lacking more than she'd realized. She'd been growing increasingly aware of what was missing from her existence—a husband, a family, a relationship with her only living parent that didn't involve a massive lie—but she was now faced with the possibility that there could be entire sides of life she'd never even considered experiencing.

Her father would be delighted with the story Jonas had written, but Harriet struggled to accept it. It sounded nice on the page, but it couldn't possibly be *real*.

"Are you ready, miss?"

Harriet jerked her attention to the door, where Elsabeth stood with Harriet's bonnet and reticule in hand.

"Of course." She pushed up from the chair and strode to the door with a purpose normally reserved for crossing the street ahead of speeding carriages or avoiding unwanted conversations. She'd declared her intention to go into town and visit the modiste on something of a whim earlier, but perhaps that was exactly what she needed. She was only ruminating over Jonas's words because she had no other task at hand to think about.

Then she had to buy a book before going to the modiste because she'd walked past the shop and was seven doors down at the bookshop before she'd realized it.

Then the modiste asked her three times which shade of green she wanted the new spencer jacket to be.

Harriet departed the shop, determined not to lose her focus again, and nearly knocked Mrs. Miller over. In response to Harriet's profuse apologies, the other woman insisted Harriet join her, as she was on her way to take tea with other ladies from the church.

Surely an actual conversation would be enough to distract her mind.

Then she forgot to ask for milk in her tea.

Fortunately, the concentration required to choke down the bitter brew while still maintaining a smile took her mind off Jonas's story for a few moments.

On her way back through town to meet her coachman, she gave her attention to every passing conversation, every public interaction, every solitary mutterer. Most were nothing but noise, though the effort helped her stay in the moment, but one young boy stood in front of a shop window with a friend, lamenting his inability to buy a displayed ribbon for his sister's birthday.

Finally. Here was something she *did* know what to do about.

Harriet noisily dropped her reticule as she slowly walked past, pretending utter absorption in whatever was happening across the street even though it was nothing but a couple of men entering a tavern. In the corner of her vision she saw Elsabeth slow her own walk, putting more distance between her and Harriet in order to keep an eye on the reticule in case the boy did not behave as desired. Only once had that ever been an issue, but they were still careful.

"Beg pardon, miss," the boy called.

Harriet turned, eyes wide in inquiry.

The boy scooped up the reticule and ran forward. "You dropped this."

"Why, so I did. How clumsy of me. Thank you, kind sir." Harriet smiled as she reached into the reticule to procure a coin that should more than cover the cost of the ribbon he'd been eyeing. She pressed the coin into the boy's hand. "Such honesty deserves a reward. Thank you for coming to my rescue."

Then she gave a small nod and went on her way as if she wasn't giving the encounter another thought. Her smile widened as she heard the boy scamper through the shop door.

Unfortunately, the pleasurable consideration lasted only until she returned to the library in anticipation of Jonas's arrival. His latest writing still sat on the desk. Mocking her. Challenging her. Making her question far more of her life than she liked. Clearly one of them didn't have a firm understanding of the world.

She was reading over it once more when the soft shuffle of footsteps stopping just inside the library door drew her attention.

Jonas looked at her through narrowed eyes. "What's wrong?"

"Why would anything be wrong?" she asked. He couldn't possibly know how his writing would affect her.

He stepped closer and nodded toward her. "Because you're sitting at the large desk and fraying that quill to shreds."

A brief glance down revealed that yes, she was indeed mangling the feather in her hand. She carefully set it aside and folded her hands in her lap.

He approached the writing desk, still sitting perpendicular to the large desk, eyeing her the entire way. "Should I work over here today?"

"That won't be necessary." She cleared her throat and arranged the papers he'd most recently written on the desk in front of her. "I read over your writing from yesterday, and it's clear you need far more supervision."

And that was not what she'd meant to say.

"I beg your pardon?" he asked, eyebrows raised and head tilted.

Where was the gentle questioning she'd practiced in her mind during the visit to the modiste? She straightened her shoulders and plunged on. There was no taking the statement back now. "I know fiction is often fanciful, but I do wish this book to be realistic." She waved a hand at the words that had plagued her all morning. "This is not what people do."

Jonas circled the desk and leaned over her shoulder to see the passage she was indicating. Disbelief shone on his face as he turned his gaze to her. "'Tis a walk in the woods."

Harriet nearly sputtered as she pointed to a particular paragraph. "She wades through a stream."

"How else is she going to cross it? She came in a carriage, so she'd hardly be on horseback."

"There should be a bridge."

"In the middle of the woods? I don't think so."

"But she's on a path."

He shook his head and stepped away from the desk. "That only means people have walked there before. Nearby, there's a perfectly good road, presumably with a bridge. Why would someone take on the hassle and expense of building a footbridge over a crossable stream?"

Everything he said made sense, so why did she find it so bothersome? Father always said the world held no borders for her, but did that include the invisible boundaries of proper transportation routes? Was this the sort of natural world experience he wanted her to have?

If so, she'd been farther from the mark than she'd realized all these years. No wonder he was never satisfied. Apprehension swelled within her so strong it resembled anger as she flicked at the edge of the paper.

> *The water trips toward me, tickling my toes as they strive to stand firm upon clusters of rocks made smooth by years of slipping water. It's a feather-soft kiss on my skin, washing away more than mere dust and taking my weariness as well.*

Harriet's breath rushed from her lungs to ruffle the page. The passage was as wonderfully sensory as everything else Jonas wrote. Harriet could almost feel the pull of the water and the coolness of the shadows. Would it be like a cool breeze on a warm day? Or perhaps more like fresh tea in the middle of winter?

Maybe that was the true problem here. She was going to tell her father about this glorious experience, and she had no idea what it actually felt like. This hadn't been a problem before. She had no burning need to see fantastic buildings or foreign cultures, but this . . .

"It's too good to be true," she said so quietly that Jonas tilted his head down to catch her words. "I don't want my, er, reader to dream of an experience that is unattainable."

Silence fell over the study. Only the ticking of the clock and the occasional crack of a log in the smoldering fireplace marked the passage of time.

"Have you never walked in the woods?" Jonas asked, a note of softness in his voice. Was that how he calmed fretting horses? It certainly sent a blanket of warmth over her, though she didn't know if the sensation it created was better or worse than her earlier agitation.

"I don't . . ." She took a deep breath and let it out in a rush. "No, I don't suppose I have." And how disappointing was that? It wasn't as if she had to travel across the world to experience such a thing. There were woods aplenty right here in England. She didn't know where they were precisely, but her carriage had driven through them many times, so they definitely existed.

Maybe life could hold a few adventures without requiring her to devote her life to indulgent travel. "Does a similar spot exist near here?"

Jonas rubbed a hand across the back of his neck. "It's not exactly like I described, but there's a place about two miles north of here called Seven Springs. Near Exning."

A wide smile stretched across Harriet's face. "Perfect. Let's go."

Jonas didn't look nearly as excited about the idea as Harriet was, but she hadn't noticed him getting all that excited about anything else either. She pushed away from the desk and rounded it to move toward the door.

He didn't follow. "You've only two hours until tonight's dinner. Besides, the sun will be setting soon."

Postponing the trip was disappointing, as it had been a long time since she'd been this enthusiastic about doing something merely for herself, but she did need to be practical.

Mostly because Jonas would never agree to anything else.

She sighed. "When can we go, then?"

"I could . . . give you directions?" He shrugged and shifted his gaze toward the fireplace. "You can go whenever you like."

"Are you suggesting I go for a walk in the woods *alone*?"

"You have footmen."

But she'd invited him. In a way. It had been implied. Besides, it was his idea. In a roundabout fashion.

His reluctance revealed another way she could make his life better. He needed to learn the joys of human interaction. It would make him happier. She could even make him feel needed while she taught him the lesson. Hadn't that been what Sophia said he liked best? "I might do it wrong."

He frowned at her. "Do what wrong? It's a walk in the woods."

"Which I have never done. I need a guide."

He looked at her.

She looked back. Held her breath. Pinched the skin between her thumb and forefinger. Curled her toes within her slippers. Anything she could think of to help her hold his gaze while remaining silent and still. Relatively speaking.

Finally, he shook his head with a sigh and dropped his gaze to the carpet. "I don't work Thursday morning."

Her triumph could not be contained, and her smile grew until her cheeks twinged with the effort. "I'll clear my schedule."

He peeked up at her, then shook his head again before looking away.

Harriet couldn't be certain, but she thought maybe, just maybe, he'd been smiling a little.

Twelve

"Once upon a time . . ."

—Jonas, in his notebook after his first day working with Miss Hancock, the page then promptly ripped out and thrown into the fire

Aaron and Mr. Knight could insist that Jonas take a half day off from his tasks twice a week all they wanted, but they couldn't convince his body to use those hours to sleep. He was up and dressed in his rough work clothes at the same hour he always was.

Only today he didn't know what to do with himself. He agreed with Aaron's reasoning—rest was a biblical idea after all—but a man needed something to occupy his time. About a month ago, he'd discovered no one said anything if he tended Pandora on his own time, so he tromped down to the stable as usual.

The mare nuzzled at his pockets, and he laughed as he pushed her nose away. "No treats for you today, lass. Anything you're smelling is there because this shirt was hung to dry next to the cook fire after it rained last week."

He checked her hooves and combed out the abundance of hair, then grabbed the large saddle to settle it on the horse's back. "You get to stare at a different four walls today, but we'll take the long way around to get there, hmmm?"

The horse turned her head and bumped her nose against his chest. He rubbed behind her ears before snagging her bridle from the hook. He kept his voice low, almost at a whisper, to keep it from echoing through the stone arches of the stable. "I'm going to the woods today. I thought to ride you there, but we'd have to take an extra groom to look over the horses while we walked. I'd rather limit how many people know of this farce. Besides, it's only a two-mile walk."

After leading the mare out into the morning air, he mounted up. He had hours to fill until he had to be at Miss Hancock's, but he refused to mope about Hawksworth. The sun was barely peaking over the horizon as the buildings faded behind them. "At least it's a pretty day."

Pulling Pandora to a stop in the middle of a secluded paddock, he considered his options. Plodding through the countryside held little appeal. Racing the mare over the Heath wasn't a draw either. As much affection as Jonas was finding for the horse, she would never be able to give him a run that competed with flying on the back of a thoroughbred.

He *could* train her.

His mind balked at the idea. Sophia was the horse trainer. He'd assisted her at the circus, but that had never been his life.

Then again, hadn't he been thinking that his life needed more purpose in it? *Any* purpose? He could do only so much for Sophia now. Maybe going back to the techniques he'd learned as a child would start him on a new path. He needed something to keep him from becoming completely numb.

Fleetingly, he considered the box of art supplies shoved beneath his bed and the notebook full of scribbles tucked in his dresser drawer. Those were merely hobbies, not purposeful pursuits. If he was going to dedicate large chunks of time to anything, it should be meaningful in some way—useful or helpful or tangibly successful.

When they'd been forced to sell their late father's school and all the horses but their personal mounts, Jonas had thought the days of training were behind him. Working with Prancer and Rhiannon had been his way of mourning, of keeping the memory of finer times alive. Then training had become a way of earning a living, meager though it was, in the circus.

Could he find something more by working with Pandora?

It took a great deal of searching, but he finally found four long, thin items: a branch from a nearby tree, two boards from a recent fence repair that hadn't yet been hauled off, and a long, coiled lead rope left behind by a stable hand.

He laid them out on the ground, then remounted Pandora, trotting her slowly in a circle before aiming her at the series of obstacles. The horse's natural inclination to lift her legs higher as she crossed the various items was far from the lifted gait that would eventually be the target, but it was a beginning. Several more passes, and the raised steps continued for two or three paces past the obstacles.

Even as he lavished praise and encouragement on the horse, Jonas searched his soul for a sense of meaning and purpose. Other than the satisfaction of a job well done, he found nothing.

He could almost hear his father's voice dissecting the horse's performance, noting what they should do differently next time and boasting over his children's mastery of his own passions.

But Jonas couldn't find it in himself to care.

If Pandora were his horse, maybe it would matter, but only from the perspective of creating a more enjoyable ride. Sophia craved the display and challenge of the trickier accomplishments. Jonas just enjoyed riding a well-trained horse.

He'd also prefer to interact with a well-trained female instead of the unpredictable woman awaiting him. Sophia would kick him if she heard such a thought, but he didn't mean it in the same way he meant for his horse. He just wished Miss Hancock were more gracious and less volatile.

Not that it mattered. She was so far above him in class that he'd be in torment if she was as appealing in personality as she was in presence.

For the past two days, he'd tried to find a little excitement about this outing, but whatever thin stream of anticipation he'd managed was gone by the time he knocked on Miss Hancock's door. This morning's excursion would simply fill his time and meet the expectations others had for him. Rather like the exercises he'd put Pandora through.

He kept his hat and coat as Lawrence showed him in, hoping to be inside for but a moment. The sooner he got this over with, the sooner he could return to work and stop feeling the need to examine his life and uncover what it was missing.

Miss Hancock was already in the drawing room, standing by the sofa, book in hand as if she'd been waiting on him. Her smile was broad as she set the book aside and clasped her hands together, obviously bursting with more enthusiasm than a jaunt in the countryside should merit.

The woman walked through town almost daily. Why was this walk any different?

Her frilled and pristine walking dress and delicate embroidered boots made him thankful for many years of practicing an impassive expression. He had to say something, but he didn't want to insult her. Actions spoke before words, so he shrugged out of his coat and laid it over his arm while moving toward a chair.

"Aren't we leaving?" Her smile pinched into a confused frown.

"Of course." He kept his face carefully blank. "But aren't you changing?" Best to pretend he assumed she knew her clothing was ridiculously inappropriate.

"My mind?" Her shoulders straightened and her chin lifted. "Certainly not."

"Your clothing," he said slowly before gesturing with his unencumbered hand toward her dress and shoes. "That isn't going to hold up well to water, briars, and mud."

She blinked at him, her face expressionless apart from her wide eyes that indicated no, she hadn't considered her clothing inappropriate. This was what a lady of means wore when she went walking because she would stay to the roads and tended garden paths.

Her hands clenched together in front of her, and her gaze dropped to the floor for a moment before popping back up to his. "Of course I'm going to change clothing. I won't be but a moment."

Then she dashed out the door, leaving Jonas murmuring Bible verses to hold on to his sanity.

HOW HAD SHE NOT THOUGHT of the mud? She was planning to put her foot into a stream. Of course there would be mud. It wasn't as if forests came equipped with nicely planked walkways. Hadn't that been the entire point of the original discussion?

She'd been tempted, just for a moment, to go in her current clothing and deny Jonas the pleasure of being right, but this was one of her favorite dresses and the boots were only a few months old. And she was fairly certain she'd heard the words *hasty*, *fool*, and *folly* in Jonas's mutterings as she left the room. Indulging her pride wouldn't have won her anything. He'd simply think her more foolish than he already did.

Leaving him for too long in the drawing room was rather stressful as well. What was scattered about the room that he might use to entertain himself? Harriet enjoyed reading there in the mornings, and several of her favorite books lined one of the shelves. Normally she didn't give their public display a single thought, but now she couldn't stop wondering what Jonas would think of them.

Given that he usually occupied her library, it was something of a nonsensical worry, but would he judge her for having those particular books set aside? Why did she care if he did? Yes, he was the focus of her attention now, but soon he would return to being nothing more than the brother of her friend. His opinion did not direct the course of her life.

Not that her well-read copy of *The Heroine, Or, Adventures of a Fair Romance Reader* would alter that opinion. She rather doubted his view of her could crawl much lower anyway.

And wasn't that something of a depressing revelation.

She nearly tripped over the top step and braced a hand against the wall to steady her balance before rushing into her room and ringing for Elsabeth. Harriet pored through her wardrobe, searching for something suitable. What should one wear to go traipsing about in the woods?

Jonas's sister was an outdoorsy sort, always riding horses and mucking about in the sunshine. She would be a fine muse for this situation.

Unfortunately, Harriet didn't own a great deal of clothing as plain as Sophia's normal choice of garb. In fact, Harriet was doing all she could to ensure Sophia didn't own such plain clothing either. If she wanted to earn the trust and regard of ladies who might hire her, she needed to look the part.

That didn't help Harriet pull the proper selection from her existing wardrobe, though. Were they riding to the woods? She refused to send someone to the drawing room to inquire. She'd already looked like something of a cake once this morning. If it was possible to avoid doing so again, she would greatly prefer it.

She stood in the dressing room, glaring at the riding habits to her left, walking dresses straight in front of her. Which to choose?

Since Jonas had commented only on the quality of her dress and not its style, she moved toward the walking dresses. She spied one from three years ago that she hadn't discarded because she liked the fabric pattern. It would likely get a stain or two on this outing, but it would still be enjoyable to look at.

Elsabeth rushed into the room with wide eyes. “You rang, miss?”

“Yes.” Harriet whipped the old gown out with a flourish. “I wish to change clothing.”

“You’re going to wear that?” The maid’s voice was thin and hesitant.

“Yes. And we need to find my oldest boots.” Harriet grinned, the excitement that had bubbled throughout the morning making a swift reappearance. For once she’d be exactly what her father had always wanted her to be—a woman who grabbed life with both hands and demanded it give her everything it had to offer. “I am going to wade through a stream.”

Thirteen

"?????????????"

—Jonas, in a circle around Miss Hancock's name in his notebook

There was a time, not so long ago that Jonas couldn't remember it, when Miss Hancock had been merely a regular if somewhat annoying presence at the edge of his life, her connection to his sister the only reason she was granted importance in his mind.

That was before seeing her tromp across a field, smile wide, eyes bright, one hand slapped atop her bonnet as she tilted her head back to catch the sun full on her face. This dress was still far too fine for such a walk, but she charged forth as if she were garbed in rags, trampling any reminder that their stations were far apart.

Her sheer, unhidden joy thawed the image of a calculating society diamond.

Her laugh joined the trills of distant birds as they strode through the grass, following near-nonexistent paths normally trod by horses and servants.

It jarred the already cracked image he had of her. Who was

the real Miss Hancock? A month ago he'd have thought that a ridiculous question because her character seemed blatantly apparent, but now . . .

Moments like this made him wonder.

Jonas glanced over his shoulder at the footman who was carefully placing his foot with each step as he searched the grass for who only knew what. The man had been brought along at Jonas's insistence for the sake of propriety, but he was falling behind.

"Perhaps we should slow our pace," Jonas said, though it pained him to do so. They were already striding at far less than his normal speed. "Lawrence seems to be having difficulty."

Miss Hancock cast a glance over her shoulder and sighed. "I should have requested Thomas. The maids needed a footman to go with them to the market, though, and I didn't want to wait." She nudged Jonas with her elbow. "I suppose you're now going to set me straight with some verse about how haste makes waste."

Was that how she saw him? He dropped his gaze to the grass. Yes, he tended to attribute Bible verses to everything because it helped keep his own life grounded, but had he inadvertently taken to using them as weapons against other people? It was possible. It had been so long since anyone besides Sophia had been in his life for an extended period of time that he might have loosened the walls around his tongue even as he erected more around his heart.

If he was using the Bible as a defense, or possibly even an offense, without conscious thought, he might have damaged someone else's faith, dented their belief and trust.

That could not continue. "I hadn't intended to, but I could think of one if it would make you happy."

She gave an exaggerated gasp. "You mean you haven't got one at the ready?"

This was a pointless chain of conversation that would not end well for him no matter which way it went. "Your man is still falling behind."

Her head swung about in an exaggerated perusal of the surrounding area. "We've quite a while before we need worry about being out of his sight. Anyone who can see us can also see Lawrence, not that they're going to care one way or the other."

"You don't think the people of Newmarket would find your walking across the fields alone interesting?"

"I'm not alone. I'm with you."

"A fact that would make the news even more tantalizing."

She frowned. "You don't get to have it both ways."

Jonas coughed. "I beg your pardon?"

"Either you are too far beneath me to be a proper companion, or you are an equal with whom I must guard my reputation. Do make up your mind so that I may adjust my actions accordingly. I, for one, think you have far too low an opinion of yourself."

His opinion of himself wasn't low. It was realistic. "This isn't about how I value myself. It is about the impression my appearance has when others view it. That is what reputation is based upon."

She smiled. "Then I have your permission to ignore what you think. Lovely."

Bothersome woman. "That isn't what I meant."

Her grin grew wider. "That is what you said. And I'm fairly certain a man is supposed to mean what he says. Didn't you quote that to me?"

Yes, he had uttered the verse that said a man's yes should be yes when she'd extracted his promise, but he never meant to have it turned on him in this way. "My saying what I mean does not necessarily lead to your understanding what I intended."

"You should speak more clearly."

"You should listen less willfully."

"I hardly think my independence is affecting the construction of your sentences."

"No, but it does change the context of your interpretation."

She bent a little to watch the way her skirt moved through a patch of tall wildflowers but didn't lose the conversation. "You could take the hearer into consideration before speaking."

The grin that stretched his lips was surprising and unnerving, but he could not will it away no matter how hard he tried. Was he enjoying this infernal exchange?

Thankfully, she was still captivated by the way the flower stems bent beneath her skirt and couldn't see his face.

He cleared his throat. "You could take the speaker into account when you're listening."

"Oh, I do." She turned her head to give him a saucy grin. "Which is why, whenever possible, I willfully twist your meanings to suit me. It may be wrong, but I find riling you up most enjoyable. I think, if you'll allow yourself to admit it, you find it exhilarating as well."

Did he? He must, because he was returning her grin and his heart was beating far faster than required by their current exertion. "Perhaps if you explained why you sought such an entertainment, I would see my way to enjoying it as well."

"Perhaps." She took an exaggerated step and kicked at a tall yellow flower. "I suppose it has been a while since you had to endure the veiled double meanings of English society."

"I have never had to endure English society."

Miss Hancock waved a hand in dismissal. "I doubt Irish society is all that different."

"I wouldn't know."

She frowned, her delicate brows scrunching to nearly half their normal length. "I'm certain Sophia told me your father was a gentleman."

"Who died when we were but seventeen. I never moved about in society." Birth and destiny didn't always align. He'd never expected very high connections, but even the respectability he'd been born to had been lost before he could grasp it.

"Oh."

Silence fell heavy between them, throwing a blanket over the conversation that had been light and teasing just moments before. The shift was simply a reminder that the end of the road was not determined by the beginning. Life was not a set course but rather a meandering trail with forks and paths that could lead in a variety of directions.

"Well," Miss Hancock said, her voice bright and cheery once more, swinging the mood of the moment into another sharp turn, "people are capable of hiding their true feelings no matter their class or location."

He had to grant her that one. "So you like that I am blunt?"

"I like that you allow me to be so."

What could he say to that? She sounded complimentary, and it may explain why he was enjoying this unexpected sparring. How long since he'd had the pleasure of speaking so freely with someone so quick-witted?

If only he could know she was being truthful and not making sport of him somehow. He'd like to think he was too smart for that, but she was far more skilled in the art of cutting conversation than he was.

They fell into silence once more, but this one seemed lighter.

As the woods shifted from distant shadow to distinct trees, her eyes grew wider and her smile of joy slid softly into one of awe and wonder. "I had no idea this was even here." Then she looked about the area of large fields as far as the eye could see. "*Why* is this here?"

Jonas pointed into the trees. "There's a spring. Several, actually. The waters join and flow through Exning. I don't know where they go from there. Perhaps toward the River Cam or maybe underground like the waters in Newmarket."

"Fascinating." She breathed out the word, then fell silent again, gaze fixed upon the trees.

Jonas couldn't stop watching her.

Did she truly view him as some sort of haven? A safe space where she could be herself without concern? The concept was thrilling and terrifying in turn. While it was flattering to be so trusted, he'd unleashed his pricklier comments in an attempt to keep her distant. Had he accomplished the opposite?

Had she somehow become a haven for him as well?

He tore his gaze from her profile and guided her into the shade of the trees.

She stumbled to a stop with a slight intake of breath. "Oh my. It's a great deal cooler in here, isn't it?"

It was on the tip of his tongue to make some remark about that being what happened when the sun was taken away, but he restrained himself. It suddenly seemed important that he not say anything discouraging or belittling. He may not know how he felt about her revelation, but that didn't absolve him of the responsibility it created.

He cleared his throat and shoved his hands into his pockets as he looked around for something of interest to point out. "There's more undergrowth at the edge because the sun reaches in. As we go farther, you'll see less and less of it."

She grinned. "An artist, a horseman, and now a botanist. Tell me, Jonas, is there anything you don't know about?"

There were a great many things he didn't know about, and he was quickly moving *women* to the top of that list. "Why would I speak on something I don't know anything about?"

"And you know about plants?" she asked with a grin and a shake of her head as her eyes jumped around, taking in the scene like a child at a fair.

"A man left a book on plants behind at a show a few months after we joined the circus. It was something to read."

When was the last time he'd mentioned his circus days? He didn't think he'd spoken of them to anyone since he and Sophia had left it behind back in September.

"Do you read a great deal?"

He nodded. "Lord Stildon has granted me use of his library now, but for a time the only books I had access to were the Bible and my father's horse training manuals. I think I have the latter all memorized."

"Does that mean you'll be quoting horse maneuvers to me soon?"

"Ah, no." Thank goodness the forest was dim, because there was a distinct possibility he was blushing.

"Hmmm." She turned back to face the way they'd come and called, "Are you all right, Lawrence?"

"Yes, miss." His reply was tense and stilted. "I'll be with you momentarily."

The squeal that broke through the end of that sentence allowed Jonas to pretend all his embarrassment was on behalf of the footman.

"We aren't likely to encounter anyone here," Miss Hancock replied. "Why don't you wait just inside the trees?"

"Very well, miss." Lawrence was clearly relieved.

Jonas was not.

Miss Hancock smiled at him, that edge he'd seen in her but hadn't quite identified visible in her expression once more. Then she turned and took two steps deeper into the woods.

Jonas narrowed his eyes as he followed. Had she chosen Lawrence on purpose, knowing his fastidiousness would keep him at a distance?

Probably. For a moment he'd forgotten that she was adept at making her will appear the natural order of things. It was a good reminder to keep up his guard.

"Be careful. It isn't far before you come across the springs."

"Have you come here often?"

"Often enough. A point farther up is easily accessed by horse, and the horses enjoy it. Some bring the racehorses here to drink before a race for good luck." He shrugged. "I just think the shade and water make it a nice place to rest and turn around when I'm exercising a horse away from the Heath."

It was also a good place to think, but he didn't want to share how this was something of a special place to him. Here he could forget where he was and where he'd been, feel at one with the nature around him.

She came to an abrupt stop and gripped his arm before looking at him with an expression of wonder that ripped through the wall of ill opinions he'd been carefully reconstructing. "Do you hear that?" she whispered, looking far from a spoiled, immature heiress.

Jonas could hear nothing over the blood suddenly rushing through his ears. His heart pounded as his mind struggled to remember why he shouldn't consider her beautiful. "What?" he choked out.

"Water. I can hear the water." She giggled and dove farther into the trees, ignoring the occasional twig that snagged at her hem or the squish of wet earth beneath her boot.

Jonas followed, staying close enough to catch her should a mishap occur, but his mind was several paces behind. Was this alluring, witty, independent woman the one his sister saw? If so, the friendship made far more sense. This was a woman he could get along with.

This was a woman he could care about.

Who was the real Miss Hancock?

He swallowed hard, part of him hoping this was an anomaly and the prickly, irritating woman would soon return. If he lost his ability to dislike her, would this new admiration, curiosity, and yes, attraction take over? That would doom him to a heartache he'd rather avoid.

She wrapped her arm around a tree trunk and leaned over the steep bank that cut down to the first branch of flowing water. Her bonnet strings snapped through the air as her head swung about, allowing her to take in the stream and surrounding plant life. "You were right. This is so much different than riding over a bridge in a carriage."

Jonas blinked at her. "Is that the only way you've seen a stream before?"

She shrugged. "I've been on boats in lakes, and I've crossed the ocean."

"That's rather different too." At least, he assumed it was. He'd been on a lake, but the closest he'd come to the ocean was the crossing from Ireland to England seven years ago.

"Yes. The ocean has waves, and the water is so vast but also so far beneath you that it seems unreal at times. But this . . ." She ran a hand over the bark of the tree and smoothed a leaf between her fingers. "This is real. I can see it, touch it." She took a large inhale. "Smell it."

How did this woman, who had done more than he could ever imagine—if even half of the rumors about her were true—make him feel as though he'd experienced more of life than she had?

She sighed. "You wrote that Elsabeth walked in the stream. I want to do that."

Did she intend to roll headfirst down the incline to the water below? Jonas seized her shoulder to keep her in place.

The glare she sent him in response had him sighing, both in frustration and relief. There was the Miss Hancock he knew. "This isn't the best place." He pointed to his right. "Down there would be better."

Her smile returned. "Well, then, lead on."

He nodded and picked his way down the gentle slope. He'd brought her here because it was a good wading spot. Sometimes, when he rode out here, he would take off his boots and stroll in the running water while he prayed. The current crossing his feet felt like God Himself was walking with him.

Now he was going to share that with Miss Hancock. Would it forever ruin this place for him?

The ground became even with the water as two more springs joined the first to create a slow-moving pool. Large rocks and a fallen tree made the perfect place to sit and remove one's boots or simply enjoy the peace of this pocket of paradise. There was a great deal to like about Newmarket, but he frequently felt exposed by the large expanses of flat fields and pastures.

Here was peaceful solitude.

He plopped down on the tree and waved his hand toward the pool. Because the flow of the water here was slow, it was also murky. Not that upstream wasn't also full of plants and twigs, but they were far more difficult to see when the water bubbled and trickled quickly over rocks. Would the condition of the water change Miss Hancock's plan?

It would seem not, as she walked right up to the edge, nearly touching the water with the toes of her boot.

"Elsabeth felt the cool water between her toes," she said.

"Yes." He knew where this was going, and he shouldn't be bothered by it. No one in their right mind waded into a stream in their boots unless it was to get to the other side and keep hiking.

"I should remove my shoes, then. One can't feel anything between their toes if they are encased in leather."

She came to sit by Jonas on the log and then frowned at her feet. Did she not know how to remove her own boots?

"I didn't bring a hook. Do you think I'll be able to get them back on?"

Once again Jonas had misjudged her. Normally he was inclined to give people the benefit of the doubt, to think the best of them. That he'd been expecting the worst of Miss Hancock at every turn made him ashamed. Whatever was coloring his view of her was clearly his own problem and not hers. It was time to set his issues aside and give her the consideration every person deserved.

"We'll find a way to get them back on. Do you need assistance removing them?"

"I don't think so." She shifted the hem of her dress just enough to reveal an old, worn walking boot. Brown laces held the leather molded over her ankle and up beneath her skirt. Untying and loosening the laces seemed to take Miss Hancock hours, but eventually she tugged the shoe loose and held it aloft with a triumphant smile. "Aha!"

Jonas couldn't help but grin.

Moments later, she held the other boot aloft as well, then set them both neatly on a nearby rock, her stockings draped over the edge and making him blush. Her bonnet joined the small pile.

Then she stood and gave her toes an experimental wiggle. They peeked out from beneath the hem of her dress, and Jonas couldn't tear his eyes away. When was the last time he'd even seen a foot other than his own? Had he ever seen a woman's? The delicate curve of the arch and the tiny toes were mesmerizing.

He didn't fully realize he was staring until she stepped out of his field of vision to approach the edge of the water. Jonas blinked and shook his head before quickly pulling off his own boots. The sooner he got those feet covered by murky water, the better.

Fourteen

"The boat has fourteen cabins and three masts."

—Harriet, in a letter to her father written in a hotel room in Dublin, Ireland, as the boat she was supposed to be on, bound for the Caribbean, set sail without her

"But how was your trip?"

—Gregory Hancock, in his response

The air was chilled enough for Harriet to wish she'd brought a cloak, so she expected the stream to be cold. Bracing herself for the sensation of stepping into cooled bathwater, she slid one foot forward until her toes were completely immersed and discovered how incorrect her assumption had been. A shiver worked up her leg and along her spine. Was this what it would feel like to step into a vat of ice cream?

It would have been far smarter to take this outing in the middle of summer, but by then the opportunity would be gone. Jonas would be working on his own writing endeavors, and she would be pretending to be on a ship bound for England and the start of her own life.

Besides, it was too late to change her mind now. She refused to let Jonas think she found nature intimidating.

Though she did. She truly, truly did.

This was why she could never be the adventurer her father wanted her to be. Despite having two days to plan for this moment, she'd donned the wrong clothes, given no consideration to the weather, and her heart and body seemed to be vibrating with nerves to the point that she was likely to spend the evening in bed recovering.

New experiences were wonderful, but she couldn't handle more than one at a time.

She'd realized the failing only a few years ago and had never been able to admit it aloud. It was yet one more reason she would never be able to conquer the world and perform daring exploits.

Jonas's passage had inspired as much envy as it had awe and confusion. How did other people have the nerve to claim such adventures? In the safety of her library, she'd thought she could be just such a person for an afternoon, long enough to experience a small piece of it herself.

Now she wasn't so sure. She swallowed hard. "Do I just step in?"

"Unless you intend to jump." He came from behind her and stepped past her, not even hesitating as his feet plunged into the rippling pool of water.

He'd removed his boots and stockings as well, and his breeches stopped a few inches below his knee, revealing a strong calf with a sprinkling of red hair across the skin. His feet in the shallow water looked large and distorted.

Then his hand slid into view, palm up, with fingers extended toward her. It was covered in calluses and the fine lines of long-healed cuts and scrapes, so unlike the gloved hands that offered to escort her onto dance floors or into dining rooms.

In its own way, reaching out was also an adventure.

She placed her hand in his, and if the tightened grip was as much for moral support as it was for physical stability, only she knew.

It was just water. She stepped into water all the time when she took a bath. Why was she hesitating?

Because her bath had never glinted at her with a ray of sunshine that managed to pierce through the covering of limbs over her head. There had never been a plant waving to-and-fro with the movement of her bathwater. A fish had never scurried in and out of sight.

She pulled in a deep breath through her teeth as she plunged the other foot in. The air shuddered out of her chest as the icy shock rolled over her body. The bottom was far closer than she'd anticipated, and she nearly tumbled forward as her foot came to rest on a rock. Though the stone surface was smooth, it jutted up in a way that bent her ankle in an unfamiliar direction. Her other hand grasped tightly onto Jonas's forearm as she curled her toes around the edge and took another quick step to catch her balance.

Once assured that she wasn't destined to fall headlong into the pool, she took mincing steps forward, adjusting to the chilled water and marveling at the way the hem of her skirt floated on the surface.

A delighted laugh bubbled up as she experienced exactly what Jonas had described. Water flowed over and around her toes like silk. Occasionally, something—whether fish or plant she didn't know and wasn't going to ask—would brush her leg.

Her gaze lifted and took in the expanse of water before her. "How far is it safe to go?"

When Jonas didn't answer, Harriet pulled her focus from the rippling surface of the moving water and turned it to him.

He wasn't watching the water.

He was watching her.

And he looked as if he'd never seen her before.

"Jonas?" she asked with more than a little hesitation. She pointed toward the middle of the pool. "Can we go farther?"

His eyes met hers. In the shadow of the trees, she couldn't see the fascinating green depths, but she could feel his gaze. It seemed he was spearing her with it, poking at her to see what was real and what wasn't.

What would he find? Over the years she'd buried her desire for a cozy life of family and close friends under layer after layer of carefully crafted façades intended to improve the lives of those she cared about. Did they hold up to his scrutiny?

"Yes," he said, his voice soft yet rough, as if his throat was now coated in rocks like the ones beneath her feet. "We can go deeper."

He offered her his arm, and she clung to it as they slowly made their way forward. He pointed out areas where she needed to take more care and never rushed her as each foot felt out the next step before moving forward. Eventually, the water swirled just below her knees as the bottom of her dress danced along the top. They moved into an area unprotected by the natural canopy overhead, and sunlight glinted off the surface like dozens of tiny candles.

She tilted her head back to feel the warmth on her face. It contrasted with the chill around her feet, making her aware of everything in between in a way she'd never experienced before. It was as if she could trace her blood through her veins.

"This is glorious," she said. "I feel just like Elsabeth." She closed her eyes and took a deep breath, smelling the trees and the earth and a dozen other scents she couldn't identify. "Is all of nature like this? Does it all make one feel so small and yet so powerful at the same time?"

Jonas's voice stayed low, protecting the reverence of the moment. "I've always found it to be the best way to remember who I really am. There is so much of God in nature, whether it be the flow of a stream or the beauty of a horse or the tickle of a breeze. The fact that everyone feels the same wind or wades through the same water regardless of who they are or where they were born reminds me that God sees us all the same and loves us equally."

Harriet held her breath, afraid her heart would shatter at the depth of healed pain Jonas was revealing. Or perhaps she would shatter at the idea that she could be loved for nothing more than being herself, with no expectations to meet or requirements to achieve.

His voice became little more than a whisper when he continued. "I need to remember that sometimes. When it feels like life does nothing but cut me down. Not so much now as before."

"I think," Harriet said slowly, not even sure what she wanted to say but knowing she had to give him some sort of response, "I could believe in a God like that." She looked around at the trees and rocks and plants. "I could love a God who didn't weigh people by their birth or accomplishments or money. I can't imagine what that would be like, but I like the idea."

Was that what God was truly like? Was the perfect deity not sitting atop His throne in heaven, waiting to see who would rise above the rest of humanity and do their part to improve the world? She'd been to church all her life and remembered sermons about thinking of others more than herself and avoiding the horrible sins, but here, where the water followed its course and the sun and plants worked together to make a cathedral of natural glory, she had to wonder if she'd gotten it all wrong.

She lifted one foot and wiggled her toes, letting the water cool the spaces between. Jonas was experiencing this gift the same as she was. She could bring along her maid and the woman who begged near her church and even Caroline, Princess of Wales, and they would all feel the same thing. The water would be just as cold, the current just as swift, the sun just as warm. It wouldn't matter.

God had made this place and put no restrictions on who could enjoy it.

Did that mean there wasn't some secret number of people she had to help before God could accept her?

"Harriet."

The whisper of her name was so soft, so low, that her heart

jerked. For a moment she thought it the voice of God coming to her on the slight breeze weaving along the streambed behind them.

But it was Jonas. Saying her name. Her real name.

Her head swung in his direction.

"I believe I owe you an apology."

She frowned. "What for?"

"I—" He glanced away and swallowed before looking at her once more. "I may have misjudged you."

Her middle clenched, her heart jumped, even her eyebrow twinged as too many emotions whirled through her in response. That he might be coming to like her made her giddy, while also feeding a fear that his initial assessment might not have been wrong. Then, of course, there was curiosity over what that assessment might have been and anger over the idea that it apparently wasn't positive. Finally, trepidation that she, too, might hold faulty understandings of other people trickled through her mind.

Since her heart could not pick an emotion to settle on, she focused on the statement itself. It wasn't exactly definitive. "That seems a very rickety sentiment. Let me know when you decide one way or the other."

A grin tickled one corner of his mouth. "I didn't think you the type of woman who would wade into the middle of a stream. I certainly didn't think you'd see the beauty in it."

Since she wouldn't have guessed that about herself either, she couldn't blame him. "This might be the most beautiful place I've ever seen in my life."

He shook his head and swept his gaze over the tree-lined water. "I thought you were, well . . ." He swallowed. "My opinion has not been the highest. You deserve my apologies."

The war of emotions settled into a heavy lump in her middle, a weight of sadness and possibly even shame. She'd known he hadn't considered her a friend, but it would seem his opinion had been far lower than neutral. She whispered, "What did you think of me?"

His tone matched hers. "I'd rather not say. Can we leave it at my realizing I was at least partially wrong?"

Partially? Once more anger swirled through the emotional pit, throwing everything into turmoil. She would prove him wrong.

But could she? After all, she *was* lying to him. It was for the greater good, but it was still deception.

"How do you see me now?"

He gave a short laugh and a one-shouldered shrug. "At this moment I'm questioning everything I thought I knew." He turned his head to meet her gaze, and it stole her breath. "I suppose I'm now determined to know who you really are."

And if that wasn't a statement to melt a girl and freeze her in terror all at once, Harriet didn't know what was. Not even she was daring enough to embark on such an adventure. She was a daughter, a friend, a community supporter, an employer. Was she supposed to be something on her own as well? "Will you let me know what you find?"

He smiled. A real smile. The type he gave to other people. "Yes."

He kept looking at her. She looked back at him. Around them the breeze blew and the trees swayed. The water trickled on, but time seemed at a standstill.

"'*He hath made every thing beautiful in his time.*'" The words seemed to breathe out of him, becoming part of the encompassing swirl of water and wind and sun.

Unlike the society men who doled out an arsenal of compliments, Jonas wanted nothing from her except for her to perhaps leave him alone. He wasn't predisposed to flattery, but he had just called her beautiful.

In his own strange way, of course, but somehow that made it more touching.

And more believable.

A leaf drifted down and landed in his hair. Before she gave it a thought, she'd reached up and plucked it free, her hand drifting through the cool strands of hair and across his cheek as it fell back to her side.

He swallowed, a visible jump in his throat. It would be so easy, so simple to lean forward, to brush a kiss across his cheek.

That such a bold, forward thought would even occur to Harriet had heat surging through her chest and up her neck. The breeze brushed her cheekbone, and her heart lurched as if she had followed through on her wayward, crazy notion. A tingle ran from her cheek to her middle, far warmer than the rays of the sun working their way to her shoulders.

They were standing so close, her arm wrapped securely in his to keep her steady. Details the shadows had stolen before were visible now—the green in his eyes, the spot of bristly stubble he'd missed when shaving that morning. Her wet skirt dragged against his legs instead of flowing freely with the water.

Moments passed.

Was he thinking what she was thinking? If this were a moment in the book, how would he describe it?

"We should make our way back." His words were quiet and rough, an obvious attempt to break the moment as gently as possible but somehow only making it more thrilling and terrifying.

Harriet hadn't one iota of breath in her lungs with which to form a response, so she blinked an answer, then turned and headed toward the shore.

Fifteen

"Miles is feeling under the weather. I'm taking his jobs today, so I won't make it for dinner."

—Jonas, in a note to Sophia on the Sunday after his trip to the springs

Some would consider Jonas's behavior over the next four days an example of cowardice, but he preferred to think of hiding amongst the horses an act of self-preservation. Hadn't David said *in the time of trouble he shall hide me in his pavilion*? Well, there wasn't a great deal of difference between a pavilion and a stable, and Jonas could definitely use a refuge at the moment.

He'd seen her delight in something simple.

He'd been slapped in the face with the unexpected and unexplainable urge to kiss her.

He'd called her Harriet.

Jonas rolled his shoulders in an attempt to shrug off the reminder niggling at the back of his mind that *the honour of kings is to search out a matter*. Other than the horse manuals, the Bible had been his only choice of reading material for a long time, so many of the verses were embedded in his memory. Usually, his mind chose one to focus on and help him make decisions.

Now was not the time for it to start confusing him with conflicting references.

Perhaps it was a sequence instead of a conflict. Even if he wanted to, Jonas couldn't avoid Harriet forever. All he needed was a few days to put their walk and all its revelations into perspective.

Wheels on the gravel drive had two Hawksworth grooms moving swiftly toward the door. When the noise didn't continue toward the manor house, an invisible band tightened around Jonas's chest. Was it Harriet coming to see why he'd missed two writing appointments?

Jonas retreated to Sweet Fleet's stall, giving the horse an unnecessary second brushing.

Moments later Harriet's frowning face appeared between the bars that formed the top portion of the door to the racehorse's stall.

"Jonas Fitzroy," she said in a voice loud enough to make him wince as it echoed off the stone walls for everyone to hear. "Are you avoiding me?"

Yes, he was, but he had nothing to gain by admitting it. "I've a job to do, Harriet."

Her eyes widened, and Jonas gave all his attention to perfectly aligning the hairs on the horse's shoulder. What happened to his intention of returning them to a certain formality? He cleared his throat. "Not every decision I make revolves around you."

At least it shouldn't. Lately, though, far too many did.

"You've two jobs, if I recall, and you haven't been showing up for the second."

"You don't pay me." He shot a glance her way. Black eyebrows scrunched into deep curves above her frown.

"I offered to."

"No, you offered to pay my expenses so I could"—Jonas flipped the hand holding the brush through the air—"follow my muse or some other such nonsense."

He was willing to—*wanted* to—work for his wages. This freedom he'd gained was too new, too refreshing to risk by relying on someone else's charity.

Though he'd faced away from her, he angled his head to watch her exasperated movements at the edge of his vision. A huffed sigh. Arms crossed over her chest. Shoulders swaying as if she were resisting the urge to pace.

"Very well. I'll pay you to work on the book, then."

Jonas sighed and rested his forehead against the horse's neck for a moment before turning to face her, taking three steps toward the door so she knew he was giving her his attention. "I agreed to help you. You don't need to pay me." Especially since he'd agreed in order to keep a closer eye on her and determine her intentions with Sophia. It would feel wrong to accept money, considering his motivation.

Not that he'd been doing a great job of that either.

She pressed her lips together, then blew out a frustrated sigh. "You've been hiding since Thursday. That's four days. Even Jesus came out after three."

A laugh spilled from Jonas's chest before he could stop it. Harriet's frown cleared, to be replaced by an expression of mild pride. He shook his head and shrugged. "I'll be there this afternoon."

He'd always planned on returning to her library, and that was all he was agreeing to do. He would keep his head down, write his pages, and leave. There would be no more outings, and all discussions would be about the book unless she wanted to talk about something concerning Sophia. Once he got their interactions back under control, there would be no reason to avoid her.

"Good." She beamed at him, making him question every resolve he'd just made.

"Good," he repeated, his voice revealing more tension than he'd realized he felt.

They stared at each other in several moments of awkward silence before she announced an intention to visit with Bianca and fled from the stable.

It was fifteen minutes before Jonas turned back to the horse.

BECAUSE JONAS was a man of his word, he saddled Pandora that afternoon.

If he stalled by taking the long way to Harriet's under the guise of giving the mare a bit of exercise, only he knew it.

Mostly because no one else was aware he'd done it.

Was that a good thing, that he could now go about his business in any way he wanted without anyone the wiser? Did it make him free or alone?

Was riding about the countryside a waste of time? Should he have spent the time training Pandora more?

The conflicting questions with no definitive answers left him irritated as he walked into Harriet's house.

He'd never been overly personable—had certainly not encouraged an indulgence of personal chatter—but today he tossed little more than a greeting of acknowledgment into the room as he crossed to the large desk. It should have been awkward, even embarrassing, to call out when he hadn't even looked around to see if the room was occupied.

But she was there.

Somehow, he simply knew she was there.

He was being rude, but he'd never claimed to be a man without fault. He kept his head down, gaze focused as he prepared his paper and pen, but then he froze. Ink welled at the tip of the nib before dripping to the paper beneath. Jonas set the pen aside and stared at the circular blemish on the paper.

What was he meant to write? The last thing he wanted to do was write a piece that would inspire another outing. If the story had a natural next step, he didn't know what it was. Could this collection of writings even be called a story? Nothing was happening. If he'd found this book in a library, he'd probably use it to level a wobbling table.

He'd promised to write today, so he couldn't leave until he'd put words on the paper. That required an idea.

Asking Harriet would be the most expedient way to attain one, but he wasn't willing to open the conversation. Instead, he read through his previous writings, hoping for inspiration. Two of them were missing, but he wouldn't ask about those either. They were probably on the other desk waiting for her changes.

He read through everything twice—it didn't take long—and was as frustrated at the end as he'd been at the beginning. From an objective standpoint, he could admit the writing was decent. Exhibiting false humility was pointless, especially in his own mind. He'd been reading one book a week since moving into Lord Stildon's stable, and he could see the strengths in his own writing.

What he couldn't see was a story.

Each page was interesting by itself. Here was an account of Elsabeth trying a new food, and here she watched a local street performer. Of course, there was her experience dipping her feet into the stream. All together, though? As a book? Who would want to read this? Perhaps it should be a serial magazine column—*The Adventures of Lady Elsabeth*.

He set the pages aside and finally lifted his gaze. It immediately pulled to Harriet sitting across the room, bent over a travel book, a small pucker between her eyebrows as she flipped the pages.

Maybe people would prefer *The Adventures of Elsabeth Ridley, Heiress*. Someone more accessible. Someone they could believe had enough bend in her neck to try the spicy fare of a market food vendor.

Did he see Harriet that way? A few weeks ago he'd have thought her the stiffest-necked member of Sophia's entire friend group. She certainly enjoyed swanning about in society the most. Despite her lack of title and heritage, she seemed to think it her due for everyone in a room to crave her attention and feel honored by her presence.

Jonas shook his head. He wasn't here to make sense of the woman. He was here to make sense of the story, and coming up with a name wouldn't do that. These snippets simply didn't go together.

Rectifying that required a conversation. "This isn't a good book."

Harriet looked up, her frown smoothing into a smirk. "That seems rather harsh, as you're the one writing it."

"It isn't the writing. It's the story—or lack of one."

She cleared her throat and dropped her gaze before turning a page of the travel book. "Of course there's a story. She's traveling and writing letters home to her father."

"That's not a story, that's . . ." Jonas struggled to come up with the right word, because her confidence made him doubt himself even though he knew he was right. "It's an existence."

She paused and lowered the book, leaving her staring at nothing as she flatly stated, "An existence."

"Yes."

"Meaning what?"

Jonas frowned. Was she all right? "Meaning that's just who she is. It's not giving her life purpose."

She smoothed the pages of the travel book with one hand. "And life needs a purpose to be a story?"

How could she think otherwise? Had she ever read a book? Despite a few years when he'd had little access, Jonas had read hundreds of books in his life. Some good, some bad, some set aside and forgotten until he'd come across them again days later. The uncompleted ones all had one thing in common: he hadn't cared about what happened enough to pick the book up again.

That had to mean something, didn't it?

"Something needs to tie the scenes together," he said, trying to sound like he knew what he was talking about when his own thoughts were only a word or two ahead of his mouth. "If you can flip them around and still have them make sense, it isn't much of a story. People can quit reading whenever they feel like it."

She set the book aside and smoothed her hands over her skirt before clenching them together in her lap. Her entire focus was fixed on him as she asked, "Does the same apply to life?"

Was she talking about viewing others' lives or her own? "I suppose. Without purpose we'd be wandering in the desert, with no way of knowing when to turn to the right or the left."

The fog cleared from her face, and she gave him a small smile. "Another Bible verse, I assume."

A suspicious heat flared across the tips of his ears. "No. That's a Fitzroy original statement."

"Hmmm." She picked the book back up and seemed engrossed in the pages for several moments. He'd about decided to write a few more thoughts on early mornings when she asked, "What's yours?"

"I beg your pardon?"

"If life is supposed to have a purpose, what's yours?"

He opened his mouth, but nothing came out. Months ago he'd have said it was to provide for and protect Sophia while keeping her healthy and possibly even happy. Now he didn't have much purpose at all, but he wasn't ready to admit that aloud. "Your book is upside down."

She blinked and flipped the book over only to frown and put it right side up again. "No it wasn't."

"But you didn't know that. What are you over there thinking about instead of plotting Elsabeth's meaningless path?"

She sighed and snapped the book shut as she rose to her feet and crossed the room to the desks. The small writing desk now sat parallel to his large one, both facing the far seating area, and she set her book on its surface before running a hand over its cover and lifting her dark eyes to meet his.

It made him want to scoop up the nearest book and pretend to read for a while.

"I *was* thinking about where she should go next until you said she had no purpose. Now that's all I can contemplate."

Elsabeth. They were discussing Elsabeth and her fictional dilemma. "She needs a grander idea, something that propels the reader to move along to the next adventure."

"What do you suggest?"

Jonas ran a hand over his face. How had he gotten himself into this conversation? Since he couldn't not perform a task to the best of his ability, he plunged forward. "Books with romance in them are often in the bookstore window."

His cheeks heated even as he made the suggestion. If the book needed romance, all he had to do was rewrite the passage about the stream as a journal entry. Harriet's silence could indicate she'd had the same thought.

Not that he would ask.

Unfortunately, he couldn't think of another solution with that memory crowding his mind. His heart tripped faster at the idea of plotting a fictitious romance with Harriet. It was dangerous. There had to be another option.

"Or . . ." He cast his eyes around the library in search of other book themes. "We could give her a mystery to solve."

"I can't put her in danger," Harriet cried. She crossed her arms over her stomach and mumbled, "And a romance would give the reader ideas."

"Isn't the point of a book to give a reader ideas?"

"It would give her father ideas, then."

"He isn't real."

She took the three steps needed to pace the length of the writing desk. "We have to pretend he is. That's what gives the story life."

"By that logic, we can pretend the same of a beau. Or a villain."

With a groaning sigh of frustration, she spun away from him and crossed the room to look out the window. "Heiress adventurers are a lonely sort. Who could she fall in love with?" Her voice dropped to a whisper. "No one is in her life long enough to form an attachment."

Were they still discussing the book? Jonas walked back through the conversation, and it all *seemed* to pertain to the book. Any current unease had to be from the discomfort he'd arrived with. That could be ignored.

"She's traveling through Europe," he said. "We could add a guide to her entourage. Or the coachman could be a duke in disguise, hiding from his responsibilities. Don't readers like that sort of thing?"

"They do." She gave a short laugh. "That seems a ridiculous way to hide, though."

"The best hiding spots are the ones no one would consider."

"Then he should find a small town to invest himself in. Perhaps one a few days' ride from home. No one would look there."

Jonas shook his head. "The duke isn't real either."

"Which is exactly why we can't include him."

Were they having the same conversation? Jonas frowned. "Are you saying Elsabeth is real?"

"No."

"But we're writing a story about her."

"It's for her father."

"Is her father real?"

A slight moment of silence weighed heavy on the room before Harriet sighed. "No."

"Then what is the problem?"

This wild ride was giving him a headache, especially since it seemed there was something here he should be seeing but wasn't, some key that would unlock this entire confusing business. At least the ridiculousness of this conversation was proving the confusion of the springs to be an anomaly. While he was now willing to admit that Harriet might not be entirely as conniving as he'd once thought, she was still proving to be the haughty heiress determined to get her own way without any consideration for another's view of the situation.

With her arms crossed and her chin lifted, she said, "A duke in disguise will take too much focus away from Elsabeth's life experiences."

Jonas settled into the desk chair, feeling relaxed for the first time in hours, perhaps even days. This was a version of Harriet he could handle.

Mostly because he didn't much like her.

"A guide, then." He picked up his pen.

"Are you so very keen to write a romance?" Harriet dropped the haughty look and strode toward him with the same gleam in her eyes he'd seen before she convinced Lady Adelaide to serve beef instead of fish. "Are you pining for a romance of your own? A few public assemblies are occurring over the next two weeks."

As if he would attend an assembly. Local tradesmen and their daughters might attend on occasion, but no one of his station would dare darken the door, even if they could afford proper clothing and the subscription fee.

If he said that, though, she'd appear at the stable tomorrow with a tailor and a voucher. Instead, he said, quite truthfully, "I'll be far too busy with the April Meetings to attend the assemblies."

"Hmmm, yes." She frowned. "And after the races everyone hies off to London." Then she smiled once more. Like a cat. "Perhaps we invite a few additional ladies to dinner Tuesday? I'm sure the others won't mind, as it's for a good cause."

That she would even offer such after their moment in the woods stung him more than a little. All notions of tenderness must have been in his head.

Not that he was looking to start a romance with Harriet. Or anyone else.

How had this conversation become about him? "We've strayed from the point. Elsabeth needs something to *do*."

"She's experiencing life like her father requested."

Jonas sighed. "That's boring."

"No it isn't. It's fascinating."

"As individual scenes, perhaps. You should submit the writing to a magazine."

Her arms dropped to her side, excitement lighting up her face. "You'd let me do that?"

Jonas frowned in confusion. "Do what? It's your story."

"But you'd let me submit your writing?" Her shoulders shifted forward. Was she preparing to pounce on the desk?

Jonas sat back in his seat. "You are building upon what I write, aren't you? Changing it? Making it your own?"

She waved her hand in the air. "Yes, yes, but your writing is so captivating that I'm not altering much."

Which meant it was as meandering and unpublishable as he thought. "We've veered from the point again."

"No we haven't."

"Aye, we have."

She frowned. "No. We're discussing how good your writing is."

"The quality of my writing is not the point."

"So you agree that you're a good writer?"

Maybe. Perhaps. That didn't change the current problem. "The story has no substance."

"Your writing is good enough to circumvent what some would consider a lack of story."

An unfamiliar agitation swelled in Jonas's chest, and it wasn't until he shoved his hand through his hair, yanking the strands with clenched fingers, that he realized it was anger. "She's done nothing but go for a walk in the woods and eat from a street cart."

"And you've written it so lovely that I don't care! I'll read about Elsabeth sitting in a carriage all day the way you write it."

He was flattered, but she was impossible. "Books don't work that way, Harriet."

"I'll have you know I read a great deal, and I find exemplary writing far more important. Just look at the popularity of poetry. Lord Byron put out that collection of thirty poems that had not a thing to do with one another."

Jonas had read Lord Stildon's collection of Byron and could only roll his eyes at Harriet. "We are to ignore his other works, then, which are hundreds upon hundreds of lines of narrative poetry that do, indeed, have a story to them?"

She sniffed. "I didn't realize you'd read those."

Because during the years they'd been published he'd been scraping by without leisure time or access to books? Jonas lifted his brow. "Books tend to lie about for years, you know."

"I didn't mean . . ." Her eyes widened, and she swallowed. "We can consider Elsabeth's story a series of vignettes."

"People won't buy that."

She flung her hands wide and looked up at the ceiling in exasperation. "I don't really care if they do."

If he dropped his head on the desk really hard, would it knock him low enough that he could move on to tomorrow morning, when he would once again be working with the horses? They, at the very least, made sense. "Why am I doing this then?"

"Because I asked for your help, and you like being of assistance."

It was true, but how could she know such a thing?

The answer came as swiftly as the question. Sophia. His sweet sister might not be the innocent victim he'd thought her to be. That was a matter to consider later.

Slowly, he rose to his feet, forcing himself to not be distracted by the door she'd unwittingly opened. "Why a book if you've no intention of publishing it? What else would you do with it?"

She watched him, eyes wide, mind clearly churning. No immediate answer meant she was having to formulate one. Would she confess?

"You're right. That doesn't make sense." She moved to the writing desk and picked up the travel book. "If you were to give her a romance"—her voice dropped to a near whisper—"what would it look like?"

Her acquiescence did nothing to aid his understanding. It did force them to perpetuate the pretense a little longer, though.

He sat back in his chair and cleared his throat, fighting to keep his mind clear of memories better off ignored. "It's your story. It can go however you want."

She eased into the chair behind her desk, sitting sideways, not fully facing him but occasionally looking his way. "If she did . . . I mean, if we gave her a guide and their interactions became . . . personal, do you think they would make it? Would he eventually come home with her?"

"I suppose it depends." His voice was as quiet as hers.

"On what?"

"Whether or not he fell in love with her. If there was a place for him in her real life. If he could have a purpose."

She sighed. "And we're back to that. Do you think I have a purpose in life, Jonas?"

Was driving him insane a purpose? Because it seemed to be all she did of late, and she was very, very good at it. As to her tendency to involve herself in other people's lives, he couldn't decide what sort of purpose that would entail. "I can't answer that for you."

"I think I have one. You've even inspired me to tie a Bible verse to it."

"I have?"

She nodded. "I heard it in the sermon last week." She shrugged. "It seemed to fit, so I claimed it."

"That's not how the Bible works."

"Why not?" She shifted so she could drape one arm over the back of the chair and look at him directly. "You always attribute verses to things."

But he didn't go seeking a verse after making a decision. "The verse is supposed to come first, not the application."

She frowned. "Can't God inspire people in the opposite direction?"

"Well, yes." How had they gotten onto this topic? "He guides through the Bible."

Her mouth pressed into a thoughtful moue as she tilted her head. "Not always."

"Why would you say that?"

"Because they didn't always have the Bible. Someone had to be guided through living it first."

Jonas felt something was off with that logic, but he couldn't find it. On the surface, her sentence made sense, but it seemed too open-ended for him, as if she thought people could still add to the Bible. "We aren't writing new books."

"That doesn't mean God can't still work in those ways. Perhaps He revealed my purpose another way until I could unearth the passage."

Again, Jonas couldn't put his finger on what felt skewed about her opinion, so he claimed the idea that *he that shutteth his lips is esteemed a man of understanding* and moved on. At least she wasn't quizzing him about what he was doing with *his* life again.

He ran a hand over his face, afraid to ask but desperate to understand what drove this woman. "What verse are you claiming?"

"That we are to rescue those who have been beat down in life and move them to places where they can heal and start afresh."

"That's not a quote."

"It's still in the Bible."

Again, he couldn't argue. Why were Harriet's thoughts so difficult for him to grasp? Was she illogical, or was he?

"We've lost the point." He gave her a dark look. "Again. We need to give *Elsabeth* a purpose."

"Very well. Have her fall in love with the guide." She pointed at him as her body turned in the chair. "But if it all falls apart and she returns to her father brokenhearted, I'm blaming you."

What did he care? By then he'd be back to seeing her only from across the room when his sister guilted him into attending dinner. "It will sell a million copies. People love experiencing another's desperation."

"Only people who have yet to experience their own," she muttered before opening her book and avoiding Jonas's gaze.

This time, it really was upside down.

Sixteen

"Your description of the view from your window was wonderful. Your mother watched people that way. She would have loved sitting next to you."

—Gregory Hancock, in his reply to the first letter Harriet sent with Jonas's writing

Harriet dropped her father's letter on the desk with a sigh.

She'd finally made him happy.

Why didn't she feel better about it?

Ignoring Jonas's piece about the street food, Harriet pulled her blank paper forward and bent her head to write.

Dearest Papa,

I've decided to hire a guide. If this is to be the last leg of my adventure before I come home, then I want to be sure I miss nothing. He's a local man, or he is now. He's traveled the country quite a bit and has a great respect for all it contains.

She sat back in her chair. In some ways Jonas was turning out to be a guide. Not of the local sights, though she had to wonder what other nearby treasures existed that she'd never considered.

No, Jonas was making her venture into herself in ways she'd never done before.

And she didn't know how she felt about any of it.

Her gaze fell to the paper covered with the strong slant of Jonas's writing. He saw so much more than she would have guessed. For the writing to elicit so much emotion, the author had to feel it, didn't he? Was Jonas not as calm as he appeared? Or was it a detached sort of emotion? Could he separate his mind from his heart and merely observe?

It wasn't often Harriet wished she'd given more attention to cultivating close friendships, but someone to talk to about this business would be nice. She could, perhaps, go to Adelaide or Bianca, but then Sophia would inevitably hear about it.

She dipped her pen in the ink and bent over the paper once more.

His name is Jonas, and I've never met anyone like him before.

FOR THE NEXT TWO WEEKS, Jonas went back to hiding amongst the horses. This time no one—not even him—could call him a coward for doing it. Working for a racehorse trainer meant the days around the April Meeting were busy. On top of the normal feeding, cleaning, and training were preparations for the races, along with extra checks of the equipment and horse health, as well as massive disruptions to the stable's normal schedule.

Jonas refilled the feed bin with mash before giving Equinox one last congratulatory pat and ensuring that he had plenty of water. The stallion had just won his race by more than a length and deserved extra attention during his rubdown.

After Sweet Fleet's race, Jonas would do the process all over again, but he had at least two hours before that happened. The stable was quiet with all the grooms watching the races, taking turns returning to the stable and seeing to the horses.

Jonas walked through, checking water and food, before wandering back out toward the Heath to watch the next race. As he passed the stairs up to the grooms' living quarters, he paused. It wouldn't hurt to take his sketchbook and pencil with him.

He found a place to sit atop one of the dykes that gave him an elevated view of the end of the course. The air itself seemed to give off a measure of anticipation as he filled his lungs with the scents of baked treats, fresh grass, and horses.

In the distance, he could see horses and men gathered around the weigh house. Watching the animals move about was fascinating, even when they weren't in the midst of a race. It was a marvel how God had constructed them.

Jonas couldn't imagine his life without horses. A patch of open grass lay to his right, and he turned to look at it, almost surprised to find he hadn't brought Pandora out here with him.

A gunshot in the distance marked the start of the race, pulling his attention back to the track. The low rumble from the nearby spectators fell to near silence before swelling to a roar as the horses came around the corner. Jonas's position beyond the finish pole allowed him to see the striving horses and the cheering crowd. The excitement of the onlookers couldn't begin to match the waves of effort rolling in front of the running horses.

Grass and sweat flew. Nostrils flared. Three horses ran even with one another, their legs moving so quickly and so close together it was a wonder they didn't kick one another. As they stretched and strained for the finish, Jonas found himself leaning with them, his breathing picking up pace, his hands curling into fists as if he were the one striving to get that last bit of speed out of the animal beneath him.

Then it was over.

Voices shouted and fingers pointed as everyone tried to declare the winner. Finally, the judge indicated that Lord Gliddon's horse had come across first, and another roar rippled through the crowd.

Jonas didn't roar, but he did snatch up his sketchbook. His pencil flew over the page as he threw down the lines that shaped that final moment as he'd seen it. The mass of horse and human writhing with ambition and determination. The depiction was crude, but he was more interested in capturing the essence than in perfecting the lines. He could redraw it later. All he needed now was something to remind him how the moment felt.

He paused, his pencil poised to finish one of the reins.

His breath thinned until he was barely breathing as he flipped to a clean page in the sketchbook. Once more his pencil flew over the page, only this time he wasn't drawing the exciting race he'd just seen. He was writing about it.

When he was finished, he felt a sense of accomplishment he'd never known existed.

HE DIDN'T GET THE OPPORTUNITY to return to the sketch right away. When the races finished the next day, most of the other grooms and two of the jockeys celebrated behind the stable. They had food, drink, and two sets of stakes driven into the ground so they could play horseshoes.

Jonas joined the festivities long enough to eat and listen to the first round of retellings. The second round included a handful of embellishments, making Jonas roll his eyes. Fortunately, he had his own account of the races. He should clean up the drawing before the adjusted accounts took root in his mind.

He returned to his room and pulled out the sketchbook to look over the lines of his crude effort. It would make a good guide for a clean drawing.

Before he could turn to a new page, his thoughts dropped to his bed. More specifically, to the box he'd shoved underneath it.

It was ridiculous to just leave it there. What sort of point was he making to anyone?

He knelt on the floor and slid the box out. With a hesitation born of fear, reverence, or a combination of both, he laid the tools in a row on his bed. The narrow chisels had an obvious purpose, but the leather pillow and wider blades were a mystery.

The manual was heavy in his hands. If he opened it, if he read and followed the instructions within, what would that mean? That he was accepting this idea of sponsorship? That he was pursuing an avenue in which he had no control over the outcome and no security? An artist could work on his talent for years and never become successful enough to support himself. He was at the mercy of others' opinions of his work.

That wasn't a future Jonas was willing to accept.

One hand drifted over the tools as he considered the possibilities, then he picked up a chisel and panel of wood. If he could draw without jeopardizing his livelihood, why couldn't he engrave as well?

Three days later, he had an engraving worthy of the kindling bucket. The final touches were evidence he'd improved over that short period of work, though. He set the small chisel back in the box and slid the engraved block away to get a better look at it.

Ernest, the quiet young man who shared his room, came in and braced against the wall, lifting one foot and bending over to begin tugging at his boot. The room had only one chair, and Jonas was sitting in it. He stood and spun the wooden seat to face the other groom and then nudged it across the floor. Ernest sat before continuing to remove his boots. "Did you finish, then?"

Jonas nodded. When he'd first moved in, he'd kept his sketches a secret from the other man, but it didn't take long to realize everyone here had their own interests. No one would think less of him for not working himself to the bone every waking moment of the day.

Still, it felt strange to share. He cleared his throat and waved at the dresser he'd been using as a desk. "I don't know that it's good, but it's complete."

Setting the boots aside, Ernest stood and leaned over the dresser. "That was a stunning moment, wasn't it?" He pointed at the carved wooden block. "That takes me back to it all over again. You could do a sequence of them. Show the whole finish."

That daunting idea made Jonas's fingers cramp. How many blocks would it take to truly show the spectacular finish to someone who hadn't been there? Five? Six? A dozen?

Whatever the number, it was far too high to contemplate.

His fingers twitched once more, only this time it wasn't in agony at the thought of scraping away that much wood. It was in memory of the fact that he had captured the moment in another way as well. The notes had been just for him, so he wouldn't forget anything, but what if he gave them the same attention he gave Harriet's writing?

The idea stayed with him the entire next day. While he fed and exercised the horses, while he cleaned the stalls and the tack. No matter how menial or complicated the task, part of his mind was consumed with documenting that exciting race.

This would be different from writing Harriet's vague ideas.

This would be his.

When he finished work, his heart pounded as he forced himself to walk sedately to his room. Once there, he grabbed his notebook and the words he'd been crafting in his mind all day flowed from his pencil.

The next day he grabbed a new block and started his engraving all over again. This time he knew how to hold the tools, what sort of pressure to put on them, the way to brace the board with the leather pillow so it was easier to make lines and curves.

By Sunday night, he'd completed a set of work he was proud of—a decent engraving with an accompanying description.

The only unsettling part was how much he wanted to show it to Harriet instead of return it to the drawer.

A FEW WEEKS AGO, Harriet had not been looking forward to the April Meeting and the influx of people and social engagements it would bring. It would take time away from her project with Jonas, and she hated to delay moving toward a goal once she'd set one.

Now, though, she welcomed the abundance of invitations and the busy schedule. Even without attending the races, she was barely home except to change clothing and depart for her next engagement.

She played cards, danced, talked, laughed.

And spent many an hour wondering what Jonas was doing with his time. Or how he'd feel about what she wrote about him in the letter to her father. Or about that last conversation they'd had about life needing a purpose.

"Did you hear?" Mrs. Wainbright sidled up to Harriet at a soiree the night after the races had completed.

"I'm assuming I did, as I heard your inquiry." It was oh so pleasant to be the town's eccentric heiress. Only the elderly titled women got away with more bluntness than she did. Harriet had to admit, though, her retort had been sharper than normal.

Was it because she'd been matching wits with Jonas, who gave as good as he got? Or the fact that she didn't particularly like Mrs. Wainbright?

No matter. It was said, and there was no taking it back.

The other woman laughed, but it was short and brittle. Harriet would guess the dislike was mutual.

"We've had our own little Season in Newmarket this year. I know of at least three engagements officially announced this week. My own daughter's being one of them."

The stab of envy was familiar enough that Harriet had little trouble ignoring it, or at least keeping it from her expression. She'd never formed a particular regard for any of the men who lived in Newmarket or even trotted through town with the horses, but there was always the knowledge that one more engagement was one less opportunity for her once she was finally free to marry. "My sincerest felicitations. You must be very happy."

"Oh yes." Mrs. Wainbright smiled. "Before the end of the London Season, my daughter will be Lady Davers."

Well, the loss of that prospect was certainly not anything to pine over. She'd never have married Lord Davers. Even she couldn't be so rude as to say such in public, though. "How nice."

The other woman smiled and went on to share who the other affianced couples were, as well as the rumors of who might be paired soon. A spark of delight flit through her upon learning Miss Sailors had been seen dancing thrice with the milliner's son, but otherwise Harriet's reactions were dim. It was as if she felt she *should* be disappointed yet wasn't.

"We're getting a grand reputation as the place to go to find a spouse," Mrs. Wainbright continued. "That's good news for you."

"For me?" Harriet glanced around, looking for something to use as an excuse out of this conversation. It didn't have to be a polite excuse, merely a believable one. If she didn't find something soon, she'd have to stoop to the timeworn and overused need to visit the retiring room.

"Why, yes. It means more men will come here, and perhaps you'll finally find one that suits your fancy. You don't want to wait too long, you know. Money is only so pretty."

Forget an excuse. Harriet was giving this woman the cut direct every time she saw her from here on out. "I suppose it's a good thing that my face is pretty as well, then, isn't it?" Harriet turned her back on the woman and walked away without another word.

She'd have loved to leave the party, but then Mrs. Wainbright would think she'd won some triumph over her. Instead, she sought out the women she'd just heard about and offered congratulations or a listening ear, making sure there was nothing she could quietly do for the fledgling couples.

There'd been a time when she lived for these sorts of evenings, but tonight, in the back of her mind, she kept thinking how much she'd rather be at one of her Tuesday night dinners.

Especially if Jonas was there.

Seventeen

"I know you would be willing to turn down this trip to America because you don't want me to be alone, but this is an incredible opportunity. Your mother wanted to see it so badly, but I couldn't be away from the factory for four months. I can't wait to hear how you conquer the former colonies!"

—Gregory Hancock, in a letter to Harriet when she was eighteen, the summer after her grandfather died

Sunday was meant to be a day of rest, but Harriet labored through the entire morning service searching the hymns and the sermon for deeper purpose and underlying meaning. When she returned home with an aching head, she took an uncharacteristic nap.

That evening, she went nowhere, dining alone as she watched the sunset. The races were over, those who had not yet departed for London would be leaving in the morning, and Harriet would be returning to her normal patterns.

And she was questioning every one of those usual activities.

She rose Monday morning, determined to put the mulling of the past two weeks behind her with a cup of tea and a large breakfast.

It didn't work.

She pushed away her tea and propped her elbows on the table before dropping her chin on her joined hands. How would she handle this if it were an acquaintance who needed to find their way out of the doldrums? What had she done for Frances, the maid who'd taken to sniveling in corners last year?

Her face pulled into a frown as she tried to remember. She'd made the girl go through everything that had happened, walking back through the days until they came to the source of her despondency: a vase she'd accidentally broken while dusting and had hidden away in fear of retribution.

Assuring the maid it was not a horrid loss hadn't worked, so Harriet had instructed a local shop owner to bring three vases to the house. Frances chose one to purchase as a replacement. Harriet had, of course, instructed the owner to quote a price that would make poor Frances feel she'd paid her debt but not put her in any sort of pinch. Then Harriet quietly paid the difference.

There was no shop to visit in this instance, but perhaps thinking back to the point where everything had gone wrong would still work.

It didn't take long to determine that what needed repairing was her working relationship with Jonas. That should be simple enough. She had a few hours to shore up her defenses before he arrived. Then she would make sure their interactions returned to how they'd been before their confrontation.

No more philosophical conversations about what should or should not be happening in Elsabeth's life. No more outings. No more interactions at all that didn't relate to him finding his passion for writing.

She closed herself in the library, poring over travel books and making pages and pages of notes on possible destinations. Those should keep him busy enough that he couldn't opine on the lacks in her life and would instead create enough stories to fill months' worth of letters until she staged her homecoming.

It was a good plan.

Until Jonas arrived, looking a bit sheepish and holding a threadbare knapsack in his hands. One look at his face and all her intentions of burying them both in work immediately fled.

He cleared his throat and set the bag on his desk. "I have something to show you."

"Oh?" Harriet's heart pounded. Thus far she had always seemed to be the one being vulnerable, but here he'd brought something of himself to share with her.

He was deliberately opening up to her, and the idea made her stomach flutter.

"Yes." He reached into the bag and pulled out a flat board and a folded piece of paper. He frowned at them a moment. "This is not me accepting your sponsorship offer. It's, well, it's a show of gratitude. I've found I do enjoy it in my leisure time, and I wanted to thank you for supplying the tools."

He set the block and paper on her desk, and Harriet reached for them with trembling fingers. She picked up the block first, and a feeling of reverence swelled through her as she softly traced the grooves.

Three horses and jockeys seemed to strain as one toward the finish line. The picture didn't include legs, focusing on the upper halves of the horses and the determination of the jockeys, but just looking at the image made her hold her breath in anticipation.

Setting the block down, she picked up the paper and unfolded it. The words put the writing he'd been doing for her to shame as she found herself creeping closer and closer to the edge of her seat as she read his account of the race. This was what he'd meant by saying writing needs a purpose. Every word on the page was building toward a climactic moment when one of the riders would win.

"Jonas, this is amazing," she breathed, relaxing back into her chair as she read through the passage again and then picked up the carving. "It must have taken so much time."

He shrugged. "It was good to have something to do in the free moments." He pointed to the carving. "That's actually the second attempt. I tried to use too much detail in the first one, and it was a jumbled mess."

His humble gratitude felt too large. Jonas didn't know it, but he was giving her far more than she'd given him. In the last letter from her father, he'd been effusively excited to hear more about her guide, her plans, and her awakened observations.

He'd been proud of her.

And while that left a bitterness in the back of Harriet's throat, she was thankful that now she could plan her return knowing he would be satisfied. Soon she'd be able to live her life in Newmarket with no restraints.

For all that, she owed Jonas more than a simple thank-you. "May I keep them?"

He looked surprised by her question but shrugged. "I don't see why not. It's not as if I've a use for them." He glanced around the room with a soft laugh. "You can display it amongst your treasures."

Oh, she would. Just not the ones he could see. No, she treasured the memory of every single life she'd made better, and his would be one of them.

BY MIDMORNING THE NEXT DAY, Jonas's entire body seemed to twitch like a horse waiting for the start of a race. Part of him was still working at the hectic pace required of him for the past two weeks, and he ripped through his tasks faster than he would have liked. He was too worked up to sit or even stand still, so drawing, writing, and reading weren't options.

On Jonas's fourth trip down the stall aisle, looking in on the needs of each horse, Mr. Knight stopped him and shoved a set of reins into his hands.

The leather brought him an immediate sense of comfort. Of course horses were the answer. Perhaps he'd try his hand at training again, or—

"The ladies' horses are outside. They'll be down shortly."

Jonas frowned. "Ladies?"

Knight gave his shoulder a strong pat. "Your pacing is making the horses nervous, so you get to escort Lady Stildon today."

Wonderful. He sighed. Riding along at a sedate pace while leading a horse with a disgruntled viscountess in the saddle wasn't the best prescription for restlessness. At least it was something to do and he'd get out into some fresh air.

Mr. Knight had said *ladies*, though. Who else would be accompanying Lady Stildon?

His answer waited on the drive. There, beside the cream-colored mare, was his sister's snow-white Andalusian. Jonas mounted Pandora and fleetingly considered escaping before the ladies could come down.

Minutes later, Sophia and Lady Stildon emerged, and two grooms assisted them into their saddles. It still jarred him to see his sister draping her habit skirts from a sidesaddle. Before they'd come to Newmarket, Sophia had always worn wide-legged trousers beneath a regular-length skirt so she could ride astride when doing the training their father had taught them or riding long distances for the circus.

Sometimes it was hard to remember that she now had enough income that her dresses no longer had to be entirely serviceable.

Jonas took the lead rope for Lady Stildon's horse and off they walked.

If glares could harm a man, he'd have been bleeding by the time they reached the first gate. Lady Stildon was a fine horsewoman, but her husband was the one who gave the orders, and very strict instructions had been given to all the stable hands—even those working for Aaron—as to how the lady's rides were to go before the baby was born.

Sophia laughed. "It's not his fault, Bianca. Stop trying to kill my brother with your eyes."

"It's humiliating," Lady Stildon grumbled.

"Which is why we aren't going to the Heath. Relax. Enjoy the breeze and the view."

Jonas had been concerned that the steady walk wouldn't calm him any, but as he settled into the saddle and swayed with the horse beneath him, some of the tingles that had vibrated beneath his skin abated.

Sophia rode on the other side of Lady Stildon, and Jonas did his best to be invisible so the ladies could enjoy each other's company. He'd likely hear a lot of gossip over the next hour, and most of it wouldn't mean a thing to him.

Still, it was nice to see his sister's smile so wide, her bearing relaxed. Life was good for her, which meant it was good for him.

"I adore the color of that habit," Lady Stildon said. "Is it new?"

"Yes. Isn't it lovely? Harriet helped me pick it."

A band snapped tight around Jonas's chest, and he couldn't take a deep enough breath to relieve it. Women assisted each other with shopping all the time, didn't they? Goodness knows he'd heard the ladies discussing colors and fabrics at Tuesday dinners.

"She does have excellent taste in clothes," Lady Stildon said.

"Yes," Sophia answered. "I almost had the modiste make my normal trousers and skirt, but Harriet was near to swooning over this new pattern, and the modiste said two other ladies had ordered similar ones that week, so I changed it to a habit. It's probably better if the other Newmarket ladies see me in proper clothing when I'm not working."

Jonas doubted the conversation had been as innocent as Sophia remembered. Yes, there was some merit to the thought, but it was clear that, once again, Harriet had suggested something in a way that made Sophia think it was her own idea.

He took several breaths, happy the conversation didn't require his participation. It was just a dress. He didn't need to confront anyone or administer any warnings. He did, however, need to keep a closer eye on Harriet in case she decided to interfere in anything truly important. He hadn't even known she'd visited the modiste with Sophia.

They rode on, plodding over the countryside, waving to the occasional farmer. The topics turned to menus for upcoming dinners and decorating plans for the nursery and Sophia's new house. Jonas let his mind wander, periodically meditating on Bible verses about nature and birds.

"Jonas!"

His sister's sharp call of his name broke into his thoughts and brought his attention jerking back to the two women.

Lady Stildon started laughing. "Well, I think we can now be assured that our secrets are safe."

Sophia rolled her eyes. "Of course they are. This is Jonas."

"What did you need me for?" Jonas asked.

She gave him a cheeky smile. "We want to know how things are going with Harriet's art sponsorship."

Jonas gave his sister a narrow look. Yes, she'd been the one to pressure him into talking to Harriet about art nearly two months ago, but they'd not mentioned it since. Why did she think he'd accepted the offer?

Lady Stildon smiled. "She's sponsoring your art?"

"No." Jonas frowned. He wasn't going to even attempt to explain the strange working relationship he and Harriet were forming over her work. Besides, he was supposed to be playing the servant today. They wouldn't be discussing this if he weren't here.

"She's not?" Sophia's mouth pressed into a tight line.

"No," he repeated before remembering the box of tools and the engraving he'd done during the race week. Keeping secrets was one thing. Lying to his sister was another. "Well, in a way."

"What sort of art are you doing?" Lady Stildon asked.

"Engraving."

She nodded. "Does that require a great deal of space? Is that where you've been going on your free days?"

Sophia leaned forward to stare at him open-mouthed. "You're making the art *at* Harriet's house?"

"No," Jonas grumbled. "I'm writing at Harriet's house."

As soon as the words left his mouth, he wanted to take them back. He just wasn't accustomed to watching what he said around Sophia.

"Jonas Fitzroy, are you writing a book?" Sophia nearly squealed.

He was not getting out of this without something of an explanation. He'd have to apologize to Harriet later. "*She* is writing a book. *I* am helping her collect ideas." His writings thus far had been a collection of concepts that wouldn't become a book until something tied them together.

Like a romance between Elsabeth and the guide.

What had he been thinking to suggest such a thing? Now he had to sit across from Harriet and imagine scenarios that drew a couple together in a way the reader would find thrilling. Not even a normal, everyday romance of practicality and simple interest. No, it would have to be something dramatic and fraught with risk.

Which should be an easy thing to accomplish, by nature of a woman like Elsabeth and a man she'd employed falling in love.

That didn't make it easy to contemplate.

"Harriet *was* always writing when I worked with her," Sophia said. "It was mostly letters, I think."

"This is to be a book of letters," Jonas said, hoping a few tidbits would be enough to satisfy his twin.

He should have known better.

"Who are they between?" She gasped. "Is it a romance? Are they sweethearts separated by an ocean, falling in love over the written word?" Her excitement faded as quickly as it had flared. "Actually, that sounds like it would take a dreadfully long time."

"Perhaps they are in the same town or even the same house." Lady Stildon tilted her head in thought. "Maybe they work there."

"Harriet could never write an entire book about a servant." Sophia shook her head. "The woman is generous to a fault but also spoiled beyond belief."

Protest rose in Jonas's throat, but he kept it to himself. Besides, which part would he speak against? Harriet's generosity? Her being spoiled? Both? He could see a certain amount of truth behind both claims, and Sophia obviously meant neither in a disparaging way.

So why did he feel such a need to defend her? Yes, the Bible said *we then that are strong ought to bear the infirmities of the weak*, but that didn't really feel like it applied to this situation.

"It is hard to imagine her writing about a lower station, isn't it?" Lady Stildon scrunched her nose. "She'd be far too bold for someone who isn't entirely independent." She shot a sideways look at Jonas and bit her lip. "And I think that was far too bold a statement for me to say aloud."

Sophia laughed. "No need to worry about Jonas's sensibilities. He's not Harriet's staunchest supporter." She leaned toward Lady Stildon and pretended to whisper. "He doesn't like her much."

"I never said that," Jonas grumbled.

Sophia jerked her head so she could see him past her friend. "Have you changed your mind about her?" She grinned. "Do you like her company now?"

Did he? Perhaps. "I am merely pointing out that I never said I didn't like Miss Hancock."

"You implied it."

"I cannot be responsible for how you interpret my statements."

"Humph. That's a fine attempt at wriggling off the hook. You know very well that communication isn't all in the wording."

"Ah, but liability is."

Lady Stildon lifted a hand to her mouth to cover her laughter.

Sophia stared at Jonas, and he adjusted his horse's pace so Lady Stildon more fully blocked his sister's view. With a sigh of frustration, Sophia turned her horse and trotted around the group until she was on Jonas's other side.

He gave her a disapproving frown. "You are meant to be riding with your friend, not your brother."

"We're providing the entertainment, and *you* are being evasive."

Was he? Given that he wasn't entirely sure what the topic was, aside from it being somewhat connected to Harriet, he didn't see how he was avoiding anything. "What is it you think I'm stepping around?"

"Harriet."

"As she is the topic of the current conversation—quite rude of us, I might add, since she isn't here—I don't think your claim holds up."

Sophia pressed her lips into a firm line and jutted her nose into the air. Jonas bit his cheek to keep from grinning at this sure sign he was winning the battle of wits. Not that he didn't usually win against his sister, considering that he'd normally given whatever they were talking about a great deal more thought prior than she had. Though that was still true in this case, he'd come to no conclusions where Harriet was concerned. In fact, he hadn't moved much beyond obliterating all the conclusions he'd previously had.

Having no solidified opinion on the subject made it very easy to avoid stating one.

Lady Stildon cleared her throat. "He does have a point," she said gently.

"Of course he has a point," Sophia grumbled as she wheeled her horse around to go back to her friend's side. "He always has a point. He's insufferable in his ability to state nothing but unarguable points."

Yet somehow Harriet always seemed able to challenge him.

And that was a very uncomfortable thought.

Eighteen

"Matthew and I are getting married. Please don't be angry. I know you'll have no trouble finding a replacement for me, especially as you've decided to return to London."

—Bernice, Harriet's traveling companion, in her resignation letter two months into Harriet's stay in Dublin

Normally Harriet didn't question the helpful impulses that came into her mind, but she spent the entirety of Tuesday morning wondering if she'd done the right thing where Jonas was concerned. She'd been so sure—was still sure—this new career would make him happier, but she had the distinct feeling he wasn't going to thank her for showing him.

She was not accustomed to this lack of surety, and she couldn't say she wanted to become so. It was highly uncomfortable.

As usual, her busy schedule came to her rescue. Adelaide and Trent were hosting Tuesday dinner, and the ladies had been invited to come early and paint. Harriet, grateful for the distraction, was the first to arrive.

Bianca appeared not long after with the news that Sophia was giving a riding lesson and wouldn't be there until the usual dinner time.

The ladies set themselves up in the parlor with paints and fireplace screens.

Then the inquisition began.

"I hear you're working *with* Mr. Fitzroy instead of merely sponsoring him." Bianca's tone was innocent, but her look was quite pointed.

Harriet busied herself by selecting a paintbrush, trying to ignore the heat suddenly flooding her cheeks. They hadn't exactly been sneaking about, but how had Bianca learned of it? Harriet attempted a casual shrug. "Yes. We're writing a book."

It was always best to stick with the truth, even if a subtly twisted version. Remembering what she had already told her father when she wrote her weekly letter was difficult enough. She couldn't possibly keep up with the details if she allowed the situation with Jonas to turn into a complete fabrication.

Adelaide tilted her head as she dabbed her brush lightly against the fireplace screen in front of her to create a small purple flower. "I didn't know you wanted to write a book."

"I didn't know *he* wanted to write anything," Bianca added.

"Why should you know anything about what he wants to do?" Harriet asked.

"Why should you?" Bianca countered, giving Harriet more attention than her paintbrush yet still managing to elegantly swirl a green vine across the screen.

"He doesn't share much when he comes to dinner," Adelaide mused.

"I think he feels out of place," Harriet said quietly, painting a tree on her own screen with far more care than she usually gave the craft.

Bianca lifted her brush and tilted her head, staring into space as she thought. "I do believe you're right. It would make more sense if his sister wasn't in attendance, but truly, he could hold his own in the conversation. It isn't as if he is without breeding or education, and the rest of the lot is utterly horse mad. If anything, Adelaide and Trent should feel like the odd ducks."

Adelaide gave a small hum in response before adding a long, thin stem to her cluster of flowers.

Bianca frowned. "We don't make you feel like such, do we?"

Adelaide glanced up from her painting, blue eyes enormous behind her black-rimmed spectacles. She looked at Bianca and then Harriet before saying in a calm voice, "I don't think either of you would have allowed me such sensibilities. You'd have run them over. Besides, Harriet isn't horse mad either."

"That's true enough." Harriet painted the lines of bare winter limbs on the tree she'd placed in the center of her screen. "Though I do at least ride."

"I can ride," Adelaide said with a scowl.

Harriet gave a small grin, thankful the conversation had turned off her and more particularly off Jonas. "At a pace faster than a walk?"

"I'm still sitting upon the horse." The sentence was spoken in a gentle, matter-of-fact tone that sent the other women into a round of laughter.

Bianca sighed as she returned to her painting. "We have digressed from the objective."

"As the point of this gathering is to paint screens and enjoy one another's company, I do not believe one can digress from the objective as long as conversation is flowing." Harriet directed her attention to the paint colors as if there were a great internal debate to be had about the shade of winter grass.

"Very well. Then we've digressed from the topic," Bianca said.

Harriet selected a tube of grey and a tube of green. Blending a paint color required she keep her gaze on her palette. "Which you chose."

"And which you are avoiding."

And Harriet would continue to avoid if at all possible. She

didn't even know for certain what she *thought* about her dealings with Jonas, so she wasn't about to *say* anything.

Was that why she was experiencing such consternation? Or was a larger, more complex issue at hand? Jonas was hardly the first person she'd helped who'd required a great deal of focused attention, but he was the first with whom she'd personally involved herself to the extent that she invited him into her home in a capacity other than employee.

Harriet selected a new brush and dipped it in her swirled paint to create the expanse of dying grass.

"Harriet." Bianca drew the name out.

"Bianca," Harriet returned.

"Adelaide," Adelaide sang to herself.

Harriet snorted out a laugh. Every now and then, the quiet woman showed a glimpse of personality that evidenced why she was such a good match for her effervescent husband.

Bianca laughed as well but was not deterred. "You are writing a book, and he is helping you gather information, correct?"

Where *had* she learned that? Harriet couldn't remember saying anything, and if she had, it would have been phrased differently.

Bianca continued, "That was all he would tell me and Sophia this morning."

And that was how Jonas described it? What else had he said? She couldn't risk contradicting him. Or revealing something he considered private or embarrassing.

"You had a conversation with Jonas?" Adelaide asked.

"He led my horse around the countryside," Bianca grumbled. "Sophia arranged it. She said it was because she trusted him not to share anything we talked about, but I think she wanted to question him somewhere he couldn't run away."

Harriet silently applauded Sophia's resourcefulness.

Adelaide blinked. "Has he been avoiding her?"

"He says he's been busy." Bianca shrugged.

"He is spending a great deal of his free time at my house," Harriet said, defending Jonas before thinking better of it.

Both Adelaide and Bianca lit up with curiosity as they stared at Harriet.

"What is it like, working with him?" Adelaide asked at the same time Bianca said, "Do you think that wise?"

Harriet happily chose to ignore Bianca and gave her attention to Adelaide. "Working with him is quiet, as you can imagine. He writes his passage, and then I, er, edit it."

"You don't talk?" Clear disappointment tinged Adelaide's question.

Harriet shrugged and switched brushes to work on the sunset of her picture. "We do. Mostly about what the next scene should be."

Adelaide sighed. "Is that all?"

Bianca laughed. "What do you mean, is that all? You haven't asked what type of book they are writing."

"Why would that matter?"

"It's a book of letters, is it not?" Bianca pierced Harriet with a questioning glare until the urge to fidget nearly consumed Harriet. A strange expression covered the viscountess's face—something that looked almost like glee but was covered with a sheen of hesitation. "Sophia thinks it's a romantic book."

Adelaide swung her wide gaze to Harriet. "Is it?"

It hadn't been. But now it was. Or soon it would be? Harriet wasn't looking forward to picking the bits of the growing tendre between Elsabeth and her guide, Robert, out of the story when she wrote to her father. It would make writing to him far more difficult.

Almost as difficult as reading the sections and not imagining her and Jonas instead. Maintaining appropriate perspective on this project was challenging.

"I do believe silence is a very telling answer in this instance," Adelaide said, causing Harriet to blush once more.

"I don't believe I've ever seen Harriet blush before," Bianca mused, "and here she's done it twice in the space of ten minutes."

"I am merely flushed. I believe I may be coming down with a fever."

"Do not lie," Adelaide said, admonishing her. "It doesn't become you."

If only she knew.

"Do tell us what sort of book it is," Bianca pushed.

"It is a travel book. Should I use yellow or orange for the sun?"

"No one cares." Bianca jabbed her brush toward Harriet. "You aren't traveling."

"It is a fictional account. I think orange would be better."

Adelaide frowned. "How does one write an account of fictional travels when one stays in the same place all the time?"

"By making it up," Bianca said. "That is what fiction means, is it not? Like that *Gilligan's Journey*."

"*Gulliver's Travels*," Adelaide corrected.

Harriet rolled her eyes. Bianca was well aware of the title of the book. They'd all read it together two months ago.

"Do you have tiny people in your book? That would make it a bit similar." Bianca grinned. "Maybe you should have giants instead."

Harriet sighed. She'd have to give Bianca something or the woman would continue to dig. "All the people are normal. It is simply a book about a woman traveling the world. She writes letters home to her father about the little things she is experiencing. The beauty in life's moments."

"That sounds lovely," Adelaide said dreamily. "I can't wait to read it."

Harriet's brush skidded across the screen as a spurt of panic shot through her. She'd never meant for this scheme to go any farther than Jonas. If more people knew, then they'd eventually expect to read a book. "It might not get published."

"It sounds boring," Bianca muttered. "Is she solving a mystery? Discovering a previously unknown city?"

No, she was making her father happy. Why was that never enough for anyone? "She has a guide."

Adelaide looked up from her screen and smiled. "So there is a romance."

"And you and Jonas are discussing how it should go," Bianca added.

Harriet groaned. "I'm only deciding where she should go next. He is putting in the details."

"Is Jonas courting you through the story?" Adelaide sighed. "That is so romantic. He doesn't speak much, so that might be the only way he knows how to express his feelings."

"He speaks plenty when he has something to say." Like how Harriet should stop mucking about in people's lives. She stabbed her paintbrush at the screen, blending the edges of her sun with a bit more force than necessary.

After the moment in the woods, Harriet had to admit a romantic inclination had flitted across her mind, but Jonas's actions since proved he felt nothing but disapproval toward her.

"Harriet," Adelaide said softly, followed by the click of her setting her paintbrush down on the little table at her side. "Is everything well?"

"Of course it is. Why wouldn't it be?"

"Because Jonas is the first man I've seen you take an interest in since we met."

Why were the quiet ones so painfully observant? "I haven't taken an interest in Jonas."

"For your sake, I hope not," Bianca said, "but you are blushing. Again."

"Only because this discussion is excessively personal." Harriet looked up from her screen and attempted to glare at Bianca. The only result was that her face grew even warmer. "And why would you be concerned?"

Bianca sighed. "I . . . don't see him fitting into your life well. That's all."

It was on the tip of Harriet's tongue to correct Bianca's assessment, but was she wrong? Hadn't Jonas himself indicated the disparity?

"I'm doing it for Sophia," Harriet blurted, desperate to redirect the conversation away from her confused considerations of Jonas Fitzroy.

"For Sophia?" Adelaide asked.

"Is she attempting to pair you with her brother?" Bianca tilted her head. "I suppose I could see that. She was rather nosy with him when we went riding."

"No, she wants him to . . . to . . ." Harriet's tongue tripped over the words and fell still. Had Jonas shared his artistic talent with anyone? It sounded as if he'd given little weight to his own abilities when speaking of the writing.

"She wants him to what?" Bianca leaned toward Harriet.

Harriet cleared her throat. "To find more in life."

"More?" Bianca frowned.

Adelaide nodded sympathetically. "I'm sure she's struggling with the idea that she's building a house with her husband while he shares a room above the stable."

Harriet didn't think that was it, but it sounded better than anything she could come up with.

"Perhaps she wants him just as settled," Bianca said.

It was time to move Bianca in another direction. "How are you finding wedded bliss?"

"Fantastic." She sighed and grinned.

Why had Harriet surrounded herself with such happily married people? It brought a constant, agonizing battle against jealousy.

She was finally taking the steps to close off this ridiculous situation with her father, but what if she was too late? What if Mrs. Wainbright was correct?

If she could redo anything in her life, it would be telling her twenty-year-old self to tell her father the truth—that she hadn't cared for traveling when she'd gone with friends, and she'd hated every single second of traveling on her own. It would have been horrible. He'd have been disappointed.

But all that would be better than the devastation that would occur now if he ever learned how she'd been lying to him. And for how long.

She would be thirty in a matter of weeks. Thirty and unmarried. That would leave her a spinster if she didn't come with heaps upon heaps of money. If she wanted a chance at a family, she needed to start soon.

And somehow find a man who wanted *her* and not the heaps and heaps of money.

Jonas wouldn't care about her money. Not that it mattered, since there was nothing and would be nothing romantic between them.

"That's the fourth sigh in as many minutes," Bianca muttered not at all quietly. "Do you think she's thinking about Jonas?"

"I hope not, considering her face doesn't look at all happy and she's flooding the sky with that angry red."

Harriet blinked and looked down to see that she had, indeed, put far too much red in her sunset. It looked like the land was bleeding. Or on fire. "Perhaps I should make it a night sky."

"Perhaps you should tell us what's wrong," Adelaide said gently.

Her friends wanted to help her, and they wouldn't quit until she let them. So she gave them the problem she didn't want to admit and they wanted to solve. "Jonas is a very appealing man."

Adelaide clasped her hands together and grinned. "I knew it."

Bianca's smile was far tighter. "He works in Hudson's stable."

"That's right." Adelaide looked from Harriet to Bianca and

back. "You should visit Hawksworth more often. You can join Bianca on her rides and arrange to have him as an escort like he was this morning."

"I believe he'd quickly become suspicious," Bianca murmured. She gave Harriet a long, considering look. "Has he noticed you?"

"There was a moment." At least, there'd been one for her. "I thought we might kiss once."

Complete silence met her comment.

Harriet deliberately dabbed paint on her screen, not even knowing or caring what the picture was, just needing to keep her gaze away from her friends.

Bianca slowly set all her painting supplies on the table and said in measured words, "Harriet Hancock, when did this happen?"

Harriet swallowed. "Three weeks ago."

"And you didn't tell us?" Bianca nearly screeched.

"Where were you?" Adelaide asked.

"There's a stream north of here." Dab, dab, dab. "Part of something called Seven Springs."

More silence.

"Nothing happened," Harriet finally said.

"Oh." Bianca sat back, a small frown on her face.

Adelaide coughed. "Have you kissed anyone, Harriet?"

"No."

"Well, so you know, the first kiss between two people is bound to be a little strange, even more so if you've never kissed anyone. Particularly if no intentions have been declared. Has he made declarations?"

Harriet just glared at her friend. What part of *nothing happened* didn't she understand?

"Have you made declarations?" Bianca asked.

"What?" Harriet snapped her head around. "Of course not."

"You're hardly given to conventions." Bianca shrugged. "Why should you stand on them here?"

"I've given no declarations because I have no intentions. We were both caught up in the beauty of the moment, and I shouldn't have said anything." Harriet switched colors and stroked her brush across the screen again, desperate to move her agitation out of her throat and into her hand. "He stayed away for four days after that and only came back to help me when I guilted him into it. I know you are both madly in love with your husbands, but it's making you see feelings in places where there simply aren't any." Harriet's throat tightened. *Heavens no, please don't let me cry about this.*

"That might be a good thing," Bianca said. "Any sort of attachment between the two of you would be rife with difficulty."

She didn't elaborate. She didn't have to. Even though they dined with a variety of social classes every Tuesday, they were all well aware that society worked differently beyond the walls of their homes. Jonas, despite his birth, was a stable hand. She, despite her wealth, was untitled. Together they would have no social protection aside from their friends.

"I am helping Jonas find a greater purpose in life. That is all. And no, his purpose is not going to be me."

Silence fell. Had the wobble she'd felt in her middle come out in her words?

Finally, Adelaide cleared her throat. "Have you a fireplace in the attic? Perhaps an unused corner room?"

Harriet blinked at her friend. "It's just me in that house. Of course I have unused rooms."

"Good." She nodded toward the screen. "Because I don't think anyone would be comfortable having to look at that every day."

Harriet blinked down at her screen. The picture wasn't awful—if one thought the painter was an eleven-year-old girl who'd held the brush with her teeth. It had a definite darkness to it that would signify the painter had not been feeling gentle at the time of creation.

Bianca came to stand behind Harriet and look at the screen. "Maybe you should forget to remove it next time you light a fire."

Then the entire mess could go up in flames and she could start over.

Too bad life didn't work that way.

Nineteen

"Grandmama and me making baskets for the village families."

—Eight-year-old Harriet, in a description of a picture she drew for Grandmama, who had gone to bed with a terrible headache the same evening a local baron held a party

Harriet freely acknowledged herself to be a woman of faults. She was easily distracted, a dash outspoken, and far too fond of sugar in her morning tea. And yes, she was lying to her father and Jonas and now her friends, but it was all in the name of making people happier, so how much was that truly a fault?

In truth, she could make a lengthy list of things she could or should do better—the vicar's sermons were full of such suggestions—but working on them didn't seem to enrich anyone's life. What was the point? If she had to twist one virtue, in this case honesty, in order to attain another, such as generosity of spirit in caring for a fellow human being, then wasn't the gain to others worth the harm to herself?

What she'd never considered was that other people might also like to twist the world for others, and Harriet had a heavy suspicion that the recently delivered card was Adelaide attempting to help her. Why else would the woman who rarely opened her home choose to hold a ball in the middle of the quietest stretch of the year?

And without seeking Harriet's assistance too. Since they'd met three years prior, Adelaide had recruited Harriet's help for any event larger than an afternoon tea.

Harriet dropped the invitation—which had likely taken Adelaide and her maid the better part of the morning to create—on the desk and walked to the window.

"It was probably her husband's idea," Harriet murmured as she sent the card a glare over her shoulder. "He does like to stick his nose into other people's affairs."

Adelaide had seemed rather enamored with the idea that Harriet and Jonas might be on the path to true love, but surely she wasn't holding this event in an effort to move that along. It was just as likely that, given time to think it over, Adelaide had joined Bianca in her wariness and hoped Harriet would find someone else.

As if Harriet hadn't already met every soul who would attend an off-season engagement.

The question was, then, had Jonas received a similar card today? If so, did he intend to use it?

Harriet sputtered out a laugh. She knew the answer to that one. The answer was an unequivocal *no*. And she wasn't disappointed by the idea.

At least not much.

Curiosity remained. *Had* he received an invitation? He would probably tell her if she asked, but what if he hadn't? Would he feel insulted? Would they have another awkward conversation about Harriet's trying to meddle in other people's lives?

She tossed a glance at the desk strewn with the papers he was working on. Two open books, one stacked on top of the other, sat near the quill, and another lay closed on the corner. Perhaps Elsabeth could attend a ball? That would open the subject without undue pressure.

How would Jonas write such a scene? Would Robert go with her or would Elsabeth go alone? Would a reminder that such a flirtation was highly impractical stop the idea of a romance before it got started?

Did she want it to?

Harriet dropped her head against the window and groaned. This infernal book was going to drive her to Bedlam. Or maybe her feelings for Jonas would.

Perhaps what this story needed was a tragedy. Jonas couldn't argue that readers wouldn't love Elsabeth enduring the trauma of seeing Robert trampled by a runaway carriage. Her father would be horrified that she'd experienced such a hardship and completely understand her immediate return to England.

And it would put an end to any more talk or thoughts of romance.

A black horse came into view, its long mane streaking back to graze against the arm and shoulders of the man sitting tall in the saddle and moving as one with the animal.

No, Harriet couldn't kill the guide. When she wrote to her father about him, she pictured Jonas, wrote him as Jonas. She did not want to envision anything horrible happening to him. Besides, asking him to write such a thing would be like asking him to relive one of the worst experiences of his life.

Sophia had been vague about the event that had nearly crippled her brother, but there'd been enough detail for Harriet to know she'd never ask him about it.

Harriet sighed as Jonas swung a leg over the horse and jumped to the ground in a single fluid motion. He just looked so right in a saddle. The horse curved around to nudge at him as he playfully patted her on the neck and spoke, a wide smile on his face.

The coolness of the window only emphasized the heat in Harriet's cheeks, and she let out another sigh. No, she couldn't kill the guide. She wasn't quite willing to kill the romance by inventing a romantic ball either.

Did that mean *she* was enamored with the idea of her and Jonas? That *she* wanted to encourage a romance between them?

She wished she had more than fifteen minutes to figure it out.

How long did it take most authors to write a book? Jonas and Harriet had spent weeks on this project, yet it seemed to be going nowhere. Granted, there'd been interruptions with the races and her need to experience the story, but there didn't seem to be many pages to show for the hours he'd put in.

He never should have suggested a change to the story. That first week he'd completed four of her requested letters. Now he was having to make changes, to consider how what happened in one would affect the others. It took more time, more thought.

More conversation.

She'd moved her desk again, and once more it was sitting perpendicular to his, though facing his right instead of his left this time. Seated behind the larger desk, he could easily see the angle of her nose, the length of her dark eyelashes, and the way that one stubborn curl fell down her back.

He shuffled through the pages, determined to move forward today with new letters. She could make the changes she'd requested in her notes. Wasn't that the end goal anyway?

"Where is Elsabeth going next?"

Harriet shifted in her chair. "Perhaps she should stay in the area a while."

"Doing what?"

Small shrug. "She could meet some people. Experience the local society."

Jonas set down the pen he'd had ready to jot notes. "Local society? You want her to go to a party?"

Harriet mumbled something he couldn't quite make out, and he leaned forward in his chair. "You want her to go where?"

With a huff of frustration, she turned to look at him. "Yes, I want her to attend a function. A soiree. A gathering. Maybe a ball."

Jonas sat back in his chair and clenched his fists to keep from rubbing his hands over his face. This wasn't about the book. This was about that small, thick square of paper he'd received that morning.

And promptly shoved beneath his mattress. He wasn't going to risk that card being seen in the kindling bucket. It wasn't coming out of his room until he could toss it into the fire himself.

"She's a wealthy woman traveling the Continent." Harriet frowned. "She's going to need some society. No one can be alone that long."

"She has Robert."

"I don't think he's enough," Harriet said softly. "Do you?"

For him, one person would be plenty. For years he'd had no close companion aside from Sophia, and he hadn't felt the loss.

His sister had, though.

The people she had around her now seemed to satisfy her. Was the same not true for Harriet? "How much more does she need?"

She blinked at him with wide, dark eyes. "You're being serious." Her low voice was tinged with pity.

Oh no, she was not going to start feeling sorry for him. He'd nipped that one, hadn't he? That was how he got sucked into this writing business. "Forget I said anything." He slapped a fresh sheet of paper onto the desk. "You want her to go to a ball? She'll go to a ball."

Harriet nodded, though her eyes were still assessing him with a sheen he didn't care for. She took a deep breath before saying,

"Readers will like seeing her dance with Robert." It sounded almost like a question.

"Robert won't be there." Jonas dipped his pen and kept his head bent over the paper, refusing to look at Harriet again.

"He won't?" The question was almost a whisper.

"No. He's her employee." They were not talking about Elsabeth and Robert. He knew it. She knew it. Neither of them were going to acknowledge it, though. This conversation would be only about the two characters.

"What if he received an invitation?"

"He hasn't shared company with anyone other than Elsabeth." Since that sounded far more intimate than he wanted to consider around Harriet, he quickly added, "And the driver and maid and other servants. Who would issue him an invitation?"

He almost gave himself a pat on the back for that one. She couldn't possibly argue his point without admitting she was no longer talking about the story.

She crossed her arms. "It's our book. We can have anyone we want receive an invite."

"It is *your* book." Jonas corrected her because he refused to become a part of this any more than he already was. "Don't you want to make it at least a little bit believable?"

"You think it unbelievable that a person of means and title would consider a working man worthy of receiving an invitation to a ball?" There was no hesitation in her voice anymore. Now it was full of strength and an emotion Jonas didn't want to linger on. "Even if they've socialized previously?"

Elsabeth and Robert. He had to keep the conversation about Elsabeth and Robert. "Given that Elsabeth hasn't socialized with anyone and I'm not even certain how *she* is to get invited to this event, yes, I think it unbelievable."

He started writing then, determined to keep his head down.

The sentences were useless, but the scratch of the pen broke the tense silence.

"Even if he received one, he wouldn't go, would he?"

Jonas paused, pen poised over the paper before decisively saying, "No."

She sighed. "Why not?"

He set his pen aside and looked at her. "Are you seriously asking me that?"

"The words came out of my mouth, yes, and I have no reason to recall them."

One side of his mouth quirked upward, but he managed to avoid an outright laugh. Very well. They'd have the conversation she seemed to want, but he refused to admit they were having it. "Harriet, we have classes for a reason."

"It's a stupid reason. Everyone deserves to be happy, no matter their station."

He shook his head. "One is not connected to the other. What will happen if Robert attends this ball?"

"He and Elsabeth can dance."

Jonas narrowed his eyes. Was Harriet a little flushed?

She continued, "And he can eat fine food and relax and chat."

"Who will he talk with?"

"The other guests, of course."

"What will they talk of?"

She didn't have a quick answer this time, and a look of consternation crossed her features before they settled into stubborn mutiny. "He is a well-traveled man. They can talk of that."

"Yes, I'm sure they'll be able to share thoughts on scraping mud from boots and keeping one's skin from turning red from too much sun."

"Or"—she drew out the word, narrowing her eyes back at him—"he could focus on the topics of commonality, such as the beauty of the views or the anticipation of seeing a new place. The conversation doesn't have to focus on differences."

It was becoming increasingly difficult to keep this discussion about Elsabeth and Robert, even on the surface. "You think the others won't bring up topics designed to put him in his place?"

"Only the addlepated ones."

He bit his cheek to keep from laughing at her assessment of higher society's members. "How many of the attendees will be addlepates?"

She opened her mouth but then snapped it shut before slumping in her chair and looking down at her hands laced together in her lap.

Perhaps if she'd continued to push, Jonas would have stayed agitated, but seeing her struggle made him admit part of him was in turmoil as well. When he was with Harriet, verbally sparring and experiencing life, he had to fight against the desire for more, the desire to hope.

Hope for what, he didn't exactly know, but she made him want something.

With a deep breath, he ended this farce of a conversation. "Harriet, I'm not going to the ball."

Her head snapped up. "So you did get invit—" She cleared her throat. "I mean, of course *you* aren't. We're discussing Robert."

"Are we?" It was sweet, in a way, that she wanted to erase the lines, to make him a part, but she didn't have that sort of power.

Harriet licked her lips. "We should be."

Jonas nodded. Admitting this discussion was about them would make it uncomfortable.

After years of next to nothing to call his own, he craved simple and stable even more than he had before. All he needed was a life with work he enjoyed and a select few people with whom to relax. Companions who were bluntly honest and didn't mind when he lapsed into long stretches of silence might be nice as well.

And that purpose he'd told Harriet everyone needed in life? Well, God would lead him to it eventually.

Now he just needed to explain that to Harriet.

"Robert," he said with emphasis, "does not have difficulty interacting with Elsabeth on her own. However, if her charity was required for them to spend time together, he would feel very different."

It was true. Away from everything else, he enjoyed his time with Harriet, even working quietly in the same room. Most of the time he forgot he was supposed to be looking for schemes that might involve Sophia.

"That doesn't paint a very promising picture for them, does it?"

Jonas cleared his throat. "Not if you want it to be realistic."

He sighed. He couldn't continue to avoid the truth, uncomfortable though it may be. Not if he wanted to sleep with an easy conscience tonight. "Harriet, look at me."

She turned toward him with clear eyes and an expectant expression that didn't look at all saddened or hurt by the idea that the moment in the stream could not be allowed to happen again. Nor could anything come from it.

Good. That was good.

Jonas took a deep breath. "I am not going to the ball."

She lifted an inquiring brow. "I don't believe I asked."

"Not in so many words, no."

With a sharp nod, she replied, "I believe you are a man who goes on what is stated instead of implied, so I don't know why you'd bring it up."

"Because we both know that is what this is about."

Harriet rolled her eyes toward the ceiling and shook her head. "I never claimed to be very creative. If I were, I wouldn't need you. There's a ball in my life, so I put one in hers. It's that simple."

Then she surprised him by directing her determined gaze his way. Color rode high on her cheekbones, and passion was clear in the glint of her eyes and the set of her mouth. Whatever she was about to say, she truly believed.

"I heard you. But I do not live my life bound by the expectations of reality and certainly not by society. I make my own rules and define my life as I see fit."

Before Jonas could answer—and he had no idea what he would have said in response—she rose and flounced out of the room.

Jonas found himself grinning as he watched her walk away, nose so high in the air she almost tripped over the edge of the carpet. Then he shook his head, picked up the pen, and started to write. Fortunately for both of them, he was a realist.

It was all well and good for Harriet to defy the rules, but one of them had to keep in mind that consequences eventually came calling. He, for one, intended to keep his heart intact when they did.

Twenty

"I danced all evening with several local gentlemen, but not with Robert. He did not attend the ball. It wasn't a place he truly belonged."

—Jonas, in the passage about the ball Harriet requested

Jonas enjoyed working for Aaron. His brother-in-law knew horses, knew racing, knew training, and knew the Heath. Perhaps his finest quality was how much he loved and cared for Sophia.

Still, it was somewhat awkward when Jonas visited his sister and encountered his employer in a private capacity. It was getting better since he'd started dining with them on Sundays, but that was a different variety of strange.

When Aaron met Sophia, he'd been living in a small one-room cottage. They both lived there now while their house was being built. The cottage didn't have much in the way of a kitchen, and Sophia wasn't much in the way of a cook, so they usually got their meal from nearby Trenton Hall, where Aaron's friend Oliver and his wife, Rebecca, lived.

Jonas always had to resist the urge to laugh at the fine spread on their humble table.

"Come in, come in." Sophia waved Jonas through the door, then bustled about the room straightening pillows, putting away a great coat, leaning a riding crop against the wall by the door.

Aaron shook Jonas's hand and then wrapped an arm around Sophia's shoulders and moved her toward the table. They sat and prayed over the meal.

When Jonas lifted his head, Sophia was staring at him.

He lifted his eyebrows in inquiry even as he reached for the food.

Sophia tore off a corner of a roll and popped it into her mouth as she all but bounced in her seat.

"You're going to break that chair," Jonas murmured.

Sophia rolled her eyes and put the roll on her plate before reaching for another dish. "Aren't you excited?"

"About the food?" Jonas looked over the table. "I suppose. It's better than the fare I eat most of the week."

Aaron laughed and shook his head.

Sophia frowned at both men. "The ball is this week. In a few days we'll be dancing and laughing in Lady Adelaide's gorgeous ballroom." She pointed across the room to where a square of parchment held a prominent place of display atop a picture on the wall. "Isn't that invitation beautiful?"

His was still under his mattress. Likely it was wrinkled beyond recognition by now. "I hope you enjoy it." He threw a forced grin toward Aaron. "Both of you."

Aaron cast his eyes to the ceiling and then bent over his plate. The other man was probably dreading the event, but he'd endure it for Sophia. She'd been dreaming of attending a ball for years. When they were fourteen, Jonas had sat with his sister in the freezing winter air so she could peer through the window at a local assembly. She'd talked endlessly of having pretty dresses one day and dancing the evening away.

Had their parents survived, it was a dream she'd have experienced years ago. Jonas as well.

Unlike Sophia, though, he had no aspirations of reclaiming the opportunity. Climbing to that level of society would require sacrifice on the part of another for him, and he'd never crave that.

Despite instigating a lengthy conversation about the ball, Harriet had said nothing about the account he'd written. There'd been no notes even though she'd made plenty on the pages he'd written since then.

"We shall have a lovely time," Sophia declared. "All of us."

Jonas did not want to have this argument. "I have no doubt I will enjoy myself Friday evening."

"Good." Sophia nodded, oblivious to Jonas's true meaning. "Bianca has agreed to hold dancing lessons. I won't be able to master them all, but I should be able to learn a few basics to keep from embarrassing myself. You are joining us for those, aren't you?"

He'd rather muck all the stalls in Hawksworth. "I don't see why I should."

"Because you'll look rude if you stand in the corner all evening. It's one thing to do it at dinner amongst people who understand and are accustomed to your aloofness. It's another to do it in front of the whole of Newmarket."

"Then I shan't do it."

She smiled and almost started bouncing again. "You won't?"

"I can faithfully promise you that I will not stand in the corner of Lady Adelaide's ballroom."

She narrowed her green eyes. "What will you be doing instead?"

Jonas shrugged. Her direct question brought an end to his evasive statements but didn't change his intentions. "Possibly playing cards. If we aren't too tired, the men sometimes sit in the common room for a game or two. I might do a bit of drawing." Or engraving. As much as he might wish Harriet hadn't given him those tools, he was enjoying the challenge of learning to use them properly. "If it's been a long day, I'll just go to sleep."

Sophia's mouth dropped open. "You don't intend to go?"

"No, Sophia, I don't intend to go. Balls are not the entertainment of the working class. I must be up before dawn to help with the horses. I can't be out until midnight."

"You could have the next morning off."

"That's not something you can offer."

She pointed at her husband. "He can."

Aaron lifted his hands. "Please don't bring me into this."

She frowned. "You don't want him there?"

"I don't think he wants to be there." Aaron nodded in Jonas's direction but held his wife's gaze with his own. "Unlike me, he doesn't have a reason to suffer through the stares and the questions and discomfort."

Sophia glared at Aaron, who didn't seem at all perturbed by the possibility of his wife disliking the truth. There might be a discussion later, but for now she apparently considered Jonas the more pressing problem.

Her narrowed gaze swung back to him. "Give me one *good* reason why you won't attend, and it can't have anything to do with what other people will think of you because you've never cared a jot about that in your life."

If need be, Jonas could come up with a dozen reasons so long as he didn't have to give her the real one. He didn't want to watch Harriet dancing and flirting and laughing with other men.

Fortunately, he didn't have to answer to her. Jonas loved his sister, and he'd sacrifice anything for her, but the truth was he wasn't her whole life anymore. She needed to not be his as well.

"I'm not going, Sophia."

Sophia frowned. "Everything that comes out of your mouth is just obstinate and ornery."

He gave her a meaningful look before stabbing a potato with his fork. "Sophia," he said slowly and decisively before stuffing the potato behind his grin.

THE CONVERSATION STAYED with Jonas throughout the week. He knew Sophia could not be the focus of his life anymore, but he'd yet to replace her with anything else.

Anyone else.

It was *not good that the man should be alone.*

Tonight his sister would attend a ball. She'd broached the topic twice more this week, but he'd refused to respond every time. It wasn't until she'd handed him a box with a brand-new evening ensemble inside that he'd told her flatly to cease.

She had.

The clothes were now under his bed beside the engraving tools. If this kept up, he'd have to ask Ernest if he could use the space beneath his bed as well.

It was strange, living in a world where all the lines were blurred and his place within it wasn't obvious.

Tonight he could be in a ballroom.

Harriet would be there.

He could dance with her.

He could dine with her.

He could spend an evening in her world and have a new experience like he'd given her. The difference was that while the spring had been as welcoming to Harriet as it would be to anyone, the ball would not be welcoming to him.

He stood in his room, staring at his bed as if he could look through the mattress and see the crumpled invitation and the box of clothing beneath. He'd been building to this moment for weeks, possibly even months. Life was no longer about survival. His world was no longer confined to his sister. His future was no longer unimaginable.

And it was time he started living as if all those things were true.

He'd never been a coward, and he wasn't going to start now. *And let us not be weary in well doing: for in due season we shall reap, if we faint not.*

He splashed water into a basin and washed the day's grime from his face and arms.

It was time to make a few changes.

BALLS, ASSEMBLIES, SOIREES, MUSICALES. Harriet had been to them all. A fine line sat between the eccentric who made everyone nervous and the one who made everything fun and interesting. She liked to think she walked that line fairly well, which was why she could attend any gathering she wished. And avoid any gathering she wished. She'd attended parties out of boredom, obligation, intention, and enjoyment.

Never before had her heart pounded with nerves the moment she crossed the threshold. Yet, here she was, standing near the punch bowl, watching the door.

Normally she would be looking over the people, seeking out those who didn't seem to be having a good time or might need rescuing from an unfortunate conversation.

Not tonight.

Would Jonas come? She wanted him to. Dozens of times in the past two weeks she'd looked at him, his head bent over the desk, and opened her mouth with the intention of returning to the ball attendance discussion.

Each time she'd changed her mind because her desire for his attendance was selfish. She couldn't honestly claim that he would find a single enjoyment this evening, but still she wanted him to be a part of it.

It was a strange feeling, wanting her own satisfaction over someone else's. It created an itch between her shoulder blades that she had to meticulously ignore. If he came, she would find a way to make it advantageous to him. She would.

But she doubted she'd get the chance.

Besides, what could she truly give him? He didn't crave connections or affluence or even the position he'd once had as the son of a working gentleman. If he did, he'd be far more consistent with his attendance at the Tuesday night dinners.

Adelaide had hired a quartet, and music drifted through the ballroom. It seemed to flow from the raised alcove where the musicians sat to bounce around the large room, swelling until it reached the far corners. The sensation was one only a crowded ballroom could create with the sounds of rustling skirts, dancing feet, and conversation blending with the music. Harriet let the harmonies of life seep into her bones, swaying a little as she sipped.

Jonas hadn't come to dinner Tuesday, unsurprising since Bianca had been hosting. He never attended when all he'd have to do is walk across the drive to the Hawksworth manor house. Sophia had been there, of course, and she'd been able to talk of little else aside from the ball.

At least one Fitzroy twin wanted to be part of Harriet's world.

Even as she considered the thought, she felt the unfairness of it. Jonas's rejection of this evening wasn't a rejection of her.

It only felt like it was.

Everyone—or at least everyone Harriet was watching for—had arrived, aside from Bianca and Hudson. They were her last hope. Jonas wouldn't come alone. He'd ride in someone else's carriage because he'd succumbed to their prodding and inviting.

Then the couple stepped into the room, Bianca radiant in a loose green gown and Hudson in black finery.

And no one behind them.

Not until just that moment had she realized how much hope she'd been holding on to. Jonas wasn't coming. He didn't want to be here.

He didn't want to be with her.

She made her way back to the punch table as much for something to do as a need to pour something down her suddenly parched throat. She greeted people as she went, even participating in a conversation or two. It wouldn't do for anyone to see her distress. Harriet was never distressed. Bold, generous, and occasionally bored, yes, but never distressed.

After she gulped down a second glass of cool liquid, she felt somewhat back to normal, at least physically. With a smile pasted on her face, she engaged the people nearby in conversation, and when a man asked her to dance, she accepted.

She made sure they lined up beside a young lady who was known for forgetting the steps. Tonight, though, Harriet was determined to give her partner as much attention as she gave the ladies. Soon she'd be living in Newmarket with her father's knowledge and it would be time to settle down. No harm in perusing the available marriage prospects in the meantime.

And if tonight they all seemed far too tall and annoyingly polite, well, that was something she'd have to learn to move past.

SURPRISINGLY, JONAS TURNED OUT to be decent at throwing horseshoes. Participating in the conversations with the other grooms was somewhat beyond him, but they seemed satisfied that he stood in the group, sipping ale and occasionally nodding at whatever was said.

It was more than the simple discomfort of putting himself out there, though. Jonas had been raised differently from these men. If asked, he'd have never considered the education and homelife of his formulative years something that would set him apart from others, but it was proving to be so.

Not that he wasn't enjoying his time at the gathering behind the stable. The other grooms had been welcoming—even excited—when he'd turned the corner.

That didn't mean Jonas felt like he belonged.

When he returned to his room this evening, this would merely be the way he'd spent his time.

He strolled to where Ernest was watching Miles and Andrew throw horseshoes. If he was going to make the effort to form a friendship with any of these men, the one with whom he shared a room seemed the logical first choice.

Except neither of them were talkers, and five minutes later the only words either of them had uttered had been "Pardon me" when they'd had to jump out of the path of a wayward horseshoe and Ernest stepped on Jonas's foot.

"Do you want to challenge the winner?" Miles extended a horseshoe in Jonas's direction.

Because having something to do made everything easier, Jonas took it and went to stand by Andrew. The man's normal toothy grin was solidly in place when he said, "You can pitch first."

Jonas did, his horseshoe bouncing in the grass a few inches from the pole.

Andrew's first throw bounced off the pole before landing atop Jonas's horseshoe, sending the clang of metal through the area.

A few other men came over to watch, and conversation about the horses swelled until an unknown voice called out and another group of people rounded the corner of the stable. Two men carried stringed instruments while another had a barrel of ale on his shoulder. Four ladies followed, and soon they were flitting about the group, talking and laughing with the maids who had come down from the house and some of the grooms.

Before long, the clang of horseshoes was joined by the strains of music, laughter, and the shuffle of feet on grass as several couples got into formation for a reel.

Quietly, Jonas eased his way to the stable and leaned on the wall, watching the crowd from the shadows. He could join them. That was what he'd come down here to do. But the truth was the scene before him was almost as unappealing as the ball.

Especially when the only people he wanted to be with were nowhere in sight.

Twenty-One

"I danced and ate food and met new people."

—Twenty-one-year-old Harriet, in a letter to her father, pretending a party she attended in London had actually taken place in Canada

Harriet was having a terrible time.

When had balls ceased being entertaining, or at least interesting? Even when Harriet didn't care for the gathering itself, she always attended with a second, more enjoyable goal in mind. Success was its own sort of fun.

Yet she wasn't finding her normal pleasure in helping young ladies through a dance or rescuing trapped daughters from uncomfortable conversations.

She was even considering leaving early.

Perhaps she just needed to step away for a moment and gain some perspective.

A scattering of people had drifted out onto the terrace, though the ballroom wasn't stuffy enough to drive many into the night air. Harriet easily found an unoccupied patch of shadow to step into near the stairs that led to the lawn. The wide-open space between the terrace and the lights of the stable wasn't a temptation for those seeking privacy, but Harriet couldn't help but be drawn to the direct escape the area offered.

She stood, debating whether to retreat or return to the ballroom.

A dark figure came to stand near the bottom of the stairs, and Harriet took a hasty step closer to the house.

"'Tis me."

The light Irish brogue eased her fears and sent her heart into a quick patter. "You came."

"Not really." Jonas climbed the first half of the stairs, remaining in the darkness, though his pale skin was now visible. "I was curious to see what it was like. I haven't looked in on one since I was a boy."

Harriet grinned. "You snuck around to peek at balls when you were a child?"

The shadow shrugged. "Sophia wanted to go."

And he would do anything for those he loved.

The closest she'd come to such caring was her grandfather, who bought the house in Newmarket and included it in her inheritance so she would always have a place of her own no matter what she did in life.

"What do you think?" Harriet asked.

"It looks like a party."

"Is that good or bad?"

"It is what it is." Jonas climbed two more steps, and a stream of pale light crossed the top of a nearby statue to slide across his features. "I don't know that it's all that different from the party behind the stable tonight, though the clothes are far fancier and the food is likely better."

Harriet smiled. "Probably. Are you coming in?"

"Dressed like this?" He shook his head and gave a short laugh. "I don't think so."

Harriet squinted until she could make out that he was in the same clothes he wore when he came to work at her house, though with the jacket he wore on Sundays thrown on top. "I thought Sophia bought you new clothes."

"Was it a conspiracy, then?"

"Not one of mine. At Tuesday dinner she told the ladies of her plans to get you here." Harriet looked from Jonas to the windows where the flickering candles and dancing couples were visible. "I don't believe this was her intention."

"Probably not."

As she stood there, watching the festivities from a distance, the agitation she'd been feeling all evening evaporated. She would eventually wade back into the dancing swirl, but it was nice to be with Jonas on the outside now.

"It's like a painting come to life," he said with an undercurrent of reverence.

It was the perfect description.

They stood, not speaking. Their soft breathing joined the strains of laughter and music from the ballroom's open doors, providing a natural accompaniment to the view before them. A waltz began, and the couples in the ballroom paired off. Aaron and Sophia twirled by the window, inspiring a wide smile.

Harriet turned to Jonas. "Do you want to dance?"

A BREATH AGO he'd been craving his notebook, but now he didn't even have air in his lungs.

She wanted to dance. With him.

He should say no. Not only was the dance beyond the doors like nothing he'd learned seven years ago, but he'd been working very hard to forget what it was like to hold Harriet in his arms at the springs. Not touching her was one of his new priorities.

Then she touched him. She glided down the steps, snagging his hand in hers as she went, and he was helpless to do anything but follow.

"What are you doing?" he asked when he finally loosened his tongue.

"You won't come to the ball, so I'm bringing it to you."

"You don't need to keep me company. I do rather well on my own."

She placed her free hand over her heart, making him once more aware that her fingers were clasping his. "I consider it my obligation in life to rescue those suffering the fate of standing to the side at a party."

"I'm not suffering."

"Doesn't matter." She shrugged. "I'm saving you anyway."

She tugged again, and he hadn't the willpower to resist her a second time. Soon they were facing each other in the shadow at the bottom of the stairs. Anyone who ventured to this end of the terrace would easily be able to see them, even if they couldn't make out who they were.

"I've not attended dancing lessons since I was seventeen, and those weren't anything special." Those lessons in Irish country dances would be as helpful now as they'd been when their mother had been trying to pretend their world wasn't falling apart.

Harriet shook her head and gave a slight *tsk*. "That's what happens when one is too stubborn to prepare for the possibilities."

He laughed. "That doesn't even make sense."

"Of course it does. Sophia has been learning to dance this week. You could have done the same to prepare for coming to the ball, even if your intention was otherwise."

"By your logic I should study the inner workings of a sailing vessel in case I find myself aboard one. That isn't logical at all."

"I never claimed to be logical." She beamed at him. "Do you know how to waltz?"

"No." And what he'd seen through the windows made him wary of trying.

"We're fortunate my feet are small." She wiggled her eyebrows. "It makes my toes smaller targets."

Then she was arranging them into the very position he'd been determined to avoid. It was another near embrace, and everything in him shouted that he should run away.

Or pull her closer.

"Consider this another experience," Harriet continued. "A new adventure. You like learning new things, don't you?"

"Yes." He also liked self-preservation. Considering that, despite everything, he was finding he liked Harriet, dancing with her did not fall under the umbrella of wise decisions.

They fumbled about in a circle, barely able to hear the music. Occasionally Harriet would giggle and push him lightly in a different direction. What they were doing couldn't truly be called dancing. It was more like walking around sideways.

"Were you a handful as a child?" Harriet asked once they'd settled into a strange sort of rhythm.

He shook his head. "No. Sophia was wild enough for both of us. If we wanted to stay out of trouble, one of us needed to think things through."

"And that was you?"

"Well, it wasn't going to be her."

"No, I suppose not."

They swayed silently through another loop before Jonas asked, "What were you like as a child?"

"I followed my father and grandparents around a lot. It was just me, so helping them was how I played."

Her smile was dim, barely visible in the darkness, but love was clearly in her tone. She didn't speak of a mother, and she'd never mentioned taking a trip home to visit family.

Jonas had avoided talk of the past, both because he saw no need to share his own and he hadn't wanted the connection such sharing inevitably formed. Still, he wanted to know more. "What did you do to help out?"

"This and that. Grandmama worked with the Ladies' Aid Society. Grandfather used to busy himself with making his managers' and factory workers' lives better. Father does that part now. There was always something to do."

"So you were raised to help people."

She nodded. "Until I was ten. Then Grandmama died and Father sent me to a girls' school."

They lapsed into silence again. This time it wasn't a warm cocoon but a cloud of energy, as if they were standing in the midst of an electrical storm.

It was like the springs all over again. He couldn't see anything but her, couldn't imagine stepping away.

Could all too easily imagine pulling her closer.

Her brown eyes met his, and she seemed as completely absorbed as he was.

Jonas stepped away. "Thank you for the dance."

His voice was stilted, and she blinked up at him, obviously still a little dazed. "I . . . yes. Thank you."

He nodded toward the stairs. "I'll wait here until you're safely back inside."

"I . . . Oh." Her gaze dropped to the ground. "Of course."

Then she turned and walked up the stairs, each step feeling like a stomp on Jonas's heart. He'd enjoyed their moment, perhaps a little too much, but she belonged in the ballroom. He belonged in a stable.

He glanced at the building across the expanse of lawn, then back up to the ballroom windows. Yes, this was where it seemed he lived these days. Somewhere in the middle with nowhere to actually belong.

Why was he here? It was a long walk back to Hawksworth, and he pondered that question the entire way. What did God want him to do with his life? Unless it was to simply exist day after day and do his best with whatever task he set his hands to, Jonas hadn't a clue.

The dancing and horseshoe throwing had stopped by the time Jonas climbed the stairs to his room, and the only remaining noise was the occasional burst of laughter from the few still gathered behind the stable.

Moonlight cast a glow across his pillow, and Jonas undressed before flopping onto his bed and pulling out his sketchbook. He didn't have a picture in mind, but the very act of moving the pencil across the paper brought a calm to his chest and an ease to his heart.

Until he saw what he'd drawn.

Harriet. Her gown was nothing more than a few bold lines, but her face, her smile, the wrinkle between her brows were all clear on the paper.

He could no longer deny the truth. He liked Harriet. A lot. There wasn't a doubt in his mind that if she were of his station, even a mere step or two above, he would ask her to go riding with him, to go on a picnic, to walk home together after church.

But Harriet was many steps above him. She could have a true gentleman, even perhaps a minor title. Jonas couldn't escort her to the theater, couldn't bring her rare hothouse flowers, couldn't squire her about town in a sparkling phaeton. In his observation, that was how the people of Harriet's echelon courted.

She deserved a man who could give her a world that included everything, not just one of streams and the occasional engraving.

He tried to put the book away, to leave the drawing unfinished, but he couldn't. His pencil flew, adding the lace that had wrapped around her waist and the flounce that decorated her skirt. Harriet could never be his, but this memory could be, and he wanted to hold on to every last detail.

Twenty-Two

"Please inform the current tenants of the Newmarket house that their lease will not be renewed next year. Do not mention this to anyone else."

—Harriet, in instructions sent to her solicitor after a disastrous fight with her father over her early arrival home from her first falsified trip abroad

Harriet hadn't been able to focus on Saturday. Sunday was something of a blur. Monday had been spent counting the hours until Jonas was due to arrive and work on the book. Now he was here and her mind still wasn't functioning right.

She turned a page of the travel book she was pretending to read and pressed her lips together. He'd arrived twenty minutes ago and gone straight to the desk. No greeting or acknowledgment of her presence.

Her desk now faced his, the front edges pushed together. In retrospect, that might not have been the smartest move, as she was afraid to look up in case Jonas caught her movement due to such proximity. She'd thought this would allow her the best vantage point from which to watch him, but she hadn't considered how it left her nowhere to hide.

Except in a book.

"I cannot write another scene of Elsabeth smiling at the flowers and the clouds and rambling on about how kind Robert was to show them to her."

Harriet looked up. The paper before Jonas was blank. She blinked. What on earth had he been doing for the past twenty minutes? "Why not?" she murmured with a nonchalance that made her proud. "That's the purpose of the letters."

"So she's not going to learn anything on this journey? All these experiences will leave her unchanged?" He dropped the pen atop the paper, and a dot of ink fell from the tip.

Harriet frowned. Was that how he saw her? Unmoved, unchanged, and unwilling to do either? Why, just yesterday at church she'd resisted the urge to have new lace anonymously delivered to a young lady because she heard the unspoken, underlying enjoyment of the fact that the lady and her daughter were planning to sit together and mend lace this week. It wasn't only about the lace itself. Two months ago, Harriet would have missed that entirely.

Now Harriet was trying to decide how to get the woman's neighbor to make too much food and share it so the mother and daughter could spend more time mending lace without worrying about dinner.

She cleared her throat. "No, I don't want her to be unchanged. Only a cold person would see the vastness of the world and its wonders and not feel anything." No wonder her father had been frustrated with her letters.

"What do you want Elsabeth to do with those feelings?"

They were talking about Elsabeth. Not Harriet. Goodness, but bluntly barreling through and arranging people's lives was so much easier than maintaining this fabrication.

What did Elsabeth need to learn? What did Harriet want to share with her father? "She is going to take those feelings and use them to form a greater appreciation for the world around her."

Jonas tilted his head, the expression of patient inquiry familiar yet somehow harder, perhaps a little more cynical.

"Robert challenges her. She may not always agree with him, but he makes her think." Harriet frowned, trying to sift through her thoughts about Jonas and pull out ones that could be attributed to Robert.

No wonder her head was a muddled mess these days.

"Does she include Robert in this appreciation?"

"It does seem that if she'd been opening her eyes to the beauty around her, Robert would be included in that." Harriet propped her elbow on her desk and dropped her chin onto her hand. It was all too easy to imagine how spending time with a man she wouldn't normally encounter would allow a woman to see his great appeal.

Jonas's mouth thinned. Was he about to say something serious? Was he going to change the topic to him and her instead of Robert and Elsabeth? She didn't want that, so she rushed to add, "Though she'd find him handsome instead of beautiful, wouldn't she?"

Slowly, the hardness left Jonas's expression, and he gave her a crooked grin. "Semantics aside, I do agree she'd include the people around her in her awakening."

Harriet nodded, waiting to see which direction he wanted to take the conversation.

He shook his head and ran his hand along the edge of the desk. "What do you want to do with this book, Harriet?"

Her brain spiraled in five directions. "What do you mean?"

He leaned forward and propped his elbows on the desk, bringing their faces closer together. Not so close that she could feel his breath or see the flecks of darker green in his eyes, but close enough for her to see his lashes, a darker red than his hair. "I mean," he said slowly, "that you have to decide what happens next. What did you think I meant?"

"That," she chirped. "That is exactly what I thought you meant. I was merely stalling."

"Because you don't know?"

"Exactly." She picked up one of the travel books. "She can travel toward the coast. There are plenty of farms and ruins she can see along the way."

"And?"

"And what? I've already marked a couple of passages."

"Will she talk about wheat blowing in the wind and birds soaring through the clear country sky? That's not overly exciting. Unless something significant happens in this book, no one will buy it."

She had no response to that.

Jonas's eyes narrowed. "That is your intention, is it not? To sell the book?"

Why was he pushing this again? Harriet didn't want to lie, not any more than she already had. Time to redirect the conversation.

He shook his head and waved a hand at the paper. "Unless you've something else for her to do aside from waxing on about the smooth ride of her carriage, I don't know if I can keep doing this."

No, he couldn't quit now. Her father was so excited about the new tone of the letters. "But that's a ruse," Harriet rushed to say. "She doesn't want to tell her father about her feelings for Robert."

Jonas frowned. "That's the only way for the reader to know."

Harriet wanted to drop her head to the desk. Were they talking about the book? Or was this one of those times when they were talking about life? About their own relationship or lack of one, depending on the day?

Which did she want it to be?

Harriet straightened her shoulders. Brash boldness had served her well everywhere in life but with her father. Perhaps it would serve her now. "Robert should say something to her."

"Something?"

"Yes. A, well, not necessarily a declaration but something Elsabeth has a reason to write her father about."

"He can't broach the subject. He's the guide. She employs him."

Harriet crossed her arms over her chest. "That seems rather unfair to make her speak first. Just because Elsabeth has the means to travel the world doesn't mean she doesn't want to be treated like a lady."

His half grin returned, looking just a little bit closer to normal. "You speak your mind all the time, Harriet. Does anyone dare treat you as anything other than a lady?"

"No. But I'm not in a . . . romantic entanglement with anyone." Goodness, but the lies were coming easier these days.

"Of course," he said softly. "That doesn't change the fact that Robert wouldn't speak first."

Harriet traced the edge of the desk with her finger. The firmness of Jonas's statement had to mean he felt the same about their real-life situation as he did about Elsabeth and Robert's fictitious one. Twice now, he'd held her in his arms. Twice they'd almost kissed. Harriet didn't want to ask for more, at least not without knowing what his answer would be.

"He could show her."

"I beg your pardon?"

"Maybe he can't be the first to say anything, but he could show her. He could . . . he could *do* something to let Elsabeth know he thinks of her as more than his employer. Caring about someone is more than simply words."

Jonas rubbed a hand across the back of his neck. "For it to show up in the letters, she would have to recognize the action for what it was."

"Obviously. If she didn't understand what was happening, it wouldn't do Robert much good."

"If she doesn't say anything, Robert won't know if she didn't understand or just didn't reciprocate."

Harriet started to sweat. Had Jonas done something? Had he thought he was making some silent overture and she'd missed it and now he thought she didn't care? Of course she cared. True, she didn't know how much she cared, but that was hardly something a lady could determine on her own, was it?

Jonas wasn't the most demonstrative of people, so he might see an act as significant when she thought it commonplace. "He should do something that requires a response from her. Something obvious that she couldn't miss."

"Anything other than a direct statement can always be misunderstood." Jonas sighed. "Even plainly spoken statements can be misunderstood. It happens all the time."

"Don't they say actions speak louder than words?"

"The Bible says, 'Let us not love in word . . . but in deed and in truth.'"

Harriet waved a hand over the paper. "There you go. Even the Bible says he should show instead of tell."

Jonas laughed and shook his head. "Shouldn't she show it, too, then?"

"What would you have her do?" Harriet held her breath. Would he give her a hint?

Jonas cleared his throat. "She could smile at him."

Harriet smiled.

"Maybe reach out to him when they're walking. She could use him to steady herself even when it's obvious she doesn't need it."

Harriet curled her hands into fists. They were sitting at desks. Even if she could reach him over the expanse of wood, she could hardly feign the need for extra stability.

"She could definitely talk to him. Even if she doesn't tell him how she feels, she would have to be the one to open conversations."

"That seems a large responsibility. What is Robert going to do?"

"What do you think he should do?" Jonas's voice was quiet, but was that because he didn't need to speak loudly to be heard in their close proximity, or, like her, he was anxious to hear the answer?

Harriet licked her lips. "He could offer his hand. Or see to her comfort. An extra pillow or a blanket."

"That's part of his job, isn't it? And his responsibility as a gentleman? How will she know the difference?"

What an excellent question. Jonas certainly treated her kindly, but was that because he was a decent fellow, because his sister had asked him to, or because he cared for her? "I don't know."

"Then poor Robert will have to wait for Elsabeth."

Poor Robert indeed. Harriet surged to her feet, hips braced against the edge of her desk as she leaned toward Jonas. "Robert," she spit out, "has to take the openings she gives him." She planted her hands on the desk so she could lean in farther and loom over the man. "If he never shares anything personal when she does open discussions, she'll think he doesn't care."

"He may not have anything to share that pertains to the conversation she opened." He rose and matched her challenging stance. "What if his life has been difficult and he doesn't want to weigh her down?"

"If they care about each other, it won't be a weight." Goodness knows Harriet had willingly picked up the weight of her father's pain. Though it made her life difficult, seeing his happiness made the load far easier to bear.

Jonas shook his head and dropped his gaze back to the papers on the desk. "It will always be a weight."

"But one she wants to carry." She kept her eyes glued to him, willing him to look at her so she could try to see the meaning behind his words.

"What if she finds she can't? What if he knows it would be too much and she convinces him it isn't? What would happen when it falls apart?"

"They won't know unless they try."

They'd both leaned in during the rapid exchange, removing most of the distance between them. She could see the flecks in his eyes now. In fact, her vision was so full of his gaze she could see nothing else. What might have happened if the desks weren't preventing them from moving forward those last few inches?

His voice softened to a whisper. "He might not know how to share."

"If he wants to get closer to her, he'll have to learn."

"That's a difficult lesson."

"It's a risk. But if she's going to take one, he'll have to as well."

His throat jerked with a swallow. His tongue darted out to wet his lips. "And if Robert believes Elsabeth is hiding something too? That she's suffering from something she doesn't want to share? Burdens can be divided both ways. Will Elsabeth give him that?"

Harriet's chest felt tight. "She might not be able to."

"You said they'd have to take risks."

"Some risks are too large."

He stared into her eyes for a long time, and a shadow grew in his eyes, deep enough to create a coldness in the space between them. He knew she wasn't talking about Elsabeth and Robert. He knew. And it hurt him.

She was hurting him.

"I see," he said softly before carefully lowering back into his chair. He picked up the pen and positioned the paper in front of them. "I'll write about the carriage journey. Robert can tell her about the wheat."

Harriet couldn't bring herself to sit down, to put more distance between them the way he had. His backing away seemed so final. "Will Robert share?"

After a moment, Jonas nodded. "This is fiction. If love can't win there, it hasn't a hope of succeeding anywhere."

TWO DAYS LATER Jonas sat at the desk again. Harriet wasn't in the library this time—wasn't even in the house as far as he knew.

Still, he'd stayed to work, hoping it would give him the answers he hadn't found on his ceiling the last two nights.

He tapped a finger on the desk and read over what he'd just written.

These pages could not be left on Harriet's desk. They didn't say what he wanted them to say. This letter was important. Their conversation two days ago hadn't been about the book. He knew it. She knew it.

It was clear the only romance he and Harriet could ever share was that of Elsabeth and Robert. Jonas didn't even care what she was doing with the book anymore. If he wrote it, he could, in a way, live out in his imagination something that could never happen in reality. It wouldn't make the realization that he liked Harriet any easier. It would likely make it harder.

He'd already learned so much about Harriet by working closely with her. Did he want to learn more? To become more personal?

Frustrated, he grabbed a pencil and began doodling on the back of one of the pages.

What was Harriet getting from this? Two days ago, she'd seemed to be looking for hope, and Jonas didn't want to give it to her. He didn't even know what he wanted in life, and he couldn't imagine her wanting to be invited along on any of his current possibilities.

He hadn't expected to like Harriet, certainly hadn't expected her to make him laugh or think or challenge his way of looking at the world, but there she was.

And here he was.

And that was about as close as life would ever let them get.

Perhaps if his parents hadn't died, if he'd been a man of trade instead of labor, the chance of love could be enough to ask her to consider the sacrifice. But he didn't have a trade. He didn't even own a home.

He glanced around the library and had to acknowledge his lack of property wasn't an issue. Harriet had more than enough.

Still, he couldn't see himself as a man of leisure. He would always want to work.

And she could be gentry if she wished.

He looked down at his sketch. Harriet stared back once again. It seemed all his mindless drawings were of her now. This time he'd drawn a man with her, holding her. His head was turned away, face hidden. Jonas hadn't been able to put the two of them together, even on paper.

Heiresses simply did not fall in love with stable hands.

Except perhaps in novels.

He slid out a clean sheet of paper and started the scene again.

Twenty-Three

"What is between the stable and a ballroom? Whatever it is, that's where I belong."

—Jonas, in his notebook the morning after the ball and stable party

He was going to Tuesday dinner.

Voluntarily.

Ever since the ball he'd been considering that there had to be someplace between the party behind the stable and the ball, a place for people like him.

Not that he'd avoid gathering with the other grooms. It had been a pleasant enough evening. The ballroom might even be doable if his friends left him alone in the corner. Still, if he was going to consider the idea that life was more than existence, there had to be somewhere he wanted to be.

The only place he knew that fell between the stable and the ballroom was the drawing room. So here he was, on a Tuesday, walking up the steps to Trenton Hall's front door.

Lord Farnsworth was in the hall when the butler let Jonas in. He'd invited Jonas to call him Oliver, and he should probably take him up on that if he really wanted to give this Tuesday-night group a fair try.

Jonas's mouth went dry. Perhaps that could wait another week.

"Dinner won't be for another twenty minutes. Everyone is in the drawing room." Lord Farnsworth waved a hand toward a doorway, allowing Jonas to lead the way.

After taking a deep breath, Jonas walked through it and took in the small groupings. Sometimes the women gathered on one side of the room while the men circled up a few feet away. Other times they all formed one massive cluster of people in the middle. Then there were times, like tonight, when both men and women were interspersed among several small conversations.

His gaze immediately sought out Harriet, and before he could give it any consideration, he moved toward her group. She was talking with Aaron and Lady Stildon, whose happy condition was becoming obvious despite the flowing skirts.

If everyone else assumed he was joining this discussion because, aside from Sophia, Aaron was the one he was most comfortable around, that was fine by him. The last thing he needed was Sophia knowing he liked her friend and becoming disappointed by his acceptance of reality's boundaries.

Jonas stepped into the circle where, to his surprise, they weren't talking horses.

"You have to do something special," Lady Stildon said, pointing a finger at Aaron. "It's her first birthday with you."

Were they already making plans for Sophia's birthday? Not that Jonas wasn't in support of a celebration, since it had been years since she'd received more than whatever treat he could scrape up the funds for, but her birthday was still a few months away.

"A party," Harriet said with a nod. "We can have it at my place."

Aaron ran a hand behind his neck. "I was thinking a holiday. Maybe two weeks at the coast."

Harriet waved a hand in the air. "Do that too. As a present."

"You think she needs both?" The dismay in Aaron's voice almost made Jonas laugh.

"Yes," Lady Stildon said as Harriet turned to Jonas and asked, "What do you think?"

"I, uh, well I don't think we've had a party since we were children."

"That's right." Lady Stildon's eyes were wide. "It will be your birthday too."

Harriet grinned. "Then we definitely need to have—"

"You will not throw me a party," Jonas cut in.

"Why not?" Harriet turned to fully face him, crossing her arms and defiantly tilting her head. "You deserve to be celebrated as well."

"Unlike Sophia," Jonas whispered to keep the news from traveling across the room in case the plans were to be a surprise, "I don't care if anyone celebrates my birthday. If I hadn't shared it with Sophia, I might have forgotten when it was."

"That's terrible."

"No, it isn't. It's just a day."

"It's not *just* another day."

"Oh, it's not?" Jonas copied her stance with arms crossed. "When is yours, then? Are you holding a party?"

She rolled her eyes. "One doesn't hold their own birthday party. That would be crass."

Jonas leaned in. "When is your birthday, Harriet?"

"Next week, but that hardly signifies. We are discussing your birthday."

"Actually, we're discussing Sophia's."

"They are the same."

"But the party doesn't have to be for two."

A throat cleared, and Jonas's stomach tightened. He and Harriet had been jabbing at each other just like they did in the privacy of the library. Heat flushed up his neck as Aaron lifted an inquiring brow in his direction.

A quick glance revealed that everyone in the room had stopped what they were doing to stare at him and Harriet with varying degrees of delight, though no one's grin was wider than Sophia's.

Coming tonight had been a mistake.

Or had it? Obviously, he was comfortable enough here and felt like he could be himself among these people. All he had to do was weather this evening and all would be well. The moment could be an anomaly soon forgotten.

Sophia nodded in Harriet's direction. "So glad someone else is having to put up with his obstinacy. You should all believe me now when I say he's a trial."

Jonas frowned at her. She discussed him with her friends?

She blushed under his scrutiny. "Er, yes, well, what was this I heard about a birthday party?"

Lady Stildon's wide eyes and Aaron's tight mouth revealed that it was indeed to be a surprise party. Jonas cleared his throat. "Miss Hancock's birthday is next week."

"Oh, how wonderful." Sophia clasped her hands to her chest. "Where is the party?"

"Oh, er, Hawksworth, of course," Lady Stildon said. "Just a small gathering. This same group, actually." She waved a hand through the room and smiled before turning narrowed eyes to Jonas. "Your brother has even promised to attend."

He gave her a slight nod in recognition of her neat maneuvering. It was either go to the party or ruin Sophia's surprise. Still, it irked him.

Did all women feel the need to manipulate others?

Small conversations swelled around the room once more. Jonas almost drifted to the fringes to listen and observe, but tonight was an experiment. He couldn't abandon it. He just needed to avoid Harriet.

He moved to Sophia's circle and made himself participate in the discussion.

Then they were called in to dinner.

His place card wasn't next to his sister, as it normally was. No, he was between Harriet and Lady Farnsworth. Lady Stildon sat across from him, making no attempt to hide her scrutiny.

It was a very long dinner.

JONAS WORKED WITH PANDORA on the way to Harriet's two days later. The horse's high steps were getting better, and the feathers on her legs made them beautiful, though that didn't smooth out the feel of the horse's gait in the saddle.

Still, it was progress.

And he didn't care.

Something about the training process was comforting and familiar, but the results didn't mean much. Especially since all the work would be for naught when he moved to Aaron's new stable.

While he had enough discretionary income to purchase pencils and sketchbooks now, he was a long way—a lifetime away—from being able to buy a horse. Particularly a horse like Pandora.

What he did care about was the fact that part of him had wanted to ride in the opposite direction of Harriet's house today.

His Tuesday experiment had gone well, but there was still a world outside their drawing room group that wouldn't accept a relationship between him and Harriet. He wasn't even sure all the Tuesday group would. For all of Lady Stildon's smiles, he'd seen her frown his way more than once. Lady Farnsworth as well.

He didn't blame them. They were only thinking what he already knew.

As he approached Harriet's stable, it wasn't Matthews or Taylor who came out to greet him. No, it was Harriet, wrapped in a riding habit and waving a paper in the air.

"This." She stabbed the paper toward Jonas. "I want to do this."

What was she talking about? The paper was covered with his

own handwriting, but at this distance he couldn't begin to read it. Was it his writing from earlier in the week? He'd finally settled on a way for Robert to show Elsabeth he cared that did not remotely resemble anything Jonas and Harriet had ever done or would ever do.

In truth, it was the most unromantic caring gesture he could think of.

"Do you mean you want to have a carriage accident?" Frowning, he swung his leg over the horse to dismount.

"No," Harriet huffed. "I want to ride double."

Jonas fell the rest of the way out of the saddle, scrambling to catch himself so he didn't tumble onto his backside. He'd been so pleased with the carriage accident that he'd thrown the last few lines down without giving full consideration to the possibility they might have an unwanted effect.

In one of those lines—one single, solitary line—he'd had Robert give Elsabeth a ride into the nearest town. He'd given no details, no sensory experience, no encouragement.

Yes, the image had reminded him of the moments he was avoiding, but it had been a mere mention.

He swallowed hard. "You want to ride double."

She nodded emphatically, her eyes bright and her smile wide. "Absolutely. It sounds exhilarating."

It probably would be, but that didn't mean Jonas wasn't going to search for a way out of it. "I don't think exhilaration would be what Elsabeth was thinking. She had just been in a carriage accident, after all."

Her brows pinched in thought. "Yes," she said slowly. "I'm not sure if I want to keep that. It's rather awful, isn't it?"

"You want to write a book without anything bad happening?" This was good. He could get her talking about the book and she'd forget about riding double.

Harriet sighed. "I just think she might, perhaps, make it sound like not quite as horrible a wreck so as not to worry her father."

"Again. Harriet. Her father isn't real." Jonas shook his head and took Pandora's reins to lead her into the stable.

Harriet stepped in front of him, making him stumble about once more to avoid slamming into her. "What are you doing?" she asked.

"Putting the horse away so I can get to work."

"But we need to go riding."

He sighed. "She barely mentions it. Doesn't describe it at all. There's nothing for you to verify."

"But it sounds fun."

Jonas snorted. "It isn't fun." He'd ridden double with Sophia a time or two, an experience far from comfortable and anything but relaxing. Most of the ride he'd been terrified she'd fall off. Jonas wasn't much taller than Harriet. Holding her in a way that kept her safe and secure wouldn't be easy.

In either the physical or emotional sense.

He braced his feet and crossed his arms. "No."

She mimicked his stance. "Yes."

"Unless you intend to somehow haul me onto the saddle and then tie yourself to me while I'm on it, you can't win this one."

She smirked. "You underestimate my powers of persuasion."

Jonas gritted his teeth. "Believe me, I have a high respect for your ability to annoy someone into giving in, but I have lived my entire life with a sister. I have twenty-three years of experience withstanding such things."

"And I have six more years of experience serving it out."

Jonas took a small step back. He'd known she was older, of course, but he hadn't known just how much. He'd thought her twenty-five, perhaps twenty-six, but twenty-nine?

"Why haven't you married?" he blurted before he could stop himself. As soon as the words hit the air, he winced. "Forget I said that. It's not my business."

She gave a sharp nod. "No, it isn't. You can make it up to me by riding double."

This was no longer a mere effort of sanity preservation. This was a war of wills, and he intended to win. "No."

"Yes."

"We've done this exchange before."

"I'll tell your sister."

As far as threats went, it was an effective one.

"I'll stop coming by," he retorted. He should do that anyway. He told himself so often enough, yet he was still here three, sometimes four, times a week, collaborating alone with her in her library.

"Ha!" She gave a bright smile. "As if you'd go back on your word."

"You don't think a hostile environment should allow me to change my mind?"

"It's not hostile." She straightened her shoulders and gave another superior smirk. "This is research. I think Elsabeth might say more about riding double. It sounds like a thrilling experience, and as you are fond of reminding me, readers want to hear about thrilling experiences."

If she was going to use his own words against him, his ability to win this argument would lessen.

Still, he could match her in stubbornness. "No."

"You already said that. Twice. We've moved on."

"You can't move on from no. It is an irrefutable completion. The argument is over."

"Not if I say yes. By its very nature it cancels out your no."

Gracious, he was going to end up hauling her into the saddle with him, wasn't he? When was the last time he'd been talked down from a firm stance?

Then again, how firm was his stance when part of him was well aware of the appeal riding double across a field with her held? Despite the awkwardness, despite the discomfort, she would be quite firmly wrapped in his arms.

He tried one more time to save them both. "You've ridden a horse before. You know what it's like."

"I'll never believe that riding double is the same as riding alone."

That's because she was smart. Not that he'd ever thought her an imbecile, but in the past few weeks he'd observed that she had far more going on in her head than she revealed.

And he liked it.

Maybe enough to overshadow the things she did that he didn't particularly care for.

In the end, he couldn't fight both of them. He liked Harriet. He *wanted* to ride double with her. It was like dancing, but on horseback, which made it better because he liked horses far more than ballrooms or crowds.

And he didn't know how to save himself from himself.

"Very well." He turned abruptly, shoved his foot back into the stirrup, and swung up into the saddle.

Harriet's eyes widened and she gaped. Jonas almost laughed. Had she not anticipated winning?

He pointed at the mounting block. "I should be able to help you onto the saddle from there."

She climbed onto the block, a wide smile on her face as she moved on from surprise to excitement.

"Don't blame me if this is a far worse experience than you anticipate."

"Of course I won't blame you." She unhooked her riding skirt and let it drape to the ground. "That is the entire point of the experience, isn't it? To see what it is really like instead of merely imagining it?"

He shifted the horse into place and moved the reins to his right hand. As his left arm pulled her up, her arms wrapped around his shoulders, effectively trapping them in the tightest hug he'd experienced with anyone other than Sophia.

He almost dropped her.

Fortunately, Pandora's back was wide. This would have been nearly impossible if he'd been on one of the thoroughbreds. Still, there wasn't a great deal of room between his torso and the mare's neck, and that was where Harriet had to fit.

It took some work, and Jonas received at least one elbow in the ribs, but finally she was seated across his legs, her skirts trailing down past the stirrup, her hands folded awkwardly in her lap. His arms were around her, holding the reins.

She looked at him with a frown, her face mere inches from his. "This isn't very comfortable."

Jonas laughed. "Do you want down?" That would keep this short and safe.

"No, of course not. If it's a horrible experience, I'd like to understand that as well. Perhaps Elsabeth can tell her father it was even worse than the wreck."

"Have you ever been in a carriage accident?" Gathering the reins, he nudged the horse into a walk, then angled his head to see around her. She needed to shift a little more to the right. Holding his breath, he grasped her waist and quickly lifted to reposition her.

She squealed. "What are you doing?"

"Making it so I can see."

"Oh." She tried to adjust her arms, and after a few moments, she grumbled under her breath as she extended one arm to wrap around his back. Her head now practically rested on his shoulder.

As the horse plodded on, rocking them back and forth in the saddle, most of the discomfort melted away, and the situation instead became far too intimate. Maybe because they were riding in silence and nothing distracted him from thinking about how her hair smelled of roses and was close enough to brush his cheek and overpower the odor of horse, leather, and earth.

He cleared his throat. "Experienced enough?"

She tilted her head to the side and turned it so she could look at him. While it did remove her hair from his nose's immediate vicinity, he now had the complication of being able to distinguish the dark brown from the black in her eyes. "Do you think," she said slowly and softly, "that Robert and Elsabeth found their journey tiresome or romantic?"

Twenty-Four

"The world is a strange place, but that only proves the majesty of God. Only a complex, unfathomable deity could create such variety."

—Harriet, in a letter to her father, copied from Jonas's writings

If Jonas were Robert, very afraid that he might be developing feelings for a woman he could never have a future with and yet unable to remove her from his life, he would find the ride excruciating torture. "As they're fictional, they can feel however you wish."

With a sigh, she slumped, driving her farther into the hold of the arm extended behind her. "I don't think I have that much imagination."

"Just pretend they are a couple you met at an assembly."

"Oh!" She sat up straight as she gasped her understanding, startling him, the horse, and the bird in a nearby shrub.

She didn't seem to notice.

"There was a couple once," she said with delight. "I noticed that Sir Martin's daughter and Arthur Craven, whose father owns that mill near Moulton, were watching each other. Of course, Sir Martin's wife wasn't looking that direction, so I made sure to remind her that my father owns a factory, which is quite similar to a mill in some ways. She had them paired up for the very next dance."

She beamed at him while Jonas stared at her.

"What if that had gone wrong?" he asked. "What if they didn't care for each other but you convinced her parents to put undue pressure on the match?"

"If they didn't love each other, it would have stopped at a dance. They got married last March. All I did was make way for a favorable opinion."

"Women marry to please their parents all the time. You can't go mucking about in people's lives like that."

"I am not mucking about," she said angrily. "I am arranging circumstances to allow them to achieve what they want most in life."

"How is that not mucking about?"

"If they didn't actually want it, it wouldn't work."

She had a point. Sometimes. She was manipulative, yes, but he'd never seen her force anything. Still, her confidence was convincing. How many of the people had regrets later?

If they did, was that really Harriet's fault? He still didn't agree with her methods, but he was seeing them a little differently as he considered her point of view.

That shift was dangerous for his peace of mind.

"Do you want to try riding faster?" That would provide a distraction.

"Oh yes." She turned to face forward once more.

Jonas gave the horse a nudge. Pandora's gait wasn't rough, but it was large, and going with the flow of it required a great deal of concentration, particularly with two perched in the saddle.

While he'd wanted something to consume his mind and stop it from wandering, the focus required to keep Harriet atop the horse wasn't much better. The way her laughter rang in his ears and she clung to his arms was going to cause him more problems when he remembered them later.

They returned to the stable, and Jonas lowered Harriet to the ground. Normally he'd be here for another hour or two, but it might be best to stay in the saddle and ride on home today.

Harriet had other ideas.

As soon as her feet hit the ground, she was hooking up her skirt while trying to walk toward the house at the same time. "I have so many ideas for what happens next," she said. "I'll be in the library when you're ready."

Apparently, he was staying. "I'll be there after I see to Pandora."

She nodded and gave a wave as she all but ran to the house.

Either her ideas were amazing or she needed a moment away from him as much as he needed one away from her. Holding on to his hesitations and misgivings was becoming a struggle.

There was so much danger in that revelation that he should mount up again and ride away. Instead, he took Pandora into the stable to find Matthews and Taylor busy cleaning out the stalls. He was thankful for the excuse to take care of Pandora on his own.

He led the horse toward a stall.

"Ho there," Matthews called. "We're not using that stall this week. Put her in the next one. Just laid fresh straw in it."

Jonas looked at the stall. The straw covering the hard-packed earthen floor appeared clean. "Why not this one?"

Matthews shrugged. "That's what Miss Hancock wants."

Just when he'd almost convinced himself he'd misjudged her.

What had she called it? Arranging circumstances? What opportunity was she providing by dictating how the stalls in her stable were cleaned? "If Miss Hancock doesn't want this stall used, why does it have hay in it?"

"It's just vacant for this week. Next week, I'll stick a horse in it."

Jonas frowned. "What?"

Matthews pointed at the next stall in the row. "Then we'll leave that one be for a week."

"I beg your pardon?"

"There's a rotation."

"You move the horses around each week?"

The stable hand gave a nod and leaned his pitchfork against the stall wall.

"Did she ever say why?" Jonas asked.

"She likes to give the horses a bit of new scenery."

Jonas looked over the small stable again. Three horses used it. Four, if one counted Pandora, and there were surely other visitors. Why spread straw in a stall and then refuse to use it? Such an unconventional and unnecessary quirk didn't sit well with him. "That's ridiculous."

Taylor shrugged and grabbed the handles of his wheelbarrow. "Miss Hancock pays well enough to be ridiculous if she wishes. She wants me to clean one less stall every week? It makes no never mind to me. It's not like we leave it dirty and cause a stink."

A few months ago, Jonas would have simply groaned and rolled his eyes at Harriet's eccentricity. He knew better now. Every quirk she had, every unexplainable thing she did, had a greater purpose. She didn't know enough about horses for it to have anything to do with them, so it had to be the grooms.

It still didn't make any sense.

Did Harriet just have a strange need to tell people what to do? Every time he thought he was getting a handle on her behavior, something like this happened to throw him sideways.

While he settled Pandora into the next stall, his mind worked. Harriet didn't make straightforward requests. This was part of something bigger. As with the book, he couldn't figure out what the master plan was, but she had to have one.

Harriet didn't make sense, and Jonas liked for things to make sense. Moving the horses around to give them new scenery when they were looking at identical boards in each stall was the thinking of a child.

Harriet wasn't a child.

As it said in 1 Corinthians, when one attains adulthood, they put away childish thoughts and understandings. Then again, *what man knoweth the things of a man, save the spirit of man which is in him?*

Before he left the stable, he stepped into the reserved stall. Only Harriet knew why she did what she did, and it was time for Jonas to decide whether or not he could accept that.

He could walk away from the book. Harriet obviously had no serious intentions with it. Walking away from it meant walking away from Harriet, though. Some of her nonsensicalness must have invaded his mind, because he didn't want to do that.

Even though he should.

He gave the hay in the corner a kick, angry that for once in his life, he couldn't make a decisive decision. More than hay flew through the air. A square of paper fluttered to the ground several feet away.

Jonas scooped it up. It was a letter. The grime, heat, and stable air had caused the paper to wilt and wrinkle, and the edges were dirty, but the direction was easily readable.

Mr. Gregory Hancock, Iron Manor, Shrewsbury

He frowned. This was Harriet's handwriting. Over the past few months, he'd come to know the gentle scrawl well. Had she dropped the letter by accident? Had the wind blown it in?

He looked at the hay. Was there any chance she'd brought it here on purpose?

His fingers itched to break the seal and read the letter, but he couldn't. This wasn't his correspondence, and he had no right to interfere.

That didn't mean he couldn't perform a little experiment.

Slowly, he tucked the letter back underneath the hay. She rotated the untouched stall every week. He'd simply have to see if next week's stall held a similar extra adornment. If it did, propriety wouldn't be enough to keep his curiosity from seeing what that letter was about.

BY MONDAY, Harriet was ready to drop a basket of books atop Jonas Fitzroy's head. The only problem was he would ask why she'd done such a thing and she wouldn't be able to articulate an answer.

She looked up from her writing desk, which she'd left facing his. Jonas was running his finger along a passage in a travel book, occasionally writing a few words on the paper in front of him before reading through another passage.

It was what he often did when he was working. In fact, nothing appeared to have changed in their relationship at all. Jonas would arrive in the afternoon. They would work on the book for two or three hours. Once or twice they would disagree on something. Then he would go home.

Everything was the same.

It didn't *feel* the same, though, which was why Harriet wanted to clobber the man. Not twenty minutes ago they'd had a verbal skirmish over whether Elsabeth and Robert could sit on the same side of the carriage.

In the end, she'd given in to Jonas's declaration that Robert had to sit on the other seat because no man would make a woman—even a maid—ride facing backward. It was a silly conversation given how Harriet couldn't begin to imagine how such a thing would come up in a letter to her father, but lately she didn't even care what they talked about.

She just liked talking to Jonas.

She thought he liked talking to her, might even be coming to like *her*.

And then there'd been that ride . . .

When he came up to the house afterward, he was as prickly as he'd been at the beginning.

Harriet propped her chin in one palm and stared at him. Thinking. Wondering. Daydreaming.

He glanced up and gave a soft laugh before returning his attention to his book. "What are you doing?"

"Looking at you." She was also imagining them together on a dark terrace again. Only this time he was in elegant evening clothes and they'd come out from the ballroom together.

With another quick glance at her, his smile grew. "I meant why are you looking at me?"

"Then that's what you should have said."

"I'm saying it now."

She shrugged even though he wasn't watching anymore. "I was simply wondering."

"About?"

Us? Your feelings? My feelings? Our future? She didn't know.

She was saved from answering by the light knock on the open library door. Harriet swung about to see her parlormaid, Frances. "Yes?"

"Beg pardon, Miss Hancock," the maid said, stepping in and gripping her hands together before giving Jonas a quick sideways look. "Might I speak with you a moment?"

Harriet rose and crossed to the woman. Poor Frances was as shy as they came, but she did excellent work. Her compulsion to tidy everything had driven her previous two employers to fire her for sorting items they hadn't wanted her touching, like private papers and jewelry. Harriet's view was that as long as Frances could tell her where something was when she asked, the maid could put things away wherever she wished.

"What is it, Frances?" Harriet asked gently.

"Might you be able to tell me what you plan to wear this evening to the musicale? I'm afraid Elsabeth has been laid low with a pain in the head."

Which meant Frances would be seeing to Harriet's needs for the evening. It wasn't that Frances was incapable, but the responsibility terrified the woman. Last time, she'd been pale as death before she pinned up Harriet's hair. Preparing Harriet for an evening out could send the poor girl to bed herself.

The other maids didn't know the first thing about dressing hair, and her housekeeper, Mrs. Wright, lectured the entire time she worked, usually on what a disappointment it was that Harriet hadn't married yet.

Harriet molded her face into the picture of sympathy, even as part of her delighted in the new plan now forming in her mind. "How dreadful. Do be a dear, Frances, and look in on her for me? To tell the truth, going out sounds dreary tonight. I think it might rain."

Frances tried to hide her relief, but it was easy to read it in her face and slumped shoulders. "Should I tell Mrs. Wright you'll be eating in tonight, then?"

"Yes, and . . ." Harriet looked over her shoulder to where Jonas was working. Hadn't he said Elsabeth would have to be the one to change the relationship? "Have her lay out dinner for two."

Frances glanced past Harriet, and her mouth curved into a tiny smile. "Yes, miss." Then she gave a small curtsy and left the room.

Now all Harriet had to do was convince Jonas he wanted to stay for dinner. "Have you plans for tonight?"

His brows were drawn together in a small frown as he looked up from the book. "Nothing beyond the normal." He nodded toward the door. "Is everything all right?"

"Yes, just a change of plans for the evening." She strolled back toward the desk, fingers twined together. "I'll be dining in now."

He looked from her to the door. "Your maid was the one to inform you of that?"

"What? Oh, no." Harriet braced her shoulders. She could do this. "Frances informed me my lady's maid is feeling unwell and has taken to her bed. Frances manages well enough as a substitute, but it is a truly trying experience for her." Harriet slid into her seat at the desk, shrugging one shoulder as if her decision wasn't significant. "It's simpler for everyone if I stay in."

Jonas laid down his pen and folded his hands on the desk as he considered her. "You changed your plans to make your maid feel better?"

"I wouldn't put it that way," Harriet said with a frown.

His eyebrows arched up. "How would you put it?"

She did not want to talk about the maids. What if she accidentally said Elsabeth's name? He would know—or at least suspect—that she'd pulled it out of nowhere that first day. "The matter of importance here is that I am now dining alone and inviting you to join me."

There was a moment of silence before he said, "You want me to stay for dinner."

"Yes."

"Why?"

Because she wanted to make sure he was eating properly, because she wanted to have a conversation with him that wasn't about the book or the world or other people, because she just wanted to spend more time with him. What she said, though, was the one reason that had the most chance of getting him to stay. "Because I don't want to spend my birthday alone."

His eyes widened. "Today is your birthday?"

"I told you it was this week."

"You told Lady Stildon it was tomorrow when she was planning the party."

Harriet took a deep breath. How to explain that she didn't like the reminder that life was passing her by? Or rather, how to avoid explaining that? "The invitation list is the same as a Tuesday dinner. There was no reason to make more work for Bianca."

He watched her silently, and no matter how closely she examined his expression, she couldn't begin to guess what he was thinking.

"Besides," she said with a cheerfulness that hopefully sounded more natural than it felt, "I am celebrating. With you."

Twenty-Five

"I do believe it's time for me to come home, Papa."

—Harriet, in a letter to her father written on her thirtieth birthday

Harriet felt strange walking into the dining room in the same gown she'd worn all afternoon, but she didn't want to give Jonas an excuse to depart, and he would certainly have used his lack of proper clothing as a reason.

She'd made no progress with her reading in the last hour, but he hadn't seemed to write much either.

The dining table held a simple spread of food and two place settings across from each other in the middle. Harriet would have preferred they sit at the corner, but this was more appropriate. She was veering into the dangerous territory where they probably should have a chaperon, but what was the use of being a rich thirty-year-old spinster if one couldn't do as one pleased every now and again?

The meal was pleasant, and the conversation was easy. They talked of growing up, and she was surprised at how well Jonas answered her questions. She'd expected him to be closed off, but if she asked, he was happy to say. That they were discussing the early years was better for her as well since she had nothing to hide about that time in her life. After the age of twelve, it became another story.

They sat at the table, plates long cleared, nursing glasses of sherry as if they both knew he would leave once the last drops had been drunk.

"Did your father ever teach you how to make iron pans?"

Harriet laughed. "Yes. I have one here." She stood, bringing her glass with her. "Come see." She left the room, holding her breath until she heard his chair scrape the floor and his footsteps fall in behind hers.

She led him to the small drawing room at the back of the house. Had she a family, this would be the morning room, but as it was just her, she'd turned it into a gallery of sorts with a few precious trinkets haphazardly displayed. Most had no value to anyone other than her, but she loved coming in here and looking at them.

"This is a beautiful globe," he said, moving to a table set prominently in the center of the room where an old wooden globe sat.

"It was my grandmother's. She would sit every night and read travel journals, then find all the places they mentioned. She had a large book of maps as well."

"Is that where you get it from? Your love of travel journals?"

Was it? No. She had nice memories of sitting with her grandmother and the globe, but the truth was she had come to both love and hate those journals. If she hadn't known about them, known how real they could make other parts of the world sound, would she have ever told that first lie?

She needed to talk about something—anything—else, so she moved to a table near the window, where she set down her glass and picked up a doll. She was heavy and ugly, with a head made from a small cast-iron pan. It was utterly ridiculous.

Jonas laughed as he came up behind her, set down his own glass, and reached for the doll. "You turned your pan into a doll."

"All I cared about then were dolls. I had six of them. My father and I made a pan, but I certainly didn't know how to cook with it, so I turned it into a doll." She smiled at the memory. "I still remember Father indulging me, helping me find the right scraps to paint and use for the eyes and mouth." It had been a wonderful day. "Everyone laughed, but he took my project seriously."

"You must love your father very much."

"I would do anything to make him proud." Including lie through her pen.

Jonas set the doll down. "I still miss my father. Mother, too, but Sophia and I spent more time with Father and the horses. He taught us everything he knew. Life's so different now that I don't think about it often. It's good to remember."

She couldn't stop her hand from reaching out to cover his. "I'm sure he'd be proud of how you've managed to come out on top of everything."

He looked at her hand on his, then lifted his gaze to meet hers. "I'd like to think so."

His voice was soft, and the only light in the room was what came in from the open door and the window. They stared, caught up in each other the way they'd been so many times before. Only this time there was nothing to break the spell. No people, no running water, no birds.

When his hand lifted to touch her cheek, her breath rushed in on a gasp.

When that same hand slid around to cup her neck, her breath solidified in her lungs.

When he eased a step forward, her heart beat fast enough to break the block in her chest and send her breath shuddering out through parted lips.

And when he leaned forward and touched his lips to hers, she forgot about everything. Her heart, lungs, and every other organ was on its own. All she could think of was the softness of his lips as they touched hers, the coarseness of his hair as her fingers threaded through it, and the gentle brush of his breath against her cheek when he tilted his head to kiss her deeper.

He pulled back, and she had no doubt that he'd taken her heart with him.

The room was so shadowed now that as his hand dropped to his side and he stepped away, she couldn't make out the details of his expression. Could he see hers?

"I should go," he whispered.

She nodded, because yes, he should, and she couldn't think of a good reason for him to stay. She certainly wouldn't be able to enjoy any conversation for a while.

"Happy birthday," he added before backing out of the room. He stayed facing her until there was no way for him to see her anymore.

Then he was gone.

HARRIET TRIED TO PRETEND it was a normal Tuesday dinner. Truly, what would be different? It was her friends gathering to talk and eat. There might be a cake for the dessert course instead of some other confection, but otherwise nothing would change.

At least, nothing should change. It wasn't as if people would bring presents. She wasn't a child in need of a new doll.

The greetings were profuse and loud when she entered the drawing room. Sophia was the first to reach her side and wrap an arm around her. "You can thank me later."

Harriet frowned. "What for?"

Sophia gave a pointed look to the corner. Harriet shifted her head to see Jonas leaning against the wall, watching the room.

His gaze flitted to her, and he raised his glass in a toast as his lips twisted into a smirk and one shoulder gave a small shrug.

Memories of the evening before warmed her cheeks. "You had to make him come tonight?"

"What was it you said a few weeks ago? All he needs is to experience the life that can be his so he knows it's his for the grasping?" She gave a short nod. "We're doing that. You with the career exposure, me with the social. It must be working because he didn't put up any resistance."

It didn't sound as if he'd been planning to avoid the evening, then. Despite Bianca's claim the week before, Harriet wouldn't have been surprised if he'd made his excuses after last night's kiss.

Sophia repeating her thoughts back to her like that made her uncomfortable, though. If Jonas were to hear it . . .

Harriet cleared her throat. "Perhaps we should keep the plan between us, hmmm?"

"Of course." Sophia laughed and shook her head. "If he knew we were orchestrating his every move, he'd lock himself in his room and refuse to come out, just to be stubborn."

Would he? Harriet wasn't so sure. She rather thought he'd decide how far he was willing to be tugged and go along until his sister—and Harriet—reached that point.

After that kiss, Harriet didn't want to lead him anywhere. She'd much rather walk beside him.

Her attention was soon absorbed by everyone coming to share felicitations and well wishes. Her cheeks ached with her smiling acceptance.

Being thirty and having nothing to show for her own life didn't feel like something to celebrate. How had she let the scheme with her father go this far?

One thing was certain. When she wrapped up her lie, the people in this room would be what she built her new life around. If—*when*—she found a husband, he would need to fit with these people.

Thoughts of Jonas crossed her mind on the heels of that conviction, and Harriet glanced about to find she'd maneuvered herself closer to his corner. No one else was in the vicinity.

He tipped his glass in her direction. "Happy birthday plus a day."

She laughed. "Thank you."

"I did a lot of thinking last night."

Harriet held her breath. "And?"

"I'd like to talk to you later, if I may. Now isn't the right place or time, obviously. I have a birthday present for you too. The opportunity may not arise tonight, but, well, I wanted you to know."

"I . . ." Harriet smiled. "Thank you."

Jonas smiled back. "Now get along. I don't want anyone else talking about us before we get a chance to."

Harriet grinned as she moved on to the next person, but she hadn't a clue what they said.

Dinner conversation turned to London as Oliver and Rebecca announced their intention to move to Town for part of the Season. Trent and Adelaide debated the merits of going to London in the midst of the crush or arranging to see their families closer to the end. Neither Hudson nor Bianca had ever experienced a Season, and Rebecca offered to introduce them around.

Harriet enjoyed what London had to offer. The shops and museums were nice, and she'd made a few friends on her visits over the years—mostly ladies who worked in charities with people Harriet knew from Newmarket.

But the Season was something else entirely. The opera. Vauxhall Gardens. Balls that made Adelaide's event look like a garden party. She understood the appeal, but enduring the chaos once had been plenty for her.

Perhaps if she hadn't felt so alone at every event she attended, hadn't met people only to never see them again, she would have enjoyed the experience.

Harriet glanced down the table to where Sophia had grown unusually quiet, pushing her food around her plate with a dreamy expression.

"We could all go," Harriet blurted. "Just for a week or two. London isn't far."

A beat of silence followed her suggestion, and then conversation rolled around the table.

"We've plenty of family between us to house everyone," Oliver said, looking about the table.

Sophia's eye grew large as she looked at Rebecca. Then her gaze went to her husband before returning to her plate. Aaron abandoned his food entirely to look at his wife, his face devoid of any emotion.

"We don't even need invitations," Harriet said. "London has plenty to offer during the Season."

"I wonder what opera is playing," Rebecca said.

Servants took the plates away and a cake arrived, causing a heated discussion on the best confection flavors.

That didn't dampen Harriet's excitement, though. The ladies could make plans amongst themselves when they withdrew to the drawing room.

She mentally walked through her dressing room. Which gowns could she loan Sophia? Elsabeth's services would be needed as well, since Sophia hadn't yet hired a lady's maid.

Once in the drawing room, the ladies talked of various entertainments, the conversation occasionally touching the idea of going to London.

Harriet casually reminded Sophia that Aaron was great friends with Lord and Lady Grableton's son and they'd assured Aaron he was welcome in their home at any time.

"It would be no problem to stay somewhere nearby," Harriet said. "Then I could loan you my lady's maid for special evenings."

Sophia sighed, that dreamy look on her face once more. "Aaron says the house is large. You could probably stay there."

Harriet's shoulders straightened a little more as a sense of accomplishment fluttered through her. She did so enjoy removing obstacles from the paths people wanted to travel.

When the men joined them, Sophia immediately crossed the room to have a conversation with her husband, who was standing beside Jonas.

Would anyone notice if Harriet and Jonas slipped away? It was terribly impatient of her, but she desperately wanted to know what he planned to say. His phrasing indicated she would like what she heard.

Then a thunderous frown formed on Jonas's face, and his gaze lifted from his sister to crash into Harriet's across the room. It was nothing like the smile and wink he'd given her earlier.

He shifted away from the couple, and Harriet held her breath. Was he coming over to her?

Her heart raced, and then everything in her fell to her toes.

He wasn't coming to her.

He was leaving.

Her gaze swept the room to see if anyone else looked upset. All were acting normal, except for Aaron and Sophia. They, too, were leaving. Her friend's small hands were clasped around her husband's arm as she rested her head against him. His shoulders curved in, and his head hung a little forward.

It was not the picture of a delighted, happy couple, and Sophia was never the first to leave a Tuesday evening dinner.

What had Harriet done?

Twenty-Six

"The striving of flesh and blood as it pounded for the finish was enough to free the hearts of the onlookers and bring them galloping alongside."

—Jonas, in his account of the race

Jonas placed Sweet Fleet's hoof gently on the floor of the stable before straightening and giving the horse a pat on the neck. The satisfaction of a completed task settled through him, but that wasn't enough to blanket the disquieting unbalance he'd been feeling all week.

He'd been ready to declare himself, ready to put Harriet's scheming mind to work with his so they could find a way to make a relationship work.

That was before Sophia had come up to Aaron, spouting excited plans, most of which started with the phrase *Harriet says*. With each sentence Aaron had stiffened until even his toes had to be tense as rock.

Finally, he'd asked his wife, "How will you feel if they don't allow me in somewhere?"

Being the illegitimate son of a marquis meant Aaron wasn't

always welcome in London's respectable places. Not to mention his father spent every Season in London, and their relationship was far from decent.

And now, because Harriet had wanted to arrange a few circumstances, the newlywed couple was facing a few very difficult conversations.

Jonas should be angry with Harriet, and he was. But he also wasn't.

Was this restlessness what Sophia had felt as they'd gone day to day, living a life that provided their needs but didn't go anywhere? Was this why she'd dreamed up elaborate goals to keep her hope alive and herself motivated?

It wasn't that he didn't like what he was doing, but wasn't it possible he could do something . . . more? Something of significance?

How many times had he claimed Paul's admonishment to *run with patience the race that is set before us* in order to find the encouragement to move steadily onward? Lately, he'd been thinking about the fact that life had a finish line. Was his only goal to die working? Or, as another verse said, was he going to run the race in a way that would earn him the prize?

All week, he'd been plagued by Harriet. Her bravado. Her boldness.

Her shattered expression right before he'd left the party Tuesday.

That had been days ago, and he couldn't get the image out of his mind. As much as he disagreed with Harriet's methods, her life had a purpose. She got up every morning with the passionate goal of making life better for those she encountered. Her methods were odd, but her heart wasn't.

He didn't want to change that, though perhaps he'd encourage her to alter her methods. And, surprisingly, part of him even wanted to help her do it.

There'd never been a grand mission in his life, never been a grand passion, but he'd been happy to propel the dreams of those he loved.

Did that mean he loved Harriet?

Not yet. But he could. She was flawed, but she never intentionally hurt people.

With one final pat on the horse's neck, Jonas let himself out of the stall, sliding the latch into place with a force that sent a *clink* resounding through the stone stable.

His hand rested on the latch, dirt smudged across his skin and caked under his fingernails. This was good work. Necessary work. The stable would falter without him and the other grooms. The horses wouldn't receive proper care. In the grand scheme of things, though, when he stood before Christ at heaven's gate, would the work be what earned him a "Well done"?

He'd never considered that before, had always assumed it was enough to do whatever he did to the glory of the Lord and with dedication and integrity. There was a verse for that too.

Which was he to believe?

Or were both true? Was God pleased with his work as a stable hand as long as he was an honorable worker? Did He also want him to have a goal? A purpose? Something to work toward?

That didn't seem right either. Jesus never commanded anyone to have a business plan and notebook of objectives. He said to *love the Lord thy God with all thy heart, and with all thy soul, and with all thy strength, and with all thy mind; and thy neighbour as thyself.*

Jonas dropped onto a barrel and stared at Sweet Fleet through the bars of his stall. He did all right with the loving God portion. At least he kept it at the front of his mind and strived for it.

Loving his neighbor was something else.

He'd lived with the other grooms in this stable for months now, and what had he done with the scattered conversations? Stored away the information like he stored everything else he learned but never actually did anything with it. Even when he shared a meal, he allowed the conversation to drift around him, nodding and commenting just enough to appear involved but keeping himself distant.

Last night he'd condemned Harriet's interference but hadn't offered a hand in finding another solution. If he was loving any of those people as he loved himself, then one certainly couldn't call him selfish.

Cold and unfeeling would be closer to the mark.

What would it look like if he—

"There he is!"

Jonas blinked, thankful for the interruption of his introspection but wary of why half of Hawksworth's grooms were moving his way. Miles led the group, a magazine in hand. Andrew and Ernest were on either side of him, both smiling like he'd just won a race. Heads poked out of other stalls, eager to hear whatever the news.

"I didn't know you had this in you," Miles declared.

"I told you he was good," Ernest said as he left the group to come stand by Jonas's side. "Didn't know you'd decided to make a go of it, though. Or that you were a writer too."

Jonas stood and busied himself with putting away the grooming tools. "What are you talking about?"

"The article, of course." Miles plopped the magazine onto Jonas's recently vacated barrel. Jonas had just enough time to make out the *Sporting Magazine* banner before the pages were flipped open.

A vaguely familiar drawing appeared on the left page.

Jonas stepped closer and examined the picture. The more he looked, the more familiar it became. He knew every line, every blank space, every nuance. Before his eyes traced the reins from the jockey's hands, he knew he'd find the horse's mouth open and eyes wide, knew another horse's nostril would be a little too large.

Knew what name he would find in the picture's description.

He shifted his gaze to the facing page, where line upon line of type marched down the paper. There, halfway down the first column, was an all-too-familiar title.

The Fight of the Champions, an etching by Fitzroy.

Words he knew well fell like stones beneath the title. The article was short, but that didn't lessen its impact.

It was his article.

The one he'd given to Harriet.

Published in a national magazine.

And he'd never sent it in.

HARRIET RAN A THUMB along the edge of the feather, carefully avoiding the ink-stained nib affixed to the end of it.

Would Jonas come today? He'd missed every workday since her birthday party. Did he no longer want to have that talk? No longer want to give her his present?

It wasn't that she craved gifts, but she really wanted *his* gift. Even if it was a rock like the one he'd mentioned painting for Sophia's Christmas present one year.

Every day, she told herself not to worry. Every day, she tried to remember that he was a man who took time to think through things and would come in his own time.

But the *Sporting Magazine* article had also come out this week.

Her copy had reached Newmarket today.

Until this very moment, she'd managed to convince herself he would be happy, that the knowledge his work was valued enough to be selected and printed would more than make up for the fact that she'd sent it without his permission.

While she'd believed that when she'd sent the article, she wasn't so sure she believed it now.

"Mr. Fitzroy, miss." The maid gave the slightest of curtsies before stepping to the side and allowing Jonas entrance to the library.

He took three steps into the room and came to a halt, his face stony and grim. "Why did you do it?"

Goodness. She'd done so many things lately, and she was afraid to assume which one he meant. Fortunately, her answer would be the same for any of them. "I like to help people."

"Help yourself to their work, you mean?"

Definitely referring to the article. Unless he'd found out about the letters to her father. He'd be even angrier about that. "I didn't claim your work for myself."

She nearly cringed as her conscience added *this time* to the end of that defense.

"Is that supposed to make it better?"

"I should think it would."

He rubbed a hand through his hair. "Those are my words, Harriet. *Mine.* My name is beneath them and everyone in town reads the horseracing section. If you think they won't connect Fitzroy with Sophia, that they won't know it was me . . ." He shook his head. "Until today only a handful of people even knew I existed, and those who did wouldn't spare me a second glance. My anonymity has been thrown away, but yes, at least I won't have to suffer the anxiety of seeing you claim my words."

She winced at the heavy sarcasm in his last sentence. With no defense, she opened the top drawer of the desk and pulled out a bank draft. "Here's the payment for the article. Made out to you from the magazine so you'll know I didn't take any of it."

He shook his head with a dry, humorless laugh. "That you would steal the article payment is the least of my concerns at the moment."

"Well, minimal though it may be, you can now remove it completely since I did nothing of the sort." She folded her hands atop the desk, realizing as she did that it was the first time she'd been sitting at this desk—*his* desk—when he arrived.

Had part of her known this confrontation was coming?

He crossed his arms over his chest, but he didn't pace, didn't glance furtively about the room, didn't bump his hat against his leg in agitation. His utter calm made the displeasure in his expression even worse. It looked decisive and complete. An unemotional fact instead of a possibility she could work around.

"You're upset," she said quietly.

"Yes."

That was it. A simple yes. No explanation, no qualification, no exception.

"I suppose I should apologize."

"That is what people tend to do when they betray another."

She frowned. "I didn't betray you. I helped you. I do realize now this would not be your preferred method of assistance, but I didn't know that when I sent it in."

"So you regret your actions?"

The note of hope shrouded in his displeasure was almost enough to convince her to say yes. But in her heart, she knew that was a lie. Even knowing how he saw things, she'd do it again. It was what he needed. "I was helping."

Disbelieving eyebrows rose above cold eyes. "How, exactly, was an article in a magazine meant to help me?"

"It would prove you have other career options."

"Because it's more respectable to be seen with a journalist than a stable hand?"

His eyes had chilled her, but his implication left her shivering like she'd walked into a snowstorm in her lightest summer frock. Not because he'd tossed it into the air as a possibility but because she was afraid he might be right. Had she sent in the article because a journalist was more acceptable in society than a man who ended each day covered in filth and sweat?

"I don't . . . that is, I . . ." She pressed her mouth into a line, refusing to believe herself that shallow. That had not been her thought when she'd sent in the article. "Having your work published means it will go farther than you can, last longer than you will."

"It's a magazine, Harriet. In a week it will be used to wrap fish down by the river."

"Sometimes people keep the pictures."

"And my gracing someone's wall or holding a page in their scrapbook means I'm worth more than I was when my only purpose in life was to keep horses alive and healthy?"

Tears burned her eyes. This was why it was better to remain anonymous. As long as people didn't feel beholden and embarrassed, they were simply grateful to God or the world at large. Or should they not be happy with their change in circumstances, not knowing whom to blame kept their anger away. "You are deliberately mistaking my purpose."

He looked to the floor with a sigh. When he lifted his head, the anger was wrapped in dark sadness. "You stole it from me, Harriet."

"You gave me the article." The excuse was weak, and she knew it, and she was barely able to force it out louder than a whisper.

"But not permission to publish it."

She wanted to argue with him, but hadn't she known this was a possibility? Hadn't she depended on his gratitude overcoming his hurt?

"I was ready," he said softly. "Tuesday night. I was ready to talk to you. To ask if you thought there was a way we could make this work. Not a hidden conversation about Robert and Elsabeth, but a real one. About you and me."

Harriet's heart leapt into her throat. "But you left."

He gave a sharp nod. "I did. I've spent the days since then convincing myself my reaction was wrong, believing I knew you better, understood you better, but I don't."

What had she done Tuesday to change his mind? The only conversations of substance had been about the trip to London.

Jonas and Aaron might not have been happy with the idea, but there had been no mistaking Sophia's delight.

"If you are referring to London, Sophia wants to go. I was simply making it possible." She might have been wrong about the article, but not about this. "I was helping."

"That's not helping."

"What would you call it, then?"

"Being controlling. Manipulating people." He took a deep breath. "Playing God."

Harriet's back stiffened. How dare he accuse her of such a thing? She was willing to sacrifice two weeks of comfort so her friend could have what she wanted. That was not selfish or manipulative. It was giving. Caring. Helpful. "I am not playing with people."

"Are you not? It's a game to you—maneuvering, adjusting, shifting, making the circumstances be what you want them to be to guide people to what you've decided is the best outcome for their lives."

"I am making people's lives better without requiring the awkwardness. Did you see her face when London was mentioned?"

"Did you see Aaron's?"

She opened her mouth to answer, but the truth was no, she hadn't seen Aaron's face. Other than his relationship to Sophia, she didn't know Aaron at all.

He shook his head. "Harriet, you can't play with people like they're dolls. They have real lives, real desires, real feelings."

"And I am fulfilling the desires while sparing the feelings. Some people get funny about receiving help." She gave him a pointed look, tired of feeling defensive.

"Don't you think they should have a choice?"

"Not if I know better."

Had those arrogant words really just left her lips? Harriet's hand flew up to cover her mouth as she dropped into the chair.

Her gaze dropped to the magazine sitting atop the desk.

His gaze followed, and he swallowed hard and closed his eyes. "This isn't some fib about laundering your dress or changing your evening plans. These are people's lives."

They both fell silent. Harriet didn't know what to feel, what to think. Was this the real reason she'd worked so hard to stay anonymous? So that no one could challenge her?

"Tuesday night," Jonas said softly, "one couple arrived with intentions of going to London. Now they're all planning an excursion because you decided what was best for Sophia without asking her."

"She has a choice," Harriet said.

Jonas nodded. "She does. A choice that will now be publicly known. Aaron could take Sophia to London tomorrow. He has all the connections. They could privately choose when and if to make that trip. Now all their friends will know if they decide to stay home. They will know it's because of Aaron."

"I didn't . . . I don't . . ." Harriet couldn't find the words to defend herself.

Jonas picked up the magazine and flipped it to the article. "But at least she does have a choice."

Harriet winced.

"What about this book, Harriet? Was my name going to end up on that too? We're a scrambled crew at those dinner parties, but I'm certainly the bottom of the lot. Perhaps you intended to elevate me?"

She jerked to her feet and snatched the magazine from his hands. How dare he dismiss her as though she were an irritating insect unworthy of his complete attention? Did he think himself so perfect?

"My grandfather worked and sweated and scraped by until the right person came upon his wares. Within three years he'd gone from creating pans one by one in a shed to owning a factory and employing a dozen people. I would never belittle a man because he works with his hands."

Jonas held her gaze with his, and then his lashes slid down, breaking the connection. "I want to believe you, Harriet, I do."

"But you don't." It wasn't a question. He still thought she wanted to shine him up like a piece of discovered jewelry, make him presentable to wear on her arm. "I don't collect people."

"Don't you?" His question was almost a sigh. "With your favors and your meddling, aren't you amassing a wall of trophies? Instead of deer and elk, you mount relationships and reputations. When you walk through town, you see face after face of people whose lives were altered by the dip of your finger. Small ways, big ways, it doesn't matter."

There was some truth to that. She did feel satisfaction when she saw them about town. But they *were* better off.

Weren't they?

She jutted out her chin. "At least I see them. You do everything you can to pretend you walk alone in this world."

They stared at each other in silence. Jonas was scarily calm, while Harriet felt as if her bones were ripping apart.

"Is there anything else you need to tell me, Harriet? Let's get it all out now. I don't know if we can be . . . friends like we were, but we're going to see each other. We should get all the unpleasantness out of the way."

She should tell him about the letters, confess about the book.

But she couldn't. That was *her* secret, not his. "No, there's nothing."

He nodded grimly. "Very well, then. Don't include me or Sophia in your future schemes."

He stepped forward and laid a package on her desk. Two pieces of paperboard tied with twine. "Happy birthday."

Then he turned and strode out the door without looking back.

She untied the string and pulled away the first board to reveal a drawing. It was her, standing in the middle of the springs, head tilted back to catch the sun.

Harriet laid her head on top of the desk and cried.

Twenty-Seven

"I hope I never see this place again."

—Jonas, in the mud at every circus stop during his second year of travel, written with a stick

He should have buried the magazine Miles gave him in the rubbish heap, had it trampled under horse hooves, or just thrown the dratted thing into the fire. Anything, really, aside from keeping it on his dresser, opened to the engraving and article.

Every morning he saw it. Every evening it plagued him. Every hour in between the image lurked at the back of his mind. Why was he obsessed with the printing when he'd never aspired to such an achievement in the first place?

There was the idea that *whatsoever ye do, do it heartily, as to the Lord, and not unto men*. Then again, *Daniel was preferred above the presidents and princes,* and even Jesus found *favour with God and man*, so he couldn't claim the limited honor of being published as the source of his discomfort.

He tightened the girth on Sweet Fleet, the idea that he was to *do all to the glory of God* no matter what he did muddling up with the other verses in his mind to leave him entirely confused.

Since he hadn't a clue what to do with his life, he'd focus on doing his job. Aaron wanted to run this horse in October, but if he didn't stop finding each wisp of a breeze distracting, his speed wouldn't be worth much. Today, Jonas was taking him out to the countryside, where there were more potential issues and more opportunities for correction than the contained area of the Heath.

He led the horse outside and mounted, waiting for Apollo to be brought out as well. When Ernest led the racehorse out and climbed into the saddle, Jonas was surprised.

"It's a trial," the quiet man said with a shrug. "Aaron mentioned he'll be needing one more man when he moves stables. Asked if I was interested."

Jonas grinned. "Wanting to get away from the gossip?"

The other man shook his head. "They chatter like magpies."

They rode out, each man content to focus on the horses and the countryside around them. There was something nice about being in his own head but not actually being alone.

Jonas kept Sweet Fleet moving forward, giving thought to the straightness of his head and the consistency of his gait but not paying much attention to his surroundings. Instead, he let his mind wander through bits of Bible verses and memories of his months in Newmarket.

"Where are we riding to?" Ernest asked.

Jonas broke from his thoughts and realized they'd traveled a decent distance north. "Have you ever been to Seven Springs?"

The other man nodded. "Should we run it?"

The two men lined up and set the horses off. It was barely a mile to the trees, so it wasn't much of a race, but Sweet Fleet never once veered off course. Maybe they needed a tree at the finish line instead of a pole.

They slowed the horses and walked them in a large circle before riding them into the woods. It wasn't the same part of the springs where Jonas had brought Harriet, but it was similar enough to inspire memories.

Here his practicality had cracked, allowing the idea of something impossible to grow, and robbing this place of the peace it had once held for him.

As the horses drank and Ernest breathed in the earthy air, Jonas contemplated.

"Do you ever think our lives are too simple?" he asked.

Ernest turned his head. "What do you mean?"

What *did* he mean? "I don't know."

The other man chuckled. "Then life isn't too simple. Otherwise we'd all be better at ciphering it out."

Perhaps that was true. Still, he had been planning to talk to Harriet, to ask if she thought a simpler life with him was something she could accept.

Maybe simple wasn't the word.

"Has anyone ever done something for you that you wished they hadn't?" Jonas asked.

Ernest scratched his head. "You mean like untacked your horse but then didn't put the bridle back right?"

"Something like that." Jonas shook his head.

"I just put it right myself. They meant well."

That was the truly painful part of this. He didn't know if Harriet *had* meant well or if she'd been trying to make him acceptable.

Would he have said yes if she'd asked before submitting his work? Maybe. He didn't have a problem with journalism, so he might have agreed to her pushing and cajoling. They'd never know.

Two sides of his mind warred with each other, and both were pulling out convincing arguments. Both even backed up their side with the Bible, and that, more than anything, didn't make sense to him. He'd always been able to find a verse to hold on to and direct his steps.

"God is not a God of confusion," Jonas said softly. Why then, when he was quoting the Word, was he unsure how to feel? *Did not our heart burn within us, while he talked with us by the way, and while he opened to us the scriptures?*

Was that what was happening here? Was Jesus pushing him toward a new understanding? He rubbed a hand over his chest.

Ernest coughed. "Er, no. At least I don't think he's supposed to be."

Jonas blinked. He'd forgotten the other man was there. "Do you ever find Scripture confusing?"

"Can't say that I read it much on my own. On Sundays it comes with an explanation."

"Do you think that's enough?"

Ernest frowned. "Don't you?"

Jonas constantly quoted Scripture, but the man who lived with him thought he found the Sunday readings enough?

Guilt slammed into him. He hadn't given Ernest any reason to think otherwise, considering how little he'd been reading the Bible himself of late. Now that he had access to other books, he spent all his time reading those. For the past few months, he'd been working with memorized verses only.

Maybe it was time to stop leaning on his own understanding.

Jonas stared into the gently bubbling spring below. "There's seven of them," he murmured.

"Bibles?" Ernest asked.

"Springs." Jonas nodded to the water. "One alone wouldn't have done more than make the area sludgy, but with seven, you get a river."

"I suppose."

The Bible was like that, its books and verses all coming together to give a complete picture of God, and here he was, picking it apart and using single verses as solitary guideposts. What he needed to do was consider them in the whole of the Bible so as to give fuller meaning to the instruction.

He'd been combing through verses, trying to find the right one for this situation, but what if the answer came in a combination? What if the answer lay somewhere in the middle, in a place where all the ideas applied? He could write pieces people might enjoy without craving their approval. He could work for the glory of God and still receive recognition.

"Jonas, I think we've known each other long enough for me to say this." Ernest pulled his horse from the water and turned back toward the edge of the woods. "You are just a little strange."

Jonas chuckled as he directed Sweet Fleet to follow Apollo.

They rode south in silence, and Jonas couldn't stop thinking about how close he was to Harriet's house. Their last meeting had been an argument, not a conversation. Should he try again? Had she been thinking through everything as much as he had? Just moments ago, he'd realized he'd been using God's Word wrong, and God would forgive him of that.

Jonas could forgive Harriet, and they could move on and grow together.

Maybe.

"Can you return without me?" Jonas pulled Sweet Fleet to a stop. "I'll finish my tasks when I get back."

Ernest opened his mouth, then closed it again and shook his head. "I'll let Aaron know."

Apollo trotted off, and Jonas waited until horse and man had disappeared over a slight rise before turning Sweet Fleet toward Harriet's.

Matthews and Taylor both stepped out of the stable as Jonas approached.

"Now, that one's a beauty," Taylor said, admiring the racehorse's lines.

Jonas dismounted and gave the horse a strong pat on the neck before leading him inside and toward an empty stall. Was this wise? Should he be here? This idea and understanding were new.

He hadn't taken the time to think it through or weigh out the options. He could give it another week to settle in his own mind.

But that wasn't how people grew together, was it?

"Use the next stall. That's the empty one this week."

Jonas moved on to the next one without a word and loosened the girth on Sweet Fleet's saddle. Taylor offered to take care of the rest, and Jonas agreed, but he didn't leave the stable.

Heart pounding, he went and stood in the vacant stall.

Slowly, he moved to the corner and dug in the hay.

There it was. Another letter. Addressed to her father.

Why put it in the stable? It would seem she put every letter down here for a week before posting it. Like before, the paper in his hand had wrinkled from the damp heat of the stable. The earth and hay had caused the edges to become discolored. The letter looked like it had made a long, arduous journey despite still being within sight of its desk of origin.

He shouldn't read it. It wasn't from him or to him, but he had to know. He had to know if there were more secrets before he gave a relationship with Harriet another chance. Before he offered forgiveness and asked for it in return.

Before he opened his soul and risked his heart.

He broke the seal and carefully opened the pages.

What he read stole his breath and stopped his heart. From the beginning the idea of a book had been a suspicious one, but he never would have guessed this was its true purpose.

Written in Harriet's delicate loops were his words. She wasn't writing a book. She was using him to lie to her father.

HARRIET WAS PUSHING ASIDE yet another cooled cup of tea when Jonas was announced.

Her heart lodged in her throat. She froze for the space of a breath before lunging for the mirror on the far wall to ensure her hair was tidy enough.

It wasn't. Dark strands flew in every direction from her head, and yesterday's curls had drooped into limp locks. Nothing short of a complete redo would make it better, but she didn't want to make Jonas wait that long. She gathered the strands together into a very loose bun and jabbed several pins in to hold it in place.

His return had to mean he'd reconsidered, seen the benefits of her interference. Otherwise he'd have simply avoided her for the rest of his days.

She met her own gaze in the mirror, took a deep breath, and skipped down the stairs to the drawing room, a wide smile on her face.

Her happy greeting was not returned.

Instead, she was met with complete coldness. Even the deepest frown he'd ever worn would have been more welcome than the chilled expression now directed her way.

He held up a paper before tossing it on a side table. "Would you care to explain that?"

She stepped forward to look at the discarded paper. It was the letter she'd written her father this week and hidden in the stable to attain the feel and smell of a well-traveled document.

Somehow he'd found it.

And now he knew just how much she'd lied.

"I can—" She stopped herself, because while yes, she could explain, she could say nothing that he hadn't already guessed or would make his obviously correct conclusions any less incriminating.

"There was never a book."

There was no question in his hard tone, and it stabbed her through the heart. "No," she whispered.

The laugh he emitted was just as chilling. "All the times I told you her father wasn't real. All the times you wanted the story to be simple and easy and happy." He shook his head. "What a fool I was not to see it."

"You weren't a fool," she hastened to assure him.

"Maybe not. Maybe I just never gave you enough credit. I'm hardly the first to get caught by you."

How could she possibly respond? This was worse than his anger. At least then she'd known he felt something. No matter what she said now, it would cast one of them in a poor light. Better that he think less of her than of himself.

He shook his head and looked away from her. "I was beginning to believe you when you said you just wanted to help people, that your heart was in the right place even if your methods were questionable."

"I do," she said, insistent. "I do want to help people. I want to make everyone's life better."

"By lying?" He snatched up the letter. "Who is this helping?"

"My father. I've been writing him for years. I never set out to involve anyone else, truly. I was supposed to help you grow your passion for art. That was what Sophia requested, but then I read your words, and all I wanted to do was help you see what a wonderful talent you possessed."

She stepped forward, fingers knotted together. "And it worked! You wrote that article." She winced. Probably not the best idea to bring up the article right then.

"Leave Sophia out of this."

It was on the tip of her tongue to push back, to tell him this had all started because his sister had been trying to help him, but that would only show Jonas he could trust no one. She couldn't bear to do anything that left him more alone than he already was.

"Exactly how is this helping your father?"

Harriet closed her eyes. She didn't want to do this, didn't want to say aloud how much she'd displeased her only living parent, how she couldn't be what he'd wanted her to be. How that failure haunted her until she'd done the only thing she could think of.

"My father wants me to be independent." His eyes narrowed at her before taking a quick trip around the room. Yes, in Jonas's eyes she was independent, but that wasn't her father's definition.

"His mother—my grandmama—never adjusted well to my grandfather's change in wealth. She was never accepted by local society, never comfortable in their larger home. When she realized the funds would allow them to travel, she was thrilled. By the time Grandfather was able to leave the factory in my father's hands, however, she was too frail to go."

Was he remembering the globe? The travel journals? She couldn't tell as he just stood there, watching her.

She plunged on. "My mother had plans too. She and Papa were going to see beyond their little corner of England, experience something bigger than London. Only she had me before they could plan a big tour. So the new plan was to wait and go when I was older."

She fell silent once more.

"What happened?" Jonas asked, his voice gentle but unyielding.

"She had another child. They were both dead within a week." Harriet took a deep breath, still mourning the adventurous mother she'd never had a chance to know. "The funeral wasn't even over before Papa started talking about all the ways I could live out her dream, that I would claim the world as my own and see and experience everything that was out of reach for most people. She'd worked out a plan for their first tour, and all my life I'd been told I would fulfill that dream as soon as I was old enough."

"Yet here you are."

She couldn't expect him to give her much grace in this moment, but the distance in his expression still hurt. "I hate traveling. I always have. I went with a girl from school a few times. It was bearable, but soon I took to spending breaks with my grandfather.

Papa was devastated when he found out I wasn't taking advantage of my opportunities."

She could still see the tears in his eyes and feel the pain of his inability to look straight at her when he learned she'd been spending time with her grandfather instead of building an influential set of friends who could lift her to a new class of society.

"I wanted to make him happy," she whispered. "When I finished school, he was smiling so wide as he presented me with my mother's notes. She'd gathered maps and travel journals. Scribbled prayers. I tried. I really did. But traveling with another family had been difficult enough. By myself with just an entourage of servants, I was miserable." She'd wanted to blame seasickness for the devastated feelings, but the misery only got worse once she was on land.

"I spent six months in Dublin, then almost a year in London, trying to learn how to happily navigate places on my own. I thought I could train myself to like traveling. In the meantime, I couldn't bear to disappoint my father, so I wrote him letters. It was supposed to be temporary. Only until I was stronger."

"But you never went."

She shook her head. "No. My grandfather included this house in my inheritance, so I finally came here. I pay a shopkeeper in London to pass our letters back and forth, but Father thinks he's a solicitor. I write every week, but he thinks the letters are several months old."

As she spoke her plan aloud, she nearly collapsed at how conniving the entire business sounded. How could she convey the love and care and good intentions behind her decision?

Jonas considered her for several moments. Then he said quietly, "What was I in this scheme?"

"I wanted to help you, too, to see that you could . . ." She stumbled to a halt as she recalled his words about the article, his accusations of her intentions.

"Be more?" he asked with a sneer.

"Yes," she whispered.

Though shorter than the average man, Jonas had never seemed small to her. Now he seemed to shrink before her eyes. An enormous sigh deflated his shoulders, and he hung his head as he gave it a slight shake. "I should have trusted what I thought I knew."

"About me?" As guilty as Harriet felt, as much as she now questioned herself, there was still room for a frisson of anger in her heart. "You were right about me?"

He nodded sadly.

"Because you thought I used people for my own amusement without a care for their actual lives?"

His wince let her know she'd been accurate in her guess. "And what about you?"

"Me?"

"Yes, you." She stepped forward and poked him in the chest. "You may not use people, but you weren't using yourself either."

He frowned and, yes, she had to admit that sentence had come out strangely. "What I mean," she said in slow, carefully articulated words, "is you were hiding."

"I was surviving."

"And how was that going for you?"

He looked down. "I'm still alive."

"But you aren't *living*."

He glanced at the letter. "Neither, apparently, are you. You're faking a life you aren't actually leading."

Harriet narrowed her eyes as she crossed her arms over her chest. "So. Are. You."

He straightened, obviously trying to intimidate her, but she was too emotional to sense a threat at the moment. "I beg your pardon."

"How many dinners have you skipped? How many gatherings have you been to where you stood at the edge of them? And you still call everyone Lord and Lady, still speak only when spoken to, still avoid acknowledging that your life doesn't fit where it's supposed to either."

Was that one of the things that had drawn her to him? The way he floated between social classes, defining his own existence? Was it strength or apathy that allowed him to do it?

"Have you made more engravings? Written more articles? I know you're still drawing—thank you for my birthday present, by the way. I'll cherish it forever." Never had gratitude sounded more like an insult, but Harriet couldn't help it. "What are you doing with those works? Setting them in a drawer? Stuffing them beneath a mattress?"

Suddenly, it was imperative that she get him to understand what she saw. This might be the last time he paid her any attention. She couldn't waste it. "Doing anything with your work would be a risk, and you won't risk anything beyond tomorrow."

"That's different."

"Why?"

"If you are correct, and I'm not saying you are, but *if* you are, then I am harming no one but myself."

"You think no one cares that you hold yourself aloof? That you reject their offers of friendship? That you know so much yet you hold that knowledge to yourself and it makes the rest of us feel like fools when we learn what you've known all along?"

His eyes widened as he looked at her.

"Yes," she said, thankful for anger instead of guilt. "We notice."

He remained silent, and the ire and desperation that had fueled her faded, leaving nothing in their wake but loneliness and pain. She stepped to the side, giving him a straight path to the door. "I think you should go now."

And without a word, he went.

Twenty-Eight

"What can we learn from the world around us? Everything if we open our hearts and listen."

— Harriet, in a letter to her father, copied from Jonas's writings

He didn't go to his room. Didn't even go back to the stable. Instead, he rode straight for his sister's.

The quickest way to her home was through the center of town. He got more than one strange look for riding a racehorse through Newmarket, but he didn't care. He had far too many other things to consider.

The two stalls in the small stable behind Aaron and Sophia's cottage were taken up by their respective horses. Jonas tied Sweet Fleet to a post, removed his saddle, and gave him water and mash. He didn't know how long he'd be here, didn't even know for sure why he'd come. What could Sophia do?

Still, he trusted no one more than his sister. If anyone could help him work through the confusion of Harriet's accusations, it was the one person who'd known him his entire life.

And if Harriet was to be believed, Sophia had a hand in starting this entire fiasco.

Jonas strode down the narrow path to the cottage, marveling

at his sister's ability to comfortably socialize in forty-room manor homes and then come home to this. Somehow, he didn't think it was the same disconnection that allowed him to return to his shared room above the stable.

After giving the front door three firm knocks, he turned and leaned his back against the side of the house, staring up at the sky as if God would write the answers in the clouds.

The door opened and Aaron looked him over. "Jonas? What's wrong?"

"Is Sophia available?"

Aaron pushed the door open wider. "Come in."

The small dining table didn't hold a full spread of food like it did on Sundays. Instead, its surface held two simple trays and a well-worn Bible.

"Jonas?" Sophia was dressed in a simple gown, and her hair floated around her shoulders in red waves. Obviously, the couple had already settled in for a quiet evening at home.

He shouldn't be here.

He turned to leave, but his sister grasped his arm with her strong fingers. "What's wrong?"

Jonas gave a dry laugh. "Do I look so wretched? You've both assumed the worst."

"It's more that you never seek me out. If you've something to say, you normally wait until I arrive at the stables in the mornings."

She led him to the sofa in the corner across from the dining area and pushed him down before sitting at the other end and curling her feet beneath her. "What's happened?"

What to tell her? He didn't want to speak ill of Harriet, to make Sophia feel she had to choose sides. Jonas felt the loss of the connection enough for the both of them, and only time and prayer would make it better. No, it was what Harriet had said about him that he didn't know how to handle.

"Do you think I hide from life?"

Sophia's eyes widened, and she licked her lips before looking to her husband for help.

"I'm going to check on the horses," Aaron said, halfway out the door before he finished his sentence.

Sophia's answering frown was almost comical.

She sighed as she turned back to Jonas. "What do you mean?"

"What do you think I mean?"

She huffed. "You are the one asking the question. As the one being asked, it is within my rights to request clarification."

"Interpret it however you wish. Do you think I hide from life?"

She wrapped her arms around her legs and rested her chin on her knees. The pose made her look so young that it was hard to remember they were the same age. Jonas certainly didn't feel young—wasn't sure he ever had.

"I think," she said slowly, "that you prefer observing life to participating in it."

She wasn't wrong. Jonas braced his elbows on his knees and stared at the floor, fixing his gaze on a knot in one of the boards. "Is that so dreadful?"

"I don't know. Maybe?" She crawled across the sofa and wrapped her hands around his arm before setting her head on his shoulder. "You've always been there for me, and I've never ever questioned how much you care."

"There's a fairly large unsaid exception hanging on to the end of that sentence."

"Who else do you care about?"

He opened his mouth, but no answer came to mind other than Harriet, and that was such a new and confusing situation that he didn't want to bring her into this conversation. There had to be someone else, though. Wasn't there? "God commands us to care for everyone, does He not? 'As I have loved you, that ye also love one another' and all that."

It was an evasive answer, and she proved she knew that by pinching him hard in the ribs.

"That is not what I mean. And even if it was, that love requires us to get dirty with both the ones we like and the ones we don't because everybody has filthy feet."

It wasn't an accurate quote, but he was fairly certain he knew what story she'd referred to. She'd understood the point if not the phrasing. He supposed that was what actually mattered.

"It's in there." She pointed toward the Bible on the dining table. "Or something along those lines. Aaron and I read it a few nights ago. The point is, you can't care for people and stay out of their lives. You keep yourself apart from everyone except me. And sometimes"—she took a deep breath, then continued softly—"sometimes I think you're even holding me away."

"Is that why you went to Harriet? Asked her to put me to work?"

Sophia pulled away and searched his face. "Are you angry?"

He gave a nod. "Yes. And hurt. Confused." This was how people made life messy. Existing on the edge was easier. "Why didn't you just talk to me?"

"I tried. You refused to get involved. Not with my friends, not with your art, not even with the other stable hands."

"It's hard to understand what's happening if you're in the thick of things. An outside observer can better see the full picture."

"So life is a museum and you're merely strolling through it? If you don't get into the thick of things, you'll never know love. Love gets in the middle and gets messy."

Was he avoiding love?

Yes. Not on purpose or by any conscious choice, but somewhere along the line he'd stopped trying to get to know people, to let them in, to make himself vulnerable.

Maybe he'd never done that.

"I like the edges."

"I know." She hugged his arm. "Maybe you can try little steps.

Come to dinner tomorrow and talk to the person sitting next to you. Oliver and Rebecca are hosting, if you need a reminder. You could call Trent and Hudson and the others by their Christian names. Or at least drop the honorific."

Jonas took a deep breath. He could do that, especially since referring to the other men the same way everyone else did would be less obvious than the formal address he was using.

And that was rather the opposite of Sophia's point, wasn't it?

"I know the men you live with play cards. Join more of those games and, I don't know, talk to them while you play."

Jonas lifted his brows and gave his sister a sideways look. "How do you know I don't talk to them? You aren't up there."

She laughed. "Have you been in the Hawksworth stable? Nothing is secret. By the way, I'm proud of you for attending their gathering the night of the ball."

Jonas groaned.

Sophia grinned. "Miles complained that you spoke even less than Roger." She gave him a pointed look. "That's really saying something, you know."

"At least I'm not as grumpy as Roger."

She shrugged. "I don't think one has anything to do with the other."

"Maybe." Even if he accepted that he had problems to work through and he wasn't living life as abundantly as he should be, that didn't excuse what Harriet had done. "Soph." He dropped his gaze once more to the knot in the floor. "What's worse? Doing nothing or doing the wrong thing?"

She grasped his chin and pulled his head around until she could stare into his face. Green eyes so like his own tried to pierce his soul from three inches away. "What happened?"

"Why do you think something happened?"

"Very well. What didn't happen?"

Jonas tilted his head and lifted his eyebrows. "I would imagine a lot of things didn't happen today. It didn't rain. The stable didn't burn to the ground. None of the horses stepped in a hole. Owen didn't stab himself with a pitchfork."

Sophia rolled her eyes and flopped back on the sofa. "You've plenty to say when you're full of fudge."

He cleared his throat. "The particulars of the situation don't matter because the question it raised is more important." He turned his head to look at her. "Which is worse? Doing nothing or doing the wrong thing?"

"I would think," she said with a somberness that showed his sister had matured more than a little over the past few months, "it would depend greatly on the situation. If you do nothing and a child gets trampled by a horse, that's a problem. But if you brought the group of children into the paddock in the first place just because they wanted to see a horse, well, that wouldn't be wise. I don't think the question is about doing or not doing things. I think it's about why you would choose either."

Questions about what he should be doing with his life had plagued him for months now, but maybe he'd been asking the wrong ones?

Or maybe he'd been seeking the wrong ways.

He needed to sit, think, and pray. Not necessarily in that order.

For all Harriet's faults, she was a great observer of human nature. It was very possible he wasn't going to like what he found.

IF THE SERVANTS brought Harriet another cup of tea, she might scream.

Yes, they were worried. She hadn't left her house in five days, and given that she'd schedule five engagements in a single day before, such languidness was unusual.

Harriet didn't care. She didn't have the energy to choose an invitation much less attend.

A far more pressing decision lay before her. Should she or should she not keep using Jonas's writings? He'd written enough that she could utilize them for at least another month.

But should she? Maybe reading all his pages had made her a better writer. Maybe she could do it herself.

She went to the writing desk she'd had moved back into her private parlor, pulled out her father's letter from six months prior, and smoothed it on top of the desk. Then she laid a blank paper next to it and prepared her pen.

Even though she tried her best to copy Jonas's style, she just didn't see the world the way he did. How did he notice all the little things? How could he be aware of how small and how large the world was all at once? She saw people and what could be done to tweak or alter their paths, but that wasn't the same as appreciating them.

She needed Jonas's observation skills to give her father what he wanted. Her attempts to replicate it after the weeks of beautiful prose he'd received would have him deeply concerned about Harriet's health and well-being.

Already he'd wonder about the gap in her letters. If she didn't want one missed week to extend into two, she'd have to send the letter Jonas had found to the shopkeeper in London on tonight's mail coach.

If she was going to do that, she might as well keep using Jonas's work.

With a sigh, Harriet pulled out another blank piece of paper and then extracted Jonas's writing from the bottom drawer. She tried to convince herself it was no longer wrong since he knew what she was doing and nowhere in that horrible conversation had he told her to stop, but she knew this was an act of desperation.

She was only a quarter of the way through the letter—thanks to the many times she had to pause and collect herself because her hand was shaking—when one of the maids entered with the post.

And another pot of tea.

A new letter from her father lay on top of the stack. Harriet frowned. It wasn't the normal day for her to receive a letter from him.

Harriet broke the seal and quickly read over the words. Bile crawled up her throat and left a bitter taste in her mouth. She couldn't swallow it down. Everything in her was frozen, weighing her down as if she'd never be able to leave her chair.

This simply could not be happening.

Her breathing sped up, ruffling the paper in her hands. His last few letters had been shorter and now she knew why.

She gripped the paper in both hands, wrinkling the sides and stretching the top until a small tear formed in the middle. Over and over she read the words, but nothing changed. The truth was staring her in the face and chiding her for every plan she'd ever made.

None of them mattered anymore.

Harriet's father was ill.

Twenty-Nine

"Any number of stables would be willing to take you on, but no households are willing to hire Sophia. If you want to stay together, you'll have to leave the area."

—An old friend of the family, in answer to Jonas's inquiry about possible jobs after the death of his father

It felt strange not going to Harriet's on his free morning. He almost mounted Pandora and rode there just to quell the restless anxiety inside.

If he could ensure that all he would endure were bittersweet ghosts of a unique time in his past, he would have done it. There was something comforting about knowing he was capable of such investment.

He was guaranteed to feel so much more, though. Pain. Regret. Maybe even the less-than-advisable temptation to forgive her, to try again, to risk another betrayal when she decided he could be of use in one of her schemes.

How was it possible to crave someone's company and find the idea appalling at the same time?

Aaron stepped up to the stall, resting one arm on the ledge

created where the framing stopped and the vertical bars began. "What are you doing in here?"

"Williams is feeling poorly, so I rode Equinox in the morning brush runs." He'd jumped at the opportunity when word came round that the jockey was ill, but now Jonas had to find something else to occupy himself and keep him away from Harriet's.

"There seems to be a contagion going around." Aaron was silent for a moment. "Needing to stay busy?"

Jonas considered either denying it or pretending he didn't know what his employer was talking about, but that went against this new idea he was trying—attempting to get to know people and let them get to know him. "Yes."

Aaron gave a nod toward the end of the stable. "Come on. I'll show you what I do every day. There's a good chance I'll be going to London in a few weeks, and you can step in for me."

Jonas didn't wince even though the admission burred under his skin and stabbed at the wound Harriet had opened. "You're going?"

"Yes, but we won't stay with the group the entire time. It's a balance. Sophia would stay home with me and never say a word, but she was so happy at the idea I couldn't let her do that."

Jonas fell into step beside Aaron as they moved to the corner of the saddle room Aaron used as a makeshift office and said, "She's always struggled with the isolation we found ourselves in. People were around, but most didn't stay long, and they weren't always the best of company. It was enough for me, but I could tell she craved more."

"She has it now."

Jonas glanced at his brother-in-law. "And you'll put up with anything to make sure she keeps it?"

"I don't know about *anything*." He gave a small shudder. "But I will suffer a great deal."

Jonas nodded. He wasn't inclined to tuck himself away in a

remote cottage forever, but he'd never felt the need for close confidants like Sophia did. Was that because he didn't need them? Or did he want to avoid the challenges they brought along?

"Ho, Fitzroy." Andrew stuck his head into the room. "There's a bloke out here asking for you."

Jonas frowned as he stepped outside. One of Harriet's grooms was there, holding the reins of her horse and looking exhausted.

A trembling started in Jonas's knees and worked up his spine. "Matthews?"

The man extended a paper. "I'm to deliver this straight to you."

Jonas accepted the paper but didn't open it, waiting to see if Matthews would say more.

He did. "If you don't mind my saying, things haven't been right since you stopped coming by. Don't blame you, though. Not everyone appreciates Miss Hancock's special blend of care."

How was Jonas to respond to that?

The man continued, "My brother got a job in the duke's stable. Miss Hancock won't admit it, but I know it's because she talked about him. Charles said he heard how she claimed she'd considered hiring him herself but then she would have to let both me and Taylor go because he was so efficient."

"You didn't find that insulting?" Jonas asked.

Matthews shrugged. "Hard to be angry when she didn't fire me and my brother's got work. Not here to jab about that, though."

"Is Miss Hancock well?" Jonas could barely get the question through his tense throat.

"She's fit as a horse, health-wise, but that doesn't mean I want her riding off on one by herself. She's smart enough to see that too." He pointed at the note. "That's why she sent that."

The note wasn't sealed, and Jonas quickly opened its folds.

There was only one line.

I need you.—H

Jonas spun around to go saddle Pandora, only to find Aaron leading the horse out the door, all tacked up and ready to ride.

Jonas swung into the saddle with a nod of thanks and kicked the mare into a run, Matthews on his heels.

Taylor was waiting in the doorway of the stable, and Jonas tossed Pandora's reins his way before jogging toward the house. He'd have run full out, but then he'd have to catch his breath before knocking on the door.

It took several minutes for a maid to answer.

Jonas stepped in. "I received a note from Harriet."

Another woman, more finely dressed, entered the front hall. "I'm glad to see you, Mr. Fitzroy."

Jonas lifted his eyebrows, certain he'd never met this member of Harriet's household.

"Miss Hancock has been in something of a tizzy for the past three hours. She ordered the carriage once, then changed that order, then bustled around the house before locking herself in her rooms. She only came out long enough to dispatch Matthews with a note. I presume it was to you."

She folded her hands in front of her and took a deep breath. "I shouldn't be telling you all this, but you've been a friend to her. She was relaxed while working on your book, but now . . ."

The two women looked at each other before the one he didn't know but guessed to be Harriet's lady's maid continued speaking. "It's obvious she's interfered in a way you don't like, but that's just her way. She doesn't mean any harm. I'm glad you're here, Mr. Fitzroy. I'm worried."

And just that quickly, Jonas's concern grew to worry as well.

A hefty dose of frustration also rolled through him. Harriet had roped her entire household into her crazy schemes, making them believe that mucking about in people's lives was beneficial, even endearing.

Still, it did seem something was very wrong with Harriet. He couldn't walk away from that. "Will you take me to her?"

The woman took him to a part of the house he'd never been in and knocked on a door.

"Who is it?" Harriet's voice drifted through the wood, and despite the muffledness of it, its shaky quality was enough to make Jonas frown.

"Elsabeth, miss."

Jonas sighed. Of course there was a real Elsabeth. Harriet likely had to pluck the name from her mind at the last moment.

"I'll ring for you when I need you," Harriet called.

"Mr. Fitzroy is here."

The door cracked open enough for Harriet's face to appear. The maid gasped. He refrained from doing the same—but only just.

Harriet's dark hair was a wild tangle, and her eyes were streaked with red and surrounded by puffy, raw skin. Even a child would know she'd been crying. A lot.

One arm shot through the opening, and Harriet's hand wrapped around Jonas's arm. The door opened wider, and he was pulled inside, the wood slamming shut behind him.

He looked around. "Harriet, this is your bedchamber!"

She swiped her hand across her eyes. "Technically, this is my private parlor."

There wasn't any way she could truly be that naïve. "I can see your bed."

"Through a doorway." She waved a hand in dismissal. "It can easily be closed."

"These are still your private rooms." And the door was still shut, and she was still beautiful, and his worry was weakening his anger.

She sniffled. "Yes."

He ran a hand through his hair. At this moment where they were wasn't really of concern. A staff as loyal as hers would never spread tales about his visit. It wasn't as if they'd never been alone together in other rooms of the house.

"What is going on, Harriet?" He kept his voice as gentle as possible.

"I'm going to lose everything," she said on a sob before taking a deep breath and wiping her eyes with the heels of her hands.

How was that possible? "Someone's taking the house? I thought your grandfather bought it for part of your inheritance."

Harriet frowned. "The house? This isn't about money."

"You said you were going to lose everything."

"Everything that *matters*. My father is ill. I must go to him, but then . . . he'll know. He'll know I've been lying to him. I don't know what to do. No one else knows about him, about me. I know you're angry with me, I know you don't want to see me, but I can't think. I need help, and I didn't know who else to turn to."

"I'm here." Jonas placed a hand on each of her arms and rubbed them slowly up and down, the way he'd done for Sophia when they were younger. He may not be able to build a life with Harriet, but he still cared about her. He wouldn't abandon her in a moment of true distress. "I'm here."

"If I don't go . . . if I wait . . . if he . . . if he . . ." Tears poured down her face. "I'll never forgive myself. Either way I lose."

Only one way was the loss irreparable, though. "He'll be happy to see you."

"But he'll no longer respect me."

What was the value of respect earned through lies? Now was not the time to mention that. "Respect can be restored. A lost opportunity cannot."

Her sniffle was hard enough to make her shake. "You're right. I must go home." She pressed her hands into her eyes. "I'll ride out first thing in the morning."

"He lives in Shrewsbury, yes?" That had been the address on the letter.

She nodded and sniffled again.

"Harriet, that's three or four days' ride away." Obviously, she wasn't using all of that sly mind right now. "You can't go that far on horseback alone."

"My staff doesn't know what I've been doing, and I don't want them to. I need a sanctuary to return to."

Jonas dragged a hand through his hair. He'd wanted to sever his connection to this woman, to sort through the mess she'd made of his mind and the insecurities she'd created, but he couldn't leave her to manage this crisis alone. "Do you trust Elsabeth?"

"My lady's maid? I suppose. But she doesn't ride."

"I'll drive you. We'll hire carriage horses from inns and change them along the way."

Her dark eyes were watery as she blinked up at him. "But your work . . ."

"As my sister is frequently informing me, she has some sway over my employer. If need be, she can help me convince him to give me a couple of weeks." He could make it up to Aaron by covering the extra work while he and Sophia were in London.

Harriet blew her nose into a lace-trimmed handkerchief. "You would do that for me?"

Jonas couldn't quite believe it, but yes. It was the right thing to do. Despite having questions about his future, he still knew who, at heart, he was as a person.

He didn't trust her, didn't agree with her, but he'd been falling in love with her. That didn't fade with the realization that a future was impossible. "I still care, Harriet."

"Thank you."

She wrapped him in a tight hug, and Jonas's heart pounded, informing him that not all of him was quite on board with getting this woman out of his life. That fight would just have to wait a little longer.

HARRIET HAD NEARLY been lulled to sleep by the steady rocking of the carriage, but the slowing and turning brought her awake again. Beside her, Elsabeth lifted her head and blinked repeatedly. "Where are we?"

"An inn, I would assume." Harriet shifted so she could look out the window as the vehicle pulled into a yard. They'd stopped at several today for necessary breaks and fresh horses, but they would likely be staying the night at this one. The yard was already lit with lanterns to ward off the encroaching darkness.

It had been an exceptionally long day. Somehow, even though the sun had already dipped behind the distant trees when Jonas departed the evening before, he'd managed to make all the arrangements and be back at her house hooking a pair of rented horses up to her carriage when the light made its first appearance this morning.

They'd moved steadily since then, with only short waits at the toll gates. Still, this was only the first of at least two nights they would have to spend in inns along the route.

Though she'd had many reasons for moving so far from home, she resented the distance just then. For her father to admit his illness on paper meant he had to be bad indeed. The lines had been crooked and the handwriting shaky. This was far beyond a trifling cold. Was he frightened? Concerned he'd never see her again? He'd written that letter thinking it would be months before she received it.

Her throat tightened. What if she was already too late?

The carriage stopped, then shifted as Jonas climbed down. Harriet pressed her head to the glass, and she could just see his shoulder as he talked to the postboy who had come with the leased horses. Tomorrow there would be a new set of horses and a new postboy.

With the animals seen to, Jonas moved to open the carriage door and help the women down.

Harriet turned to him once she'd settled her balance and her skirts. "I shall go inside and inquire how many rooms the innkeeper has available." She glanced about the quiet yard. "The inn doesn't appear busy, so he might have three, which would be ideal. If he has only two, Elsabeth can stay with me."

"I don't need a room," Jonas said.

"Nonsense. If anyone needs a room, it's you. You are the one who must sit up top and stay awake. Elsabeth and I can doze inside the carriage if need be."

Jonas frowned. "Drivers and grooms sleep in the stable."

She knew that, of course, but she considered Jonas a friend doing her a favor, not a servant. "But you—"

"I'm here as your driver."

The sentence was said so firmly and definitively that she couldn't argue. Well, she could. Harriet was rather good at arguing, but it wouldn't change anything. She'd have to be sneaky to get Jonas to accept the use of a bed.

"If the innkeeper has three rooms to let, I'm sure he'd be happy of the business."

"I'm sure he would," Jonas said, "and if you're truly concerned for his welfare, he won't stop you from adding an extra coin to your payment. I'll not have you manipulate me, Harriet."

"I'm not manipulating you."

"Are you not attempting to get me to do what you want me to do by changing the circumstances or my view of them instead of directly asking me?"

Harriet opened her mouth, then snapped it closed and pressed it into a thin line. She sighed. "Yes, but—"

"That's manipulation. Or at least a close enough definition for identification purposes."

Why did the dratted man have to be so smart? "I'm doing it for your benefit."

"No, you're doing it for yours. I'll sleep adequately with the other servants. I do it on a regular basis."

"I don't consider you a servant," Harriet whispered.

He didn't answer immediately, his green gaze searching hers through the darkening evening. "What am I, then?"

What an excellent question. Harriet swallowed hard. "You're my friend."

He shook his head. "I'm fairly certain I'm your project, and I didn't ask to be that."

"You didn't ask to be anything," she muttered with a tinge of anger. All those moments over the past few months when he'd surprised her, when he'd become something other than a project, as he called it, and when she'd begun to care about him on a deeper level, she had not been alone. He'd been there, becoming as drawn in as she was. She was certain of it. If he hadn't been, he wouldn't have been so upset.

He'd experienced it all along with her, and now he was happy to let it slide away because she'd hurt his pride by trying to make his life better?

Her ire faded as she considered his face. No. That wasn't fair. She may have injured his pride, but she'd battered his trust even more. "Will you at least have dinner with us?"

"Servants don't dine with—"

"Oh, stuff it," Harriet growled. "I'm not manipulating or maneuvering, I'm asking. Will you *please* dine with Elsabeth and me tonight? She's a servant, and she'll be at the table."

Jonas gazed down at his hands. "I'm filthy, Harriet. There's a reason the drivers are separate from the passengers." The stoicism dropped from his face as he lifted sad eyes to hers. "The world can't always function to suit you. Needs other than your own are at play.

"My being lower than you socially makes my life different, not bad. I may not get the best food or the best bed, but I can live a good life within my limitations. It's all in how I view it. You trying to change it for me just . . ." He sighed. "It's the closest I've ever come to feeling unworthy."

Harriet gasped. She'd never considered, never thought . . .

She'd been trying to help him. Wasn't that what she was supposed to do? Surely there was a Bible verse somewhere about those who had more helping those who had less. At least it seemed like a very Christian sentiment.

That she didn't know for sure made her question more than just her principles.

"Go inside, Harriet," Jonas said softly. "We've a long ride tomorrow."

She nodded dumbly and moved toward the inn. She had a lot of thinking to do.

Thirty

"An adventurous opportunity I cannot deny has arisen. I don't know when I shall return, but I promise to write while I'm away."

—Harriet, in her notes to Adelaide, Bianca, Sophia, and Rebecca, notifying them she would not be at Tuesday dinner for the foreseeable future

Their third day on the road, it started raining hard enough to make Jonas consider staying at the inn they came to in the early afternoon. According to the hostler, their destination was less than five miles away and the roads stayed decent in the rain, so they pressed on after making arrangements for the postboy to collect the horses later so at least *he* could stay in the warmth of the inn.

As much as Jonas detested driving a carriage through bad weather, he was less inclined to spend the afternoon avoiding Harriet's well-meant invitations. At least he was making this final stretch alone atop the box seat. There was no one to witness his torrent of rain-fueled emotions or Harriet's reunion. This was going to be difficult enough. Harriet didn't need anyone spreading tales through her childhood town.

Jonas pulled the team to a stop in front of a decorative iron arch marking a long drive. He knocked on the roof and leaned over the edge of the carriage. Harriet's face appeared in the rain-streaked window.

"Is this the place?" Jonas yelled so he could be heard without her having to open the door and allow the rain to enter the vehicle.

She looked about, bit her lip, and nodded. Even through the glass, rain, and exhaustion, he could see her wariness, note the paleness of her face. Her skin was ashen, stark against her black hair and making her appear almost ghostly.

His heart pounded for her. Though Jonas had never been confronted with years' worth of deceit, he knew what it was like to approach a door unsure of a parent's health. He could only imagine how difficult it would be to face both at once.

As much as he wanted to be there for Harriet, to support the kind, funny, caring woman he'd worked with for months, he couldn't. Not only had they severed the delicate connection that would have allowed him to do so, but he couldn't add another betrayal to the omissions she'd already had to confess.

Their flirtation, if that was what one called it, was over. There was no reason to make her father aware of the remnants that hadn't yet faded.

And they would fade. Even the most beautiful flowers died without water.

He tried to peer at the surrounding view through the rain, but he couldn't see more than a few feet in any direction as the horses trudged down the drive. What shadows he could see looked like a small, tidy village. He would probably have to take a stagecoach to London and then another to Newmarket in order to get home.

The prospect of several more long days of travel made him groan.

He sneezed and urged the horses to move faster than a plod, hoping he'd soon be ensconced in a cozy kitchen before a warm fire belowstairs as he continued his servant role. His stomach growled at the thought of what else a kitchen could provide.

The drive wound through a small park. It was mostly wild but grew more maintained as they approached the house. The fine home was made of grey stone and was more than comfortably sized. Though a little smaller than Harriet's house in Newmarket, no one would doubt the success of the family in residence.

After hearing Harriet describe her father's aspirations for her, he'd expected something ostentatious. This home was a definitive but modest statement of wealth, not the flaunting of a fortune. The factories that had earned the Hancocks' money had to be somewhere nearby, but it was easy to imagine this house as the home of a member of the gentry.

He pulled the carriage as close to the front door as possible. Unlike the grand homes around Newmarket, the entrance was level with the drive. Harriet and Elsabeth wouldn't have to take more than a dozen steps in the rain, and that was if they chose to walk delicately.

The front door opened as Jonas descended from his soggy perch with a wince. Though his old injury from Prancer's accident didn't plague him much now, sitting on the driver's seat for three long days had aggravated his tailbone something fierce.

Perhaps he'd wait a day or two before climbing aboard that stagecoach.

The butler stood in the open doorway, waiting to see if the unexpected guest was worth his striding into the rain.

Jonas approached him and pulled the hat from his head in a gesture of respect. It was soaked through to dripping, so it wasn't useful aside from preventing the rain from dropping directly into Jonas's eyes. "I've Miss Harriet Hancock and her maid in the coach."

The butler's eyes widened. "That's not possible. Miss Hancock is out of the country."

"There's a lady in there who's claimed the name for years. Dark hair. About my height." Gorgeous eyes. Lips a man could dream of kissing.

"Where does she hail from?"

"We came from Newmarket." Jonas shifted his weight. He was not going to have this argument. "I don't want to let the ladies out if you mean to make them stand in this weather. Will they be granted entrance?"

With a small frown, the man nodded and stepped to the side, remaining within the safety of the house.

That would have to be good enough.

Jonas grabbed the step from the back and opened the carriage door, acting as outrider as well as driver. When he'd been urging the horses to move faster than a plod, he'd been ready to curse the languid nature of the rented horses. Now he was thankful for their penchant to not move unless they had to.

Harriet huddled in the far corner of the seat, eyes fixed on the house, trembling hands clutching tightly to her reticule.

Jonas's heart broke for her. Yes, he was angry with her and hoped she'd learned a lesson about honesty, but he still wished he could make this moment better for her. He hated that she had to face this alone. There was only so much he or Elsabeth could do.

"You'll have a short burst through the rain, but there's no standing puddles, and the door is open. You shouldn't get very wet." Would the practicality of the statement break through Harriet's fear?

She blinked at him. "You're soaked to the skin."

He gave her the best grin he could muster. "That does tend to happen when a man rides in the rain."

"You should have been in here with us."

Fear really did addle the mind, it would seem. "You think those horses knew the way on their own?"

"Oh." She blinked. "Yes." Nodded. "Right."

Jonas reached a hand into the carriage and kept his voice gentle. "Sitting out here won't make your situation any better, and it can't get any worse. It is what it is at this point, and facing it is better than dreading it."

She reached out and wrapped her fingers around his, squeezing them far tighter than necessary to keep herself steady as she stepped out of the carriage.

Once on the ground, the butler's sharp inhale of surprise was audible even over the storm. Instead of propelling Harriet forward, it adhered her feet to the ground. Jonas handed Elsabeth down.

The maid tugged at Harriet's arm. "Miss, we need to get out of the rain."

When that wasn't enough to move Harriet forward, Jonas placed a hand at her back and gave a light push. It moved her one step, but that was all, so he pushed again, continuing until she was all the way into the antechamber. At least she could stand there and be out of the rain.

The butler was barking orders to several servants within the house, then paused to turn to Jonas. "Are the horses rented?"

Jonas nodded and told him which inn the postboy had stayed at. He had to pause in his telling to sneeze.

"Drive around back to the carriage house." The man pointed to where the paved path curved on around the house. "Our boys will see to the horses while you warm yourself at the kitchen fire. Are there trunks?"

Jonas nodded, then went to unstrap them and pull off the oilcloth he'd covered them with to keep them as dry as possible.

A footman appeared to help him cart them into the house. Jonas grimaced as his boot crossed the threshold, instantly creating a puddle.

"I will see to them from here," the butler said in dismissal. It wasn't rude or unkind, given he had no way of knowing that Jonas was anything more than a hired driver. As far as the butler knew, he wasn't even in Harriet's extended employ. He'd acted like a man who was as temporary as the horses.

And that was all he needed to be.

Jonas said a prayer for Harriet, his mind searching for the right verse to focus on but stumbling over several, leaving him to focus only on the truth that God cared for His children even in the midst of their struggles and that He never withheld forgiveness when it was asked for.

Jonas could only hope that Harriet's father was of the same mind and that she would be humble enough to admit she'd been wrong to mislead him.

Also that he was well enough to hear her out.

Following the butler's instructions meant Jonas soon found himself installed by the kitchen fire, a hot mug of tea clasped between chilled hands. He'd changed into his dry clothing and been served a simple, filling meal. He didn't have another pair of boots, but his stockings were wool and free of holes. He wiggled his toes in them, glad he could now do so without pain. He'd felt the chill every inch of that last mile.

He wanted to ask after Harriet, wanted to wander about the house until he found her and see what he could do to help. But he couldn't.

His only hope was to stay tucked in the corner, as inconspicuous as possible, and hope that Elsabeth had reason to venture belowstairs soon. Otherwise, he was doomed to wonder.

He shifted his hold on the mug, stared deep into the flames of the fire, and recited every Bible verse about worry he could bring to mind.

It took a long time to find them comforting.

HARRIET STOOD in the middle of the hall, activity flowing around her. Trunks were whisked up the stairs, and Elsabeth disappeared after them. A maid dried the wet floor. Other servants rushed to and fro, seeing to things she couldn't begin to guess about.

And through it all she stood there, staring at the ceiling as if she could see through the floor to her father's bedchamber.

Idly, she hoped Jonas was changing into dry clothes and finding a fire to sit in front of. Maybe she should have stood in the rain until she was soaked enough to require such attention before seeing her father.

"Miss Harriet?"

The gentle voice broke through her numbness, and Harriet pulled her gaze from the ceiling. The activity in the hall had abated, leaving only her and Mrs. Kemp, the housekeeper they'd had since she was a child, standing in the silence. Harriet wanted to greet the woman, but her mouth was too dry to form more than a croak, so she nodded and gave her a slight smile.

A kind, knowing curve of the older woman's lips was the response. Then she gestured toward the drawing room. "Your father is sleeping. Perhaps a bit of refreshment before you go to him?"

Harriet could do nothing but nod as she turned to enter the indicated room.

She couldn't sit, so she wandered the room. It was an aimless stroll, her hand trailing over items that were familiar and others that had been added since her last visit. The clock on the mantel was the same, but the upholstery on the sofa was new. The large painting on the wall was one her grandfather had purchased for her grandmother when Harriet was a child.

The door opened, and Mrs. Kemp appeared once more, tray in hand. Hair that had once been as brown as the trees was now more than a little grey.

Life had moved on without Harriet.

She'd thought the letters had kept her enough a part of it, but now she felt like a stranger in her childhood home.

Suddenly, her legs didn't feel capable of holding her up. She reached for the arm of a sofa and lowered herself to the seat.

Mrs. Kemp gave her a teacup and sat on the chair to Harriet's right. The housekeeper didn't say anything, just kept Harriet company while she drank the tea.

Harriet didn't look at the other woman until her cup was nearly empty. "How is he?"

Mrs. Kemp folded her hands in her lap and looked down at them. "We were worried for a while, but he seems to be much better. The fever still comes and goes, but the doctor expects him to recover. He's . . . he's going to be happy to see you."

"And disappointed in me," Harriet muttered. After her mother died, much of Harriet's maternal guidance had come from Mrs. Kemp. She'd been the one to take Harriet to Ladies' Aid Society meetings and help make baskets for the factory workers at Christmas.

And now her face wore a sadness that was only a glimmer of how her father was going to look at her.

"He'll still be happy," Mrs. Kemp said. "He was afraid he would never see you again."

Harriet set the cup aside. "I need to see him. I won't wake him if he's asleep. I'll just sit there and wait. But I need to see him."

Mrs. Kemp nodded. "I'll take you up."

Harriet knew the way, but she was glad not to walk alone.

Harriet paused in the doorway, afraid of what she would find. She'd heard tales of the sickroom, stories of people looking wan and thin as if they were wasting away amid the covers. Would Papa look like that?

The drapes had been pulled back to allow in the little light available despite the grey weather. Harriet stepped forward, pleased that the lump in the bed didn't appear smaller than it should and that it rose and fell with regularity.

Papa's face was pale in some areas and flushed in others. Several weeks' growth of beard covered his cheeks, and a sheen of sweat made his brow glisten. He was far from well but not at death's door.

Harriet's shoulders slumped with relief as she sank gratefully into the high-back chair near the bed. She would wait. It wouldn't be a hardship. Even ill, he was a sight she was aching to drink in. It had been so long. In that moment, she couldn't believe she'd ever thought staying away was the right thing to do.

Correcting her error wouldn't be easy. So many difficult conversations and probably more than a few tears were ahead of her, but more than ever, she felt this was the right thing to do. Not the safe thing, or the pleasing thing, or even the most gratifying thing, but the right thing.

That knowledge settled a blanket of peace on top of her dread.

Eventually, her head lolled against the back of the chair, and she, too, found sleep.

Thirty-One

"My darling daughter, I know you're nervous to be away from home, but you mustn't squander this opportunity."

—Gregory Hancock, in a letter to his daughter when he learned she'd gone to the races with her grandfather instead of to Scotland with schoolmates

It was impossible to know how much time had passed while she dozed. When she woke, the windows were still pale squares of grey light, and her eyes felt gritty.

She rubbed a hand across her face and blinked several times before turning to the bed.

Where her father was awake and staring at her with eyes rimmed in red and anguish.

"Harriet?" he rasped before going into a bout of coughing.

Harriet rose, arm outstretched, ready to go to him.

"No," he said sharply, stopping her in her tracks. "The doctor said it might be contagious."

"I don't care, Papa."

The look he gave her, despite the weakness from the fever, clearly stated that he cared, and that was the end of the discussion.

Harriet sank back into her chair.

The door opened, and Robinson, her father's longtime valet, slipped into the room with a tray bearing three mugs, each with steam curling from the top. He set it on the table and presented one to her father. "Your tea, sir."

Papa chugged the steaming brew quickly enough to make Harriet wince. Was he not burning his mouth with that? "Father?"

The look of bliss on her father's face as he pulled the mug away indicated he suffered no discomfort from the drink at all.

"Nothing feels better than a hot drink," he said, voice still raspy but sounding far more comfortable than he had before.

"You've a mug of medicine from Mrs. Kemp," Robinson said, drawing a frown from her father. "Then another mug of soup. All are hot, but they'll cool rapidly."

In answer, Papa took another long drink of tea, his gaze meeting Harriet's over the edge of the mug. "Speak while I drink."

Harriet folded her hands together. "I wasn't in Europe."

"Obviously." He finished the tea, and Robinson traded the empty mug for another.

"Nor was I in Africa." That was where she'd claimed to be during the war. She hadn't wanted to worry her father, so she'd pretended to go somewhere that wasn't constantly on the front page of the papers.

"The Caribbean? Canada?"

She shook her head. "I'm sorry, Papa. I did try, that first time. I made it to Ireland, and I was miserable. I'd barely been able to sleep on the boat, and I couldn't bring myself to board another. Staying in a hotel was just as awful. The unfamiliarity of the people and surroundings. I didn't know anyone outside of my servants, didn't know where the streets went or who served the best food or the names of the people I saw in church."

Her father coughed and made a face at his mug. "That is the point of new experiences, Harriet. In order to learn something, you must first be ignorant of it."

"Yes, Papa." Harriet closed her eyes on a sigh, allowing the memory of those long days in Ireland to crash over her. "I stayed there for months. I would lie awake at night, staring at the ceiling, breathing hard enough to nearly rattle the windows. My heart near broke my ribs."

She opened her eyes to see her father finish drinking the second mug of liquid, only to go into another bout of coughing. Robinson leaned over and helped her father sit up more, rubbing at his chest. To give them a measure of privacy, and perhaps to give herself a bit of distance with which to compose herself, she rose and crossed to the window.

"My maid who was to act as my companion fell in love and got married," she said, "and I couldn't manage to do much more than visit the baker once a day."

Rain still pelted the glass, and the distant buildings looked like nothing but shadowy blocks.

She glanced over to see her father settling back onto his pillows before accepting the third mug. His attention turned toward her once more. "We don't have to have this discussion now, Papa. I'm not going anywhere. It can wait until you're better."

"Then I'll have nothing to do but lie here and wonder," he groused, sounding a little more like himself.

Wonder what? What she'd been doing? Where he'd gone wrong? Why she'd started the lie?

Which question was she to answer first?

"I don't know what you want me to say."

"The truth," he bit out.

"As you know," Harriet said, before pausing to take a deep breath, "France was a difficult experience for me that first time."

He narrowed his eyes over the mug of soup. "You were a child."

There was some truth to that, but Harriet hadn't felt any more capable of handling the situation at twenty than she had at twelve.

She simply didn't have the adventurous spirit of her mother or the inquisitive craving of her father.

"While I was in Ireland, I decided I needed to learn how to be in an unfamiliar area, so I went to Dublin. That's where I was when I got your first letter."

"I sent it to Canada."

Harriet shook her head. "You sent it to my solicitor. Because he was handling my accounts, he knew I was in Dublin."

He stared at her, alternating between sipping soup, coughing, and sinking deeper into the pillows.

"Truly, this conversation can wait—"

"Why?" It was more of a command than a question, a demand that she get to the heart of the issue. They could cover the how of it all later.

"You were so happy in your letter," Harriet whispered. "So adamant that Mama would be proud of me." Tears filled Harriet's eyes until everything in the room grew blurry. "I didn't want to disappoint you. I'm so sorry. I just wanted to make you happy."

She sniffed and pressed the heels of her hands into closed eyes. "I didn't know what to say, so I didn't answer. After four months, I decided I had to go on with the trip, so I sent a letter saying Canada was wonderful."

Her control broke then, and she sobbed hard enough to nearly collapse on the floor. "But when I got to the docks, I booked passage to London instead. I just couldn't do it."

"Oh, my darling." The groan in her father's words broke the last of Harriet's restraint, and she slid to the floor in a heap by the window. Her father was alive and that was wonderful, but now she must mourn the relationship she could have had, the years they'd lost.

An arm gripped her shoulder, and the crazy idea that her father had crawled out of bed entered her mind as she opened her eyes, blinking rapidly to clear them of tears. It was Robinson, guiding her back to the chair that had been pulled up beside the bed.

She sat and reached out to wrap both of her hands around her father's lying atop the covers.

"Where have you been?" he rasped.

She grimaced. "Newmarket. Grandfather bought property there and included it in my inheritance, telling me I could lease it while I traveled. I think, maybe somehow, he knew."

Her grandfather had loved going to that area of England. He took her to Newmarket to watch the horses and to Cambridge to see the fair. They'd gone far more often than her father realized, and he hadn't liked the number of times he'd known about, complaining about why a person would want to visit the same place twice. To Harriet, though, the idea of a place that gave both quiet solitude and energetic society seemed a dream. The best of both worlds.

"First I spent nearly a year in London, hoping I'd find the nerve to try travel again."

Her father's eyes were growing glassy and drooping, but he was fighting sleep to hear her story. What did he need to hear so he could rest?

"When I got your answer to my letter from Ireland, I . . . well, I couldn't be the one to break your heart. I was all you had left, the only one who could live out the dream Mother never got to see. You wanted me to be brave and bold, and I tried, but I . . ." Her voice fell to a whisper. "I couldn't."

"Oh, Harriet." His eyes drifted slowly closed, and Harriet waited to see if he was thinking or had fallen asleep.

After several moments, his eyes opened again, and he licked his lips. "You came home after London?"

Yes, she had. He'd been happy to see her.

For a while.

"You said I shouldn't waste my life." Harriet clasped her hands in her lap. How to explain in a way that didn't accuse him?

The truth was that yes, her father had pressured her, had voiced expectations she hadn't wanted for herself, but she'd never corrected him. She'd never said she wanted something else. *She* was the one who'd placed this burden on herself. In his mind, he'd been nothing but encouraging. If she'd told him she wanted something else, would he have supported that?

Neither of them would ever know.

She took a deep breath. "I had been given a gift. You and Grandfather gave me the opportunity to change the world and show how strong the daughter of a tradesman could be. But I am not strong, Papa. Adventure made me feel ill. I didn't want it."

"What did you want?"

"A home. A family. Hidden smiles and late-night laughter like Grandfather and Grandmama had. Like the stories you told about Mama. Friends who visit for dinner and a chance to make a difference in a community. Everywhere you go, people smile. I've seen you arrange to have food delivered when your workers were sick. You've paid for weddings and helped with rent, all without anyone knowing. You made the people in this town happy."

Harriet looked up, eyes burning with the threat of renewed tears. "I wanted to be that person for you."

Father's eyes slid closed. "Harriet."

The word wasn't accusing, wasn't pitying. It was simply . . . accepting. When he opened his eyes, they were filled with resignation. "All those stories . . . You didn't do any of them?"

She shook her head. He'd had a dream, and she was killing it. "No. I tried to put my real life in there. The bits between the descriptions."

"I talked of you in the pub."

Harriet winced.

"I told them how my daughter was conquering the world."

"I'm sorry, Father."

"I am a liar." His gruff voice broke with pain.

Harriet choked on a sob. "No, I am."

When he looked at her, his face was hardened with so many emotions that she couldn't begin to name them all. "Then you made me a liar. I may have pressured you more than I knew, but, Harriet, you have robbed me."

"I know. I stole your dream."

"No." He reached over and gripped her hand tightly in his own, an indication of health she was more than happy to hold on to. "I thought I was encouraging you, giving you wings to go where you wanted. You stole my ability to be part of my daughter's life."

Then his eyes dropped closed once more, and he fell asleep.

Harriet continued to sit there, holding his hand, desperately trying to remember why she'd felt she'd had to do what she'd done.

Thirty-Two

"There is a purity in stillness, which I experience only as I travel the road between destinations. The lulls of space allow me to find myself."

—Harriet, in a letter to her father, copied from Jonas's writings

Jonas could finally feel his toes again, but he wasn't keen to slide them back into his boots. Despite their proximity to the kitchen fire, he doubted they'd managed to dry out yet. He couldn't stay by the kitchen fire all night, though.

Not that he knew where else to go. His ability to blend in with the furniture had made the servants forget that no accommodations had been made for him, but he was loath to call attention to that fact. If he sat anywhere other than the kitchen, he'd lose any chance of learning how Harriet's reunion went.

Gossip was flowing freely about the room, and a great deal of it had to do with Harriet. Most of it was questions and speculation, a mix of indignation and understanding. There was no mention of her father's reaction or even if they'd spoken yet.

As much as he wanted to, he couldn't seek her out. He wanted to support her, but he didn't belong anywhere in this house except the bench he was currently occupying.

He stared into the fire and gave his heart and mind over to prayer, asking God to help her father move past the betrayal and enjoy spending time with the daughter he'd seen little of in the past several years. He prayed the illness wasn't severe and that recovery would be swift.

He also prayed that Harriet had learned the true value of honesty.

It was too late for them, but it didn't have to be for her and her father. No matter how much Harriet had learned, she'd already proven Jonas wasn't enough for her. He'd known that, of course. What socializing heiress wanted to limit her life by marrying a man who worked with his hands? She'd probably have expected him to quit, to live a life of luxury with her. What would he do with himself all day?

The answer came swiftly as he pictured them in her library once again, this time the desk strewn with his drawings and writings. Magazines covered a table in the corner, open to articles that carried his name. She would curl up on the nearby sofa, reading, embroidering, or . . . or . . .

Jonas frowned. What did Harriet do with all her time?

She did whatever she needed to move along her current project.

Jonas sighed as the idyllic though somewhat uncomfortable image in his mind drifted away like smoke.

Whatever Harriet learned on this trip wouldn't matter to him or his heart. It couldn't matter. There were too many reasons why he would never fit into her life.

Still, he wanted her to be well. To be happy and fulfilled.

She could learn how to do that here. Beneath all the speculation and talk, he heard genuine caring, at least among the older servants, the ones who'd probably known Harriet years ago.

That would be enough. It had to be.

Rain pelted the kitchen windows, and Jonas sighed. It was time he watched for a slackening off in the weather so he could move to the carriage house. He'd find a place to sleep there, and then tomorrow he'd start mapping his route home.

He slid one foot into his boot, grimacing at the chilled clamminess of the inside.

A maid entered with a tray, and Jonas paused in the middle of reaching for his second boot. A man followed behind her. He'd been to the kitchens twice before, once to retrieve a tray of mugs and once to bring it back. From the conversation following both appearances, Jonas surmised he was Mr. Hancock's valet.

And he was looking right at Jonas.

Several gazes followed the direction of the valet's. Once they landed on Jonas, small frowns of confusion crossed their faces. They'd all truly forgotten he was there.

The valet crossed the room. "You are the coachman?"

Jonas nodded. He felt ridiculous sitting there with only one boot on, but sliding the other one on or the first one off while enduring this man's direct attention didn't feel right. He did his best to ignore the unbalanced feeling as he stood to greet the man.

"I am Robinson, Mr. Hancock's valet."

"Jonas Fitzroy, at your service."

A hush fell over the room. Any person who'd been trying to politely ignore the greeting before was now staring directly at him.

Robinson glared over his shoulder. "Did no one think to ask this man his name?"

All the servants immediately ducked their heads and went back to work.

"He's going to want to speak to you," Robinson said as he turned back to Jonas.

"Me?" Was he referring to Mr. Hancock? Because Jonas could think of a lot of other people he'd rather see right then.

"Yes. Miss Hancock's arrival—" The man stopped and took a

deep breath. "It is troublesome to find the content of the letters have been untrue, but your being here, well, it brings into question how much was untrue. He will have questions."

Great galloping stallions, had Harriet written about *him* in her letters? By name? "Well, I—"

"Have you eaten?"

"Yes."

The valet nodded. "Then perhaps you could finish putting on your boots, and I'll take you upstairs."

"I don't—that is, does he feel up to having a stranger visit him?"

Some of the starch left the valet as his shoulders slumped. "At the moment, his agitation is keeping him from resting. The doctor says he needs sleep and time. Therefore, we need to quiet his mind."

Jonas bent to pick up his boot. "Miss Hancock—"

"Has retired for the evening."

Or, more likely, she'd finally fallen prey to emotional exhaustion.

Jonas slid his foot into the second damp boot and gave the valet a sharp nod.

Soon he was seated at the bedside of a man who bore a striking resemblance to Harriet. Dark hair, dark eyes, and an expressive face that didn't look welcoming or well.

"This is Miss Hancock's coachman," Robinson said.

"Not really," Jonas broke in. "That is, I don't actually work for her. I work for her friend. I drove her here as a favor."

Both men watched him with expectant gazes, though Robinson's mouth curved a little more than Mr. Hancock's. What else did they want to know?

He swallowed. "I normally care for and exercise racehorses, but I've driven a team plenty. I was a safe driver." It was a ridiculous assurance given the journey was over and done with. What else would they need to know?

"His name is Jonas Fitzroy," Robinson said.

The frown cleared from Mr. Hancock's face. "You're real?" he rasped.

Jonas looked down at his clothing. It was workman's garb, clean and presentable though wrinkled from being in his bag. The boots had seen better days, but that was to be expected. "I'm not sure how to answer that, sir."

"She mentioned a Jonas in her letters recently."

So she had written about him. "She did?"

"Yes. Her, er, guide."

Heat crept up Jonas's neck. Obviously, she would have adjusted any reference to Elsabeth, but why turn Robert into Jonas? It would have been simple enough to leave the fictitious man in place if she included him at all.

Which writings had she sent? How much of the growing connection between the couple had she left in?

Jonas swallowed. Did Mr. Hancock think him a suitor for Harriet's hand? A man grasping for her fortune? "I'm a stable hand, sir."

The older man laid his head back in the pillows with a tired sigh. His eyes slid shut, but he still spoke. "She wrote about a man named Jonas who showed her how to wade in a spring. Was that real? Did you do that?"

"Er, yes." *Please, God, let Harriet stick to the truth from now on.* Jonas didn't think he was capable of doing anything less, and he didn't want more harm to come to the father-daughter relationship.

"And the horse race?"

"I beg your pardon?" The only horse race he'd written about had been the one in the article Harriet sold.

Mr. Hancock started to speak but fell into a fit of coughing. Robinson came forward with a glass of water. The valet turned his head to look at Jonas while his employer drank.

"She wrote about attending a horse race and befriending a female jockey. Do you know if that's true as well?"

Jonas cleared his throat. "Yes, sir. The jockey is my sister."

Mr. Hancock handed the glass back to Robinson and speared Jonas with his stare. "Then you are more than her friend's employee."

Jonas straightened his shoulders. He had no reason to cower before this man. "My sister is her friend."

"You work for your sister?"

"I work for her husband."

"Sounds difficult."

"Better than my previous job."

"Which was?"

Jonas didn't need to impress anyone, but the heat in his neck increased as he fought the temptation to alter the truth. Never before had he been faced with stating his past aloud. He'd simply allowed the people in his life to know whatever they needed to know and then moved on.

Much as he might want to, he couldn't be rude and ignore the man's questions, but he was beginning to understand how Harriet had given in to the desire to tell her father what he wanted to hear, particularly when she was a child. "I worked for a traveling circus."

Silence pressed into the room until a light knock sounded on the door. A maid entered, carrying a tray with three steaming mugs. Robinson took the tray and set it on the table before handing a mug to Mr. Hancock. After taking a long drink, the man looked to Jonas again. "How old are you?"

"I'll be four and twenty soon."

"You are aware that Harriet is thirty."

"I am." Jonas swallowed hard. "With all due respect, sir, I think you should be asking your daughter these questions."

"I don't think I can trust my daughter."

"You've no more reason to trust me." Jonas couldn't go to Harriet and offer any sort of comfort, but maybe he could help her in another way. "Ask her, sir. She won't lie to you."

"She already has."

Jonas couldn't refute that, even as he was coming to understand it. "That motivation is gone now. She cares about you a great deal."

"Perhaps. But she doesn't trust me."

Once again Jonas couldn't deny it.

"The letter about the stream was more personal than anything she'd written in a very long time. I thought she was finally claiming the world. I'm glad to hear that much was true." He closed his eyes, took another long drink, then said, "Not that it matters. I can hardly go back through and pick apart what I can believe and what I can't."

"I took her to a stream, and I do think she saw the wonder nature possesses." He volunteered nothing else. Mostly because he didn't know what he could say that would help.

The man nodded. "I see."

Jonas had no family remaining aside from Sophia, and he could only imagine how devastating a division between them would be. He didn't want that for Harriet and her father. If he could encourage them toward a reconciliation, then . . . well, then nothing. It was just the right thing to do.

Just because Jonas knew he could never trust Harriet again didn't mean the older man was in the same position. The relationships were hardly the same.

Jonas sighed. "Mr. Hancock, I won't claim to understand your daughter, but I do know a few things. She loves you. She's had a strange way of showing it, and I don't know how you'll get past it, but that part isn't a lie."

Mr. Hancock finished his drink and reached for the next mug. "Now I just have to decide if everything else is."

THE NEXT MORNING Jonas asked the head groom to help him make arrangements to get home. Before he departed to Shrewsbury to catch the mail coach to nearby Birmingham, he scribbled out a note for Harriet.

Only he had no way to get it to her, and in the end, he stuffed it back into his pocket. Perhaps it was better simply to leave it like this.

With a final prayer and a last look at the manor house, Jonas left Harriet behind.

HE LEFT without saying good-bye. It would have been difficult for him to get to her, but had he even tried? The way he didn't look back as he left, didn't see her standing in the window, told her the answer was likely no.

Then again, she hadn't gone down to him either.

Despite everything, last night had been the best hours of sleep she'd had in a long while, and she'd awoken with a fresh perspective. She could make things right. Perhaps there would still be scars and areas of weakness, but relationships could be repaired.

"I'm not giving up on you, Jonas," she whispered to the empty landscape beyond the window. There were important issues for her to settle first, though. Important lessons for her to learn.

She had to give all her efforts to repairing her relationship with her father first. How could she do that? When could she do that?

Conversations such as the one they'd had last night could not be good for his healing. Until he was better, she would restrict their conversations to nothing more serious than books and cards.

Maybe then, when he was finally well, he'd be ready to listen.

And maybe by then she'd know what she wanted to say.

Thirty-Three

"Don't dance twice with any of the men, Harriet. You won't be staying there long, and it wouldn't do to give them ideas."

—Gregory Hancock, in a letter to Harriet after she told him of the assembly she attended in Ireland

Harriet had eaten a lot of dishes in her day, but she'd never been very fond of exotic food. Humble pie just might be the worst dish she'd ever had to swallow, and it wasn't even real. But it was the only chance she had of fixing her relationship with her father.

Three weeks hadn't brought them any closer to a resolution. If anything, things between them were worse.

The house was quiet, and walking into town felt as foreign as her attempts to travel the world. She missed Sophia, Adelaide, Bianca, and Rebecca—and their men. Obviously, she missed Jonas. She wanted to talk to him, wanted to ask him how he would write out this scenario.

It was strange. She expected to miss the community and the busyness, but it was the weekly dinners, the rides on the Heath, and her talks with Jonas that drifted through her mind when she sat in quiet sadness.

At least Father was healing physically. He was walking for small stretches, and he had a table set up in his room where he could sit and eat. Harriet joined him for every meal.

As she'd planned, they kept their conversations light. That first week she'd stayed away except for meals. Then as his wakeful times grew longer, she joined him for a game of backgammon or sat and read to him.

They were the politest strangers anyone could ever hope to meet.

Today he'd ventured all the way to the family parlor, and she was sitting with him. He was reading. She was holding a book.

The situation was untenable. What would Jonas do? Aside from the fact that he wouldn't have ended up in this position to begin with. A grin tugged at her lips as she realized exactly what Jonas would do. She could almost hear him pulling out the perfect Bible verse to spur her into action.

If only she knew what that perfect verse would be.

What she did know was not a single person she'd ever learned about in the Bible had solved their many issues by pretending they didn't exist.

Slowly, she closed her book and set it on the table. "Do you feel up to talking about it?"

Papa looked up from his book, his coloring nearly returned to normal, his cheeks far less sunken. "About why you lied to me?"

She folded her hands in her lap. "Yes."

"Very well. What would you like to add to your explanation?"

For weeks she'd been preparing for this moment, and no matter how she considered it, this was going to hurt. She could only trust that God would be able to heal them both when it was over.

"Do you remember the time I was on school holiday and Joanna Caster's family had invited me to go to Denmark with them but I chose to come home instead?"

Papa frowned. "That was sixteen years ago, at least."

"So you do remember."

He gave a short nod.

"Do you remember being so disappointed in me that you didn't come home from the factory in time for dinner for three days?"

"I . . ." He blinked at her. "Well, no. I can't think I would have punished you that way, Harriet. It must have been a coincidence."

"Whether it was or not, we'll never know. I certainly didn't think it was. Grandfather didn't either."

"You talked of it with your grandfather?"

She bit her lip. "Not exactly."

"Harriet, is this entire conversation to be tedious?"

He was right. She needed to just rip her heart open and lay everything out there. As Jonas said, people should simply ask for what they wanted, and if she was going to ask for forgiveness, she'd have to help her father understand.

"What I did was tell Grandfather how much I missed our trips to Newmarket and Cambridge. We made plans during those three days, plans that had him coming to pick me up from school on alternating holidays to take me there. He knew I wasn't telling you, but we both pretended I had."

Papa grunted.

Harriet continued. "If you remembered there was to be a holiday and asked if I'd decided to stay at school, I could honestly tell you no. You seemed happy with the idea that I was traveling with other families."

It had broken her heart a little that he cared more about her experiencing the world than experiencing time with him, but she supposed he thought life in this little town with only him and his father would be painfully boring for a young girl.

"You thought I didn't want you?" His voice broke, and for the first time something other than disappointment and anger rippled across his face. "You didn't have a mother, and I couldn't bear the thought of remarrying. The only way for you to learn what you needed to as a woman was to spend time with other mothers."

"Oh." Harriet looked down at her lap. She'd never thought of it that way, never considered those benefits. "Why didn't you tell me?"

She saw the irony of the question, the way she hated how he'd tried to give her something without letting her choose. Would Jonas find it funny or sad that she was apparently just like her father?

"I thought you would resent it. I thought a more natural experience would be better." He shook his head. "I didn't want you to lack anything in life."

What fools they'd both been, trying to provide for the other without ever discussing the need. "What value was my travel to provide?"

He looked at her, eyes wide and stunned as if it should have been obvious. "Your mother always dreamed of seeing the world. Sometimes I think one reason she loved me was that I could give that to her."

"Only I came along first."

He tilted his head in grudging agreement. "But she still had plans. I wanted you to have a chance to live like she hadn't before you formed a family and made that impossible."

"But those were her dreams, Papa, not mine."

He didn't answer her in words, but the pain on his face stabbed her in the gut. Was he remembering the loss of his wife or mourning that the one piece of her remaining on this earth didn't have her adventurous spirit?

Nothing good could come of focusing on people who were long gone. Her mother, her grandfather . . . none of them mattered now. Instead, she would focus on the living. Her and her father.

"I came home for one year after school. Do you remember?"

"Of course I remember," he scoffed.

"Do you remember what you said when I purchased a subscription to the local assemblies?" Harriet clenched her fingers together and continued without waiting. He wouldn't remember, wouldn't know what sentence had stabbed her heart. "You said I was bound for bigger and better things than being the wife of a businessman in Shrewsbury."

"And you were," he nearly yelled as he pushed out of his chair. He slowly paced, one hand gliding along the back of the settee. "If you'd told me you didn't want to travel, that you wanted to just get married, we could have arranged for a Season in London. At least found you a gentleman, maybe even a baronet."

"*Just* get married?" Harriet spat out, feeling as angry as she felt guilty. "And why would I want a Season and a baronet?"

"Because then my daughter could look down on those who looked down on my mother and my wife!" His voice was a roar made all the more terrible by the harsh silence that followed it.

Harriet knew part of her popularity in Newmarket was that everyone could pretend her money hadn't come from trade. To some in Shrewsbury, Grandmama had always been the woman who'd once taken in other people's laundry. And it seemed that bothered her father more than it had her grandmother.

"That was your dream, Papa." Harriet's voice was quiet but strong as she truly came to see how broken they both were. "It was never mine. And I don't think it was ever Grandmama's. Maybe it wasn't right, but by lying to you, I gave you that dream while still being able to live mine." At least to an extent. She made a difference in people's lives. She was making her little corner of the world a better place.

"How can you think that makes this okay? I didn't raise you to lie. Good Christian people don't lie."

"'God resisteth the proud.'"

"I beg your pardon."

Where on earth had that come from? Yet wasn't it the truth?

Harriet swallowed and pressed on. "God doesn't like proud hearts. It's in the Bible. What you did, what you wanted, is no more pleasing to God than what I did." Or what she'd been doing. It was all fine and good to help people without their knowing, but there was a line to it. A line she'd crossed.

She'd determined she knew best. That it was her job to steer people's lives in a better direction. She'd followed her father's example in more ways than one by assuming she knew people's dreams.

"I believe I've grown tired," Father said. "Perhaps this was too much for one day." Then he turned and walked from the room, leaving Harriet devastated in the middle of the family parlor.

She didn't know how long she'd stood there before Mrs. Kemp came in. Hurriedly, the housekeeper set her tea tray aside and rushed across the room.

It was only as she wiped a gentle hand across Harriet's cheek that Harriet realized a few tears had leaked out. "What do I do with Father?"

"What do you want to do, child?" Mrs. Kemp guided her to the settee and they both sat, the older woman's arm tucked securely around Harriet's shoulders.

"I want to make things right."

"Then you have to remove what went wrong."

Harriet busied herself pouring two cups of tea just to do something with the restlessness inside her. "How does one take back what is firmly set in the passage of time?"

"I didn't say it would be easy," Mrs. Kemp said, accepting a cup with a light chuckle. "But, my dear, if you think that is the true problem here, you've missed the entire point."

"What do you mean?" Harriet frowned. Her father was angry that she'd lied, that he'd been led to believe she was living a different, more exciting life when she was toddling away in Newmarket. How was she supposed to remove that?

"You're like your father, you know. Always wanting to fix things, move mountains and crush obstacles until the world is a better place. It's admirable and good. But if that was all there was, people wouldn't come through tragedy stronger. Relationships wouldn't become closer after a trial. Families wouldn't walk through hardship finding more love than before. And, my dear, that happens every single day. The question you have to ask yourself is, what is standing in the way for you to claim a little of that miracle for yourself?"

Harriet thought of Jonas, as she often did these days. His life had been anything but easy. His hardships far from simple. And yet he wasn't broken. She had a feeling he'd never been one to frivolously collect friendships even as a child. It wasn't who he was. He'd taken his difficulties and learned. He appreciated the simple beauty of an experience that couldn't be bought.

Could she find her way to that sort of strength? Could she lay down her pride and refusal to be wrong? Could she allow herself to be vulnerable enough to rebuild her relationship with her father?

As Mrs. Kemp said, it would take a miracle.

Harriet hoped she could find such vulnerability, because she was afraid that was all she had left.

IF IT WEREN'T FOR MEALS, Jonas wouldn't know the week had passed.

On Sundays, Mr. Knight announced who was staying home from church to keep an eye on the horses. That let Jonas know he was supposed to eat at his sister's.

He'd taken to riding with Hudson and Bianca to Tuesday night dinners, and Hudson always sent a message to the stable an hour before the carriage needed to be ready. Otherwise, Jonas would have forgotten.

The other days blended together into a blur, with each one looking much like the day before. Living with the circus had produced a similar problem, but this time each day held the same people, the same challenges.

It made numbness even easier to attain.

He rose in the morning, cared for horses, rode horses, cared for horses again, then poked around the stable making himself a near nuisance with his need to find jobs. Then he ate dinner with the other grooms. He still didn't speak much, but he was there, and if the conversation turned his way, he didn't ignore it.

That was progress, wasn't it?

The only difference was what he did before falling into bed and fighting for sleep. Sometimes he read, other times he drew, and occasionally he wrote.

Every night he missed Harriet.

How was she doing? Had she and her father made amends? With the pretense over, would she return to Newmarket or stay in Shrewsbury?

Before he could go to sleep, he always found himself praying for her, which led to praying for Sophia and Aaron because he felt guilty praying for Harriet and not his sister. Then that led to praying for Bianca's unborn baby, and then one by one the rest of the group would filter through his mind until he was finally able to say amen and go to sleep, emotionally exhausted from the ordeal.

Aside from Sundays and Tuesdays, he avoided Sophia. The truth was he needed to learn who he was without her. She'd been with him literally his whole life, and somewhere along the way she had *become* his whole life. So he shut her out. She and Aaron went to London, and when she returned, he kept his distance.

That didn't mean he let anyone else in, though—not beyond the most basic of interactions. If he let anyone in while he was still determining who he was, he ran the risk of giving them too much influence.

But Harriet was already in. Her words were never far from his contemplations. He'd thought she was asking him to change, but what if that wasn't so much about changing as about allowing himself to . . . be?

Three weeks after returning home—and Newmarket was, he finally realized, truly his home now—he stayed in the common room after dinner to play cards with the other grooms. A week later he joined in on some of the gentle teasing that accompanied the games.

He alleviated his guilt in avoiding Sophia by talking to Aaron more while they worked in the stables. The conversations were riddled with holes because Aaron enjoyed silence almost as much as Jonas did. Anyone else would have been frustrated by the exchange, but Jonas felt like he was forming a real friendship with the man instead of merely an obligatory association.

Perhaps more important than all these new actions was the value Jonas understood them to have.

He was making friends.

They were from a variety of classes, and he preferred to interact with them in small groups and for short periods of time, but they were truly friends.

What was he supposed to do with that?

He still couldn't see himself running to Aaron for advice or asking Miles to help him groom a cantankerous horse. People didn't have to abandon themselves in order to make a meaningful life, though. They just had to open who they were to the world.

Harriet had done that for him—pushed him to share who he was with her, to invite her into his way of thinking. In return, she'd challenged him. To be more, yes. Not because the world demanded it but because he could achieve it.

Without her, he had to find a new way to bring about that challenge.

Yes, he missed Harriet, but maybe he was finally finding himself.

Thirty-Four

"I don't know how to share myself with people."

—Harriet, in a letter written to herself and maybe her father as well

Harriet sat at the writing desk in the family parlor after yet another strained dinner with her father. It seemed whenever they tried to talk about anything significant, they ended up airing buried grievances.

Those pains needed to be revealed, and perhaps some rifts were being repaired, but they were also creating new ones. Their relationship was far from being what it once was.

Or what they'd pretended it once was.

What she wanted them to have for real.

Her father was better, though since he'd started feeling well enough to leave his room he frequently pushed himself to quick exhaustion and was forced to take a nap.

Harriet had little to do but sit with her own company and occasionally Mrs. Kemp. The woman told stories as they shared pot after pot of tea, telling Harriet things she'd never known about her mother, her grandparents, and even her father.

Like how Papa had played for the local cricket team for two years after he completed school.

And how Mama had enjoyed making the meals on the cook's day off every week.

Grandfather would dress in old clothes and a large hat so he could slip into the factory and work on the line when he missed being part of the fabrication process.

And when Grandmama no longer had to care for her home herself, she'd learned to paint. She'd created the large paintings that had hung in the family parlor for as long as Harriet could remember.

More knowledge and more time to think only seemed to give her more questions.

And there was no one to give her the answers except herself. It was beyond frustrating, but she was also finding that it was her own journey of discovery that defined the answers.

One large question remained, though.

How did she remove what was wrong between her and her father?

She sat staring at one of her grandmother's paintings, searching for the answer in a journey decades past. The painting was of the French countryside, or rather what Grandmama had thought the French countryside looked like from reading her travel journals.

When her first dream had been unattainable, Grandmama had taken the time to discover what else she liked and poured herself into it. And when her hands had grown too arthritic to hold a paintbrush, she'd still had the joy of seeing her work.

If this was what her grandmother saw in her mind when they read the journals and looked at the globe, she hadn't felt the loss of travel as much as Harriet had thought.

It was painfully clear that Harriet didn't know herself. Not really.

She was learning, though. Weeks of having no one else to focus on had forced her to consider the idea. Yes, she loved to help people, to enrich lives, and for years she'd been satisfied with fixing others' problems. She'd just never considered that although nurturing people made her happy, there were as many avenues to do that as roads out of London.

There was nothing wrong with helping people, but it was more important that she help the *people* than change the circumstances. How could she use that realization to fix the rift between her and her father?

Mrs. Kemp had told her to find a miracle.

Since Jonas was constantly quoting the Bible, and he was the godliest man she knew, that was where she'd turned only to discover that she couldn't stand to read more than a few verses at a time. That might mean she had a long way to go, but she couldn't believe that God required everyone who followed Him to be a scholar, even if that Paul fellow seemed to be one. It seemed half the New Testament books started with him stating he'd written another letter.

The inkling of an idea dangled at the edge of her mind, and she stopped moving, stopped thinking, even stopped breathing in hopes the thought would finish forming.

Harriet had years of erroneous letters she couldn't take back, but perhaps she could write new ones. She could be like Paul and talk about what was going on in her life and what needed fixing and all the other things she should have shared before instead of making up what she thought Father wanted to hear.

Goodness knows Paul wasn't worried about what people wanted to read.

Harriet grabbed a pen and a piece of paper and set to writing. For years she'd been copying passages from travel books, and then more recently she'd taken Jonas's words as her own. But now . . .

As she placed her own thoughts on paper, she realized something.

Her writing was awful.

Reading it back made her wince. The sentences were stilted, the words were simple, and she'd used the word *things* fourteen times in half a page. After borrowing eloquent sentences from other writers, reading her own words left her extremely uncomfortable.

Still, they were *her* words.

She folded the paper in half and slid it under her father's door, resisting the urge to fish it back as soon as it disappeared from sight.

THE NEXT MORNING, Harriet found a note pushed under her own door.

And so it went. Day after day she wrote to her father, and day after day he wrote her back. Dinner became less uncomfortable, conversations flowed more freely, and eventually she managed to fill an entire page, front and back, with her own thoughts. Sometimes she told her father what she'd seen on her afternoon walk, and other times she talked about her fear that she'd waited too late to claim what she truly wanted out of life and would never have the chance to show those paths to a child of her own.

She started writing about Jonas too. Not for her father but for herself. It was the story of a girl meeting a boy, and each day she added a little piece, retelling a memory from their time together and sharing what she'd learned from him. The story was worse than her letters, but she wished she had the courage to show it to Jonas.

Even if it didn't make any difference.

He didn't think kindly of her, and the more she thought through how he must see everything she'd done, she didn't blame him. Perhaps they could be friends if she found a way to apologize sufficiently.

But she didn't want to be friends. She didn't want to return to

Newmarket and set about trying to find another man who didn't care about her advanced age or advanced wealth. She didn't want to spend night after night examining a man's actions to see if he cared more for family than prestige. She didn't want her children to have a father who tucked himself away in an office and got a weekly report from the servants. Her father had worked her entire life, and still worked, but he'd always talked to her, always made sure she knew that he cared about her more than his factories.

Jonas would be like that. He'd ensure his wife and children were provided for, and he'd care too much to leave the knowledge of them to someone else.

But Jonas didn't want to marry her. If the way he'd left was anything to go by, he wanted nothing to do with her.

Perhaps God would provide more than one miracle for her.

If not, she'd find another way to fulfill her dreams. She would work for it, work to make herself ready. Because if she was learning anything, it was that she couldn't float through life expecting matters to fall into place. She had to work on herself, on her life, on her relationships.

She wrote about that understanding to her father.

His response was to track her down, give her a long hug, and join her on her morning walk.

A week later Harriet finished her story and sat at the desk looking out at the fields drenched in the late July sun.

It was time to go home.

IT WASN'T THE FIRST TIME Jonas had been covered in dirt from head to toe. Nor was it the first time he'd thrown a blanket over a chair because he had to rest a few minutes to gather the energy to clean the dirt from his skin and clothes.

It was, however, the first time he'd felt remotely ashamed about the condition.

Not that he should. Sometimes one fell off a horse. Sometimes the horse kicked up enough mud and dust that it was covered in the substances by the time they returned to the stable, and cleaning it off meant getting half of it on yourself. Sometimes both of those happened in a single day. It was nothing to be ashamed of.

He could, however, curse the fact that they'd both happened on the day he finally saw Harriet again.

Why was she here? Until he'd looked up and seen her standing in the door to the common room shared by the Hawksworth grooms, he'd thought he was over the way she made him feel inferior. Comparing her sparkling presence in a delicate lace-trimmed gown to his earth-encrusted wool clothing brought it all back.

That made him angry. At her. At himself. At every niggling thought he'd had that he could someday reach for more. All the work he'd done on himself over the past few months seemed to fall away, leaving him hurt and even a little frightened.

"What are you doing here?" He hadn't even known she was back in town.

She didn't drop her gaze from his, didn't look about the humble room the grooms shared for dining and relaxing. "In Newmarket or in your home?"

Her sweet voice in his ears was both calming and painful. "Both."

She took a deep breath. "I came to see you."

The way she'd said it, the implication that she'd returned to town with him on her mind—that this was, quite possibly, the first thing she'd done since getting back—sent his heart galloping.

He swallowed and tried to harden the sentimental organ. Nothing had changed. She was still who she was, he was still who he was, and the world hadn't upended itself into one that had no problems. "Why?"

"Because . . ." She bit her lip. A shudder racked her shoulders, and the desire to help her, to provide her words when she obviously was struggling to find them, burned through him. But he'd provided her words before, and that had sent them into this mess in the first place.

"You don't need me to write a book," Jonas said. "I don't need you to peddle my hobbies to the highest bidder."

"They weren't the highest bidder."

Jonas frowned. "I beg your pardon?"

"*Sporting Magazine*." She gave a small shrug. "They don't pay the most. I sent it there because I thought you'd enjoy working for them as opposed to some of the other publications."

"That's not the point," Jonas muttered.

Harriet tilted her head. "I know, but if we're going to argue, we should be accurate in our accusations."

Jonas's fingers wrapped around the worn wood of the chair to push himself to standing, but his legs refused to join the attempt. Until this moment he'd thought himself past the anger. He'd thought he'd put the betrayal behind him, thought he'd learned what God wanted him to learn and had grown into a stronger man for it.

Apparently not, because he didn't know what to do with all the emotion rising in him as he took in her pretty face, her pleading expression, the shadows in her eyes that proved maybe she, too, wasn't quite the same as she'd been a few weeks ago.

"I don't think either one of us wants to endure a listing of accurate accusations," Jonas said.

For him, it was as if everything he could have felt, maybe even should have felt since returning to Newmarket, had been locked away, and Harriet held the key.

The urge to push these feelings away from himself strengthened his legs and propelled him from the chair. "We've been through it all already. Revisiting the ways you used me and our relationship won't help me get over it. You may have needed my writings, but I can't compete with your manipulative words. They worked on me before. I can't risk them working again. You did more than betray me, Harriet."

His chest was heaving far more than it should have been when doing nothing more than standing in a low-ceilinged room, and suddenly shame at his outburst warred with the irritation in his veins. The room closed in until he wanted to break out a window and escape.

No matter what he said, it wouldn't change the fact that what he truly felt was pain.

He rubbed his hands over his face, not caring about the mud the action disturbed. The anger burned out as quickly as it had flared, leaving him exhausted. "You made me care, Harriet. Made me want things I can never have."

She'd ripped out a heart he'd thought fully protected and proved he was as vulnerable to love as any other man.

He lifted his face and met her wide eyes, saw the lack of color in her cheeks. Then he flopped back down into his seat, closed his eyes, and laid his head back against the blanket-covered chair. "I'm sorry, Harriet. I forgive you, I do. I did. Weeks ago. I've no need to yell at you."

He cracked open his eyes and rolled his head until he could see her. "I promise you I haven't been thinking poorly of you all this time. But this?" He gestured limply between the two of them and let his eyes fall closed again. "I can't do this. What's done is done. Move on with your life knowing you did your best to better mine."

The sound of rustling fabric was his only answer. In his mind's eye, he pictured her lifting her chin and setting her mouth into a determined line before turning on her heel and gliding down the stairs.

Then the scrape of fabric grew louder, and Jonas tensed as the feeling of someone looming over him became too strong to ignore.

He eased open his eyes and saw Harriet, far closer and more intent than she'd been moments before. Her dark hair formed a stark contrast to the late-afternoon sun streaming through the window behind her, outlining her face and making her features that much clearer. He couldn't tear his gaze away from her dark eyes or full lips or high cheekbones.

She was by far the most beautiful woman he'd ever seen, and he was exhausted enough that he could no longer defend himself against the desire to kiss her, talk to her, spend time with her, learn more about her, and just have her in his life.

This was why it was dangerous for him to want things. Life was full of difficult decisions, and it was far easier to do the right thing when one didn't care much about the consequences. The right thing here was to send her away, but he was afraid that when she finally did leave this room, she would be taking his heart with her.

"I have no defense to offer," she said softly, "and I'd like to think I've learned the error of my ways."

"I'd like to think that too."

"But you don't."

Jonas sighed. "Whatever goes on in your head and your heart is between you and God. I want to believe you, Harriet, but I can trust only the actions I've seen you do."

"Those have changed."

He hoped so, but he couldn't make himself vulnerable again on mere words. "I haven't seen it."

She crossed her arms. "I've been back in Newmarket for two hours."

"Then I suppose time will tell." Except he wouldn't see because he wouldn't be looking. He'd hear tales of her exploits from his sister, but he would not be forced to witness them.

He should have stopped going to the Tuesday night dinners long ago, cut the ties before Harriet returned. He would not be the reason she lost her friends.

Soon Aaron's stable would be finished, and Jonas would be completely removed from the world Harriet frequented.

There was a good chance this was the last time he'd see Harriet's face in this much detail. He drank it in, making sure to remember the small scar near her left ear, the way her right eye tilted up a little more on the outside corner than her left eye, how her lips pressed together in a way that made them push out in the slightest of pouts.

One of her hands lifted toward his cheek, and he jerked sideways in his chair. "I'm filthy, Harriet."

"I don't care."

"You should." He glanced at her dress. "I can't imagine that's all that easy to wash."

One side of her lips quirked up in a mischievous smile. "No, but my hand usually comes clean rather easily."

Right. Because it was only he who imagined a simple touch of his cheek turning into an embrace. He closed his eyes and sighed, wanting his last memory to be of that playful side of her that had first managed to break through his defenses.

Her hand landed on his cheek, its thumb brushing gently at the smudge along his cheekbone. "I'm going to show you, Jonas Fitzroy, that you weren't wrong about me."

Jonas couldn't help but open his eyes and look at her. The intensity in her dark gaze stole his breath once more. "I thought the point was to prove me wrong."

"No. It's to show you that I've changed in how I deal with people, but you weren't wrong about *me*. You saw something in me that was worth befriending." She took a deep breath. "Maybe at one point you thought it was worth more. That's the part I want to show you was right."

His heart pounded even as his determination to avoid her from here on out redoubled. He would never survive such an onslaught. If she actually tried to win him over, how much faster would he fall? It had been bad enough when she'd been blithely going along without a thought for his opinion.

"Was it ever more, Jonas?" Her voice was barely a whisper.

He couldn't allow her to think she wasn't special to him or that he'd thought nothing of their encounters. He didn't want to hurt her. He simply wanted to protect himself. "I don't make it a point to go around kissing people I don't care about."

Her dark eyes fixed on his, and she slowly lowered her head until her lips were a breath away from his. "Neither do I."

Then she was kissing him. A bit of earth from the corner of his mouth fell against his tongue, combining with the fruity flavor of whatever jam she'd had with her afternoon tea. The earthy mix, such a combination of them both, sent his head spinning until he couldn't remember why this was a bad idea.

He lifted a hand to cup her cheek as she was holding his.

Neither of them moved, neither deepened the kiss. They simply stayed there, frozen, connected, until a bang from the stable below brought them both to their senses and she pulled away. Two streaks of dirt marred her perfect face, and Jonas was torn between delight that she hadn't cared and dismay that he'd mussed her even that little bit.

"You'll want to clean your face before you go downstairs." The roughness of his voice stunned him, and he swallowed twice in the hope he'd sound normal if he spoke again.

She moved to the washbasin at the other end of the room. Water splashed into the bowl, and she quickly saw to the necessary cleaning. When she turned back, there was no indication they'd ever touched at all.

That was as it should be.

"This isn't good-bye, Jonas."

How had she known what he was thinking?

"I may be turning over a new leaf, but that doesn't mean I've forgotten how to get what I want."

"What about what I want?" Thankfully, he sounded like himself again.

She gave him a soft smile. "My previous methods were admittedly heavy-handed and far too assuming, but I wasn't wrong. I knew what people wanted even if it wasn't what they needed. I'm not going to force anything on anyone, but I fully intend to keep opening doors and inviting people to walk through them."

"Opening doors?"

She nodded. "And helping people get what they want in life. What they need to . . ." She scrunched her face in concentration for a moment. "Run the race with patience to obtain the prize that is set before them."

Jonas blinked at her. "Did you just try to quote the Bible to me?"

Her frown was adorably frustrated. "I thought so. Did I get it wrong?"

Had she? The wording was pulled from two different verses, but what she'd said was supported by both. He shook his head. "No, you're right."

She straightened her shoulders and gave a small wiggle of pride. "I know I'll never remember like you do, but I have been engrossed in the letters of Paul of late. I feel like somewhere along the way I got a broken view of my place in the world, but I'm learning a lot from the ideas he writes."

Jonas struggled with the concept of learning from the ideas instead of the words themselves, but her smile was so sweet and beautiful that he couldn't give the concern much of his attention.

Especially as there seemed to be a strength underneath the sweetness that threatened to topple his peace of mind.

"I've thought about you a great deal," Harriet continued. "And you should know that I came home with the intention of giving up on us. You deserved an apology, though, and I wanted to give it, wanted to make sure I'd done what I could to close this chapter for the both of us."

Jonas swallowed. That statement sounded exactly like what he'd wanted, and he hated it.

He also hated how it didn't sound nearly as definitive as it should have.

She tilted her head and smiled. "I find I've changed my mind."

"Why?" Jonas choked out.

Her smile widened. "Because you kissed me back, Jonas Fitzroy, and now I'm convinced we really want the same thing. And I'm going to do everything in my power—every honest and forthright thing in my power—to see that we both get it. In the meantime, you may want to decide what you truly want in life so we don't have to rewrite the story later."

Then she swept from the room, leaving Jonas to question everything he knew about life, himself, and especially women.

Thirty-Five

"Harriet has returned. Perhaps that is a sign I should run away."

—Jonas, in the journal he'd taken to writing in daily since returning from Shrewsbury

For the next two weeks, Jonas jumped at every unexpected sound, peered around every corner, and stayed in a general state of anxious awareness.

But Harriet did nothing. At least, not that he ever saw.

Were her threats nothing more than that? Was she finding that no matter how much she liked the idea, changing her ways was simply too hard?

In a twisted sense of protection, Jonas started looking for her. He saw her from the window in the common room three times on her visits to Hawksworth. Twice he saw her riding on the Heath with Sophia, though that was at such a distance he wouldn't have known it was her if Sophia hadn't informed him of her plans.

After three weeks, he stopped behaving like a skittish colt. Harriet truly was out of his life.

Her words, however, weren't.

He'd always assumed his natural contentment meant he didn't want anything. He'd been the practical to Sophia's dreamer, but had he taken it too far? What did *he* want?

The question consumed him, particularly as he packed his belongings in preparation for the move to the new stable.

And discovered Harriet had been right because he'd kept the magazine.

And the paper she'd given him with the direction for the editor.

Both had been tucked away in a drawer buried beneath odd scraps of paper and an assortment of pocket contents he'd tossed on top.

He could—*should*—throw them out now. Instead, he tucked them carefully into the bag he used to hold his sketchbook, notebook, and pencils, then placed the bag in the trunk he'd borrowed from Sophia. Right beside the box of engraving tools he still pulled out when the urge to better his skills couldn't be suppressed.

He slammed the lid shut, then loaded the trunk onto the wagon with the other items being moved to his new home.

The wagon rolled out, and most of the horses followed. Sweet Fleet was tied and waiting for Jonas to mount up and make the short journey. Instead, he stepped back into the stable and went down the side with the narrow stalls that housed Hawksworth's less valuable horseflesh.

Grabbing a currycomb, he stepped into Pandora's stall to give her one last brushing. "I'll still see you, girl," he whispered.

The horse bumped his shoulder and shifted weight as if expecting him to do more than comb her hair.

"Someone else will ride you today." Most other days too.

With one last stroke of her nose, he slipped from the stall and went to mount Sweet Fleet. It was time to move on.

The first thing he saw when he walked into his new room was a single bed. No more sharing. Whether that was a favor to his sister or if Aaron had provided this for everyone, Jonas didn't know, but he had to appreciate the privacy his own space would bring.

The second thing he saw was the writing desk.

That was courtesy of Sophia, as was the array of pencils, pens, ink, and the large stack of clean paper.

As much as he wanted to turn it down, he couldn't.

Because part of him wanted it. Was glad to have it.

He unpacked his trunk. Though he had more to his name than he'd owned in years, it took him less than an hour to put everything away in the new room. Other than when sliding a few items into its drawer, he tried not to look at the desk too much. He had horses to settle in, a tack room to organize, and a host of other jobs to manage before he could contemplate what to do with that desk.

When he returned to his room several hours later, he didn't fall into bed. Instead, he sat at the desk and smoothed a sheet of paper over the surface. Then he prepared a pen.

Perhaps it was no longer being in a borrowed room, or perhaps it was the privacy. Perhaps it was Harriet's words that never quite left his head. Whatever it was, he couldn't resist allowing himself to dream a little.

He set the pen to paper and began to write an account of the challenge race he'd witnessed the day before. It had begun to rain shortly after the race started, and everyone was soaked to the skin as they watched one horse charge across the finish line at least two full lengths ahead of the other.

As he set down the pen, a sense of satisfaction filled him. He looked the piece over. He'd enjoyed writing it. It wasn't bad.

It might even be good.

The ink dried, then he opened the drawer in the desk, intending to slide the paper in for safekeeping.

The magazine stared up at him.

What if he sent his writing in? What was the worst that could happen? They'd say no? Then he could stick it in the drawer, just like he'd intended.

He glanced at the box of engraving tools.

Did he dare?

He took out his sketchbook and began to draw the scene. He wasn't good enough to make the picture straight onto the wood, but maybe . . . maybe he could make it work better if he thought about the simplicity of the picture first.

The sun set, and he lit a candle to provide enough light to finish the drawing. Then he sat back and examined it, his heart pounding. Was he really going to do this?

One quick blow extinguished the candle and plunged him into darkness, where he admitted that, yes, he was going to try. He would see if he could put something in his day that gave him more to care about than survival.

THE NEW STABLE was a wonder. Two outbuildings housed all the storage needs, with the living quarters for the grooms above. The hayloft had been removed from the old farm stable, leaving tall, angled ceilings. Eighteen loose box stalls circled most of the space, with a washroom and four regular stalls taking up the middle of the wall directly across from the large double doors.

It was a beautiful place to work, and though the atmosphere wasn't as familial as Hawksworth, Jonas found the professional camaraderie comfortable. Ernest had made the move along with the grooms from Oliver's estate who'd been working with Aaron. Add eight jockeys roaming in and out of the place, and it was a regular hive of activity.

It should have been enough.

Somehow it only emphasized his growing restlessness.

He'd sent the article to the magazine editor yesterday. There was nothing more he could do, except possibly write another article, draw another picture.

"I'm going back to London!"

Jonas had been so engrossed in cleaning Equinox's hooves and so accustomed to the way no one could enter the Hawksworth stable unnoticed that his sister's happy cry sent him tumbling to the hay on his backside.

Her laughter rang out as he hauled himself upright. She stood at the stall door, hands wrapped around the bars forming the top third and her face pressed into the space between, which made her enormous grin twist into a strange shape.

Jonas couldn't help laughing at the picture. He turned to pick the hoof back up. "Are you giving lessons there again?" Sophia occasionally taught riding at a girls' school near London.

"No," she said with a giggle. Then her voice dropped its light brogue in favor of an exaggerated impression of a posh Londoner. "I'm going to the opera."

Carefully, Jonas put the hoof on the ground and stared at his sister. "The opera?"

"Yes. When we tried to go to London during the Season it was too difficult for Aaron." She gave a one-shouldered shrug. "So we spent half the trip in Bath instead."

So they'd made their own decisions just as Harriet said they would.

Why hadn't Jonas known this? When they'd returned from their holiday relaxed with bright smiles, he assumed the trip had gone well. He'd been so determined to limit his dependence on Sophia that he hadn't even asked.

Clearly, he hadn't found the proper balance yet.

Jonas cleared his throat. "Why return?"

"For one thing, it's not the Season anymore. For another, Harriet mentioned this fabulous new shopping area has opened up."

Jonas's heart plummeted. Until that moment, he hadn't realized just how much he'd wanted Harriet to prove she was different now. "She did."

"Yes. She brought the news article to the house and gave it to me and Aaron. Said she thought a row of shops with a roof overhead was fascinating and that I might want to read about it as well."

Jonas frowned. That sounded rather . . . straightforward of Harriet. "How did that turn into the opera?"

"Well." Sophia moved aside to give Jonas room to step out of the stall, then trotted beside him as he went to scoop mash for the horse. "The shopping street is the Royal Opera Arcade, and it's right next to the Royal Opera House. I don't want Aaron uncomfortable, but I do want to see an opera."

Ah. Here was where Harriet's true colors would shine.

"I told Aaron that, when he was ready, this sounded like a fun addition since it would be more than just the opera. Harriet said to let her know when we decided to go because she knows people who keep boxes. She also offered to have any of her dresses altered for me so I wouldn't feel out of place. That was sweet of her, but I want to order one of my own."

So Harriet hadn't forced or cajoled or maneuvered. She'd simply . . . offered. "But you decided to take her up on the box?"

"No!" Sophia clapped in glee. "Aaron did. He presented it to me this morning even though my birthday isn't for another two weeks."

Which meant Jonas's birthday was in two weeks. He'd almost forgotten about it. Of course, twenty-four was still a good bit younger than thirty. Not that it mattered.

"He took me to the modiste this morning and told me to buy an opera gown. He isn't ready to spend a lot of time in London. In fact, we'll spend more time on the road than we do there, but he's still taking me to the opera. He's asked for Harriet's help on the whole trip, and she was there to assist me with finding the dress."

Sophia frowned. "It's funny. She usually knows what I want to buy, but this time her ideas weren't exactly right. I ended up getting something far simpler than she suggested."

Jonas's heart beat so fast he almost dropped the bucket of mash on the floor. He wrapped his free hand beneath it as he moved back toward Equinox, his sister following along, talking more than a vicar on Sunday about all her plans.

"It means I won't be here on our birthday, and I was hoping you would consider coming with us to London."

He'd missed a good chunk of her speech, but that last sentence was unmistakable. "You want me to come to London. With you. And your husband."

"We've never spent a birthday apart," she said softly.

Jonas poured the mash into Equinox's trough, gave the horse a pat on the neck, and then stepped back out of the stall. He rested his hands on Sophia's shoulders. "You're married now. It isn't just you and me anymore."

"I know, but . . ." She licked her lips and took a deep breath. "I don't want you to be alone."

"It's better than spending days in a carriage and an opera box with my sister and brother-in-law."

"I was thinking . . ." She coughed and looked away before rushing to say, "that perhaps Harriet could come too."

Jonas blinked. "Did she ask to come?"

"No!" Sophia's wide green eyes met his. "She never even hinted at it, and you know she does that sometimes."

Jonas didn't correct her. Had Harriet truly changed? She was at least making an effort.

He wrapped his sister in a hug. "Enjoy your birthday trip to London."

She sighed as they pulled apart. "We're taking a post chaise and staying with Graham's parents, so there's plenty of room if you change your mind."

"Thank you."

"I had a feeling you'd say no, though."

Jonas gave her a crooked grin. "That's because you've known me all my life. You are older, after all."

She crossed her arms over her chest and stuck her nose in the air. "How true. And because I haven't given you a present in seven years, I decided to make up for it this year."

"You can hardly call the trinkets I gave you presents."

"It was the thought that mattered."

"I appreciated that you thought enough of me to know I didn't want more clutter in my knapsack." Jonas laid a hand on the latch for the next stall. "You don't have to get me anything."

She rolled her eyes. "Since I knew you'd say no to the opera, I got you something else."

Jonas sighed. "Well, I look forward to getting it." Not really. Her happiness when he opened it would be his true present.

She started bouncing on her toes. "It's here."

A quick look about the large, airy stable revealed no packages. "It is?"

"It's outside." Sophia grabbed his hand and tugged. Two other grooms joined them out of curiosity. Even without great acoustics, everyone would have heard Sophia's excited talking.

Jonas stepped through the doors, blinking a few times to acclimate to the sunlight.

The first thing he saw was Harriet sitting atop the light-brown horse she rode when she went out with Sophia. Surely this wasn't his sister's idea of a present.

Harriet, aside from appearing beautiful and familiar in a way that eased an ache he hadn't even realized he had, looked very unsure of herself. "She asked me to come."

Jonas nodded, understanding more than that simple statement. Harriet wanted him to know she hadn't arranged this, that she hadn't cajoled or suggested.

"Of course I asked her to come," Sophia said. "You two are

miserable without each other. Harriet turns down social invitations, and you do nothing but work." His sister gave him a pointed look, her joy slowly falling. "You don't like your present?"

Jonas frowned at his sister. Was he wrong? Was Harriet actually the present?

He looked toward Harriet again and realized she had a rope in her hand.

That rope curved over to another horse—a black Friesian with a long mane and bright eyes.

"Pandora." He couldn't say more than a whisper. "You bought me Pandora?"

"Actually, Aaron bought her, but based on the two-become-one business, I assume that means his money is mine now." Jonas shot her a look, and she laughed. "He knows. I asked him."

For the briefest of moments, Jonas considered telling her this was too much, but then he realized this was as much for her as it was for him. In her eyes, he was alone now, and this was her way of changing that.

He wrapped his sister in a tight hug. "Thank you."

"You're welcome." She pushed him away. "Now go see your horse."

Jonas walked to Harriet's side first and reached up for the rope. She handed it over, but he didn't step away immediately. "I hear you didn't know exactly what Sophia wanted at the modiste this morning."

She looked down at her hands. "No. I didn't."

With his body blocking everyone's view, Jonas reached out and gave her booted foot a squeeze. Her eyes darted up to meet his, and he gave her a nod and a smile. "You did well."

Then he stepped away to see to his new horse, thankful the mare's long, thick mane could hide the way his hands were suddenly trembling.

Thirty-Six

"Today, I had toast. I know that sounds boring, but as I spent the rest of the day rearranging books in the library, it's honestly the most interesting thing I can report."

—Harriet, in a letter to her father

"I think that went well." Sophia grinned at Harriet as they rode away from Aaron's new stable.

Harriet didn't know if it had gone *well*, but at least it hadn't gone poorly. "You told him about London?"

She nodded. "I'm afraid I went on about more of the details than he was actually interested in, but I told him all about it." Sophia's shoulders curled in a little. "Then he said he wouldn't come."

"Did you really expect him to?" Harriet asked gently. The moment Sophia had produced that part of her plan, Harriet knew it was doomed to failure.

"No." Sophia straightened and looked at Harriet, eyes intense. "Help me. How do I convince him to come?"

Ideas immediately sprang to Harriet's mind, but she didn't share any of them. "He won't appreciate you putting pressure on him."

"I know."

"It needs to be his choice."

Sophia sighed. "You're sounding far too pragmatic to be the Harriet I know."

Was she? Perhaps. For now, Harriet was erring on the side of caution, trying to temper every meddling instinct she had until she learned to tame them. She may not have improved many lives over the past three weeks, but her relationships were stronger. Even this conversation with Sophia was deeper. It was real.

"All you can do is tell him everything." Harriet eyed Sophia once more. "You did tell him everything, right? And how you put it all together?"

"Yes. I know you were right when you said that would be the best chance to get him to come, but I'm truly not surprised it didn't work."

While Sophia pouted, Harriet hoped. Jonas knew what she'd done, the part she'd played, and he'd still told her she did well. She liked the idea of helping people while getting to know them. Or perhaps, more to the point, letting them get to know her. No more lies. No more manipulations.

The freedom it brought was greater than she'd ever imagined.

Did she dare hope for more? If Jonas saw her heart, would he give them another chance?

Her brain teemed with all the ways she could invade his space, all the excuses she could make so they would run into each other, all the ways she could get Sophia to talk about her so she stayed in the front of his mind.

But no. Jonas would see such machinations for what they were and would not appreciate them.

When it came time for her and Sophia to part ways, Harriet hurried home. She went straight to the library, where she'd taken to writing her correspondence since coming home, and pushed aside the stack of letters from her father. They were coming at least twice a week now, and hers to him were leaving with equal frequency. Their relationship was mending.

Could she ask God for another miracle?

She picked up the package she'd retrieved from the bookshop just this morning. Originally she'd been praying for the gumption and the opportunity to give it to Jonas for his birthday, but it felt right to do it now. Why wait two weeks if they could start moving ahead today?

Hugging the package to her chest, she said one more fervent prayer over it and then went to find a footman.

JONAS WAS GRATEFUL he'd spent his life around horses and that the care of them was second nature, because his mind was not on his work for the rest of the day. As much as part of him clung to hope after Harriet's handling of Sophia's London trip, another part—the part he was coming to realize was more than a little cynical instead of simply practical—warned that one choice did not mean a changed life.

He was so buried in the internal argument that he almost stepped on the thin package lying outside his door. Jonas rubbed his dirty hand over his pants before reaching down to pick up the rectangle wrapped in brown paper. It was hard under his fingers and shaped like a book.

Curiosity rose as he entered his room, but caution had him setting the package on the desk unopened. His eyes stayed on it while he removed his mud-splattered jacket and shirt. Nor did his gaze move as he washed his hands and arms in the basin of water on his wash table. Why did it feel like a snake poised to bite him? He didn't even know who it was from.

He shook the water from his hands and reached for the package. The dampness remaining created dark marks on the brown wrapping as he pulled the paper away. It was indeed a book but not a professionally printed one. Instead, it was a sheaf of papers bound together by book boards.

The pages curled upward as he opened the top board, and the stitches pulled at the handwritten pages. He used his other hand to smooth the paper down and started to read.

Three lines in, he dropped into the chair situated in front of his desk. This was his story, his and Harriet's. Most of the sentences were short and stilted. Sometimes it was written directly to him as in a letter, other times it read like a book as if he were on the outside looking in. Harriet hadn't been lying about being a poor writer, but he didn't care. In those choppy sentences were the honesty and vulnerability he'd glimpsed during their time together.

This was the Harriet he'd fallen in love with.

She recounted their story, sharing things he hadn't realized she'd noticed or felt. He'd never seen himself the way she saw him, never realized how amazing it could be to have someone see him that way. Strong. Wise. Caring. Confident. Dependable. The one consistent thing she could always count on, day in and day out.

The story finished with an account of her time with her father, the realizations she'd had, the notion that there were right and wrong methods just like there were right and wrong motivations. She wanted to do things right and for the right reasons.

The final page wasn't part of the story. It was a letter. Written to him, from her, not requesting anything, just offering her heart on a paper-and-ink platter.

With my father I learned that facing and dealing with mistakes will not just mend a broken relationship but make it stronger. It won't be the same. It will have scars. But maybe my relationship with my father is more beautiful now? Maybe ours can be too. I love you, Jonas. I want to learn from what went wrong and make it better.

Jonas didn't realize tears had formed in his eyes until one of them splashed down onto the paper, smearing two of the words. He quickly sat back so as not to mar any more ink.

He read through the entire book again, then slowly closed the cover and sat back in his chair.

What did this mean? Beyond a simple apology or explanation, it was a declaration of love. It was certainly a risk, as not only had she made herself vulnerable but she'd done it in writing. He could do whatever he wished with it, show it to whomever he wanted, could even sell it to a gossip magazine. Not that Harriet had ever been much fodder for any gossip papers beyond the local ones, but they still might pay for the story of an heiress falling in love with a stableboy.

And she'd trusted him with it.

It was a reverse sort of fairy tale. Could it have anything resembling a happy ending?

He dropped his gaze to the corner of his desk, where the letter from the editor of *Sporting Magazine* sat, accepting his latest writing submission but not his engraving, though they'd invited him to submit future drawings.

She'd given that to him. Opened that door. Shoved him through when he might not have done it himself.

Not that he condoned her methods, but one had to move on in the present, not dwell on the past. She was right that he had more to share and had been blind to the need and ability to share it.

Could he trust the words on the page in front of him? All his life, he'd claimed to take people at their word. Only now, when being wrong brought with it a great personal risk, was he doubting that someone meant their honest, passionate claim.

He still didn't possess a driving ambition to be a Royal Academy artist or rival Lord Byron, but Harriet had never wanted that. She wanted him to have a simple, rich, fulfilled life. That he could manage.

Could he manage the way she challenged his understanding? How she made him think about the grey area, about the context of Bible verses he'd lived by his entire life, about the intent behind a choice?

What was the worst that could happen?

The worst was a life without Harriet. A life of sameness and predictability, a life of bland security. Opening his heart to passion meant risking pain but potentially gaining so much more.

He pushed up from the chair and set about cleaning up and changing his clothing.

It looked like it was his turn to create a plan.

HARRIET HAD TO ADMIT she was happy. She had the comfort and familiarity of her old friends and her old home but also the excitement of a new relationship with her father and the challenge of a new direction in life.

Jonas hadn't reached out to her since she'd left him the book, and with each day that passed, she lost a little more hope. Still, there was something good in the pain, because it meant she herself could love and live. Through Jonas's eyes, she'd learned that life was the real adventure, no matter where she happened to be.

She'd hoped to face it with him at her side, but at least she was now ready to embrace it.

"Miss? Mr. Fitzroy is here to see you."

Everything in Harriet froze. She didn't feel connected to her body. Then she slammed back into it, heart pounding, feet running. What if he wasn't here for her? For them? What if something had happened to Sophia?

Harriet ran down the stairs, eyes fixed on the drawing room doorway to the point that she almost tripped on the bottom stair. Her slippers slid on the marble of the front hall as she crossed it and then came to a halt.

Jonas stood on the other side of the room near the window, the book she'd left outside his door in his hands. As soon as she appeared, he set it down and gave her a small smile.

"Hello, Harriet."

"Hello."

They stared at each other, neither speaking, neither moving. Why was he here? What was he thinking? She couldn't do anything until she knew.

Finally, he cleared his throat and stepped forward, one arm gesturing toward the sofa. "Would you like to sit with me?"

That was encouraging, right? Sitting was a good sign. It meant he intended to stay a while. She settled on the sofa, waiting.

"I have something for you." He reached into his pocket, and when his hand emerged, the fingers were curled tightly together.

He lowered onto the sofa, angling his legs so he could partially face her before taking her hand in his and placing a small coin in her palm.

Harriet stared at it.

What was she supposed to do with it? It was obviously old but entirely unfamiliar. She looked up from the coin to find him watching her.

"I don't like to make decisions," he said. "Most of the time I'm more than happy for things to stay the way they are. Despite the fact that you desire a home, a part of you also longs for the adventure of new experiences. The part that demands to walk in a stream and ride double on a horse."

"I don't think I've ever heard you string that many words together at once before," Harriet whispered. "At least not complimentary ones."

Jonas chuckled. "You might never hear it again, so listen carefully. This coin was my father's. It's not worth anything, but it's got St. Patrick on it, which makes it special to an Irishman. This is my promise to you. When we face a decision, you won't have to scheme, and I won't have to decide. We'll just flip the coin and let it guide our adventures."

"*Our* adventures?" Harriet's fingers closed over the coin. If this little piece of metal tied him to her, she was never letting it go.

"You said you love me, Harriet. Well, I love you too. That's the only reason I can think for why you could hurt me as badly as you did."

She took in a deep breath to apologize, but Jonas held up a hand. "You already apologized. It's my turn to forgive and do a little apologizing myself. I should have believed in you, Harriet. I should have talked to you, and then maybe we could have grown together." His sigh was strong enough to flutter her hair. "Or maybe we needed to deal with our own messes apart for a while."

Harriet opened her mouth to agree with him. She hadn't been ready to hear him before her trip home.

Jonas hadn't stopped speaking, though. "From here on out, I want to be there for you. The man at your side when you face something new and supporting your back as you change the world. If you'll have me."

She took in a deep breath to scream yes, but he held up a hand again.

She was going to break that hand.

"Before you say anything, I know we have a lot to consider. I'm younger than you. By several years. I might have been born to a similar class as you, but as far as Newmarket knows, I'm so far below you I'm not even on the ladder. I've sent in another article, but I don't know that I'll ever care enough about writing to push for a career. I've been drawing more lately, but . . ."

He gave a slight shrug, and Harriet understood. He wanted to live his life, to see to his family, to care for his friends, but he didn't care if he himself was ever extraordinary.

To her that made him amazing.

She took a small breath, not wanting to alert him that she intended to speak, but before she could get a word out, he was talking again.

"As much as we don't want those things to matter, they do. You care about the people in this community. Our children will grow up here. Love is important, but it doesn't change reality. I want us to be practical moving forward, and the coin is for that too."

Harriet frowned. Flipping a coin to make their decisions was practical?

"When we're together, we can flip that coin. Whichever side it lands on, the winner gets to ask the other a question and we'll answer as truthfully and completely as we can. No holding back. We get to know each other, we get to plan our future, and we get to fall deeper in love."

Harriet waited a moment, watching him. She could see all the problems he did, but unlike him, she knew they could get around them. They had a wonderful circle of friends who would support them despite the disparities. If that was all they ever had, their life would be full. Their children would grow up with cousins and friends who cared more about life than class.

It was enough.

She held up the coin to look at it. St. Patrick was emblazoned on one side of the farthing, while a man playing the harp and looking up at a crown was depicted on the other. She held it between two fingers and grinned at Jonas. "Let's try it out, shall we?"

He swallowed hard enough to make his throat jump. He was looking at her and not the coin. "Harriet, when we're ready, will you join me on life's greatest adventure? Will you marry me and make a life with me and remove the choice of either of us ever being alone again until one of us dies?"

Harriet rolled her eyes. "That isn't romantic, Jonas."

"It's the truth. And right now I find the truth of spending the rest of our available days together to be romantic."

"So it is." She tilted her head. "Shall we see what my answer is?"

"Wait, no—"

She flipped the coin in the air, tried to catch it, missed, and sent it flopping onto the sofa beside her.

Jonas was frowning. "That wasn't really one of the questions I meant to leave up to chance. Besides, you didn't decide which side meant we go forward and which meant we stay where we are."

Harriet sighed. "I was waiting to see how it landed first."

He looked at her, understanding slowly dawning in his eyes as his smile grew.

She was smiling as well as she looked down at the coin. "It would seem that St. Patrick is our saint of adventure." Just to make sure Jonas understood, Harriet took his face in her hands. "That means my answer is yes."

Then she kissed him.

When they pulled back, she added, "You can work with horses, write books, draw, engrave, or take up pouring tea at the local teahouse. I don't care. I just want you with me. So we're only waiting until *you* are ready, but I'm happy to wait as long as that takes." She frowned. "As long as I'm not still a spinster at one-and-thirty."

Jonas shook his head, still smiling. "You won't be. I promise. Now. How about we try that coin again?"

Harriet scooped it up, excited to go on an adventure with him but also happy that staying where they were was always going to be an option. If he wanted to, she might even try traveling again. He could help her see the wonder of new places. "What is the question?"

He took a deep breath. "In my room, I have a bag packed. Inside are the evening clothes my sister gave me a few months ago. Do you want to join my sister and brother-in-law on their trip to the London opera?"

She excitedly flipped the coin in the air. This time it landed on the floor. They both leaned over it.

"David with the harp. Stay where we are."

Was that a note of disappointment she heard in his voice? She knew *she* wasn't happy with the answer, which meant accepting the will of a coin was silly. They made this game. They could change the rules. She scooped up the coin and flipped it in the air again. "Let's go with two out of three."

Epilogue

Seven Months Later

Jonas gave Pandora's reins to Matthews and let the groom take care of the horse. Normally Jonas liked to see to her himself, but today he wanted to get back up to the house. He only worked mornings at Aaron's stable now, doing odd jobs or exercising horses.

He came in through the kitchen, stopping at a bucket of water to wash most of the dust from his arms and neck before going in search of his wife.

This morning had been her turn to host the Ladies' Aid Society—the first time since they'd married just after Christmas.

Admittedly, it had taken a while for Jonas to believe Harriet wouldn't change her mind about marrying him. He'd also wanted some time to get to know her father. Mr. Hancock had come to visit in October, and they'd started exchanging letters.

Her father had given his blessing shortly thereafter, but in a stroke of unusual sentimentality, Jonas put off the wedding a little longer. All his life he'd shared a birthday with his sister. It seemed right to share an anniversary with her too. Somehow, it made him feel like they were both bringing their spouses into the family instead of twins splitting apart to make families of their own.

He jogged up the stairs to the library and found Harriet curled up on the sofa, reading.

"What do you think about sheep shearing?" she asked. "It sounds a dreadfully strange business, but it does make me curious to know where wool comes from."

Jonas crossed to the desk and slid the coin from the little glass bowl in the corner. He flipped it into the air and caught it deftly before slapping it onto the back of his other hand. "St. Patrick. That's a yes. We'll have to see if anyone knows someone with sheep."

He dropped the coin back into the bowl and crossed the room to the wooden chair they kept for him to sit on before he got cleaned up. "How did it go this morning?"

"It went well. Lady Davers made a few remarks about how my maids must be a wonder to keep the carpet so clean, and I felt a little guilty for telling her the secret was to make sure the rug got put into full sunlight one day a week." She sighed. "As much fun as it is to think of all her rugs fading to white before October, I'll need to stop by and apologize to the housekeeper and help her find a way to work around her mistress's new demands."

Jonas laughed and brushed a dark curl back from Harriet's cheek.

"Oh!" Harriet sprang up from the sofa and rushed over to the desk. "It came in today." She picked up the latest issue of *Sporting Magazine*, waving it in the air like some sort of prize.

"Harriet, this will be my seventh article."

"And I intend to celebrate every one of them." She flounced across the room and sat on the sofa, knees turned to face him. "Besides, this is only your third engraving, so that's still special."

He gave her a nod of acquiescence and sat back, knowing she was about to read every word aloud and crow over how well he'd written them.

When she finished, she set the magazine aside with a happy sigh. Then she rose again and moved toward the door.

Jonas watched her go with a frown. Normally, once he'd cleaned up, they sat in the library for a while. Frances would bring them tea, and sometimes they talked, other times they read. Why was she leaving? "Where are you going?"

"I thought we could go ahead and change for dinner. It's at Sophia's new house tonight, and I want to be early."

The wicked smile his wife had just sent his way meant there was more to the story. As he slowly rose to his feet, he asked, "Why?"

She stepped through the door and then wrapped a hand around the frame so she could lean back in. "Because I want to ask Sophia if she thinks we should come up with rhyming baby names."

Then she was gone, and Jonas's heart had dropped to somewhere in the vicinity of his knees, its pounding making them knock together. He was stuck for the space of two breaths, and then he was chasing after his family, a wide grin on his face.

Scripture References

Chapter 2:

John 8:32 "And ye shall know the truth, and the truth shall make you free."

Chapter 4:

Hebrews 10:25 "Not forsaking the assembling of ourselves together, as the manner of some is; but exhorting one another: and so much the more, as ye see the day approaching."

Chapter 5:

Matthew 5:37 "But let your communication be, Yea, yea; Nay, nay: for whatsoever is more than these cometh of evil."

Chapter 7:

Romans 8:28 "And we know that all things work together for good to them that love God, to them who are the called according to his purpose."

Chapter 10:

1 Corinthians 2:9 "But as it is written, Eye hath not seen, nor ear heard, neither have entered into the heart of man, the things which God hath prepared for them that love him."

1 Peter 4:10 "As every man hath received the gift, even so minister the same one to another, as good stewards of the manifold grace of God."

Chapter 14:

Ecclesiastes 3:11 "He hath made every thing beautiful in his time: also he hath set the world in their heart, so that no man can find out the work that God maketh from the beginning to the end."

Chapter 15:

Psalm 27:5 "For in the time of trouble he shall hide me in his pavilion: in the secret of his tabernacle shall he hide me; he shall set me up upon a rock."

Proverbs 25:2 "It is the glory of God to conceal a thing: but the honour of kings is to search out a matter."

Proverbs 17:28 "Even a fool, when he holdeth his peace, is counted wise: and he that shutteth his lips is esteemed a man of understanding."

Chapter 17:

Romans 15:1 "We then that are strong ought to bear the infirmities of the weak, and not to please ourselves."

Chapter 20

Genesis 2:18 "And the LORD God said, It is not good that the man should be alone; I will make him an help meet for him."

Galatians 6:9 "And let us not be weary in well doing: for in due season we shall reap, if we faint not."

Chapter 22:

1 John 3:18 "My little children, let us not love in word, neither in tongue; but in deed and in truth."

Chapter 24:

(NQ)* 1 Corinthians 13:11 "When I was a child, I spake as a child, I understood as a child, I thought as a child: but when I became a man, I put away childish things."

1 Corinthians 2:11 "For what man knoweth the things of a man, save the spirit of man which is in him? even so the things of God knoweth no man, but the Spirit of God."

---

*(NQ) designates a verse that is not quoted but is referred to.

Chapter 26:

Hebrews 12:1 "Wherefore seeing we also are compassed about with so great a cloud of witnesses, let us lay aside every weight, and the sin which doth so easily beset us, and let us run with patience the race that is set before us . . ."

(NQ) 1 Corinthians 9:24 "Know ye not that they which run in a race run all, but one receiveth the prize? So run, that ye may obtain."

(NQ) Matthew 25:21 "His lord said unto him, Well done, thou good and faithful servant: thou hast been faithful over a few things, I will make thee ruler over many things: enter thou into the joy of thy lord."

1 Corinthians 10:31 "Whether therefore ye eat, or drink, or whatsoever ye do, do all to the glory of God."

Luke 10:27 "And he answering said, Thou shalt love the Lord thy God with all thy heart, and with all thy soul, and with all thy strength, and with all thy mind; and thy neighbour as thyself."

Chapter 27:

Colossians 3:23 "And whatsoever ye do, do it heartily, as to the Lord, and not unto men . . ."

Daniel 6:3 "Then this Daniel was preferred above the presidents and princes, because an excellent spirit was in him; and the king thought to set him over the whole realm."

Luke 2:52 "And Jesus increased in wisdom and stature, and in favour with God and man."

(NQ) 1 Corinthians 10:31 "Whether therefore ye eat, or drink, or whatsoever ye do, do all to the glory of God."

(NQ) 1 Corinthians 14:33 "For God is not the author of confusion, but of peace, as in all churches of the saints."

Luke 24:32 "And they said one to another, Did not our heart burn within us, while he talked with us by the way, and while he opened to us the scriptures?"

(NQ) Proverbs 3:5 "Trust in the Lord with all thine heart; and lean not unto thine own understanding."

Chapter 28:

John 13:34 "A new commandment I give unto you, That ye love one another; as I have loved you, that ye also love one another."

(NQ) John 13:1–17

(NQ) John 10:10 "The thief cometh not, but for to steal, and to kill, and to destroy: I am come that they might have life, and that they might have it more abundantly."

Chapter 33:

James 4:6 "But he giveth more grace. Wherefore he saith, God resisteth the proud, but giveth grace unto the humble."

Chapter 34:

(NQ) Hebrews 12:1 "Wherefore seeing we also are compassed about with so great a cloud of witnesses, let us lay aside every weight, and the sin which doth so easily beset us, and let us run with patience the race that is set before us . . ."

(NQ) 1 Corinthians 9:24 "Know ye not that they which run in a race run all, but one receiveth the prize? So run, that ye may obtain."

Acknowledgments

This book is for readers who, like me, have spent a great deal of life not knowing what they really wanted. Of course, even if you've known you wanted to be a lawyer since you were three, I hope you still enjoyed the story.

Whether you are nine or ninety, know it isn't too late. As long as you are breathing, God is working.

I'd like to thank the many people who've supported me over the past few years of discovering the path God is leading me to walk on. My husband, my children, my lifegroup, and my Voxer girls, know that without you this journey would be a thousand times more difficult.

Gratitude of immense proportions to extraordinary author Kimberly Duffy, who granted her exemplary assistance to the brief passages of Jonas's writings. Kim, you brought his words to life in ways I could not.

A shout-out to my Rocket Readers, who love me and support me with the patience of saints. Thank you for all the work you do for the sheer love of doing it.

Debb Hackett, thanks for making sure I don't veer too far into my American side.

To Natasha, Raela, and the entire BHP team, thank you for all you've done.

And as always, thank you, readers, for inviting my words and my thoughts into your lives. It has been an honor.

Kristi Ann Hunter is the author of the HAWTHORNE HOUSE and HAVEN MANOR series, a 2016 RITA Award winner, an ACFW Genesis contest winner, and a Georgia Romance Writers Maggie Award for Excellence winner. She lives with her husband and three children in Georgia. Find her online at www.kristiannhunter.com.

Sign Up for Kristi's Newsletter

Keep up to date with Kristi's news on book releases and events by signing up for her email list at kristiannhunter.com.

Also from Kristi Ann Hunter

When a strange man appears to be stealing horses at the neighboring estate, Bianca Snowley jumps to their rescue. And when she discovers he's the new owner, she can't help but be intrigued—but romance is unfeasible when he proposes they help secure spouses for each other. Will they see everything they've wanted has been there all along before it's too late?

Vying for the Viscount
HEARTS ON THE HEATH

BETHANYHOUSE

Stay up to date on your favorite books and authors with our free e-newsletters. Sign up today at bethanyhouse.com.

facebook.com/bethanyhousepublishers

@bethanyhousefiction

Free exclusive resources for your book group at bethanyhouseopenbook.com

You May Also Like . . .

When his reputation is threatened, Aaron Whitworth makes the desperate decision to hire a circus horse trainer as a jockey for his racehorses. Most men don't take Sophia Fitzroy seriously because she's a woman, but as she fights for the right to do the work she was hired for, she finds the fight for Aaron's guarded heart might be a more worthwhile challenge.

Winning the Gentleman
HEARTS ON THE HEATH
kristiannhunter.com

Far away from London, three young women establish a home for children to protect them against society's censure over the circumstance of their birth. But each woman also has secrets of her own and will have to choose if guarding them closely is worth risking a surprising love.

HAVEN MANOR: *A Defense of Honor, A Return of Devotion, A Pursuit of Home*
kristiannhunter.com

The glittering world of early nineteenth-century London comes to life as four aristocratic siblings try to navigate societal expectations, deep secrets, and romance. Is love worth the sacrifices they'll be forced to make?

HAWTHORNE HOUSE: *A Noble Masquerade, An Elegant Façade, An Uncommon Courtship, An Inconvenient Beauty*
kristiannhunter.com

BETHANYHOUSE

More from Bethany House

In pursuit of an author who could help get her brother published, Rebecca Lane stays at Swanford Abbey, a grand hotel rumored to be haunted. It is there she encounters Sir Frederick—the man who broke her heart. When a mysterious death occurs, Rebecca is one of the suspects, and Frederick is torn between his feelings for her and his search for the truth.

Shadows of Swanford Abbey by Julie Klassen
julieklassen.com

When Beth Tremayne stumbles across an old map, she pursues the excitement she's always craved. But her only way to piece together the clues is through Lord Sheridan—a man she insists stole a prized possession. As they follow the clues, they uncover a story of piratical adventure, but the true treasure is the one they discover in each other.

To Treasure an Heiress by Roseanna M. White
The Secrets of the Isles #2
roseannamwhite.com

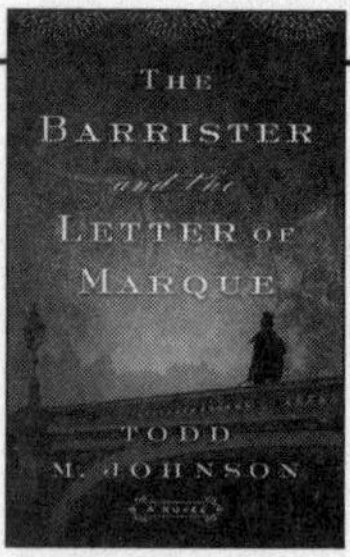

As a barrister in 1818 London, William Snopes defends the poor against the powerful—but that changes when a struggling heiress arrives at his door with a mystery surrounding a missing letter from the king's regent and a merchant's brig. As he digs deeper, he learns that the forces arrayed against them are even more perilous than he'd imagined.

The Barrister and the Letter of Marque by Todd M. Johnson
authortoddmjohnson.com